P9-DHD-456

Somewhere a Song

Books by Judith Pella

Beloved Stranger
Blind Faith
*The Stonewycke Legacy**
*The Stonewycke Triology**
Texas Angel / Heaven's Road

DAUGHTERS OF FORTUNE
Written on the Wind

LONE STAR LEGACY
Frontier Lady *Stoner's Crossing*
Warrior's Song

RIBBONS OF STEEL†
Distant Dreams *A Hope Beyond*
A Promise for Tomorrow

RIBBONS WEST†
Westward the Dream *Separate Roads*
Ties That Bind

THE RUSSIANS
*The Crown and the Crucible** *Heirs of the Motherland*
*A House Divided** *Dawning of Deliverance*
*Travail and Triumph** *White Nights, Red Morning*
Passage Into Light

THE JOURNALS OF CORRIE BELLE HOLLISTER
*Daughter of Grace**

*with Michael Phillips †with Tracie Peterson

02B

JUDITH PELLA
Somewhere a Song

BETHANYHOUSE
PUBLISHERS
MINNEAPOLIS, MINNESOTA

Somewhere a Song

Cover illustration and design by Dan Thornberg

Published by Bethany House Publishers
A Ministry of Bethany Fellowship International
11400 Hampshire Avenue South
Bloomington, Minnesota 55438
www.bethanyhouse.com

Printed in the United States of America by
Bethany Press International, Bloomington, Minnesota 55438

ISBN 0-7642-2422-0 (Trade Paper)
ISBN 0-7642-2720-3 (Hardcover)
ISBN 0-7642-2721-1 (Large Print)

Library of Congress Cataloging-in-Publication Data

Pella, Judith.
Somewhere a song / by Judith Pella.
p. cm. — (Daughters of fortune ; 2)
ISBN 0-7642-2422-0 (pbk.)
ISBN 0-7642-2720-3 (hardback)
ISBN 0-7642-2721-1 (large print pbk.)
1. World War, 1939–1945—Women—Fiction. 2. Pearl Harbor (Hawaii), Attack on, 1941—Fiction. 3. Americans—Foreign countries—Fiction. 4. Newspaper publishing—Fiction. 5. Sisters—Fiction. I. Title.
PS3566.E415 S66 2002
813'.54—dc21 2002010227

About the Author

Judith Pella is the author of several historical fiction series, both on her own and in collaboration with Michael Phillips and Tracie Peterson. The extraordinary seven-book series THE RUSSIANS, the first three written with Phillips, showcases her creativity and skill as a historian as well as a fiction writer. A Bachelor of Arts degree in social studies, along with a career in nursing and teaching, lends depth to her storytelling, providing readers with memorable novels in a variety of genres. She and her husband make their home in Oregon.

Visit Judith's Web site:
www.judithpella.com

Dedication

This book is dedicated to the memory of four World War II veterans who have been dear to me and who have passed away since I began this series: my father-in-law Harry DeMeire, my uncles Omero Betti, Richard Betti, and William Hughes. I don't know if I ever truly thanked them for the sacrifices they made in the war, but in their honor I would now like to thank all veterans who have served this country in wartime.

PART I

"I have a boy at sea on a destroyer—
for all I know he may be on his way to the Pacific;
two of my children are in coast cities on the Pacific.
Many of you all over the country
have boys in the service who will now be called
upon to go into action;
you have friends and families in a danger zone.
You cannot escape anxiety,
you cannot escape the clutch of fear at your heart,
and yet I hope that the certainty of what we have to
meet will make you rise above those fears. . . ."

ELEANOR ROOSEVELT
December 7, 1941

1

Kuibyshev, Soviet Union
December 1941

WHEN CAMERON WALKED into the dining room of the Grand Hotel in Kuibyshev that evening of December 7, it seemed quite natural to see Johnny Shanahan and Alex Rostov seated together at a table chatting. It took a couple of heartbeats for her to realize what was wrong—or so very right!—about that scene. After all, when she had left Kuibyshev several weeks ago to visit her family in the States, Alex had been in Moscow, and it had appeared as if they might be parted for a very long while.

"Alex!" she exclaimed, and forgetting all reserve, forgetting that the room was filled with gawking journalists who had suddenly lost interest in their dinner, Cameron ran toward the table.

Alex rose and met her halfway, taking her into his arms, nearly lifting her off her feet. They kissed several times before the teasing guffaws of her associates reached her ears. But it was Shanahan's voice that finally penetrated her romantic daze.

"Uh . . . I hate to be a party pooper, but you two aren't supposed to be seeing each other . . . remember?" he said cautiously but with his usual hint of sarcasm.

"Hang the police!" Alex rejoined and kissed her again.

But Cameron eased away. She had indeed almost forgotten, nearly mesmerized as she had been by Alex's intense gaze washing over her like the bluest, clearest river warmed by a summer sun. The mess with Oleg Gorbenko had nearly gotten her deported and had made her return to Russia tenuous until her visa had actually been granted. A few weeks in America had made her forget the dangers of being involved in any way, much less romantically, with a Russian citizen.

"What are you doing here, anyway, Alex?" she murmured.

"You are not complaining, are you?"

"Oh, no—never." Sighing, she melted into another of his kisses. Then she finally became clearly aware of the whistles and laughs from her friends. "What is wrong with all of you?" she asked with mock affront. "Have you no decency?"

"What?" laughed Donovan, the correspondent with the *New York Tribune*. "It ain't us spooning in the middle of a public room!"

"Then I guess we better find a more private place," said Cameron, taking Alex's hand and tugging him toward the door, though in truth, he needed little prodding toward privacy.

The only place they could find was Cameron's tiny room, which was just as she had left it several weeks ago. They experienced a bit of awkwardness at first, which Cameron attributed not only to being in her room but also to the fact that this was the first time they had been together since that day in the Moscow hospital where Alex worked when they had declared their love for each other, only to be parted by the demands of war and the NKVD. She had since then often wondered what it would be like to be with Alex on these new terms or whether they would ever even have the opportunity. Now here they were together again, and all at once the extremely unfamiliar sensation of shyness threatened to overcome Cameron. Even chitchat eluded her.

This was the man she loved. The first man she had ever made such a commitment to. Even she and Johnny Shanahan had never exchanged such words. But then, some part of her had always known she never really loved Johnny, not in the real way she had discovered was possible with Alex. No, if anything, she loved what Johnny represented to her as a journalist and mentor. They were like-minded souls, yes, but never had their hearts touched. Johnny had lacked some elemental, though nebulous, thing that Cameron's soul needed in order to be fulfilled. That *thing*, and she still wasn't certain exactly what it was, had been there with Alex. He seemed to complete something within her, or he held the promise of such completion.

Suddenly Cameron was aware of the key she wore on a chain around her neck. Alex had given it to her when he learned the police were going to keep them apart. It had belonged to Alex's mother and was the key to her house in Leningrad. The woman had been forced to leave that home before the Great War, forced into exile because she was a revolutionary. She had died before returning to Russia. Alex had given Cameron the key as a promise that one day they would fulfill his mother's dream and visit her house. They would do it together.

That seemed a dim dream now that Leningrad was a city besieged by German invaders, a city gripped by bombardment and famine and God only knew what other horrors. No foreigners were allowed into the city, and only those Russians who could be slipped past the blockade in order to offer aid to the city were permitted entrance. Yes, the hope was dim. But here was Alex, now defying the odds, sitting near her. It must be true, then, that anything could happen. Even in Russia.

"How long will you be here?" Cameron asked, breaking the silence that had fallen between them.

"As long as they can do without me in Moscow," he replied. "As you can imagine, the casualties are pouring in."

"The war is going well, though, isn't it?"

"The Red Army seems to have stopped the German attempt to take Moscow, for now at least, but the balance of power shifts like the wind on the Volga. Morale, though, is high in the city, and a Russian counteroffensive has been launched."

"Winter will be an ally."

Alex shrugged with little enthusiasm. "Winter has hit the Russian Army as well as the Germans. What many foreigners don't realize is that it will actually be easier with the freeze. The mud and rain are really more of a detriment. And make no mistake, anything that is a hardship for the Germans is a negative for the Russians, as well."

Searching his face, she saw the strain of the last weeks clearly evident. The boyish element of his stunning good looks was almost absent now, replaced by a drawn weariness that she had missed in the initial bliss of their meeting. "Was it terrible for you, Alex?"

The slightest of shudders preceded his reply as he raked a hand through his golden hair. "A nightmare, Cameron. It took me two days away from Moscow to cease hearing the echoing of cannonade in my ears. The wounded, the dead. Dear God! The dead! So many—" Stopping abruptly, he added a moment later, "You don't need to hear this."

"Of course I do—I mean, I want to hear what is in your heart," she replied emphatically.

"Not on your homecoming." He forced a smile. "Anyway, I always wanted to be in a frontline medical unit, and that is probably as close as I will come. Now all I want is for the fighting to end."

An awkward silence fell between them, and attempting to fill it, Cameron said, "With all that, I am surprised you could leave Moscow at all."

"The hospital had to make room for the influx of wounded, so all patients who could be moved have been evacuated. Yuri was kind enough to arrange for me to accompany the train of evacuees here to Kuibyshev. I didn't know you'd be gone."

"There was no way I could let you know."

"I understand." His eyes roved over her as if he were afraid to believe they were together.

"How did you happen to be at the hotel?"

"Johnny found out from the embassy when you were returning. He told me, and I wanted to be here when you arrived. I prayed the flight would not be delayed."

"Which it was in the final leg over Siberia. We had a little engine trouble and were forced to land in a small airport. I'm not even sure where it was."

"Johnny found out about that, so we didn't have to wait too long."

"I am so glad it worked out."

Alex reached out and took her hands in his. He was seated on the one chair in the room, and she was sitting on the edge of the bed.

"You haven't said anything about your visit home," he said.

"The least said the better," she answered, making little attempt to mask her bitterness. How many times during her difficult visit with her family had she longed to talk with Alex? Now she just wanted to forget it all, pretend she was in a world that could no longer be touched by the strife at home. But that kind of fantasy better suited her mixed-up sister, Blair. Cameron was a realist . . . usually.

"That bad, eh?" Alex said sympathetically.

"I should have known better than to have let that little bug of optimism intrude on my natural pessimistic self. I let myself forget just how strongly my father could hold a grudge."

Shaking Alex's hands from hers, she jumped up and strode to the little window that looked out onto a small side street. A woman carrying a basket, probably heading to the market not far from the hotel, passed by below. The snow on the ground had turned to dirty slush. Cameron thought of the unfinished letter still tucked in her typewriter case—the letter she had written to her father on the plane ride back to Russia only hours before. It now evoked more pain in her than hope.

Her father had rebuked all her efforts to reach out to him. What made her think he'd regard a letter any differently? Knowing him, he'd take it as another sign of weakness on her part, a sign that she did not have the courage to confront him face-to-face. He would not allow that she had tried.

"I thought his illness might have mellowed him," she said to Alex, still staring unseeing out the glass now frosted by the cold. "I hoped it might have made him more appreciative of the bonds between him and his daughters. But it seems he has only become more bitter and selfish." Sighing, she ran a hand through her hair. "I'm sorry. I don't want to ruin our time now by talking about it."

"It might help to talk—"

"No . . . it doesn't. It just makes me feel helpless." How she hated feeling helpless! And she became just that much more angry at her father for causing such a sensation in her.

Alex rose and came up beside her, slipping his arm around her and drawing her close. "You can't lose hope—"

"Sometimes I do feel hope, then something happens to crush it. I will not live that way—reaching a height, then plummeting down. It does no good to raise one's hopes only to eventually have them smashed."

"You can't be saying you'll never hope again!" His arm tensed slightly but remained in place.

"I think it's safer that way."

"I never took you for a coward, Cameron."

"What? I'm not!" Her voice rose to an ominous edge.

"Then why back away from the risk of hoping for good?"

"You don't understand."

"There is a way to hope without risk."

"And what is that?" She heard the challenge in her own tone and knew she should recant, but she was growing a bit miffed at Alex. He was supposed to make her forget about the troubles at home, not goad her into facing them.

"By trusting God," he said.

Almost involuntarily she jerked from his hold. "I better get unpacked before the wrinkles become impossible." She strode away, hoisted her suitcase onto the bed, and opened it.

"Can we talk about this?" he asked quietly.

She jerked a dress from the bag. It was a dark green crepe with a delicately beaded neckline that she'd bought with thoughts of wearing it while dancing with Alex. She took it to the closet and hung it up, feeling slightly foolish for her frivolity in buying it. What else had she been frivolous about in the last months?

Returning to the suitcase, she reached for a blouse, then saw the book that had been tucked under the dress. On the front of the black leather cover were the words *Holy Bible*. How did that get there? Her suitcase had never—Jackie! It must have been her youngest sister. She had checked in the suitcases while Cameron and her mother had talked alone for a few moments at the airport. Cameron wanted to fling the book across the room. But she didn't, maybe because it had come from dear Jackie. Maybe because she sensed such an act would hurt Alex. Instead, she removed the blouse, ignoring the Bible except to surreptitiously push another garment over it so that Alex would not chance to see it and question her about it. She wanted no such questions now.

She shook out the blouse and hung it next to the dress. She kept unpacking for a few minutes with dogged determination until Alex came and put his hand on the hanger she held.

"Talk to me, Cameron," he said with that soft-spoken intensity she'd come to love about him. But she saw now that when it was directed so uncomfortably at her, she did not like it as much.

She jerked the hanger from his grasp. "There's nothing to talk about."

"Why are you angry at me?"

Shrugging, she returned to her task.

He wouldn't let it go. "So that's it? We suddenly have nothing to talk about? We made certain commitments to each other before you left, and now you are saying we have nothing to talk about!" His voice rose at the end with dismay and frustration, she was certain, not with anger.

She dropped the skirt she was holding and turned. Her eyes, she knew, were glistening with tears she would not permit to spill over. "Alex, I don't want to fight on my first day back, or any day for that matter." She took a step closer to him and met his gaze. "There are so many other things we can talk about. We've always had something to talk about." She raised her hands and cupped his face in them. "Please, Alex . . ." She didn't know what else to say. She wasn't built for begging. She wasn't even certain what she was pleading for. Peace, she supposed, and love—the very things she had not received at home.

He seemed to understand, because he wrapped his arms around her once again. His embrace was tight, secure. His clean-shaven cheek, pressed against her hair, was warm, and she detected a fervor in his closeness that made her feel sure he desired the same thing. They did have something good and strong. It meant nothing that there were certain touchy areas between them. That was normal to all couples. Wasn't it?

But all Cameron's fears and uncertainties suddenly shrank in importance the moment her room door burst open.

"Johnny!" She'd been facing the door and was shocked when he exploded into the room.

He immediately noted the two standing there in an embrace and, suddenly remembering himself, became uncharacteristically awkward.

"Oh . . . uh . . . sorry. Forgot myself—" Then Shanahan seemed to shake off his momentary self-consciousness. "You gotta hear this. The Japanese have bombed Hawaii—Pearl Harbor—a surprise attack."

Cameron and Alex fell apart from each other and stood gaping at Johnny. Cameron understood enough of world politics to realize the import of this event. It meant America would soon be in the war. In an instant Cameron knew that each one of them, when asked years in the future, "Where were you when Pearl Harbor was bombed?" would remember this moment vividly, how they stood in stunned silence, how even Cameron could not dredge up so much as one question.

Alex, in typical fashion, voiced the first and foremost concern of such an event. "How bad was it?"

"Devastating," Johnny said. "We were taken by surprise. Initial reports are still confused, but the entire U.S. Pacific Fleet was likely crippled. Loss of life is sure to be high."

The three continued to stand in strangulating silence, a silence wrapped around insensibility and numbness.

Finally Johnny said, "It's not entirely unexpected."

His words were like a release, and Cameron realized she needed to talk. She blurted out in rambling fashion all the questions that now popped into her head. Johnny had few answers, but they all offered much speculation. Once America declared war on Japan, Germany—Japan's ally—would declare war on America. Stalin would soon have his Second Front. The only question was when. Could America stage a war in the Pacific and also in Europe? Anything could happen now that the country had finally been roused.

Suddenly Johnny spun around and headed toward the door.

"Where are you going?" Cameron asked.

When he looked up, she saw his jaw was set and his eyes were flashing. The gears of his mind were spinning.

"I'm going to the cable office," he said. "This is my ticket out of here!"

Cameron knew that Johnny had been growing more and more disenchanted with the frustrations of reporting the Russian War. All the correspondents had been frustrated by Russian bureaucracy and repression, made worse by the evacuation to Kuibyshev, which was more remote and more backward than Moscow ever was. Johnny never ceased to complain about the restrictions imposed upon them that prevented them from reporting the true situation here.

"Don't get your hopes up," Cameron said. "You are a veteran here, and the *Journal* isn't going to sacrifice your experience in order to provide you with a more exciting life."

"You wanna bet?" He looked like he might do something crazy. "They are gonna want their best man covering the big story, which now is in the Pacific."

"No false modesty here," said Cameron drolly.

She would say no more to burst his bubble, especially in front of Alex. But had Johnny forgotten the fact that he'd only gotten this assignment in the first place just to spite her? Her father had thought to use his power as publisher of the *Los Angeles Journal* to keep her and Johnny apart by sending him to Europe. He hadn't expected Cameron to take a job with a competitor newspaper and be sent to Europe herself. But even if her father hadn't had an ulterior motive, Shanahan's past mistakes would have kept him far from a foreign assignment. Still, he had proved his competence on this job, so perhaps he had indeed made himself indispensable to the *Journal*.

Only then did Cameron realize how Shanahan's disposition might affect her. If he was transferred, would Max Arnett, her publisher for the *Los Angeles Globe*, insist on keeping up the silly cat-and-mouse game he'd begun over a year ago by sending Cameron out as a competitor against Johnny and the *Journal*? And how did she feel about the possibility? As a journalist, following breaking news was her first instinct and desire. Russia was still a major player in this war, but it was a sure bet that Americans were going to be more interested in reading about American battles rather than about ones in a land so far removed from them, not only geographically but culturally and politically. Cameron had come to enjoy the front-page status her reporting had earned her. Stories about Russia would no doubt now be shuffled to the inside pages. Her pulse began to race as visions of following U.S. troops through the Pacific filled her mind. This was the dream of every war correspondent.

Then, almost as if to taunt her, she felt Alex's presence next to her. Guilt washed over her.

Would it really be that easy for her to give up what she had with Alex for a little glory? Had her commitment to him been that shallow? She truly did not believe it was. Couldn't she have both? Yet logic indicated that if she left Russia again, her chances of returning would be poor, and Alex's chances of leaving were little better. How certain she had been not long ago that she and Alex would not become victims of the constrictions upon them. And she had been even more certain that she would fight for their relationship. How could she toy with the idea of placing her career over him?

"You look pale, Hayes," Johnny said, breaking abruptly into her dismal reverie. "Doesn't she, Doc?"

Alex turned to face her, his gaze intent. It was almost as if he could read her mind.

"I think she's worried the *Globe* is gonna drag her away from here," Johnny said. "You know, in order to keep her competing with me when I go."

Cameron looked from one man to the other, feeling oddly torn between them, as she had in the past. She knew she did not love Johnny, but he represented a part of her life she did love. More than Alex?

She licked her lips. "No one says you are going anywhere, Shanahan." Her voice was puny.

"We shall see." With that challenge, he made an impressive exit.

"Have you ever seen such an arrogant man?" she said weakly.

"Is he right?" Alex asked.

"No. Of course not. Nothing's going to change."

He must know she was lying. Everything would change—everything *had* changed! Who were they to think they could escape? Yet for this moment Cameron wanted to believe her words. So, it seemed, did Alex. They melted once more into an embrace. Neither would admit they were actually hiding in each other's arms, hiding from an uncertain world.

Los Angeles, California
December 7, 1941

THE BALMY SUNLIT DAY belied the fact that it was almost winter. Not that this was unusual for Southern California, but this did make it difficult for Jackie to concentrate on readying herself for final exams next week. Nevertheless, when the stoplight on the road turned green, she pressed the Ford's accelerator and continued on her way to the UCLA library.

It was Sunday, and she had just left church. Several of her friends had decided to take advantage of the beautiful day and go swimming and have a barbecue at one of their homes. Jackie had declined the invitation, wanting to use every chance she could for studying. She'd all but forgotten school in the previous weeks, what with her father's illness and Cameron's visit. Now she had to apply herself. She had only one more semester left before graduation.

The song "Only Forever" was playing on the car radio, and Jackie couldn't help humming along with Bing Crosby. She should be thinking about the periodic table if she planned to pass her chemistry final. But she didn't turn off the radio. She just let her mind continue its ramble and wasn't surprised when she began to wonder what Sam was doing right now. She could forget the library and chemistry in a heartbeat if it meant seeing him. But there was no way she could pop in on him unexpectedly. No, it took some rather clever maneuvering for them to get together these days.

She had seen him twice since the night of her father's heart attack. She had needed Sam desperately that night, and despite the fact that both their families had strictly forbidden them to see each other—at least, his would have if they had known—he had come when she had called. That night they had declared their love for each other. And she still could not believe they had done anything wrong. She was white; he was Japanese. There were laws in California against them, but in her heart she knew God had brought them together, and she knew God had not sanctioned such bigoted laws.

Still, they had to sneak about in order to be together. They were clearly meant for each other but felt like criminals because of the intolerance of others.

If school wasn't such a pressure just now, she would indeed turn the car toward Inglewood, where Sam lived with his parents on their produce farm. Now that he had finished his bachelor's degree from UCLA, it was harder than ever for them to see each other. He was taking only a couple of classes toward his master's degree in English. Since there was no ready employment, he worked on his family's farm, providing the necessary help so they wouldn't have to hire anyone and thus freeing money to put toward his college expenses. But the farm work was demanding, and he seldom could get away. With just a hint of ire, Jackie thought of his unsuccessful attempts to find work last June and in the months after his graduation. He wanted a job in which he could use his education. He eventually wanted to be a writer, but until he could make a living at that, he had hoped to teach English somewhere. He'd known all along that Japanese graduates seldom found work in their chosen fields—most ended up at menial jobs—but he had kept hoping for months until finally the rejections piling one on top of the other had worn down his optimism. His parents needed him on the farm, and that option seemed better than taking some menial job from strangers.

Jackie sighed, feeling the weight of the unfairness of life. She uttered a prayer, asking God to remove that weight and to help her focus more on Him. She knew how easy it was for despair to settle in when she took her eyes off her Lord.

Just then the music on the radio stopped. The "Chattanooga Choo Choo" had taken Bing's place, and she hadn't even noticed.

An announcer's voice spoke. "We interrupt this program to bring you a special news bulletin. At approximately 8:00 A.M. Hawaiian time, the Japanese bombed Pearl Harbor in Hawaii. I repeat, Pearl Harbor has been bombed by the Japanese in a surprise air attack."

Stunned, Jackie only chanced to glance up and see the yellow light.

She slammed on the brakes and stopped just as the light turned red. With hands trembling as they gripped the wheel, she gasped in a breath. Had she heard right? An attack on Pearl Harbor? Of course she knew Hawaii was a U.S. territory, and thus it meant the Japanese had attacked the United States. This was different than the Japanese aggression in the Far East. Now America would have no choice but to respond.

This meant war. With Japan.

A sick feeling clutched at Jackie's stomach. Only the screaming horns outside the car made her focus. The light was green again, and other vehicles were impatient. Had they not heard? Didn't they know? The world was crashing in on them.

The library entirely forgotten, she turned around at the first opportunity. She had only one thought now.

Sam.

Quickly leaving the city behind, she was soon surrounded by orange groves and open fields. The groves were picturesque, the trees dotted with oranges almost ready for harvest. Some of the fields were green with crops, others fallow, waiting for spring planting. This was a rich, fertile land, a beautiful land. Without the encumbrance of a frozen winter, there was no end to the possibilities here. But in view of what she'd just heard on the radio, Jackie suddenly realized that this region of the country was also now a prime target. Would the Japanese stop at the Hawaiian Islands? What was to keep them from striking the West Coast of the mainland? Perhaps there were planes even now—

"This just in . . ." boomed the announcer's voice over the radio.

There had been continuous talk after the first announcement, but it had been mostly a discussion of the political situation over the last few months between America and Japan. Jackie, consumed with her own thoughts, had blocked out the talk until now, when the voice seemed more urgent.

"Preliminary reports indicate Japanese aircraft have made a devastating strike against the American Pacific Fleet. American lives have been lost, but no figures have been ascertained at this time. . . ."

With the taste of bile stinging her throat, Jackie could barely concentrate but forced herself to focus. She had never been to the Okuda farm and had only a few remarks by Sam to guide her. He'd mentioned a store and a gas pump on the corner just before the turn to the Okuda place. She was driving so fast she nearly sped past the store. It was surrounded by groves, so no wonder she had nearly missed it. Slamming her brake pedal and turning sharply on the steering wheel, she made the turn. There should be a sign over a driveway reading *Okuda Produce*.

There it was! She made a more conservative turn into the drive. On both sides were fields. The farm was largely invested in strawberries, but a couple of acres were devoted to a variety of other produce, as well. She didn't see the house until she eased around a curve. The building that came into view was a single-level sprawling structure with little overall design, as if rooms had been added by necessity over time. It certainly was no Beverly Hills mansion, but neither was it squalid and poor. All was sturdy and clean, with flowers in front and vegetable gardens growing close by the walls.

Taking all this in, she was startled by a figure darting into the path of the car. Slamming the brakes again, she stopped ten feet from the man. Only then did she realize he was Sam.

He ran up to the driver's window. "Jackie!" The look on his face and the surprise of his tone were not entirely welcoming. "What are you doing here?" His gaze darted toward the house before returning to her.

"I didn't know what else to do," she said. "Sam, listen—"

"Not here, Jackie." Jogging around the car, he opened the passenger door and, pausing only a moment to brush dust and bits of dirt from his work-worn clothes, jumped in. "Go!" he ordered, with one more glance toward the house.

Jackie glanced at the house before making a U-turn and wheeling back down the drive the way she had come. She understood his reluctance toward her meeting his parents. They must wait until the time was right—and she knew better than he that this definitely wasn't the right time. She checked the house again in the rearview mirror and thought she saw a face looking out one of the windows of the house, but it was shadowed and unclear.

She didn't stop until she reached the store at the corner. Sam then directed her to another back road that took them up a grove-covered rise. He finally told her to park at the end of this dirt road. She fought back a touch of ire at the whole situation. It wasn't fair that she couldn't visit him at his home, meet his parents and brother and sisters. Then it hit her—his parents weren't U.S. citizens and were now enemy aliens! The bile continued to clog her throat.

"Sam, have you heard the news?"

"I've been working all day. We had a problem with the irrigation system, and I had to miss church. What's wrong?"

"The Japanese bombed Hawaii this morning." She could barely get the words out. "Pearl Harbor."

He just stared at her a moment, then closed his eyes and murmured, "Dear God."

Unlike many Americans who didn't pay close attention to the conflicts going on in other parts of the world, they both were fairly aware of the world situation and understood at least the most obvious meaning of what had happened. They both sat silent for a good five minutes. Sam rested his head against the back of the seat, his eyes open but unseeing, his jaw working spasmodically. For the first time in a long while, Jackie noticed his Japanese features. She studied his thick, black, straight hair, his slanted eyes. She even fancied she detected a yellow tinge to his skin.

Suddenly she realized she was being caught up in a loathsome mania—one that had already begun to infiltrate California and one that she feared would only get worse. He was not the enemy, just as his skin was not yellow. It was, in fact, tan and ruddy from working in the fields these last few months. He was Sam, the man she loved.

He turned to face her. "Jackie . . . I need you!" His eyes, black like onyx, glistened.

She only nodded, because words caught in her throat.

He slid close to her and reached his arms around her. His lips found hers, and he kissed her several times with a fervency she'd not felt from him before. She knew the intensity of his kiss came from more than love. She sensed, like herself, he needed to touch her on a level that blocked out all the barriers between them. He needed to sense the love they felt, if only for a moment, before the ugliness of war intruded.

They clung to each other for a long time. No words were necessary. She felt his breathing and the warmth of his skin. She detected the fragrance of earthy dust from the fields about him. And it all washed her with a sense of security. Nothing else mattered.

It fell to Sam to shatter Jackie's fantasy.

"I must tell my parents," he said.

"Can't we—?" She stopped herself, knowing her wish was futile.

They could not be alone on an island apart from the rest of the crazy world.

He moved back from her a little so he could gaze fully on her face. "Everything will change now."

"But not for good." Her voice trembled as tears filled her eyes.

"You and I . . ." Tears were in his eyes, as well. "We have something to hold us together no matter what." He lifted her chin with a finger encrusted with dirt, but she didn't care. He gave an encouraging smile. "Pray with me, okay?"

"Okay." She sniffed, trying to rid herself of the clog of tears.

They grasped hands, bowed their heads, closed their eyes.

"Father," Sam prayed, "only you know what will become of us all. Help us to find strength in the knowledge that you are in supreme control of our destinies as individuals and as a world. Help us to find courage in that, for we are really afraid. I feel like we might lose sight of who we are, that we might doubt our love, maybe even our humanity. But always keep us aware of the fact that despite everything, we are your children. No one can take that from us. No one can rob us of your love nor of the love you have put in our hearts for each other. Those two facts will always be, even if the world ends. Your love, our love. With that we can face anything. Amen." He paused and then addressed Jackie. "It's true," he said. "Don't doubt it."

"I won't."

"I've got to get back now." He reached for the door handle. "I don't know when I'll be able to see you again."

"That, too, is in God's hands." She hoped she sounded braver than she felt.

She reached for the keys to turn on the ignition, but Sam laid a hand on hers. "I'll walk back."

She knew this wasn't the time to talk about meeting his family, so she let him go. He said he'd call her soon. He stood watching as she drove off. She kept glancing in the rearview mirror until she could no longer see him. Her heart swelled with the intensity of her love for him. By the grace of God she had found a good man to love, a tenderhearted man, a man of honor, a godly man. She was to be greatly envied in her good fortune. Nothing could shake that.

3

THE MOMENT THE CAR was out of sight, Sam turned and cut through the orange grove, taking a shortcut he knew. He did not hurry, though neither did his feet drag. He needed to tell his family the news, but he wasn't anxious to do so. He had little concept of how this might change their lives, but he had no doubt it would. His parents were not citizens and would be considered enemy aliens now. As such, they could very well be arrested or deported, but Sam did not for a minute believe that would happen. This was America! Certainly these people who had lived here for over twenty-five years would be treated fairly.

Yet Sam was not unaware of the racial intolerance to be found in the States, in California in particular, where there were several sizable Japanese communities. This terrible evil had been present as long as there had been minorities. Sam had experienced it on a personal level. It could only get worse now that the face of the enemy was a Japanese face.

It took Sam ten minutes to get home. Much to his dismay, the whole family was gathered in the house for the Sunday midday meal. He'd hoped to break the news to his parents alone. But the youngsters would find out eventually, so perhaps it was best they were all together.

The screen door slammed behind him as he stepped inside. His mother had made a warm, cozy home for the family. True, the furnishings were not stylish, and most were rather old, but there were vases of cut flowers everywhere, along with evidence of the needlework his mother enjoyed doing, which brightened dull corners and scratched surfaces. The wallpaper in the kitchen where he found everyone gathered was cheerful, with an array of bright yellow daises placed in an irregular pattern, and the table and chairs that dominated the room had been built years ago by his father. The fragrance of fish soup permeated the air, underscored by the aroma of spice cake—Sam's favorite.

Pausing a moment, he took in the scene, studying his family as if he might not see them like this again, and truly, he probably would never see them in this carefree light again.

Sam was the oldest of five children. Next after him was his sister Kimi, eighteen and engaged to be married to the son of the Japanese man who owned the little grocery store down the road. Sam's brother, Toshio, was the only other boy. He was sixteen and went by the nickname T.C., for his favorite baseball player, Ty Cobb. The "little sisses," as the family often referred to them, were the youngest girls, Miya, eleven, and Mika, ten. They were ten months apart in age and as much alike as twins.

The noise level in the kitchen, the largest room in the house, built by Sam's father and added to over the years, was quite high at the moment with everyone seeming to be talking at once. The little sisses were jabbering to their mother about the costumes they needed for the upcoming Christmas play at school. Sam's mother, Hoshi Okuda, was scolding them for not letting her finish preparing lunch. At the same time she was prodding Kimi to finish setting the table, but Kimi was involved in a conversation with T.C., who apparently had heard a rumor about Kimi's fiancé taking a job on a fishing boat.

Only Hiroshi Okuda, Sam's father, was silent. He sat in his chair by the rock fireplace in the living room, easily visible through the large archway between the rooms. He had a Japanese-American newspaper in hand, his pipe smoking between his lips. He was, as always, an island of calm in the maelstrom of family life. Tall like his eldest son but a good deal thinner, he was a very spare man. He ate like a horse but just never could keep on much weight. Sam's eyes now rested upon this figure of unflappable repose. He was a stoic man, even rather stern at times. He never raised his voice, in fact, he seldom said anything, but when he did open those thin lips, his words were always listened to, almost always respected. Sam thought of himself as quite different from his father in many ways, but he hoped that he would one day be the kind of solid, responsible, respected man his father was.

Sam's observations occurred in mere seconds. The screen door had hardly banged against the doorframe before his thoughts were interrupted by his mother.

"Where did you go, Yoshito?" she asked. Sam's given name was Yoshito. His middle name was Samuel, which was given him to honor a close friend of the family, a white friend. He suddenly realized he had never told this to Jackie, and she knew him only as Sam. He wondered why he had not mentioned his full name. But his mother was still railing at him. "And is that a friend of yours who was here? How rude is she that she not even stop to greet your family?"

Sam's mother's English, which she spoke now, was quite good, and she worked hard to properly pronounce *r*'s and *l*'s. Unlike her husband, whose command of the language, even after being in the country for twenty-five years, was tenuous at best. Of course, because of his taciturn nature he practiced little. If Hiroshi was involved in the conversation, they almost always spoke Japanese. If only the children were conversing, especially the little sisses, whose command of Japanese was limited, they usually spoke English.

"What kind of people you meet at that college?" she went on. "Don't they teach manners there?" Hoshi was a petite woman, a bit on the plump side. She often complained about the unfairness of the fact that nothing her husband ate put a pound on him but *everything* she ate padded her hips. She also contradicted all the stereotypes of the timid, obedient Japanese woman. She spoke her mind often and loudly, at least among her family and friends. She was more circumspect among the outside world of strangers.

"She wanted to come in, Mama," Sam tried to explain. "But I wanted to go for a ride—"

"You ashamed of your family? That it? It looked like a white girl—"

"I saw them together at the movies once," broke in T.C.

"Shut up, T.C.!" blurted Sam, frustrated. He did not want to go that route now. There were more important things to discuss.

"What is this?" came the soft voice of Hiroshi Okuda, clearly heard, though he sat in the other room. He had no problem *understanding* English!

All heads turned toward the head of the family. For him to ask the question meant this was an important issue. Indeed, he would be as opposed to a child of his consorting with a white person of the opposite sex as anyone in the white community would oppose an interracial relationship.

But this was not the time for such a discussion, and Sam had the means at his disposal to nip it in the bud and make everyone totally forget the mysterious white girl in the Ford. And he used it.

"Listen to me, everyone!" he said as forcefully as his father, though a good deal louder. He spoke Japanese to make sure his father clearly understood. "I have important news. You must all hear this. Earlier this morning the Japanese bombed Pearl Harbor." He repeated the message in English to ensure that his sisters understood.

Six voices clamored at once, but two rose above the din of the other responses.

"What is Pearl Harbor?" Sam's mother asked.

"I did not bomb anyone!" stated Sam's father.

Naturally Sam addressed his father's comment first. "Papa, you know what I mean."

"*I* did not bomb anyone!" The older man said again unequivocally.

With a resigned sigh, Sam corrected himself. "*Japan* has bombed Pearl Harbor."

Hiroshi gave a curt nod of approval of the semantic change, but his wife was not going to be ignored.

"I want to know what is this Pearl Harbor! I never heard of it." She put a hand on her hip, demanding satisfaction.

"Mama, it is part of Hawaii, which is a territory of the United States. It means Japan has attacked America!"

"Does this mean a war?" asked Kimi, a worried frown creasing her pretty features.

"Yes," Sam replied. "Almost certainly." He turned back to his father. "Papa, you know what this means? You and Mama are not citizens."

"We tried to be citizens!" Sam's mother said, affronted. "They will not let us be Americans. Mrs. Lombardi came here from Italy. She grows very nice tomatoes, by the way. She became a citizen. But if we are born in Japan, it is against the law. This I do not understand. But even so—"

"Enough, wife!" Hiroshi said as he lurched suddenly to his feet and strode into the kitchen. "This is not the time for complaints. Feed the children. Yoshito, come with me."

Sam followed his father down the hall to his parents' bedroom.

From the kitchen he could hear the sounds of chairs scraping and creaking as the rest of the family took their places around the table. If they were like Sam, they probably had no appetite, but they would not balk at their father's order. Anyway, the meal would provide distraction.

In the bedroom Sam's father began to open and search through dressers. He asked Sam to get an empty box, and this he filled with papers—old letters and newspapers and a few documents.

"What are you doing?" Sam asked.

"In case the police come," Hiroshi replied, again in Japanese. "They must not find anything incriminating."

"These are just letters from our family in Japan."

"Everything from Japan must go. Look carefully though the chest."

Gradually the box filled up. The last thing Hiroshi placed on top was a beautiful silk Japanese flag, its white field pristine and the red circle in the center sharp and clear.

"My father gave this to me when I left Japan," he mused, mostly to himself. "It is the only thing I have left of his."

"Papa, no one expects you—"

But Hiroshi shook his head adamantly. "There must be no doubt where my loyalties lie. Take these things to the incinerator."

"But Papa—"

"Do it, son. Burn them. Now!"

Later that evening Sam knew for certain what a wise man his father was. The family was seated around the radio listening to The Jack Benny Show. Though they tried to distract themselves with the humor of the show, no one had forgotten the terrible news of the day. Even if they might, frequent news reports came on to remind them. More details had come in from Hawaii, none very encouraging, though it would be a while before exact figures of the real extent of the damage were ascertained. But many Americans had been killed or injured in the attack, and American ships and planes had been hit hard. This horror was not going to disappear.

No wonder the family tried to lose themselves in the amusing banter of Jack Benny, Rochester, and company. The laughter felt good after the shed tears. The little sisses didn't fully understand it all, but they wept because their mama wept. Mama wept when she learned

Sam had burned all the letters from home—from Japan, that is. They were all she had to remember her family, whom she knew she would never see again. Sam did not mention the possibility of deportation, that she might very well see them after all.

Everyone was startled when a knock came on the door. They hardly ever had surprise visitors, especially at that hour. Sam answered the door. Two men dressed in gray suits, wearing stern but impassive faces, greeted him.

"Is this the home of Hiroshi Okuda?" asked one of the men.

"Yes," said Sam, a knot growing in his stomach.

Hiroshi came up to the door. "I am he," he said in clear, precise English.

"I am Agent Foster, and this is Agent Brown with the FBI. We have a warrant to search the premises."

"Why?" asked Sam. "I mean, on what grounds?" Because of Hiroshi's difficulty with English, it was Sam's habit to take the lead in dealings with whites.

"You come in," said Hiroshi, who apparently thought this important enough for him to take charge despite his choppy English. "What you look for?"

"Contraband," said Agent Foster.

Hiroshi's brow creased over the unfamiliar word.

The agent explained curtly, "Weapons, radio equipment, anything suspicious."

"We don't have anything like that," said Sam defensively.

"We'll be the judge of that."

The agents made a thorough search of the house while the family watched in numb silence. The men came up with three rifles and two hunting knives. Sam tried to explain that they were used for hunting only. The agents appeared dubious and laid the weapons on the kitchen table. T.C. noted this and jumped up.

"What're you gonna do with those?" he demanded as he jerked his head toward the rifles. Sam knew one was brand-new, a gift to T.C. for his birthday two weeks ago.

"We have to confiscate them."

"What!" T.C. protested. "You can't do that!" He reached for the new rifle, but the agent grabbed his hand, firmly restraining him.

"Easy, son! None of that. All items will be tagged. Maybe after we lick you Japs you can have it back."

Sam put a calming arm around T.C. "We'll get it back later when everything settles down." He knew he was just blowing wind, but it seemed wise to appease his brother a bit.

Outside in the tool shed more "contraband" was found. The agents were especially interested in the ham radio they came upon. Sam had gotten the radio when he was a kid but then had lost interest in the hobby. Over the years the set had been cannibalized for other projects. What remained, completely useless though it was, apparently was very incriminating. There was also a half-full box of dynamite. Again Sam tried to explain it was left over from when they had cleared a new field last year.

Nothing he said mattered. The stuff was gathered up and loaded into the trunk of the FBI vehicle. Sam did not feel much relief when the agents drove away. Somehow he felt this was only the beginning.

After driving around for a while, Jackie returned home. Studying was out of the question now.

Her mother greeted her at the door. "Oh, Jacqueline!" she exclaimed as she threw her arms around her daughter.

"Then you've heard," Jackie said, clinging to her mother as she remembered the comfort to be found there.

"It is so terrible. I still can't believe it. There are two families at church with sons stationed in Hawaii. They don't know if they are alive or . . . oh, dear! War . . . it seems impossible."

The Pacific Fleet had only left Long Beach for Honolulu last year, so of course there would be many in Southern California personally touched by what had just happened. They would have sons and husbands and fathers wounded or killed. Jackie had selfishly forgotten that in her own grief. She could not keep from also being reminded of how this connection would cause hatred of the enemy to run more deeply on the West Coast.

"Where's Dad?" Jackie asked as she and her mother moved into the living room.

"He's at the office. I tried to tell him he shouldn't go. It has been only a few days since his release from the hospital. But this is war, and he certainly won't miss that. He has been a proponent of American involvement from the beginning." They sat beside each other on the sofa, still clinging together. Cecilia continued, "I never thought I'd have to live through another war. They said the last one was the war to end all wars. But your father says this one will be far worse than the last one, taking in the entire world. And with the Japanese involved, they could actually strike mainland America. What's to stop them? Our own homes could be—"

"Mom, we mustn't panic. Japan is too far away, and besides, our military would never let the enemy strike our land." Jackie made herself believe her own words. She knew that panic would be the worst thing that could happen to the Japanese community in California.

"Your father called the gardener and told him not to come back to work."

Jerry was Japanese. His real name was Jiro, but they had always called him Jerry because they had been uncomfortable with the foreign name. He came twice a week. Jackie had stopped to chat with him occasionally, but she had never known him, hardly even noticed him. He wasn't the enemy, though. He spoke good English, and she thought he was even a citizen but didn't know for certain. Her stomach knotted. How many others like Jerry were getting similar phone calls? How would they live now? What would become of them?

Them?

She could not think of these people in such a detached manner any longer. Her life was far too intricately wrapped up in their fate. She eyed her mother. What would she think if she knew? How many times had she wanted to tell her mother that she had found love with a good Christian man? But she simply hadn't had the courage to face the inevitable shattering it would bring to her family. Just the mere rumor last month of her friendship with a Japanese boy had, she feared, brought on her father's heart attack.

She and her mother tried to eat dinner that evening. But they kept the radio on during the meal, and every time a news bulletin interrupted the usual programming, their food became harder and harder to digest. Thus the evening passed into night, but neither woman could go to bed. Cecilia said she wouldn't be able to sleep until Keagan came home safe and sound, and he had already been gone for hours. It was too much all at once.

Around eleven Jackie felt her eyelids grow heavy. Maybe she'd be able to find sleep after all. She curled up with her feet on the sofa and her head resting on a throw pillow propped against the arm of the sofa. Just as she was about to give in to encroaching weariness, the front door creaked open.

Keagan strode into the room. His broad face was flushed with excitement, nearly matching his graying red hair. He was dressed in a blue serge suit with a maroon necktie and looked almost too dapper in light of present world events. The tie was loosened at the neck though, and there was a crease in his brow that contrasted with the aura of energy about him. The events and exertions of the day tolled equally upon him.

"Keagan, I was starting to worry." Cecilia set aside the book she had been absently reading and leaned forward in the upholstered chair where she sat.

"For heaven's sake, woman! I am not a child. I can come home whenever I please!" He lumbered toward a chair. His step was definitely not as light as usual, and for a big man, he'd always had an exceptionally graceful way about him.

"Can I get you something to eat, Dad?" Jackie swung her feet from the sofa, ready to rise.

"I had a bite with some of the boys earlier." He plopped into the chair.

"Tea, then?"

"I don't suppose you'd fix me a nice Bushmills on the rocks." There was a slight sneer to his tone. He knew very well the doctor had told him to cut out alcohol. "Never mind that. There's more war news that I doubt you've heard on the radio yet." His voice softened in an unusual way for him. The crease between his ruddy brows deepened. "A short while ago, the Japs started bombing the Philippines."

Blair!

Jackie's stomach twisted.

Cecilia gasped.

Keagan pulled himself from the chair and went to sit on the footstool by Cecilia's chair. He laid a hand over her hands resting in her lap. "Blair will be okay," he said. Jackie had never heard him speak so gently.

Cecilia rubbed her lips with a shaky hand. "H-how do you know?"

"They will only be striking military targets. The airfields, ammo dumps, perhaps the harbor."

Blair had gone to the Philippines two months ago in an attempt to repair the marriage she had damaged by her deceptions. Her husband was in the Army, stationed in the Philippines. Would she indeed be away from military areas? What if she were visiting him? What if—? Jackie forced herself to cease that path of thinking, especially when she glanced in her mother's direction and could tell from the older woman's eyes that she had been thinking the same things.

"Mom, Blair will be all right. Gary will take care of her," Jackie said, rather lamely to be sure but not without a bit of certainty. After all, Lieutenant Gary Hobart was a good man, and even if Blair had hurt him, he would die protecting her if he had to.

Jackie jumped up and went to her parents. Kneeling close to them, she put a hand on each of their shoulders. She wanted to feel close to them. They all needed one another now. She got the sense that even her father needed them, for he did not pull away from her touch. Instead, he snaked an arm around her waist.

Manila, Philippines
December 8, 1941

BLAIR STRETCHED LANGUIDLY in her bed, letting wakefulness overtake her as gradually as possible. The morning was warm, the lazily turning ceiling fan hardly stirring the humid air. She was surprised to see on her bedside clock that it was eight-thirty, much earlier than she usually awoke. But last night had been Sunday, and she hadn't worked as late as usual.

Watching the fan make its endless rotations, Blair wondered what she would do with the day, especially now that she had so much more time than usual. And it was her day off, as well. Maybe she'd do nothing at all—a very popular pastime in the tropics! But then, the heat made impossible the kind of activity one was accustomed to in colder climes, even places like Southern California. Not that Blair was complaining. Since her arrival to the Philippines she had come to enjoy the tropics and the rather lazy lifestyle of the islands. She'd only been here a couple of weeks, but after the twenty-seven-day journey on the ocean liner that had seemed to stop at every possible port in the Far East, she'd been ready to embrace any solid ground. She supposed she had inherited her father's deep distaste for water and ships.

"Miss Blair, you awake already?" A voice came from the doorway of her bedroom. On the other side of the curtain of beads that made the door stood the petite form of Blair's maid.

"Yes, Claudette, I guess I am." She gave a relaxed sigh.

"You want me to fix breakfast?"

"Just some coffee for now."

"Yes, miss." Claudette scampered away.

Even at her wealthy parents' home in Beverly Hills Blair had never had a personal maid. But here it was different. Help was so cheap that any foreigner could afford it, and there was so much poverty one hardly had the heart to refuse giving employment whenever possible. Blair had met Claudette on her first day in the islands. Unable to find Gary because he was on an assignment "in the hills" that would last several days, Blair, feeling rather dejected, had gone to a movie theater. The Barbara Stanwyck movie *Stella Dallas* was playing. Blair had seen it before in the States, but it was better than roaming the strange streets in the heat of the day. In the cool theater she would try to figure out what to do next.

On the way inside Blair, deep in her own thoughts, bumped into a little girl, and Blair's box of popcorn went flying. The girl was mortified, begging a hundred pardons. Blair was equally mortified that the girl was so upset.

"It's nothing," Blair said. "I can buy another."

"I made it spill. I should—"

"I wouldn't think of it."

But ignoring Blair, the girl actually went to the ticket window, cashed in her ticket, and tried to give Blair a peso of that money. She had obviously spent her only money on the ticket. Blair was in shock. She'd seldom witnessed such poverty.

"I will not take your money," Blair said firmly. "I bumped into you! I wasn't looking where I was going."

She then took the girl's hand, marched her back to the ticket window, and was about to instruct her to repurchase her ticket. But instead, Blair gave her own money for the girl's ticket. And bought her a bag of popcorn and a soda, too. The girl tried to protest, but Blair would have none of it. They watched the movie together.

It wasn't until afterwards, outside the theater, that they made introductions.

"I'm Blair Hayes." Blair had decided not to use her married name until things were settled with Gary. "This is my first day in Manila."

"I am Claudette Colbert. This is my fourteenth year in Manila!" She grinned at her wit.

Blair grinned back. The little Filipino girl hardly looked as old as fourteen except for a small blossom of adolescent maturity about her that was not noticeable until one really looked. She was pretty despite her smudged face, with masses of curly black hair tied into a ponytail with a dirty ribbon. Her faded pink dress was more like a sack, and she was barefoot. Blair was surprised they had allowed her into the theater dressed in that manner.

"You speak very good English," Blair commented as they walked down the sidewalk.

"Gotta speak English to get by in Manila," the girl said. "And to watch American movies. I learned most of it from the movies."

"Is that how you came by your name?" Blair asked as they walked together down the sidewalk. "Your parents must like movies, too."

"I chose it myself," Claudette said proudly. "I like movies, and Claudette Colbert is my most favorite actress. I have seen *It Happened One Night* ten times!"

"Well, we have something in common. I like movies, too. I was in a movie once. It probably hasn't come to the Philippines yet."

"You're a movie star?"

"No. I had a very small part. I thought I might like to become an actress—well, once. I'm a singer . . . well, unemployed at that."

"I'm unemployed, too."

"Where's your family, Claudette?"

"I'm an orphan kid—little orphan Claudette, huh?"

"But you must live someplace, an orphanage or foster home?"

She shrugged. "I got too big for the orphanage, so I left. I think I do better on my own."

Blair was aghast at the idea that this poor little girl thought her present ragamuffin life was better than living in an orphanage. "But who takes care of you? How do you eat? You're only fourteen!"

"I get by."

Her rather superior shrug seemed to be a bit pathetic when contrasted with her little-child looks.

"I run errands for many businesses along Dewey Avenue. I eat good most of the time." Pausing, she looked up at Blair. "Hey, Miss Blair Hayes, you have errand for me? I do it for free for you buying me popcorn. I never can afford to buy popcorn."

"I just got here . . . I don't know. Wait. Do you know of a good place to stay?"

"Follow me."

Claudette led Blair a short way down the broad avenue to the Manila Hotel. Blair looked up at the place, which even she knew must be the most opulent hotel in town. Once Blair would not have thought of staying anywhere else, but her finances were limited. Jackie had loaned her some cash, and she'd had a little saved, enough to purchase the ticket on the liner and enough for about a week or two of living frugally. The Manila Hotel did not fit into such a budget, though in her fine American clothes, she probably looked like Manila Hotel material to Claudette, who had seen only movie stars dress as elegantly as Blair and naturally thought all Americans were rich.

Blair smiled weakly at her new friend. "Anything else?" Then she added, "Maybe I should find a job first."

"You want a job. You say you sing? I know a place."

It probably looked absurd to anyone taking note, her being led about by this child, yet Blair was certain little Claudette Colbert was a godsend. For one thing, Blair thought it would be a good thing if she were settled and independent when Gary finally did return. She must be prepared for the worst, for the possibility of his rejecting her. But the last thing she wanted was for him to take her back because he felt sorry for her. She and Gary had enough problems to solve without tossing that in for good measure.

Claudette took Blair to a nightclub called the Casa Mañana. There Blair met the proprietor, a woman named Silvia Wang. She was half Chinese and half Spanish, a woman of about forty. Tall, shapely, and beautiful, she wore her coal black hair in a chignon with a white orchid tucked behind her ear. Dressed in a silk Manchu-style dress of a coral color with dragons and lilies woven into the fabric, she moved and spoke in a refined manner that hardly fit with the Manila nightclub scene. Blair later learned that Silvia's father had been a Chinese diplomat and her mother the daughter of a wealthy Manila family. The mother had been disowned by her family when she bore an out-of-wedlock child of mixed blood. Silvia's father, no doubt to save face in the diplomatic community, had not claimed the woman or the child. But Silvia's mother had not been left destitute by her family, and she and her mother had lived well, with Silvia attending fine private schools. When her mother died, Silvia used her small inheritance to buy the Casa Mañana.

She looked Blair up and down, and Blair noted that around the edges of the woman's refined beauty there was the shrewdness of a street vendor.

"I already have performers," Silvia said.

"Miss Blair was in a big Hollywood movie. She's a movie star," put in Claudette.

"Not a big movie," demurred Blair.

"Never heard your name," Silvia said. "Are you related to Helen Hayes?"

"No. But I'm a good singer, and I play the piano. I've done a rather popular act in a Hollywood nightclub." She knew she was stretching the truth just a bit, but that disastrous stint at the Treasure Cove ought to be good for something.

"A solo act?"

"I worked with a band sometimes, but mostly solo. I could work with others, though. I've been in a chorus line. I also have my own costumes, and I know many of the latest tunes from the States."

Silvia tapped her chin with a slim finger that ended with a long, bloodred painted nail. "Well . . . I have to say it would be a coup to have an American performer. I could fit in another act, but I can't let go my other performers, which means I couldn't pay you top dollar or even top peso. I have to be honest—you might do better elsewhere."

Blair didn't like the thought of pounding the sidewalks in the tropical heat looking for work and trying to sell herself over and over. Besides, she liked Silvia, who, though shrewd, had a forthright manner about her.

"If you won't require a contract, I'll take the job." Blair had been burned at the Treasure Cove by signing a contract, and she didn't want to be caught like that again.

"It's a deal, then." Silvia held out her slim, well-manicured hand. "But just for drill, as they say, I should perhaps hear you sing first."

Blair laughed. "Oh yes, by the way!"

Claudette cleared her throat to make her presence noted. "Miss Blair, now you have job, maybe you need a good maid, huh?"

"Oh . . . well . . ." The suggestion took Blair totally by surprise. She thought Claudette must have little concept of the value of a dollar and what the salary of a low-paid Manila nightclub singer could afford.

Silvia interjected quickly, "Claudette, could you do me a small favor?"

"Sure thing, Miss Silvia."

"There's a loaf of bread on the counter in the kitchen. Could you wrap it up and take it down the street to the newspaper vendor? You know Manuel, don't you? I promised him bread, and I may not get away for a time. While you're gone, I'll show Blair around."

Claudette scampered into the kitchen, and in a few minutes Blair heard the back door squeak open, then slam shut as she left. Blair suspected Silvia had more in mind than just delivering bread in sending Claudette away. She turned to the older woman.

"I hope I didn't hurt her feelings by my hesitation," she said. "She's a dear girl, but I just got to Manila today, and my finances aren't very secure. I have no idea what an apartment will cost. And there are other things I'll need."

"I thought maybe you were new here. Come and sit for a minute. Would you like something to drink?"

Without waiting for a reply, Silvia gestured to one of the round tables on the main floor of the club. It was early, and they weren't open yet for business, so the room was empty of patrons. When Blair pulled out a chair and sat, Silvia went to the bar, where a pitcher, frosty with cold, sat on the counter. She got two glasses and filled them with an amber liquid, then she brought them to the table and sat across from Blair.

Blair sipped the drink. "Oh, this is good iced tea. I'm from Southern California, but still I am finding the heat here to be something else."

"The dry season is just beginning, so it should feel a little better soon." Silvia paused, sipped her own drink, then continued. "Blair, we're practically strangers, but since you are new here, maybe you wouldn't mind some advice?"

"I'd appreciate it. I really don't want to offend anyone."

"I think you could do worse than taking on Claudette as a maid. She'll work for peanuts, maybe even just for room and board—and she would be appreciative, I am certain. Goodness, I've often thought of hiring her myself, besides for just the few errands I find for her to do. But I have more servants than I need right now. It's hard to turn them away when their need is so great."

Blair smiled and thought that Silvia probably considered her a poor waif as much as Claudette. The least she could do was take the woman's advice and in the process help another as she had been helped.

"Say no more!" Blair grinned. "I'll tell her the news as soon as she gets back. I've had a feeling from the moment I met her that I needed that little girl as much as she needs me."

Blair's words proved true many times over as Claudette made herself indispensable to Blair, not only showing her around town but teaching her local customs, as well. The two settled into a three-room apartment over a single-family home, and the girl took on her regular duties as maid, which really translated to cook/housekeeper/friend/confidante. Fortunately for Blair, who was a rather inept cook and housekeeper, Claudette shined at these tasks, although, since she had learned to cook at the orphanage, there was always more soup or hot cereal or stew than they could eat in a week. But it was in two capacities that Blair appreciated her maid most—as a friend and confidante. At first it seemed odd to Blair to have a friend who was almost ten years her junior. But for all her childish looks, Claudette sometimes seemed like an old lady disguised as a child. They made a good pair, because often Blair felt like a child in the guise of an adult.

And in the confusing times ahead, after Gary finally showed up, little Claudette proved her worth over and over.

BLAIR CLEARLY RECALLED every detail of that night, now a bit more than a week ago, when she saw Gary for the first time. Blair was performing at the Casa Mañana, wearing a gown of royal blue, trimmed with sequins and rhinestones. She gripped the microphone and crooned the words to one of her favorite songs. The quartet accompanying her got most of the notes right.

" 'Falling in love with love is falling for make-believe. . . .' "

Her eyes closed, she intoned the tune with depth, each word filling her, each note vibrating through her. This was when she loved music most, when she could so completely lose herself in it, when she and the words and the melody were all that existed. The audience faded to a blur if she saw them at all. She no longer cared about the various conversations underscoring her performance, the clinking of glassware, or even the bursts of laughter from patrons who were paying little or no attention to her. In moments like these, all that mattered was her and the music.

But eventually the song must end. Her voice trailed away with the final line. The quartet played the last notes. Applause rippled through the crowd. Blair opened her eyes and grinned, her gaze sweeping the tables of patrons, making certain all were graced with her appreciation. She didn't care to admit that she enjoyed this part as well as the singing itself—no, never as well, but the response of the audience did invigorate her in a way she could not describe. They liked her. That meant something, too.

Suddenly her sweeping gaze jerked to a stop as it lighted upon the uniformed man seated at a table in the rear of the room. She usually didn't notice the customers in the back, away from the footlights flooding her, but this man was not one to be casually glossed over.

Gary! Her heart leaped in a dozen different directions. For a fleeting moment she could only see the Gary of their sweet honeymoon in Santa Barbara, when they had been together and it had seemed as if their dream world would go on forever. But too quickly that image fled and was replaced by the scene of their last confrontation at the Treasure Cove, when all her fantasies had crumbled to dust.

Gary was here. And Blair wanted to run into his arms and run in the other direction all at once.

She'd been in Manila for a week by this time. She'd known he'd be back soon from his assignment, but she hadn't known if he would come looking for her when he received the messages she'd left at the base.

"Ladies and gentlemen," she said into the microphone, her voice amazingly steady, "I'm going to take a short break now, so enjoy yourselves and do try to stay for my eleven o'clock performance. Thank you all so very much."

The quartet began playing dance music, and as she threaded her way between tables, customers were rising and heading for the dance floor.

Gary rose from his chair as she approached his table. "Hi, Blair." There was nothing in his tone or in his expression that she could read, only a cordiality that could be taken for common politeness.

"Hi, Gary. You found me." A foolish thing to say, but her throat was so constricted and her mind so benumbed she felt lucky she could utter anything even remotely coherent.

He pulled out a chair and gestured toward it. "Can you join me?"

She eased into the chair, carefully trying not to tangle the flared train of her gown around the chair legs. "Thank you for coming to see me," she added simply. It took some effort, but she was getting back a portion of her equilibrium.

"What else would I do?" The curtain that enclosed him—that was the best way to describe it, for it was not a full-blown wall—began to part a little, and tiny shards of pain slipped through the crack like moon rays on a cloudy night. She suddenly knew he was grasping as desperately as she for control. How sad for both of them. She had her acting ability to aid her, and he had that well-trained military reserve of his, which he seemed to quickly pull back into place. " 'Falling in Love With Love,' " he said. "It was the first song I heard you sing."

Her father's fiftieth birthday party, less than a year ago. Goodness, a lifetime had passed since then. But Blair could remember, as clearly as if it had been yesterday, dancing with Gary and singing the words to the song softly into his ear as the orchestra played the music. She remembered how drawn she had been to Gary from the first moment. Drawn but scared to death, too! He had been like no man she had ever known. He had regarded her as something special, not a woman to be ogled and pawed for her beauty but rather one with a heart and a soul to be touched with tender respect.

But she had killed it with her lies and deceptions. All at once something hard and protective rose within her.

"Maybe I should have sung 'South of the Border' instead," she said wryly. That's what she had performed at the Treasure Cove that last night, with every saucy, provocative move she could muster so he'd see the real Blair.

"What are you doing here, Blair? This is crazy, even by your standards." Little amusement touched his words. The curtain around him was fluttering dangerously.

She was tempted to reply, *What else would a wife do but follow her husband?* But she could not bring herself to mention their marriage. She could hardly even think the word *wife* without her insides careening wildly.

Instead, she said simply, "It's what I had to do, Gary." She wasn't going to say more. Why torture herself further? Maybe she had expected him to take her into his arms and forgive all as he covered her with kisses. That obviously wasn't going to happen. So why not just let it go? He'd left her with good reason. In reality he had not so much *left* as he had decided his assignment in the Philippines would be a good time to think things out, giving them both a time apart to work out how they felt about all that had happened. Blair knew those kinds of words were almost always tantamount to a very polite brush-off. Maybe she had been crazy to think coming all the way to the Philippines would make everything all right.

Suddenly his protective curtain dropped completely. His gaze was both stark and tormented. "You've got me so mixed up, Blair, I don't know what to think . . . what to do. My head's going to explode!" And to her shock and dismay, moisture washed over his deep-set eyes, though none spilled out.

"I'm so sorry, Gary!"

"Let's get out of here, go someplace to talk."

Pausing only for Blair to let Silvia know she'd be gone for a few minutes, they strode from the nightclub. The sultry air was a relief after what had hung over them in the club, but it only lasted a minute before the same tensions clung to them again.

The Casa Mañana was not on the main thoroughfare of Manila but rather was on a side street. Still, it wasn't long before Blair and Gary reached the main street, Dewey Avenue, where they encountered a great deal of activity for ten o'clock in the evening. But it was Friday night, and Manila was well known for its teeming night life. Many of the pedestrians were American military men, and Army khaki, Navy whites, and Marine blue were in abundance, mingling with the casual dress of the islanders.

Blair had already discovered that the Philippines was a multilayered nation. It was deeply American in many respects, since the United States had taken over the islands nearly a half century ago, and a building spurt had followed, which included much of the development along Dewey Avenue. The American architecture here had the same look of many cities in middle America. The presence of the U.S. military added to this layer, along with billboards that advertised products from the States and department stores filled with American merchandise. But long before America impacted the islands, the Spanish had spread their influence. Red-tiled rooftops, wrought-iron gates, adobe walls dripping with Spanish moss and bougainvillea, and ornate Catholic churches all colorfully echoed the Spanish hold. Yet the final layer made its impression as well—the exotic sway of the Orient. Mostly Chinese, but Japanese as well, and other cultures of the Far East had drifted to this island paradise.

Blair had never been to a place quite like this. But at the moment she could not think of the appeal of palms gently swaying in the warm tropical breeze. Her entire focus was upon the man at her side, the man who had caused her to be in this faraway place. He said nothing as they walked, and she decided to follow suit. Words would be spoken soon enough.

After a short walk up the street, Gary paused by an Army jeep. Saying nothing, he opened the passenger door for her, and she silently climbed in, her gown hardly suited to the military vehicle, but she managed. He got in behind the wheel, and with a lurch forward they moved into the dense flow of traffic. They passed brightly lit buildings, music escaping the doors of nightclubs. One of the first practice blackouts had taken place the previous night, dimming the brassy neon lights, but all was "business as usual" tonight.

Dewey Avenue curved around the waterfront of Manila Bay, providing a picturesque backdrop with moonlight sparkling on the expanse of water. Gary drove for about ten minutes while Blair tried to concentrate on the sights around her. Tonight they did not hold her, and her gaze drifted, almost unconsciously, to the man beside her. He was so handsome, like a movie star, with his dark eyes and hair that was almost as black as a native islander's. His features were as perfect as a bronze statue, but he was in no way cold or hard except for the times when he let his military aspect, schooled at West Point, have rein.

But now, seeing beyond his good looks, Blair noted that his hands gripped the wheel as if for dear life. His gaze was focused forward and his lips set in a firm thin line, while his jaw twitched, belying his schooled expression. She dared not read anything into that look, but she could not keep from remembering the glaze of moisture over his eyes before. Were the unshed tears for what was lost or for the hope her presence might evoke?

Soon he pulled off the highway, turning onto a bumpy dirt road that in a few minutes came to a dead end. Gary stopped the motor. They were on a rise that overlooked the bay. It could have been such a romantic scene, with the water sparkling at the foot of the low hill and moonlight glittering at their shoulders. But with the tension rippling between them, Blair would not let herself think of romance or of the feel of his lips on hers, which she still remembered so vividly, or the smell of him when he was close, or the security of his arms encircling her. She might never experience those things again. This might easily be the final stop for them.

"Someday I'll take you into the jungle," he said quietly, his hands still gripping the wheel, his eyes forward. "You don't have a true feel of this place without that. The heavy air, the tangled growth, the squeal of monkeys darting among the trees. Until I came here, the only place I'd seen an orchid was on my date's corsage for the senior prom. But here, hundreds of them are draped around the boughs of trees like pearls. It's beautiful."

Blair's throat tightened. Nearly all she'd heard was "Someday . . ."

Would there, then, be more for them? She thought of the song that had become her signature as much as Judy Garland's, but she could barely think of it without her heart tearing. *Someday I'll wish upon a star and wake up where the clouds are far behind me. . . .*

Was she finally somewhere over the rainbow? Were his words offering her hope? She wanted to leap at those words, grasp them to her, make them true.

"Gary, you said you were confused and mixed up. Well, I am, too." She had vowed to be honest with him and with herself, too. "Don't say things like 'someday' unless . . . there is a chance."

"I'm sorry. I wasn't thinking."

"Oh." Her world plummeted.

"That's not what I meant, either," he added quickly. "I mean—" he raked a hand through his coal black hair—"you came thousands of miles, Blair. I need to know why."

"I told you. I had to come." She must be honest, yet she didn't want his pity. "At home I . . . I was heading back into my old life. I hated it. I hated myself. I . . ." Nothing was more difficult to say, but she had to tell him everything. No more lies! "I'm certain I would have killed myself."

"Dear Lord . . . no, Blair . . ." he groaned.

"Don't feel sorry for me!" she said with all the force she could muster. "I don't want that. I don't want you to think I'm using that as a threat to hold you. If I had killed myself, it would not have been your fault. Anyway, I am not in that frame of mind anymore. I have moved forward, and coming here was a large part of that. Like it or not, you are wrapped up in my life now. I couldn't go forward without settling what there was between us."

"Do you mean—?"

His dismal tone made her cut in sharply. "Gary, would you let me finish? Hear me out so we don't get things mixed up and muddied again. I lied that night at the Treasure Cove when I said I didn't love you."

"I knew that."

"Of course, love wasn't enough just then," she went on as if he hadn't spoken. She had to get these things said before she lost her courage. "There was so much more to repair—in me, you understand? It took sliding into a pit before I finally realized I had to make changes.

I did come here to get you back, but not the way I did before."

A small smile cracked his somberness. "I do see a change in you. Blair, have you . . . have you found God?"

The ring of hope in his tone tugged at her, and she realized how easy it would be to use that hope to have her way. The thought made her shudder. "No . . . not yet." Again the words were hard to force out. Honesty. "And this is where it all gets even more confusing. When I was pretending to be a Christian, I was never happier. But if I seek God now, will it be just to win you? And how will you ever know if I am sincere or performing? How will I know?"

"I ask myself the same thing all the time," he said. He now turned to face her. "I've questioned God, as well, asked why He would let all this happen when I faithfully prayed about you and felt our marriage was truly His will. He let me down."

"No, it was *I* who let you down," she said. "Only I."

"I've told myself that a million times, believe me! I've berated you often, blamed you vehemently. You are lucky you were so far away that you couldn't feel the anger I directed at you. But Blair, I knew you loved me. I knew it so deeply in my gut that I could not truly hate you. I always saw the hurt little girl, never the hardened vamp you tried to be at the Treasure Cove."

"I think I want you to see me as a little of both. That is, I don't want your pity. I don't want you to perceive me as helpless, needy. I do need you, Gary, but I don't want that to be at the core of whatever we find together. If we have a *together*."

"That's what I want, too. But God must be in the center of it all."

She nodded. "I believe this is called a conundrum."

"A sticky one."

"A scary one."

He reached toward her, and for the first time that evening, for the first time since their honeymoon, he touched her. Only her hand, but he took it firmly in his. The warmth of his touch tingled through her. This kind of thing was likely to add even more confusion to their bewildering relationship.

"Why don't we just go back to the beginning?" he murmured softly, as if he was afraid to utter the words too loudly. "Let's pretend we are starting over."

"Pretend. . . ?"

"In a good way."

"I don't think we can make believe our marriage . . . our honeymoon . . . didn't happen." Even she was not that good of an actress.

"No . . ."

And she saw in his eyes that he had never forgotten, either.

"But let's do the best we can. Let's see if we can build again what we had, only this time for real, even better. Truer. With God."

"I do want God," she confessed. "I know I was better even when my faith was fake. Imagine what it would be like if it were real! But I won't jump into it and risk . . . I don't know. I guess losing it again. And it must be something I find apart from you—though heaven knows how that will happen, because I feel you are such a big part of it all. Kind of like pulling a single thread out of a tightly woven cloth."

"We can only try."

There was a moment then when they could have so easily melted into an embrace. She wanted to hold him and be held by him. She knew he felt the same way. The flicker of inner passion was like a visible wave of heat. But they did nothing. The moment passed like a victory. Their collectively caught breath released.

She knew "trying" would not be easy. Being real and honest had always been hard for her. Yet she'd heard something once. "Keep your eyes on the prize." That's what she must do, and the prize was not only Gary but that soul-deep peace that had eluded her all her life.

6

NEARLY TWO WEEKS had passed since that first meeting of Blair and Gary. As Blair lay in bed on that morning of December 8, she realized they had seen each other only a handful of times because his duties often took him out of town. He was involved in training new Filipino recruits, and often they went on training missions in the jungle. In a way, this was a good thing, because it forced them to rebuild their relationship slowly. But it was an exercise in patience for both of them. Blair wondered often just how they would know when the time was right, when they could once again reclaim the marriage that had been lost.

Stretching in her bed again, she was about to swing her legs out when the beaded curtain parted and Claudette entered, carrying a tray.

"What have you there, Claudette?" she said, a touch of scolding in her tone. How many times since taking the girl in as a maid had Blair tried to stop her from waiting upon Blair hand and foot?

"Relax, Miss Blair. This is your day off—"

"You are not serving me breakfast in bed!" For emphasis she flung back the covers and fairly leaped from bed. "Take that tray back out to the front room, put it on the table, and you will eat with me."

"But that is not how it's supposed to work!"

"You have seen too many movies, *Miss* Claudette. Now march!"

A bit dejected, Claudette scurried back through the beads. Blair grabbed her wrapper and was about to join her when the phone, located by the bed, rang. Blair picked up the receiver on the third ring.

"That you, Blair?" came a familiar voice at the other end of the line.

"Gary! I am so glad you called. Today is my day off and—"

"Blair, listen, okay? I gotta hurry. Just a few hours ago, the Japanese bombed Hawaii. This is war, Blair."

Stunned, Blair plopped on the edge of the bed. "Was it bad?"

"We can't get details. But bad enough, I'm sure. The thing is, the Philippines will be next. I don't know why it hasn't happened already. Probably the weather in Formosa is stalling the Japs. Blair . . . are you there?"

"Y-yes," she squeaked out. War. She couldn't believe it. Sure, everyone talked about it all the time. Gary had said it was only a matter of time. But no one really expected it this soon or believed that the Japanese would actually have the gall to attack the United States of America. Blair had never given a hoot about all the war talk. It had always been far away, never a part of her world. That was Cameron's world, not hers.

But now was she about to be right in the middle of it?

"Gary . . . what should I do?" Sudden helplessness consumed her, wiping out the independence she'd worked so hard at maintaining around Gary so he didn't need to feel sorry for her. Now her voice shook, and she thought she might cry from fear.

"Just stay put for now. The Japs are going to concentrate on military targets. I think Manila itself will be spared for a time. But there are some things you can do without going far. Are you with me, honey?"

Honey—the word indeed sounded sweet. He'd never called her that before, and in such a gentle, soothing tone. Like a husband.

But she mustn't think of that. Other matters pressed upon her like a vise. War!

"Blair?"

"I'm here, Gary." Her voice sounded far away even to her.

"Okay, listen. If you have money in the bank, get it out now and change it all to American dollars."

"W-why?" she managed.

"I've got to be straight with you, Blair. Anything could happen now. We were depending on the Pacific Fleet to protect us from the Japs. With it destroyed . . ."

His voice trailed away, and she thought she heard a shudder across the line. If he was shaken, what was going to happen to them?

He continued, his voice once again firm and confident. "You have to be prepared for any number of contingencies."

She purposely did not ask him to enumerate those "contingencies," and he went on.

"Go to the market and get whatever tinned meat and nonperishable food you can afford. Also, buy first-aid supplies, as much quinine as you can get. Then pack a few personal necessities, no more than one suitcase each for you and Claudette, and a suitcase for supplies. I'll see if I can get you a car."

"Then we'll be going away?"

"You need to be prepared for that. But should Manila fall, your choices would be to stay, be an enemy alien and almost certainly be interned, or to evacuate."

"What would you do, Gary?"

"Evacuate." He didn't even hesitate.

"Oh, g-goodness!" her voice trembled.

"But look, that's only the worst case. It isn't going to happen. Still, it doesn't hurt to be prepared. I'll try to come to you later, but I don't know if or when I'll be able to get away. I'm up at Fort Stotsenberg right now. We are all on alert. No leaves."

The very idea that he might not come to help her crushed her, made rubble of her so-called independence.

"Gary!"

"I'll do everything I can."

"Please . . . Gary!"

"Be strong, Blair. You can go to Reverend Sanchez. He'll do anything for you."

The pastor of the little Baptist church in Manila that she had attended with Gary was a nice man, soft-spoken, very intellectual. A widower with two sons, one in the Army and the other sixteen, he had impressed Blair more as a person than as a minister. She rather expected fiery sermons from a preacher and secretly thought that's what she would need to find God. Fire and brimstone stuff. But Sanchez delivered sermons that were more like college lectures. They made Blair want to look things up in the little Bible Gary had loaned her, but they didn't shake the rafters of her soul. Still, that's not why she took little comfort from Gary's words now.

She didn't want Reverend Sanchez. She wanted Gary! She needed Gary. She couldn't face a war alone. Internment by the Japs or evacuation? These were not things she had been prepared to face in her life.

"I have to go now, Blair. Just remember, God will be with you."

She managed a strangled good-bye, but as the line clicked dead, all she could think was that his promise of God being with her was weak indeed. She had been trying so hard to work out her faith, but thoughts and doubts would always snake around her mind and make her question. Reverend Sanchez said there was a balance between blind faith and questioning, though he did seem to believe questioning was all right. But she thought her questioning was different from the kind Gary sometimes did. He always came out with assurance. She came out more confused than ever.

"Miss Blair, the coffee is getting cold." Claudette's voice broke into her thoughts.

Her head jerked around. "Claudette, there's war!" she blurted out. "The Japanese have bombed Hawaii, and we're next."

"What're we gonna do, Miss Blair!" exclaimed Claudette. Blair had hoped Claudette would be the steady one. She forgot that the girl's tough street-urchin persona was little more than a veneer, as much as was Blair's independent act.

"I don't know! We could be bombed at any time. I . . . don't know!"

Claudette ran to the bed and put her arms around Blair. "Please, you will keep me with you?"

That plaintive request was like a slap to Blair. Most of the time she didn't know who was taking care of whom. But now it was clear—Claudette was a little girl. Blair was the grown-up. No matter how much she wanted to roll up in a ball and weep, someone had to make decisions, and it appeared she was the one. Maybe she could do it if . . .

She tried to imagine she had a role in a movie, one about war coming suddenly to a sleepy tropical island. Her part called for her to be a tough Barbara Stanwyck type. She had to rally the forces of good. She was the heroine.

"Claudette, Gary called and told me what to do. We can get it done quickly if we split up—"

"Please, Miss Blair, don't leave me alone. Stay with me!"

That was an easy request to grant. Blair didn't want to be alone, either. "Let me get dressed, and then we'll go together."

Gary thanked the clerk for the use of the telephone. He knew it was a great favor because personal calls were strictly limited. He had never felt more helpless. Yesterday he'd been sent here to Fort Stotsenberg to deliver papers to General Wainwright. The cavalry was based here, and Gary had thought it would be a choice assignment because he'd have a chance to see one of their famous polo matches. But now all he could think was that it had put him seventy-five miles away from Blair.

The news about the Pearl Harbor attack was now hours old, the first reports having arrived within an hour of the attack. By breakfast it had become general knowledge, and everyone was on alert. His commander at Fort McKinley, his base, called and told him to stay put, that he could be more use there than on the highway for the two- or three-hour drive back to base. Gary had to follow orders. Other guys had wives and girlfriends scattered around the islands. They were all hamstrung by duty.

Gary had hated to wait so long to call Blair, but he knew she usually slept late, and it would have really shaken her to get such news after being roused from a deep sleep. She was shaken enough as it was. He knew she wanted to be strong. She always talked with admiration of her older sister. But Blair was vulnerable, maybe even frail. He prayed she'd have the stamina to do what had to be done. He wanted to find a car for her, because if she had to leave, he didn't know how she would make it without a vehicle. More than that, though, he wanted to see her, but that was impossible for the time being.

A report came in that Camp John Hay, about two hundred miles north of Manila, near Baguio, had been bombed. Camp John Hay had little strategic value, and he couldn't imagine why the Japanese would target it. But reconnaissance reported fog over Formosa, where the Japanese airfields were located, so perhaps the enemy had missed its intended target.

Around midmorning Gary was given papers to take over to Clark Field, the U.S. Army's main airfield in the Philippines. It was located just adjacent to Stotsenberg. There was a war on, and they had him ferrying papers! He'd thought he'd have something important to do up here, but it seemed he was just being used as an errand boy. He was itching more than ever to forget his orders and head back to McKinley, which was only seven miles from Manila.

It was nearly noon, so he dropped off the papers and went to the mess hall for lunch. He saw a couple of men he knew and slid his tray onto the table next to them.

"What're y'all doin' in this neck of the woods, Gary?" asked Lieutenant Frank Woodburn, or Woody as he was called. He was a lanky, towheaded mechanic from Dallas, Texas, and spoke with a lazy drawl.

"Came up yesterday to deliver some reports. Thought I'd get to take in a polo match."

"Sorry to disappoint you," said Lieutenant Andy Mankowitz. "All we got is a war to offer."

"Don't that just beat all," said Woody. "I barely fell into bed after that party for General Brereton in Manila last night. What a rude awakening! I still got a hangover."

"How come the bombers and fighters are back on the ground?" Gary asked.

Earlier that morning the B-17s had been sent aloft for their protection, and the fighters had been sent up to respond to reports of approaching Japanese aircraft. They had just returned to base.

"Didn't see any Japs," Andy said. "They're gonna refuel and go back up this afternoon, I guess."

Just then the drone of aircraft could be heard overhead. Several of the men wandered outside to see what it was, including Gary and his friends. Shading his eyes from the sun, Gary looked up into the clear sky. He counted twenty-seven planes in nine tight Vs.

"Well, look at those B-18s!" Andy said.

Slowly Woody shook his head. "We don't have more'n a handful of B-18s left in all the islands. They can't be ours." Woody had been around a long time and knew his planes.

Someone yelled, "Yea! Here comes the Navy!"

And a moment later the bombs fell. First they hit Fort Stotsenberg's pristine white walls and the polo fields. Initial shock overwhelmed the onlookers as they at last saw the big red "meatballs" on the sides of the aircraft and realized they were Japanese Mitsubishi bombers and Zeros. But the sudden explosions quickly galvanized them into action. The aircrews raced for their grounded planes. Some who were already in their aircraft revved up their engines, but there wasn't time to taxi them into position for takeoff. They attempted to use their guns from the ground. Others headed to man antiaircraft guns, but the ack-acks had been seldom used, and much of the ammo was old, corroded useless. Those that did fire fell far short of their targets.

Gary raced with several others to a supply dump, grabbed a helmet and rifle, then dove into a monsoon culvert for cover. He fired at the low-flying Zeros, knowing he was doing little good. But it was all he could do—that and watch the airfield go up in smoke.

A couple of the Army P-26s tried to take off, but a Jap incendiary caught them both, turning aircraft and crew into a fireball that skittered into a line of other fighters, all going up into flame. A few men jumped to safety but not many. Gary groaned at the sight and, shaking with rage, leveled his rifle at a Zero. The enemy plane strafed his culvert. He ducked for cover, but something hit him anyway. A sharp pain seared the back of his head, and only then did he realize his helmet had flown off. Reaching a hand back, he felt stickiness in his hair. Blood covered his fingers. He choked back a wave of dizziness. He might be all but helpless, but no way was he going to spend the rest of the attack unconscious. Neither was he going to spend it in a culvert.

The field was littered with wounded men who needed to be moved. The mess hall and barracks were in flames, along with warehouses of vital supplies. Swallowing bile and a mouthful of grit, Gary rolled from the culvert and, crouching low, ran to a truck where men were attempting to load the wounded.

The bombers, having made two devastating passes over Clark Field, turned to head for home, their lethal loads spent. That left only the Zeros, but they rained even more death and destruction over the base with their strafing. Zigzagging between the deadly spray from the Zeros, Gary hoisted a wounded pilot over his shoulder, turned back toward the truck that waited about fifty feet away, and crumbled to his knees in shock as the truck took a hit in the gas tank and burst into flames.

Gary's head spun, and he finally lost his lunch. Another Zero's fire ripped up the ground around him. He dropped the pilot and flung himself on top of the wounded man. Something bit into his thigh, but that was all, and he got to his feet when the Jap fighter circled away. Unable to lift the man as he had before, he grabbed the pilot under his armpits.

"Leave me!" the pilot gasped. "Get to cover."

"Not on your life!" Gary struggled to run the gauntlet again, nearly blinded by smoke, dust, and debris.

His own pain and dizziness threatened to bring him down, but the weight of the pilot in his arms and the sense of usefulness it gave him goaded him forward. Another truck pulled up, and he loaded the pilot, unconscious but still alive.

The attack lasted less than an hour, but Gary was hardly cognizant of time. It seemed more like an eternity with those Zeros ripping holes into anything that moved and anything that was immobile, as well. When the last enemy plane flew out of sight, the frantic pace did not end. After the wounded were taken care of, the debris had to be sorted through, and all that was useful had to be separated. This was only the beginning of the war, and even if it appeared to be a total defeat for the American forces, Gary had no doubt this was not the end of the fighting. They were going to need every salvageable scrap to fight an enemy they had sorely underestimated.

How had such a disaster happened? What monumental command foul-up had caused them to be so unprepared? Unlike Pearl Harbor, they had had hours of warning. Had a message been sent that had never gotten through?

Soon word came through of a simultaneous Japanese attack on the fighter base on Iba Field, the next most important airbase on Luzon and the location of one of two important radar stations on the islands. The losses at Iba were almost as bad as those at Clark—a total of half the B-17s lost, leaving only seventeen, many of which were heavily damaged. Fifty-three P-40 fighters along with thirty other aircraft were also gone. Eighty men had been killed and one hundred wounded. And before the day was done, other bases on the islands would surely be hit, as well.

Gary was tearing through the debris of one of the barracks, looking for more wounded, when he finally crumbled. A medic had to drag him from the bombed-out building.

Palpating Gary's head wound, the medic asked, "When did you get this?"

Gary shrugged. "I don't know. A couple hours ago."

"You've probably lost a lot of blood, and you need stitches."

"I'm okay. I can walk."

"Your leg's bleeding, too. Only place you're walking to is the hospital, buddy," insisted the medic.

Gary struggled to gain his feet, but his legs had turned to rubber, and his head spun. He wanted to fight it. There was still so much to be done. And he couldn't get stuck in a hospital, because he had to get back to Blair.

"No . . . I'll be fine—" He tried to wrench away from the medic's hold, but the sharp movements were too much, and his stomach heaved. It wasn't the first time that day his insides had rebelled, but now his defenses were completely gone. He hit the ground again, retching.

"You've put in your time, Lieutenant. If you want to fight the rest of this war, you better come with me."

For Blair, Gary thought as the medic half carried and half dragged him to an ambulance. I'm no good to her dead.

In the hospital sleep came quickly after he was cleaned and stitched. His last thoughts were a prayer. *Lord, help me get to her before the Japs bomb Manila!*

AROUND NOON Blair and Claudette were returning to her apartment from the expeditions Gary had suggested when an air-raid siren began to shriek. The explosions that followed were distant, at least some miles southwest of town. She knew that was the direction of Fort McKinley. Claudette said there were also some airfields that way.

Fort McKinley was Gary's base, but she remembered he was someplace else. Fort St . . . something. She'd never paid much attention to all the military talk she'd heard since coming to the Philippines. Gary had mentioned other bases, but—God forgive her!—she just hadn't cared enough to listen.

Now as the distant blasts reverberated in her ears and the ground vibrated under her feet, she tried to dredge up the conversations she had heard in the last weeks. But it was still all meaningless to her even if her mind could have brought any of it into focus. She was an empty-headed fool, just as her father had always believed her to be. Perhaps that had served her well growing up, for if her father expected nothing of her, then she didn't risk failure. Being glib and shallow had been safe, especially nurtured as it had been by a life of wealth. Cameron had fought their father tooth and nail, and Jackie had somehow risen above his harsh expectations. Well, Blair was no saint like Jackie, and she certainly was no fighter like Cameron. That's what scared her now even more than the fear of death. She had no resources within her to deal with the uncertainties she now faced. If her world crumbled, she was sure to go with it.

Blair and Claudette headed to the air-raid shelter the landlady's brother had built for her in the back of the house. Several others were already gathered there.

"Where's Fort Stot—I don't know, something like that?" Blair asked her landlady.

"You mean Stotsenberg?" Mrs. Acosta asked. Her landlady was a Filipino woman Blair had not gotten to know well because she always seemed so stern and unapproachable. The sound of bombs exploding in the distance hadn't changed her. She appeared quite unshaken.

"Yes," Blair answered, trying unsuccessfully to keep the tremor from her voice.

"It's near Clark Airfield, about seventy-five miles north. That where your soldier boyfriend is?"

"I . . . I think so."

"Well, I'm glad I am a widow with no children. I just have myself to worry about. I feel sorry for you." She didn't sound all that sorry. "But I guess we will all be in hot water if the Japs invade. My husband fought in the rebel Army when you Americans took over the Philippines. I don't hold you any bad will, though, and neither did he. We came out pretty good in the long run, I suppose. My husband made enough money to buy some real estate. Oh, my house isn't in the best part of town, but . . ."

The woman droned on, and Blair wondered how she could go on talking as if nothing were happening.

It was Claudette who gave the most comfort to Blair. She clung close to Blair and whispered, "He'll be okay, Miss Blair. He will! He's a long way away from here."

But later, after the all-clear had sounded and they were back in the apartment, they heard on the radio that Clark Field and Fort Stotsenberg had been bombed at the same time as Iba, the field whose bombing Blair could hear from Manila. Panic gripped her. Her insides wrenched.

Where was Gary? Why hadn't he called? Something awful had happened. She knew it.

That night Neilson and Nichols Fields and Fort McKinley were bombed. They were all within ten miles of Manila, and the deadly bursts of light from the explosions could be seen from the city. Some people watched them as if they were a Fourth of July fireworks display. Blair shuddered and cried and clung to Claudette as much as the girl clung to her.

When they went to bed that night, they pulled the mattress from the bed and shoved it under the bedsprings for protection, and there they slept, on the mattress under the bed, in each other's arms. Though sleep was hardly the best description for the fitful bouts of sheer weariness that forced their eyes closed every now and then. Any deep sleep was shattered by the sounds of explosions. Once during the night the air-raid siren sounded, and they stumbled down to the shelter, returning to their bed around four in the morning with the all-clear signal.

When daylight arrived, the ordeal of trying to sleep ended. Claudette went to the kitchen to fix breakfast, though neither had much appetite. Blair used the time to deal with the boxes of purchases that had been delivered yesterday afternoon, a result of her shopping with Claudette. She'd been so frightened yesterday she hadn't even thought about them. She was no less so now, but she had to take care of things. If Gary came for her, she must be ready.

If!

Oh, Gary, where are you? Why haven't you come?

Doggedly, she hauled suitcases onto the living room sofa and dragged out her steamer trunk. She knew the trunk was too large to take, but Mrs. Acosta said she'd store it for Blair. Into that she put all the belongings that she wished to keep but were not practical to take to . . . wherever it was she might go. She packed the evening gowns she used for her nightclub act and a couple of framed photographs, one of her and Gary on their wedding day—he in his full dress uniform and she in that simple but lovely ecru gown. They looked an idyllic couple, not even a slight shadow across their happy faces of the disaster that came two days later. The other photograph was a family portrait that had been taken the day of her father's fiftieth birthday celebration. She still had no idea why she had dropped it into her trunk the day she left the States. Maybe her family meant more to her than she wanted to admit.

Her mind wandered as she looked at the happy faces staring back at her. The faces were smiling, but true happiness had been an elusive thing for the Hayes clan. What were they doing now? What did they think about the war? All of a sudden she missed them. Crazy, considering her history with them, especially her parents. She'd spent her life rebelling against them, but what she wouldn't give now to be home, at least to be with her mother and sisters. She knew her father probably disdained her now more than ever. On the day of her marriage to Gary, she had almost won the man's approval because finally she had done something to please him. Then she had ruined that, and she could still remember the look on his face when he learned of her deception—a look that said he wasn't surprised at all. That had hurt far more than the look of disappointment on her mother's face. The picture reminded her that she must send a telegram to let them know she was okay. Her mother and Jackie would worry.

"Miss Blair, breakfast is ready," came Claudette's voice, a welcome interruption.

Blair dropped the photo into the trunk and turned to the table. Her stomach was in knots, but she forced herself to eat. She might need the strength of food for . . . for what, she didn't know.

As she and Claudette ate a meal of sliced papaya, toast, and scrambled eggs, the radio, which they had playing continually, came on with a news broadcast. Manuel Quezon, president of the Philippines, made a statement regarding the war. It was brief but moving as he called upon God for protection and reaffirmed Filipino loyalty to America.

The day wore on, but by Wednesday the attacks seemed to have been stepped up, and the hours were punctuated at more frequent intervals by the drone of the air-raid siren and treks to the shelter. Once Blair gathered her nerve and joined a few others out on the sidewalk to watch an attack. Nichols Field and Fort McKinley were being hit hard. Billows of smoke and tongues of flames marked the destruction. Nearer at hand, Cavite Naval Yard was also being hammered. Most of the Navy ships in the bay had escaped out to sea, but Cavite itself had become a burning pyre.

As they watched the sky, the worst reality was that few American planes rose to meet the enemy attack, and near the end of the day, the Japanese were completely unchallenged. Ack-acks fired at the enemy but made little difference. Blair almost smiled then. Ack-acks. A week ago she didn't even know this term for antiaircraft guns, and now she was using it like a veteran. Oh, how she wished she truly was a veteran, taking it all in stoic stride instead of jumping from her skin at every explosion.

Rumors only added to what the eye could not see. There was frequent talk of "fifth columnists" and Japanese landings. These rumors brought Silvia Wang to Blair's apartment.

"I'm leaving town," the nightclub owner said. The woman's usually cool aplomb was noticeably shaken. "You'd do well to do the same."

There were many evacuating the city, Blair knew, but she could not leave before she saw Gary.

"I can't go until I hear from Gary. He said he'd call. I can't go!" She was partly convincing herself. Everything inside her was urging her to run away. But where to? She raised this very question to her employer.

"My family has a summer place in the hills to the north. You are welcome to come."

"I've heard rumors the Japanese will land in the north."

"Yes, but it will be safe in the hills. Safer than here, at least for me. The Japs hate Chinese. I'll kill myself before I'll fall into their hands."

"Oh, Silvia, it can't happen! We will stop them. Help will come from the States."

"How, Blair? The Pacific Fleet is destroyed. And your president has given all military supplies to England and Russia. What will they have left to send to us? It'll be too late before they have manufactured enough to defeat the Japanese."

"I don't believe that. Help will come. We have many resources."

Sadly Silvia shook her head. "Whatever helps you get by, honey. As for me, I'm not going to take any chances. What are you going to do if your soldier doesn't come for you?"

Blair shuddered and felt tears, always close to the surface, sting her eyes. "He will come."

"Okay, sweetie." Silvia's voice softened. "It's okay. He just might. With you waiting, he just might." Pausing, she opened her purse and withdrew an envelope. "This is your final pay plus two weeks' severance."

"Oh, Silvia, you didn't have to do that!" Blair stared at the envelope, appreciative of the gesture but wondering what good money would be to her.

"Take it. It's all in American dollars. I've got plenty, and you might need all you can get, especially if you stay." She thrust the packet at Blair, who reluctantly wrapped her trembling fingers around it.

"Thank you." She could barely get the words out.

Silvia gave her a motherly kiss on the cheek. "I hope I see you again sometime. If not . . . well, you take care. I put a little map in the envelope with directions to my place. You are always welcome there."

Weeping, Blair threw her arms around Silvia, but she could not get any words out. Through a veil of thickly falling rain, feeling another lifeline had been cut, she watched her friend go. Claudette and Silvia were the only people she knew and could trust in the city. Of course, any soldier would help her if she could get to them, but if she could get to them, she should be able to get to Gary. But how? And if he was back at McKinley, surely he would have called.

Then she remembered Reverend Sanchez. She didn't know him well, but Gary said he would help her, though she wasn't sure just how. He did have a car. Perhaps he could loan it to her or drive her himself out to Fort McKinley so she could look for Gary. All reason, however, told her that that was a more cockeyed plan than her coming to the Philippines in the first place. McKinley was a war zone, and the military would not tolerate a silly female roaming about looking for her man.

Nevertheless, she hated to risk leaving her apartment in case Gary did try to call or come. And she couldn't ask Claudette to stay behind all alone. So she continued to wait. Thursday was the worst day. Formosa was socked in by unseasonably late monsoons, and the Japanese were grounded. There were no air raids, only the expectation, the fear never realized. The anticipation was almost as bad as the actual bombings. Blair felt like a brittle twig, ready to snap at any moment.

Finally by Friday she could stand it no longer. It seemed as if all the American bases had gone up in smoke, and rumors of Japanese landings were sounding more and more real. She implored Claudette to stay at the apartment, promising she would be gone only a half hour. Bravely, the girl agreed.

The parsonage where Reverend Sanchez lived was several blocks from Blair's apartment. A brisk walk got her there in ten minutes. Sanchez opened his door, greeting her with a perplexed expression.

"I am surprised you are still in the city," he said as he welcomed her into the little stucco house. He was a short man, slender, and scholarly in appearance. His dark hair was slightly gray and ringed a balding pate. His wire-rimmed glasses added to the look of a man more at home with his nose in a book than in socializing with humans, though he was personable enough, even if it seemed to come as an afterthought.

Sitting on his sofa, she explained about Gary being missing. "He told me to stay put unless Manila falls. What if he comes and I am gone?" Her emotions fraying, she added, "I just don't know what to do."

Nodding sagely, he replied, "I understand your dilemma. But you will have to leave before long. Many might choose to remain in the city and take their chances as prisoners of the Japanese, but I would not recommend it."

Gary had told her the same thing. "Is it really that bad, Reverend Sanchez? The Japanese can't really win this thing."

"They say there have been landings in the north. I don't know if it is true—"

"It must be true," came a new voice. Blair looked up to find Reverend Sanchez's sixteen-year-old son, Mateo, had come into the room. "And now, Papa, will you continue to make me stay here when men are needed at the Front?"

"This is not the time, Mateo," Sanchez said, though his tone was more of a request than an order.

"It is never the time," groused the boy. He was taller by five inches than his father, with strong, handsome features. His flashing dark eyes were quite the antithesis of his father's warm, benign eyes.

"We have a guest, son. Show some manners," scolded his father.

A tinge of humility momentarily shadowed the fire in the boy's expression, but it was obviously an effort for him. He bowed politely toward Blair.

"I am sorry if I offended, Miss Hayes. But—"

"Mateo!" warned Sanchez, with more than a hint now that he meant it.

"That's okay, really," Blair said quickly. "We are all on edge these days."

"My son thinks he should be allowed to join the Army at age sixteen. To me, he is but a child." Sanchez sighed. "But the need is great. Perhaps it is time. . . ."

"Do you mean it, Papa?" The fire of excitement returned to Mateo's expression.

"We will talk of it later. Maybe it is time. Our Lord only knows what we will all be called to sacrifice before this is over. Now, Mateo, why don't you bring us some coffee while Blair tells us the reason for her visit."

"I haven't much time," she said. "I promised Claudette I would not be gone long."

"Claudette?" Mateo paused at the kitchen door. "She is well?"

Blair suppressed a smile, the first time in days she had even felt like smiling. Claudette, who had a few times attended Sanchez's church with Blair and Gary, was quite smitten with the minister's son. She would probably forget all about the war and her fear when she found out he had asked about her.

"Yes, she is, but I don't like leaving her alone with all that is going on." Blair lifted baleful eyes to the minister. "I had to talk to someone I could trust, and Gary said for me to come to you, Reverend Sanchez. I don't know how you can help. I just could not sit still any longer. Waiting . . . oh, and not knowing if Gary is okay. Is there any way I can find out? I tried calling the base, but they know nothing—that was when I could get through. Now I can't even reach them. I thought if I could go out there—"

"You mustn't even think of that," Sanchez said quickly. "I am afraid it will be a shambles out there and far too dangerous, since there are still attacks."

"But I am going out of my mind with worry!"

"Can I pray with you?"

That was the one thing she did not want to hear. It seemed a lame and futile gesture. She wanted action. Not some empty words. She didn't want to denigrate the very thing she had been trying to seek these last months. Yet she did not think this was the time for religion. Maybe others could find comfort in it, but for her it was just too nebulous.

"Forgive me, Reverend, but I—it's just that . . ." How could she say what she felt without being rude?

He spared her. "I know it seems rather insufficient. But truly, prayer does have far more power than it appears on the surface." Steepling his fingers and tapping them against his chin, he added, "I suppose you were thinking more in terms of some action. But there is precious little action left to you, my dear young woman. That's just when prayer can be most effective."

"Well, I won't stop you from praying if you want," she conceded, mostly from good manners.

"Mateo," Sanchez called, and the clatter in the kitchen stopped.

"Yes, Papa?"

"Would you come join us in a time of prayer?"

When Mateo seated himself at the other end of the sofa, Sanchez bowed his head. Blair did the same. She closed her eyes, too. But her mind was racing too fast to really hear the minister's words. All about God's protection, His help in troubled times. All fine, solid praying. But it did Blair no good. The knots were still in her stomach, and the fear still clung to her heart. But she said amen with the others and smiled her thanks when all heads were lifted.

Perhaps Sanchez sensed her ambivalence, for he said, "I've just had a thought. I was going down to Fort McKinley this morning to help out. I can ask around."

"Could I go with you?" she asked quickly.

"Gary would have my hide if I took you out there."

"Please, Reverend Sanchez. If Gary is there, he may not be able to get away, and it might be the only chance for me to see him."

"Papa," put in Mateo, "sometimes in war we cannot always do what is safe. Miss Hayes should be able to take a chance if she feels it is necessary. Shouldn't she?"

Blair was rather taken aback by the young man's words. So was his father. Sanchez stared in wonder at his son. He shook his head as if in defeat. "My son has more wisdom than is good for him. But I must confess he is right. I think Gary would understand. Okay. Let's have some coffee and a bite to eat, then we will go."

"What should I do about my maid? I told her I would be back soon."

Again Mateo piped up with the solution. "I will go to her if you like. I'll tell her what is happening and stay with her till you get back." He seemed most eager for this task.

"That is kind of you, Mateo!" Blair thought it best not to mention that Claudette would probably swoon when the boy showed up.

SANCHEZ NEGOTIATED the snarl of traffic through the city like a taxi driver, and he mentioned that he'd paid his way through school with that very occupation. In the best of times Manila was as congested and harrowing as any city, but added to that now was the frantic rush of citizens desperate to evacuate ahead of the enemy. And in one of those ironies of war, many from the country were pouring into the city, hoping for sanctuary.

Blair was grateful she did not have to drive, for the streets were as dangerous now as a battlefield. Drivers raced at breakneck speed whenever there was an opening through the clogged streets, ignoring traffic signals, other vehicles, and even pedestrians. The chaos extended to other aspects of the city, as well. There had been a run on the banks, and food was running low because of hoarding. Blair felt a little guilty for the quantity of supplies she and Claudette had managed to buy, but she was also glad for Gary's wisdom in making the suggestion early on.

Word of Japanese landings in the north and south of the island were more than rumors now. They were frightening fact. Still many miles from Manila, the enemy was close enough, and talk and rumor now centered on whether MacArthur would let Manila be declared an open city. That would mean the departure of American and Filipino troops. Blair didn't know if this would affect her one way or the other, but if Gary, as part of the military, was forced to leave, what would happen to her? He had told her she might need to evacuate. But when? How? And where would she go? Perhaps she should have left with Silvia. How would she find her friend now with a hundred miles of jungle in between?

Blair's frightened thoughts did not prevent her from seeing the effects of war as Sanchez steered them toward the suburbs of town, nearer to where the bombings had done the most damage. Little remained of Nichols Airbase, only ugly black smoke drifting up from shattered buildings. The soldiers, looking dazed, roamed about picking through the rubble. Tears stung Blair's eyes as she thought of Gary in this condition.

A village near the airbase had also been hit, making refugees of those who had survived. They clogged the road, but every time a military vehicle drove past, these people waved and made the victory sign with their fingers.

A sentry let the minister's car pass with relative ease. Reverend Sanchez had some kind of military pass since he had often acted as chaplain in the Filipino Army. They had to pull over frequently to let troops pass. Blair searched every face, but none was the one she was looking for. When they passed through the gates of Fort McKinley, Blair was nearly devastated by the abandoned look of the place. She hadn't even considered that the men on the road were from McKinley.

They drove around the fort, asking those men who remained about Gary. Only one knew Gary, and his information gave Blair her one lift that morning.

"I saw him this morning," the sergeant said. "Came down from Clark with a medical convoy—"

"Was he wounded?" Blair gasped, hardly able to consider such a thing.

"Everyone's banged up, miss. He was on his feet." The man scratched his head, his own bruises and cuts evident all over his head and face. "You know, I think he went over to Nichols. I remember he groused a bit 'cause he came all the way here from the hospital in Manila, and then they turned right around and sent him off again. He was pretty tired, of course, but who isn't?"

Reverend Sanchez eased the clutch of his DeSoto into gear and turned around.

"Reverend," said Blair, "I thought you had business here."

"They don't need me here. Let's find Gary, then I'll be about my own business."

Blair realized the man had probably just invented the story in order to offer her help.

The hopefulness of the sergeant's words did not last long as Blair quickly began to despair again of ever finding Gary in the surrounding chaos. They might well even pass him on the road and never know it. What had he been doing at the Army hospital in Manila—at least she assumed it was Sternberg Hospital the sergeant had referred to. Why hadn't Gary called her from there? It was closer than the fort. She mentioned these questions to the reverend.

"I'm sure he would have if he could," Sanchez said. "But you must remember, Blair, he is in the Army and must follow his orders. Perhaps he did call while you were at my house."

Blair's stomach twisted with guilt. She had begun to be a little miffed, thinking Gary might have come through Manila without calling her. Now it was possible her own impatience had caused her to miss his call. How could she be so selfish? He must be frantic—no, Claudette would have told him where she was. Still, she had to begin to think of others besides herself. But she was so afraid. How she wanted to be brave! How many times growing up had her father told her to "suck it in" and "show some pluck." It was Cameron who had the pluck. She'd not be trembling now or her mind ready to explode with fear.

Out of nowhere Blair thought of that baseball game she'd played in when she was thirteen. The newspaper was having a picnic for its editorial staff, and a father/son baseball game was planned. Blair's father was not going to be left out just because he was stuck with daughters. He made Blair and Cameron play. Lucky Jackie was too young.

That silly game proved to be one of those landmarks in Blair's life, a time always remembered, like an epiphany, but not in a good way. Cameron's first time at bat, she hit a home run, but she'd played before, always muscling into the boys' games at school. Blair had never even touched a baseball bat. But Keagan didn't care. He thrust it into her trembling hands and told her not to be a sissy. She walked on shaky legs to the plate and tried to mimic the other batters' stance—at least she was good at mimicking. Watching the ball hurtle toward her, she felt like a sitting duck, scared to death, but that fear was not as great as the fear of failing her father. Her first swing was a strike, but it could only be called a strike because she moved the bat as she ducked away from the lethal missile aimed, she was certain, right at her face.

The outfield all moved in, and she knew this was meant to humiliate her, and it did. The opposing team shouted all manner of degrading chatter at her. But the worst came from her father.

"Show a little pluck. Don't be a pansy!"

She determined not to duck with the next pitch. She stood like a statue even when the ball was obviously making a direct line for her face. She wasn't going to duck; she wasn't going to be a sissy.

Wham! The ball made contact with her nose. Luckily the pitcher had moderated his fast ball in deference to her ineptitude. She only got a nosebleed and a big bruise. But she screamed and howled in pain. She was going to make her father suffer as much as she. He tried to hush her as he led her away from her humiliation. Clearly it was *his* humiliation, as well, and that was the only pleasure Blair had received in the incident. Keagan told her to quit blubbering and "act like a man." She cried harder and kicked him in the ankle. He would have spanked her for that, but the nosebleed protected her—he didn't dare strike a wounded child.

That had been the time she first began to see the utter impossibility of trying to please her father. "Act like a man" indeed!

Yet how she wished she could do that very thing now. But this was far more terrifying than being on the receiving end of a baseball. She still could not bring herself to hold a bat or even watch a game. Yet wasn't there something inside her, some reserve of strength she could draw upon now? She didn't know. She didn't think so. Yes, she had come out here to find Gary, but even that endeavor had been driven more by fear than bravery.

One thing she knew: she had to find a way home, away from all this war. She did not belong here. Once she found Gary, she would do just that. There had to be a way to get back to the States. She'd find it. Some people just weren't meant to be brave.

They drove around Nichols Airfield for nearly an hour, but as it happened, it was Gary who found them. He recognized the DeSoto from a distance and started yelling. They heard and turned around. He ran to meet them—half running, half hobbling. Blair jumped from the car the moment the reverend braked to a stop. She ran into Gary's arms, not caring that they hadn't hugged or kissed since their honeymoon or that they still had made no commitments to each other. Gary hugged her back, and that was all that mattered. She was finally safe.

Blair blurted out all her fears. "Where were you? I waited and waited. What happened? You're hurt!" She touched the bandage wrapped around his head. It was soiled with sweat and grime. Her heart quaked that he had been wounded.

"Whoa!" he chuckled at her flood of questions and comments. "I'm okay. And everything's going to be okay. We're together now."

She nodded, still in his arms, security washing over her. "What happened?"

"I got stuck up at Clark. Those crazy doctors said I needed stitches, maybe even a blood transfusion. I talked them out of the blood, though it helped that they didn't have enough except for the most serious cases anyway. When I heard they were evacuating patients from Clark to Sternberg Hospital, I volunteered to go as a guard. I got back late last night just in time for an air raid. When I finally called you this morning, you were gone. Claudette told me where you were, and I knew you were in good hands—until now." He turned toward Sanchez, who had gotten out of the car and was standing close by. "Never dreamed you'd bring her out here, Reverend." There was just a hint of recrimination in his tone.

"She was going out of her mind, Gary. It seemed the only way to calm her."

"Well, I guess I'm glad you did. I don't know when I'll get away."

"You guess?" Blair put in, a bit affronted, as if she had a right to be.

"You know what I mean. Who knows when the bombing will start up again." He put an arm around her and nudged her toward the DeSoto. "Let's go sit in the car."

"I'll be back in a few minutes," Sanchez said. "Looks like they can use some help loading those trucks."

He obviously wanted to give them some time alone. Blair would have to thank him later.

She and Gary ducked into the backseat of the car. It was nice to be a little closed off from the awful sights surrounding them, not to mention the stench of smoke that saturated the air. They talked for a time about their experiences over the last few days. For all her fears, Blair realized she had been sheltered compared to what Gary had been through.

"All those years at the Point, training and practicing . . ." He shook his head, still bewildered. "No one can prepare you for the real thing. Sometimes I wonder why I ever wanted to be in the military in the first place. I never thought of this aspect of it. Seeing friends die—" he stopped suddenly. "I'm sorry, Blair. You don't need to hear this."

"Please, Gary, you don't have to protect me." She knew she was lying. She wanted desperately to be protected from it all, but she knew Gary wanted a caring, giving woman who could put aside herself for the sake of others. Was she acting again then? Or just trying to be a better person? She wanted to be all that, though she doubted it was possible. But she'd try at least.

Gently he brushed back a strand of her platinum blond hair. "Maybe some other time I will tell you all about it. But I guess we better make some plans."

"P-plans. . . ?" her voice stammered over the word because she didn't like the sound of it. The last time they had made plans, over the telephone four days ago, she hadn't seen him in that long.

"Blair, I am not going to be able to stay with you—"

"Oh, Gary, no!"

"I have to stay with my unit. I've got my duty."

"What about your duty to me?" Tears sprang to her eyes, and she knew she was whining but didn't care.

"There's a war going on. We have to do what we have to do."

At least he had the grace not to question just then exactly what duty she expected from him. The duty of a husband?

He went on, "All over the world men are having to leave their women for war."

"But their women aren't in the middle of that war," she argued petulantly. "I am!"

"You've got to be strong, Blair. Brave—"

The sudden peal of the air-raid siren cut him off, and she was actually glad for it. She did not want to hear what he had been about to say.

"We gotta get out of here!" he said and flung open the door. Blair followed him out of the car and headed toward the door of the front seat, but he grabbed her arm, jerking her away. "No," he said. "A moving vehicle is just the target they'll be aiming at. Come on!"

With his hand clamped around her wrist, he started running, pulling her behind him until she caught her balance and was able to run on her own volition. She barely noticed that the men loading the trucks were racing in the same direction, Reverend Sanchez among them.

When they came to an irrigation ditch, everyone jumped in except Blair, who hesitated at the edge, pulling against Gary's urgent tug at her hand. He let go his hold.

"Jump!" he shouted.

Overhead, she could hear the drone of airplane engines. Soon the bombs would fall. But below in the bottom of the ditch was some slimy green stuff. She wrinkled her nose and shuddered. No one else seemed to care, but she had on one of her best silk blouses. Then she realized what a fool she was. Still, when she did jump, she closed her eyes and held her breath. She landed right in it on her seat, and the stuff oozed around her blue linen skirt and splattered her pale pink blouse. It smelled awful, as if the ditch had been used as a latrine.

She forgot all about her discomfort when the explosions came, ducking her head and covering it with slimy hands. Trembling hands. This was worse than anything she had known in the previous days. This time the explosions were not miles away but mere feet! The ground shook like a California earthquake. Debris showered over them. Something sharp hit Reverend Sanchez, cutting his head, but he stopped the bleeding by pressing his handkerchief to the gash. Blair ventured a glance up when he yelled but then ducked and covered her head again, no thought in her own fear to offer him aid.

The explosions made her ears ring, and it was moments before she realized her own screams were mingling with the ringing sound. She felt frozen, numb. In one respect she was part of the wrenching mayhem of bombs and guns strafing the ground yet somehow detached, as well. All she could feel beyond her fear was Gary's nearness.

They were an hour in that ditch before the all clear sounded. But even at the drone of the siren, she did not rise from her tightly wound cocoon. Gary gave her shoulder a gentle shake.

"It's over," he said.

She lifted her head an inch from the dirt wall where her face had been burrowed.

"Are you all right?" Gary asked. "You were so quiet except for—"

Her screams?

Gaping at him, she wondered if he had expected them to make conversation during that nightmare. “Perhaps we could have finished the conversation that ended so abruptly in the car,” she suggested snidely—or at least as snidely as her trembly voice could manage. “Or we could have conversed about the weather. Maybe the reverend could have produced a pot of tea for us—” All at once, she clamped her head between her grimy hands. Was she going crazy? Gary was just trying to be kind, doing the best he could.

Why couldn’t she be good and selfless just once? Where had she learned to be so selfish? Not from her mother . . . well, maybe if her mother had stood up for her once in a while against her father, Blair wouldn’t have had to be so concerned about herself. Blair gasped inwardly. She certainly hadn’t realized that particular resentment against her mother was in her. It was true, then, that adversity brought out the worst. But to try to lay blame on her mother, valid or not, didn’t justify Blair’s present behavior. Was she going to spend her life blaming her parents for her weak character? Or was she going to try to repair her flaws?

“I . . . I’m s-sorry,” she stammered. Her voice sounded as stiff with disuse as the muscles in her body felt.

“It’s okay,” he murmured.

Others in the ditch were climbing out. Gary would want to go, too, but she could hardly move, she had been in such a taut, tense ball for so long.

“Wait a minute, Gary,” she said, clutching his arm.

“Okay.” But he glanced toward the other men.

That’s right, he has his duty, she thought bitterly, not even realizing her resolve to change was slipping not five minutes after it had been made.

As if he read her thoughts, he said, “I’m going to have to go soon, Blair. Nothing more can be done for this airfield now, and my unit is moving out. We have to set up defensive positions north of here.”

She didn’t care about any of that. “Gary, please don’t leave me.”

“I don’t want to,” he breathed.

Hot tears stung her eyes. She tried to scrub them away with her fingers, but the dirt—and what else?—on her hands only made her eyes burn and tear more.

“Don’t leave me alone!” she cried.

“Blair, you are stronger than you think. I know you can be brave.”

There it was again, and anger like an incendiary bomb momentarily burned away some of her fear. "Stop it!" she yelled. "It's bunk, you hear? *Be brave, be strong,*" she mimicked the words harshly. "I won't be! I don't have to be! You have to stay with me. *That's* your duty, curse you!" It was useless trying to be a selfless saint. She couldn't do it! She just couldn't! Tears filled her eyes, not only of fear but tears regretting her utter failure.

"Stop it, Blair!" he grabbed her arms and gave her a shake, none too gentle this time.

"No! I won't! I won't! I—"

Another hard shake cut off her tirade. "For once in your life, Blair, quit being so selfish. I thought maybe you'd changed, but you haven't. Back home it was selfishness, too, that drove you. Your lies, all so *you* could have what *you* wanted. Yes, you came to regret them, but maybe only because you got caught. Now you are doing it all over again."

"I'm not!" she protested, refusing to listen to the truth in his words.

"Listen to me, Blair! You are a speck compared to all that is happening now. Do you hear? A speck! Men are dying—" Grasping her chin between his fingers like pinchers, he jerked her head so that her eyes faced the field. Two bodies lay, unmoving, ten feet away. Men who had not made it to the ditch in time. "The whole world is on fire, and it's not going to stop for you. It doesn't care if your silk blouse gets muddied or you break a fingernail. I can't stop for you, either. God knows, I want to, but I can't."

"But I need you, Gary," she whispered.

He closed his eyes, the muscles in his jaw working furiously. Finally, with great difficulty, he said, "I can take you back to town, but after that I must leave."

One of the soldiers passing the ditch yelled down, "Hey, Gary, I just talked to the captain. We're moving out in an hour."

Gary raked a hand through his hair, obviously torn. Blair wanted to release him, but she could not do it. It just wasn't right, him putting the Army over her, the war over her. That's not the way it was supposed to be. In the movies, the hero moved heaven and earth to protect his lover.

"I will see her safely back to town," suggested Reverend Sanchez.

Blair had forgotten he was there. His handkerchief was still pressed against the side of his head.

"I would," Gary said. "I'd have to go AWOL to do it, but I would—"

"Never mind, Gary," Blair said sharply. She meant to release him, but she wasn't going to do it with grace. "I'll be fine," she added icily.

He hesitated, as if trying to decide if he should answer her tone or her words. He apparently chose the latter. "I don't know when, or if, I'll get back. You may have to evacuate. Reverend, are you—?"

"Gary, I have committed myself to remain here with my flock as long as there are any remaining. But . . ." he paused a moment in thought, then went on, "I will give Blair my car. If only she will take Mateo with her."

Blair gaped at the man as if he had suddenly sprouted horns. What was he thinking? Giving her his car was one thing—wonderful, really. But also entrusting his son to her? Couldn't he see she could barely care for herself?

"Thank you, Reverend," Gary was saying. Was there relief in his tone? Of course. He'd been spared his duty toward her.

Blair wanted to protest this whole business. She wanted to tell them to shove duty and cars and sons, that she could take care of herself. But even she would not believe that. She couldn't have Gary, so she'd better take what there was.

Gary turned to Blair. "You do understand, don't you? Please tell me you understand."

She looked at him coldly. "Yes. I understand why you haven't been able to make a commitment in all the time I've been in the Philippines. I understand now what is most important to you."

With that she climbed out of the ditch, slipping a bit because she refused any helping hands. Her clothes were nearly all brown now with slime, and she didn't even care. But her shoes! Oh, her shoes. They were Italian, purchased before the war, and impossible to replace. Ruined! You idiot! How can you think of shoes now?

Gary gave her one final look, soulful eyes pleading still for understanding. But she turned away and walked to the car. He headed toward a truck.

She and the reverend climbed inside the DeSoto. Miraculously it had survived the bombing, with only a line of bullet holes from strafing along the driver's door. Sanchez started up the engine, put the clutch into gear, and pulled into motion.

"Gary!" Blair suddenly cried.

It finally hit her what a fool she was. Selfish was only the beginning of it. There had to be a better person hiding somewhere inside her!

Sanchez hit the brake. "You want to go back?"

She looked through the back window. Gary was nowhere to be seen, and the last truck, obviously with him aboard, was bouncing across the field, a billow of dust following it. They might be able to catch it, but what then? He still had his duty, and she still ached at having to accept that. Maybe he would think she was just acting again. Maybe she was.

Perhaps, after all, it was best this way. There was still too much between them. Maybe this war would somehow bring them private peace. Or kill them in the search.

"Yes," she said suddenly. "Go back!"

Sanchez hit the brake again. He had amazing reflexes. The wheels spun a bit in the dirt, then caught, and soon they were racing after the truck. In a moment, a figure jumped from the back of the truck and ran toward them. When the DeSoto was close, Sanchez braked, and Blair fairly leaped from the car.

She ran to Gary, but they both stopped short of flying into each other's arms. A reticence suddenly prevailed.

"Gary, I am sorry for what I said—" she began at the same moment as he spoke.

"I don't care if I am AWOL. I'm going with you."

"No, you don't have to do that. It is wrong of me to expect it. I'll be okay." Pausing a moment, she added, because it had to be said, "Honest, I will."

"I hate this," he said. "We can't seem to get a break, can we?"

"We could be thousands of miles apart," she said glibly. "At least we are in the same country."

"You will be okay. I can see that."

"Help will come, Gary. I know it will. There won't be any evacuating or anything. I'll bet a fleet from the States is on its way right now." She gazed into his eyes, searching for confirmation. But he wore that schooled, unreadable military expression of his. Then it changed to a tender nod.

"Of course, it must be. But Blair, just in case . . ." He reached into his shirt pocket, unbuttoned the flap, and withdrew a couple of items. He handed her a scrap of paper. "This is the name of a missionary family I know in the hills on the Peninsula and directions to find them.

It might come in handy . . . that's all."

She took the paper without looking at it. She wouldn't need it.

Then Gary held out his hand with palm open, and in the center lay a gold ring, a plain band with three tiny diamond chips set into the band. Blair stared at it, her mouth slightly ajar, but she made no move to take it. This was her wedding ring. The last time she had seen it was in California at the Treasure Cove when she told her greatest lie of all—when she told Gary she didn't love him.

"Take it," he said. Her eyes skittered to his face, then quickly away, afraid of what she'd see in his expression, and perhaps also afraid of what he'd see in hers. "We haven't had much of a chance to work anything out. I guess it is my fault. I wanted to avoid it because I was really afraid, Blair. Your coming should have told me enough about how you feel, but I was still unsure about God, and I didn't want to risk finding that He didn't mean for us to be together. I thought there would be time to sort it all out. I still don't know what to think, but please take the ring as my promise that I haven't given up hope, that next time we see each other, I won't avoid it again."

Blair knew that to expect more would have been to expect too much. Of course she wanted a movie ending now. Yet she realized with the world literally exploding around them, hope was the best gift he could give her.

Instead of taking the ring, she said, "Gary, thank you so much for the hope you give. I will hold it close in my heart. But you keep the ring until you know—until *we* know it is the right thing to do." She smiled coyly. "I never thought I had it in me to wait for something important like this, but I believe it will be good for me."

"To hope, then. . . ." Gary said. He slipped the ring back into his pocket. "Hope . . ."

She was nearly overwhelmed with the desire to embrace him and sensed he felt the same need. But they didn't. She held hope in her heart, and that had to be enough for now. He did bend down and lightly brush her forehead with his lips.

"I'll see you soon," he said, as if they were parting from an evening of dining and dancing.

"Yes, I hope so." Her tone, too, was light as air, not tainted by smoke and war. There were times when a little acting was necessary.

Kuibyshev, Soviet Union
December 9, 1941

WHEN CAMERON CLIMBED up the stairs to her room in the Grand Hotel about three in the afternoon, the winter sun was already dipping toward the west. Only a few minutes before a bus had dropped off her and several other correspondents. They had been given a tour of several *kolkhoz,* or collective farms. She supposed the Narkomindel, the Foreign Office, had decided that the reporters, especially the American contingent, needed a distraction from the news of Pearl Harbor.

Cameron was glad of it, though she had not wanted to leave town while Alex was there because she didn't know how long he would be staying. She could not call him, and sending messages was risky. There had only been one other meeting besides that first one, and it had been brief.

Nothing had changed in her room, and nothing much had changed in Kuibyshev, or in Russia, for that matter. She turned the knob of the radiator, giving it a couple of kicks as well, in an attempt to coax some heat from the ancient object. She read for a while, then started to freshen up for dinner.

As she was applying her lipstick, a new tube called "passion pink" brought back from her visit home, a knock came to her door. Her heart leaped as she hoped it might be Alex. It turned out to be only the boy from the cable office. He gave her a cable, and she handed him a coin before closing her door. Puzzled, she stared at the folded missive. They were seldom delivered to her directly. Instead, she was usually notified that there were cables to be picked up at the cable office. She noticed that this one was not from the *Globe,* and a knot rose in her stomach. The last cable from home had informed her of her father's heart attack.

With unsteady hands, she tore open the seal. It was from her mother.

CAMERON HATE TO BE BEARER OF BAD NEWS AGAIN STOP BLAIR CAUGHT IN PHILIPPINES DURING JAPANESE ATTACK STOP NO WORD ABOUT HER AND CANNOT BE REACHED STOP FRIENDS IN GOVERNOR GENERAL'S OFFICE HAVE NO INFORMATION STOP PRAY SHE IS ALL RIGHT STOP WILL WRITE WITH MORE DETAILS STOP LOVE MOTHER

Cameron's knees suddenly went rubbery, and she gripped the side of a table for support. Blair!

She'd heard the Philippines had been hit, but that news had been little more than a footnote beneath the huge splash of Pearl Harbor. She had, of course, remembered her sister was there, but with the attack so fresh there had not been any way to get information, so rather than go crazy with worry, Cameron had convinced herself that her sister could not possibly be in any danger. But her mother's telegram slammed home the reality of all her suppressed fears.

Quickly Cameron grabbed the telephone receiver. It took several minutes to find her way around the Russian operator—where was Sophia when she needed her? Finally she got through to the American embassy, or what passed for it in Kuibyshev, and was put through to Bob Wood.

"Bob, do you know any details yet of the bombing in the Philippines?"

"Not much more than when we last spoke, Cameron. Rather overshadowed by Hawaii, I'm afraid. But rumor has it the reason for silence might be more that it was quite a debacle over there."

"What do you mean?"

"They had several hours' warning after the Pearl Harbor attack," he replied. She could almost see him shaking his head. "But—this is off the record, Cameron. This is not for print."

"I understand, Bob. I'm interested only because my sister is there."

"I am so sorry!" He was sincere. "It was bad. All the major airfields on the island of Luzon were destroyed, as was the naval yard. I only know this because the father of one of the fellows in my office is a colonel over there. Is your sister a nurse?"

"No, a civilian." Cameron sighed, a pall beginning to settle over her. "What kind of casualties?"

"High, I'm sure, but I have no figures. I wish I had something more positive for you. Manila could well fall to the Japanese soon."

"I think my sister is in Manila."

"Cameron, I am so sorry," he said again.

"Thank you, Bob. I . . . I better go."

"I'll keep you posted whenever I hear anything."

Cameron hung up the phone and gasped in a deep breath. She felt as if she'd taken a fist to the stomach. It just did not seem conceivable that Blair could be in the middle of something like that.

Could it actually be possible that America's entry into the war had already claimed a life close to her? The idea was staggering. And Blair of all people. Dear, beautiful, confused Blair . . . only twenty-three years old. Blair had not even begun to live her life yet; she had not even begun to work out all the kinks and twists that had come her way.

No! Cameron simply could not comprehend such a thing. Yet if Blair was there, some terrible premonition told Cameron that her sister was more than likely to be in danger. She simply did not use the sense God had given her to keep out of trouble.

Cameron threaded her fingers through her hair, compressing her skull between her hands. Feeling light-headed, she jumped to her feet. She had to have some air. She felt as if she were suffocating. She paused only out of learned necessity to don a coat before rushing out of her room.

By sheer ill luck, in the corridor she ran into Mr. Hatenaka, one of the Japanese correspondents. The Soviets were making an attempt to keep the Americans and Japanese separate since the bombing, a near impossible feat in the small hotel. But there had been surprisingly few rows. Donovan had taken a swing at one of the Japanese correspondents last night over some minor disagreement. But that was all.

"Miss Hayes," Hatenaka said, bowing politely.

She stared at him. She'd felt no animosity toward her colleagues from Japan—until now. It was the first time since the bombing that she really looked upon him as the enemy.

When she did not speak, he went on, "Please to know the sinking of your fleet was a political matter. I myself bear you no personal ill will." He smiled and bowed again, the light glinting rather sinisterly off the lenses of his spectacles.

In a daze she just shook her head and hurried past him.

Outside, the sun had been down for about an hour, and the temperature had dropped considerably. This was no time for a stroll, but as if to honor her sister, she ignored good sense and did not return to the shelter of the hotel. Air, even icy air, slicing through her lungs was better than the cramped quarters of her small room that had suddenly begun to close in on her. She put on the thick gloves and wool scarf she kept in the pocket of the coat and pressed her fur cap down over her ears. Then she walked.

The shabby wooden buildings of Kuibyshev, many dating back to the times of the tsars, offered little comfort to Cameron and no easing of her shattered thoughts. All she could think was that Blair's life perhaps had been wasted and her own seemed to be hanging about her in tatters. She tried to shut out such grim thoughts and convince herself that Blair might be perfectly all right. But hope was a commodity slipping from Cameron by sure degrees. First was her complete botching of the escape attempt of Oleg and Sophia, then her father's heart attack and her hopeless visit home. Then there was Alex. What kind of relationship could they hope to have with so much against them? Sometimes she wasn't sure of the foundation of that relationship, even without having problems with the police. Whenever he spoke of his newly found faith—and that was more now than ever before—she felt a gnawing discomfort. What was to become of them?

And now Blair. That seemed the final straw. Her mother had told her to pray. But how could she pray to one whom she secretly doubted really cared?

"Cameron!"

The sound of her name, dulled by the icy air, reached her ears as if much farther away. It might have been only her imagination. The thudding of footfalls in the snow as they came up behind her barely registered. She was too wrapped in a blanket of cold and despair.

A hand jarred her shoulder before she finally responded. She turned, and there was Alex.

"They told me at the hotel you'd left on foot," he said, great puffs of steam punctuating his words. "What are you thinking? It's thirty below out here!"

"I . . . I needed air."

"This air could kill. Come on, let's get inside."

"Alex, I just got a cable from home—"

"Your father?"

She shook her head. "My sister is in the Philippines. The Japs bombed it." She shuddered. Saying the words out loud made them seem far too real. "She can't be reached, not even with my parents' contacts. The destruction there was far worse than we'd heard. The last time I saw Blair she was happily attending Hollywood parties. Now . . . oh, Alex! What if she is . . . dead?"

He wrapped an arm around her as he nudged her back toward the hotel. "You mustn't think the worst. Most likely only military targets were hit. She wasn't in the military, was she?"

"How do I know what she might have done since I saw her last?" she burst, as if accusing Alex of something. "She's impulsive, crazy, confused." Cameron gasped in a breath. "I . . . didn't know her . . . not really. But I love her. She's my sister. . . ."

The words were scarcely spoken before tears erupted, oozing from her eyes and freezing as they touched her icy cheeks.

Alex leaned close and kissed her gently. "There, there . . ." he murmured. They had reached the hotel, and he opened the door.

By the time he got her up to her room, she had begun to shiver. He took off her gloves and rubbed her hands vigorously in his large warm ones. She didn't want to think how secure they felt. Yet his attention seemed to help get her blood flowing properly again. Like a ministering angel, he took off her wet shoes and stockings and rubbed her feet as she sat on the edge of the bed. Then he applied some less gentle force to the radiator to get it to emit a little more heat.

When her lips stopped trembling with cold, she said, "Thanks, Alex. What brought you here anyway?" She remembered her despair over their relationship, her sense of hopelessness. But here he was when she needed him most. That must say something. Perhaps she had been too hard on God after all.

"I just had a need to be with you." He gazed at her in a way that made her warm all over despite the malfunctioning radiator.

"It's almost as if . . ." But she paused, unable to risk the completion of her thought.

"As if what?"

"Nothing, but it is a nice coincidence you came when you did, when I needed a friend most." It was easier to admit her need than to admit the intervention of some higher power.

"A coincidence, yes . . . or perhaps God's providence."

"Oh, Alex—"

"Cameron, it's all I have to offer you," he cut in, but his voice was barely above a murmur. "Please accept it. God can and will comfort you."

She could not refute him, not because she believed what he said, but because she could not hack down his faith when he was being so loving and when she needed him.

"Won't you give it a chance?" he entreated.

"I don't know. . . ." She desperately didn't want to shut him down, yet she was growing frustrated at his persistence. "You can't expect me to toss off a lifetime of beliefs overnight."

"I shouldn't think it would be too difficult to part with cynicism and bitterness."

"Is that what you think of me?" her voice rose almost imperceptibly.

"No, but it is a part of you, and one element that I'd think you'd be thrilled to replace with something more positive."

"Or maybe you would just like to replace it. Maybe you can't accept me the way I am—"

"You know that's not true." But instead of looking at her, he went to the radiator and gave it another blow, this time with his foot. She had the feeling that was not all he'd like to kick just then. "I just want you to be happy."

She cringed at how lame his words were. A very lame cover for what was appearing more and more clearly to be the truth. They had tried to ignore it, but was this . . . this *thing* between them growing completely out of their control?

He turned and strode to her, sat on the bed, and wrapped his arms around her. "Cameron, I only wanted to comfort you. I am sorry for my rotten bedside manner."

"You've always had wonderful bedside manners, Doctor." She made a concerted attempt to lighten her tone. She couldn't find it in herself just now to push him away.

"I try."

"It is just your cantankerous patient—"

"My dear, sweet patient."

She laughed. "Sweet, Alex? That's overkill, isn't it?"

He lifted off her hat and ran his hand over her hair. "I love you, Cameron!" There was no humor in his tone now, only that fervent intensity she had come to identify with him. It made her shiver and feel warm all at once.

She told herself everything would be okay—with Blair and with Alex. There was something about him that gave her hope in spite of herself. She even began to think their disagreements were nothing. All they had to do was refrain from talking about religion. That shouldn't be hard. It had never been a problem before.

Alex wrestled with these matters for several days, almost relieved the police kept him and Cameron apart. However, in its own way, this was dismaying, as well. Cameron was the women he loved, yet the awkwardness springing up between them was nearly unbearable for him, more so than for her. He sensed she believed they could just avoid their "little" problems about religion. He knew that could not be.

When he heard Yuri Fedorcenko had come to the Kuibyshev hospital on an inspection tour, he was thrilled. He desperately needed someone to talk to, since the person who used to fill that need was growing distant from him.

"You are a godsend, Yuri," he said as they paused in their rounds to share a cup of tea in the doctors' lounge.

"It appears as if everything is under control here and I am not needed at all," replied the elder doctor.

They sat at an old table with chipped cups of steaming brew before them. The facilities for doctors here were far more dismal than in Moscow. Not for the first time Alex thought of the comforts and riches he had sacrificed in leaving America. Of course, none would have been his had he remained there, not after losing his license. Yet at times he could not deny a pang of regret for his mistakes and the price of them. The worst cost had been the loss of his faith in God. And though that was now restored to him, he was finding his joy conflicted.

With a sigh Alex replied, "All is well at the hospital, yes. In my life . . . not so, I am afraid."

"Are the police still dogging you?"

"They try, but the poor fellows can't keep up with me—they weren't built for doctors' hours. Nor have they the manpower. There is surveillance to be sure. But it is not the police. . . ." Toying with the handle of his cup, he suddenly found it very difficult to make the admission that the love he'd been so certain of a month ago was now crumbling by slow degrees. "I'm concerned about Cameron . . . and me."

"I heard she has returned from the States."

"Yes, but I don't think it went well with her there."

"Her father, wasn't it?"

"He is still alive and recovering. But their relationship has never been a congenial one, and I believe it even worsened during her visit. She won't talk about it. I made the mistake of suggesting that she trust God—" Yuri's ironic smile made him stop for a moment, then he added with a self-deprecating shrug, "I know now it was a huge mistake. I was caught up in the zeal of my personal enlightenment and thought everyone ought to experience the same."

"It is never a good idea to bludgeon our loved ones with it."

"I should have known better," Alex admitted. "I can still remember how I felt years ago when my parents tried to force their faith on me. I had to find God in my own way and in my own time."

"We are only human, Alex. It may not be a good idea to overwhelm our families with our faith, but it is hard not to do so when we want so desperately for them to share the wonderful thing we have found."

Alex nodded, but his aspect was still dismal. "I find I am hanging on to what Anna said of Cameron, that she was softening toward God." Yuri's mother, Anna, and Cameron had been sheltered together one day during an air raid, and they had had a long talk while they waited out their confinement. Anna had been encouraged because Cameron's mother was a Christian and Cameron had grown up around her faith. "I don't know, Yuri, but since she returned from California, it seems she has gone back several steps. Before, she was rather indifferent; now she seems far more touchy about it."

"Maybe that's a good development."

"What!" Alex gaped, slack-jawed, at his friend.

Yuri grinned, laying a hand on Alex's shoulder. "I am reminded of an animal caught in a trap, though I hate to liken faith in God to a trap. But bear with me a moment. What does an animal in such a situation do? He fights like the devil against it. And as long as that animal fights, there is a kind of hope. Only when he gives up, turns indifferent, if you will, to his plight, is all hope lost. A poor analogy, I know, but I do think your Cameron is in a much better place now, even if she is actively hostile, than when she was indifferent."

"I never considered it in that way before," Alex conceded. "Still, it makes it no easier."

"No, it doesn't—for either of you."

Alex was silent for a long time before finally admitting what had been eating away at his heart. "Yuri, sometimes I think about going back to where I was two months ago, to my own indifference."

"You mustn't do that, Alex."

"Perhaps there is hope in her fighting, but I fear with all else that is conspiring against us, this issue of faith may be the breaking point." He shrugged helplessly. "I fear I am not strong enough myself. I cracked under pressure before, turning to the oblivion of drugs. And look at the pressures besetting me now. Besides Cameron and the police, there is my work. I survive on a couple hours of sleep a night. Tea is my drug now, for what good it does, but what if. . . ?" He gave his head a sharp shake. He didn't want to think of that or speak of the fact that he'd experienced times, all too recently, when the bottles of amphetamines sorely tempted him. Trying to be positive, he added, "At least here in Kuibyshev I don't have to deal with such a heavy load, so it helps."

Yuri looked away for a moment, licking his lips before reluctantly speaking. "That makes it all the more difficult for me to say that you are needed in Moscow. Your skills are wasted here. Nevertheless, I would not recall you if I had the final say in the matter."

Alex closed his eyes and inwardly groaned. "Dear God . . ." he breathed, "what am I to do?"

"I cannot completely control the decisions of the powers over me, but I will forestall it as best I can. In the meantime, I have another suggestion. Perhaps some fellowship with other Christians would help to strengthen your faith."

"I would be grateful for that, but beyond the Orthodox churches, I haven't had time to seek out contacts such as I am sure you mean."

"I may be able to help. I have friends who evacuated from Moscow and have started a fellowship here. Nothing formal, mind you, and nothing . . . well, out in the open, so to speak."

"A secret fellowship? I didn't think such a thing was necessary these days."

The war had brought greater tolerance toward worship in Russia.

Stalin could not very well ask for aid from Western and Christian nations while continuing to carry on his program of religious persecution. Not only the Orthodox Church, but other denominations as well, was now able to meet openly—at least that was the official stance.

"I know I have been called the eternal pessimist," Yuri said wryly, "but I am not the only Christian who doubts this current religious freedom will last much beyond the war. Stalin's antireligious tendencies run too deep to permit it beyond the call of expediency. At any rate, many fellowships feel it is prudent to maintain a low profile now so that when the freedoms are removed, they will not be crushed in the certain backlash. This particular group I am thinking of meets in a small gathering of about a dozen. They make their way by stealth to the specified meeting place, as in the old days. If they are discovered, well, they are not doing anything illegal. If not found out, their precautions will preserve them for when times get hard again."

"It is still risky," Alex said. "What if they are taken for a conclave of spies instead of worshipers?"

"These people have known far greater risks. And that seems a small one for them to deal with." Yuri paused, giving his friend an intense perusal. "Are you interested?"

Alex could tell Yuri feared these current adversities in his life might wear away at Alex's renewed faith. Alex feared it, as well. He knew he needed the support of other Christians. Perhaps it was worth the risk.

"Yes," he said with resolve.

"They are meeting tonight—for my benefit, actually. I will take you there, since at first you must go with someone they know."

"I understand."

"I must return to Moscow tomorrow. First, however, I need to speak with Cameron."

Alex cocked a curious brow. "You do?"

"Not to preach to her, I assure you. It is about a matter regarding Oleg." When it was apparent Alex remained curious, Yuri added, "I have a feeling this is one of those matters where the fewer people who know about it the better."

Alex shook his head ruefully. "I understand that, as well. You don't know how often I have to remind myself of why I came to Russia and of how important practicing medicine is to me. Except for that, it would be so easy for me to leave."

"You should not think of leaving, Alex."

"What do you mean?"

"Do you really think such a thing would be permitted?"

Alex feared not, adding to the many weights upon him. He had often considered Cameron's inability to fully comprehend life in a police state because of the freedom she had known all her life. But he was in much the same place. Technically, he understood his position now in Russia, but there was still a large part of him steeped in freedom that simply could not comprehend or even accept the lack of it. Three years in the Soviet Union, yet he still had thoughts that he could pick up and go where he wished, as if he were traveling from Illinois to New York.

"I will miss you, old friend," Alex said, walking with Yuri back into the corridor.

"I, too, but I will do what I can to ensure I don't see you for a good long time." Yuri grinned.

"As with much in my life these days, that has a double edge. I will have to look upon it as a time to truly learn to trust in God."

10

CAMERON WAS SURPRISED when she received a note from Dr. Fedorcenko requesting that she come to the hospital for a checkup to ensure she had fully recovered from her accident. The note was a thin deception at best because of the unlikelihood of the chief of staff of the Moscow hospital where she had been a patient having the need to examine her, especially with her own doctor present in Kuibyshev. Nevertheless, she did not quibble. If Fedorcenko's deception didn't deceive the police, she could easily think of another reason for going to the hospital.

Snow lay thick on the ground as she trudged through it. Traffic was backed up because of the weather, and walking seemed a far more reliable manner of transportation than a cab or bus. Today she had on her fur-lined boots and a warm wool sweater under her heavy coat. The cold shouldn't affect her as it had recently with Alex. Besides, a little sunlight was penetrating the morning sky.

Certain that Dr. Fedorcenko did not want to examine her, she naturally wondered just what he did want. Was something amiss with Sophia? Or other members of the family? His mother, Anna, was not a young woman, and the hardships of war must be especially difficult for one of her advanced age. Of course only negative reasons for this meeting occurred to her. If she had any optimism left in her, it was slowly being eroded by life, especially by the growing tension she felt whenever she was with Alex. He had been the one bright spot that had carried her through her difficulties at home. Now even that was tarnished.

She rued her relief when she found Dr. Fedorcenko without running into Alex. Some romance that was! But the last time they had seen each other there had been some sharp words spoken. Shanahan had been with them for a short time and had mentioned hearing of a banquet for some British and American dignitaries in which Stalin had invoked God's blessing on their countries. She and Shanahan had guffawed heartily about the lengths Uncle Joe would go to in order to garner foreign sympathy. Their jokes never denigrated religion per se, but she supposed they might have degenerated into some rather irreverent pokes at religion. At least, Alex had taken it so and become offended.

Now that Cameron recalled the incident, she supposed she might have made those jabs just a bit pointedly. She might have been trying to provoke Alex, though she had not a clue why she would do such a stupid thing. Did she want to sabotage their relationship? Shaking the unsettling thought from her mind, she followed the doctor into one of the examining rooms.

"Have a seat." Dr. Fedorcenko indicated a chair rather than the examination table.

"I take it that I am not to be given an examination?" she asked wryly.

"I thought it best to at least make an attempt to camouflage our meeting. In Russia, discretion is always the better part of valor." He smiled, taking the seat opposite her in the small room that smelled strongly of antiseptic. "So how have you been feeling?" he asked with a decided medical tone to his voice. "Keeping away from explosions and such, I hope?"

"I have since coming to Kuibyshev. It is nice to have a break from the air raids. And no blackouts—that is grand. As for my health, I am in tip-top condition, I assure you."

"How did you find the States?"

"Just fine," she answered shortly, then, so as to cover the discomfort she felt about the topic, added, "I found Americans were wonderfully happy and smug in their isolation. I actually met people who had little, if any, clue about the extent of the war over here."

"I suspect that is as much the fault of the Soviet government as it is of those Americans."

"It will all be changed now for the Americans. They are in it now." She was only vaguely aware of her use of *they*. "But I doubt their interest in Russia will change very much."

The conversation lulled a moment, then the doctor said, "I wish we had more time to visit, but I have to squeeze in a couple of meetings today before I go to the airport after lunch."

"You are returning to Moscow?" When he nodded, she added, "Is your family well? Do you see Sophia?"

"The family is well. I have seen Sophia once since she joined the Women's Brigade. It is very hard for her." Pausing, he swallowed, and she could see the effects of his worry over his daughter etched around his dark eyes. "But she is a brave girl. I am proud of her."

"She is a very special young woman. I miss her company."

"I suppose I should get to the purpose for this meeting." He didn't appear especially anxious to do so. "I saw Oleg a couple of weeks ago."

"Has he been released?" Cameron asked hopefully.

"No, I am afraid not. I was permitted to visit him in prison. He was ill, and I used what little clout I have left in official circles to obtain permission to examine him."

"It is not serious, is it, Doctor?" No matter what anyone said, she would never cease feeling responsible for what had happened to Oleg. "Has Sophia seen him?"

"Unfortunately she has not, but at least I could report to her that he is doing as well as can be expected. He was hit hard with dysentery and severe dehydration, which put him in the prison hospital. He is on the mend from that, but while I was with him, he wanted me to pass a message along to you."

"Me?" Cameron was assailed with deep misgiving.

"When Oleg was first admitted to the infirmary," Yuri went on, "he was in a great deal of pain and discomfort with his illness. Another patient was a great comfort to him. According to Oleg, this was a man of middle years, about my own age, though Oleg said he looked much older, which no doubt could be attributed to the fact that he had been in the gulag for nearly twenty years. I myself never met the man because he died a couple of days before I arrived. Oleg said he was kind and gave my son-in-law hope."

"I'm glad to hear that, Doctor, but I don't see what this has to do with me."

"Perhaps nothing at all, but Oleg felt compelled to tell me so that I would pass the incident along to you. Oleg and this man—I believe his name was Yakov—talked often, and in the course of their many conversations, Oleg mentioned his involvement with an American reporter. This man was Jewish also, and I suppose Oleg told him about what he saw at Dniepropetrovsk, and that is how you came into it."

That was also how the trouble with Oleg had begun. He had been in the Dniepropetrovsk area when he had escaped German captivity. In the course of his escape he had surreptitiously witnessed the German massacre of several thousand Jewish residents. The boy had not been wise enough to keep quiet about this horrifying incident. He'd thought Cameron, as a journalist, could publish this German atrocity to the world, gathering world support for the Allied cause. Oleg viewed the world in black and white terms and could not conceive of any other reception for his story. But Cameron had been faced with many opposing ramifications, none pleasant to hear. Even if his story could be believed—and many would simply not accept such a thing as possible—there were more than a few out there who could not find much fault with Hitler's racist views.

Despite that, Cameron had managed to enlist the aid of Bob Wood, an embassy official, to make an attempt to get Oleg and his story out of the country. The escape plot had failed miserably, and Oleg had ended up in prison. And still the fool boy was spouting his story to strangers. Cameron was quickly losing her sympathy for him.

She let out a sharp breath. "Doctor, surely Oleg realizes the risk he takes in such idle conversation? How did he know this man wasn't an informer?"

"You know Oleg. . . ." mused Dr. Fedorcenko with a helpless shrug. "He is a fine boy but so very impulsive. However, he felt certain this man was safe. And the fact that he died so soon after of natural causes indicates that he was perhaps not with the police. Oleg watched the man die and in fact was by his bed holding his hand until the very last. At any rate, let me tell you what this man, Yakov, said."

Suddenly something registered with Cameron. "Yakov . . . you say?" She felt her heart skip a beat. Her mouth went dry and she had to force out her next question. "What . . . was his surname?"

"Luban."

"Are you certain?" Cameron breathed, not really needing an answer.

"Do you know this man?"

"What did he tell Oleg?"

Seeming to not notice that she had ignored his question, Fedorcenko answered hers. "He told my son-in-law that during the Great War he once knew of an American journalist named Hayes—"

Cameron was too caught now to even react to the stupidity of Oleg giving her name to his man.

Yuri continued, "Luban wondered if the Hayes Oleg mentioned and the man he knew were the same. When Oleg said the journalist he knew was a woman in her midtwenties and could not possibly be the same person the older man had known more than twenty years ago, Yakov just sighed and said it was too good to be true anyway. He also said something to the effect of, 'And even if the two were related, what good would it do anyway?' "

Leaning forward with breath held, Cameron managed, "He said nothing else?"

"The man grew steadily weaker not long after that. He was in the last stages of liver cancer."

"Did he ever speak of his family to Oleg?"

"He did. Yakov's wife died before the Great War. He had a son, but the child was taken from him when he was arrested. No doubt the child was placed in an orphan home, and if fortunate, he was adopted."

"Surely even the Soviet regime could not be so heartless as to completely cut a man off from his only son." Cameron rubbed her hands over her face, not knowing whether to feel despair or elation over this amazing coincidence. If the Yakov Luban Oleg met in prison was indeed her mother's lover, then his death must sever the only link to finding the child. Yet, on the other hand, that he should surface in this way after so long offered hope, as well. It was like stumbling upon fresh tracks during a hunt. They might lead nowhere, but they were fresh, and that was something.

The largest question, however, was whether she was indeed on a hunt. She hadn't even had the heart to open the envelope of old letters and photos from Yakov that her mother had given Cameron before leaving the States a week ago. It lay untouched, still in her suitcase. Wasn't it possible that finding her brother could hurt more people than it would help? If he was still alive, he had a life of his own and might not wish the complication of an American mother. And what of Cecilia? Would knowing her son lived be any use if she could never see him? That might prove an even greater torment to her. Then there was Keagan. Cameron did not even want to think what her father's reaction might be to hearing his wife had had an affair in Russia that had produced a child—the son Keagan himself had been denied.

Finally, the biggest question of all. If she was willing to put aside all those snarls, could she even risk a hunt? One step out of line with the police, and she would likely be deported.

"Cameron, are you all right?" Dr. Fedorcenko asked.

Still in disbelief, she shook her head. "This is stirring up some skeletons in my parents' lives. They were in Russia during the Great War and also during the famine in the twenties. I only found out about certain past events recently. I never dreamed they would reach out and grab me like this. It is incredible."

"Too bad this fellow died," offered Fedorcenko. "But if it is any comfort, it is highly unlikely you would have been permitted to see him even if you had known he was in prison."

"Doctor, do you know why he was in prison?"

"Political reasons, I believe." He reached for his medical bag, opened it, and took out a large brown envelope. "I brought these in the hope I might find you here or at the least leave them with Alex to give to you. These are the man's effects passed directly from him to Oleg. Oleg gave them to me to take from the prison, thinking they would be kept safe that way. He also thought that if you did know Luban, you might be interested in seeing them. He did ask, however, that you be extremely careful with them, for they are special to him."

"What does it contain?" Her gaze was on the envelope. Secrets revealed? Or more questions raised?

"A letter and a book."

"A letter . . . from his son. . . ?"

"I did not look closely. But if so, perhaps our government is not so cruel as imagined, eh? I do not defend the government, but Luban did have a life sentence, so perhaps it was well meaning for them to sever the ties with his son. Do you want this?"

She took it more with resolve than with eagerness. Balancing its weight in her hands, she wondered where it would lead. Staring at that packet she immediately realized there was within her a stronger instinct than self-protection—her innate curiosity, her intrepid inquisitiveness, her downright odious inability to let go of a matter once she had sunk in her teeth. Her mother no doubt had been counting heavily on those aspects of her eldest daughter's personality when she had confided her secret.

"Dr. Fedorcenko, how difficult would it be to find a missing person in Russia?"

"For you, my dear, impossible, especially if that person happens to be a Russian citizen. For one such as me, practically impossible. You know what poking around in dark corners can do. Some things are best left alone, especially in Russia."

"Yes . . . of course . . ." But Cameron's tone lacked resolve.

She knew herself too well, better than the doctor did, and she knew she was not one to leave things alone. Despite the fact that she still felt the sting of her failure with Oleg, she knew her *modus operandi* if nothing else was poking in dark corners and shining light on whatever demons might be lurking there. Being in Russia these many months, with her hands tied and her natural instincts quashed by the government, she had grown dull in this respect.

And with good reason.

To raise a crusade to discover the whereabouts of her half brother could be the most imprudent thing she would ever do. It could, indeed, have disastrous results. For once in her life she must move, if she moved at all, slowly, cautiously, though every instinct she had urged her to charge forth like an avenging army.

11

ALEX WAS IN A fine mood that morning. He joked and quipped with his patients and hummed a little tune as he strode the hospital corridors on his morning rounds. He'd slept better last night than he had in months. Reason enough for his energetic mood.

He did not want to attribute it to the meeting he had attended the night before. To him that would almost be assigning some kind of magic to it, and that seemed, frankly, incongruent. He balked at approaching faith in that way. He was far more comfortable with logic and reason. Yet . . .

He could not deny he had been caught up in a certain charisma the moment he had entered that small apartment. It had been a typical middle-class home right down to the faint odor of cabbage in the air and the samovar on a sideboard, which had been nothing fancy, just plain stainless steel, and steaming with current use. It had reminded him of his parents' home in America and Yuri's home in Moscow. He'd felt immediately comfortable.

But it had been more than the surroundings that had captured him. There were about fifteen people present. All sorts. Old peasant women with scarves on their heads, women rather fashionably dressed for Russia, men in nice suits, men in work clothes. Some were quiet and sullen, some loud and friendly. But all were welcoming. He was especially taken with the hosts of the meeting, Vassily and Marie Turkin. She was around forty years old, tall, elegant, attractive. He was short, fifteen years her senior, balding, bespectacled, rather artless in his movements, having the appearance of an absentminded sort.

Yet there was a sincere warmth in his vague eyes when he was introduced to Yuri's friend. "Such a pleasure! Yuri has spoken of you highly." The hand he extended to Alex was smooth, untouched by manual labor. Alex was certain he must be a professor. But his grip was firm, even fervent. Smiling, Turkin introduced Alex around. They all seemed to be using their real names. This was surprising, yet how much caution really was necessary?

Marie Turkin was far more reticent than her husband, and Alex guessed that came in part at least from shyness. She offered tea with the graciousness of a countess.

After a time of visiting, Vassily called everyone to gather together in a rough circle, some on seats, others seated on the threadbare carpet because there were not enough chairs to go around. Alex headed to an empty place on the floor, but Marie Turkin laid a slim, shapely hand on his arm.

"You are new and a visitor. Tonight you will have a proper chair." She seemed slightly scandalized that anyone in her home should be sitting on the floor. Alex assumed they had far more comfortable quarters in Moscow and were making do while evacuated here in backwater Kuibyshev. Yet he never had the sense of snobbery even from Mrs. Turkin.

He tried to protest but to no avail as he was firmly planted on a high-backed dining room chair. Then one of the guests brought out a small Autoharp and began to play. Alex recognized the tune as "What a Friend We Have in Jesus." He'd only heard it sung in English, and the Russian words had a rather odd discord with the music.

After they sang several more hymns, Vassily asked everyone to bow their heads, launching immediately into the oddest prayer meeting Alex had ever attended. He had heard of this process called "conversational prayer" but had never experienced it. His parents had approached their faith more formally. They had come to their faith from atheism, not Orthodoxy, yet their Russian pasts had been rooted in the Russian church. Though they attended a Protestant church in America after becoming Christians, it in no way dabbled in new trends.

This prayer session lasted well over an hour, but what was surprising was that Alex hardly noticed the passing of time. It was indeed like a conversation, only heads were bowed and eyes closed, and they were talking to God, not to each other. All chimed in, though, in proper turn, speaking in sentences that tended to be short and to the point rather than the long ecclesiastical prayers Alex was accustomed to hearing from the church pulpit. Most of the prayers were petitions to God for loved ones at war, for protection, and for strength. Some prayed for the country in this harrowing time. Some even prayed for Joseph Stalin!

Others lifted praises to God. Alex was surprised that the most moving of these came from refined Marie Turkin.

"My precious Father, you are too wonderful for words, mighty, omnipotent, yet as dear to me as my own papa. I don't understand how this can be, but I come before you now with utmost gratitude that you can be friend to my heart and listener to my smallest word! Yet you still balance the weight of the world on your shoulders. I feel your love as if I were your only child, yet you do the same with all your children. You are a wonder to me, my Lord!"

Alex could not resist opening his eyes to gaze at the woman. He immediately felt guilty for doing so, because he saw tears seeping from her closed eyes. Indeed she was speaking to her best friend.

Alex did not pray that night. He wanted to, even got that light-headed feeling indicating his turn to speak was coming. He had never been a reticent public speaker before. That was not what held him back. He wasn't certain what did. Perhaps just being new stopped him. Yuri prayed, and hearing his friend almost urged Alex to also do so. Only when Vassily closed the session with an "Amen!" did Alex realize the cause of his sudden reserve. Only one problem had echoed in his head, demanding prayer. "Pray for her!" But he could not bring himself to pray for Cameron in front of these people, because he knew she'd take it as a kind of betrayal. Yes, he prayed for her silently often, but this would be different, and he could not do that to her. Nevertheless, it left him with an unsettled feeling. His love for her was even in this way pulling him from his love for God.

The meeting closed shortly after the prayer time. No sermon or teaching at all. Yes, it was all quite peculiar. And Alex was certain he wanted to attend again. Even despite his confliction about Cameron, he had to admit that perhaps there had been a kind of magic to the gathering.

Still humming that tune, Alex visited his last patient of the morning and headed toward the operating room where his schedule of surgeries would begin. He hadn't given the tune much thought before now, though it had been the same tune all morning. Now it came to him. "What a Friend We Have in Jesus." He remembered Marie's prayer and suddenly knew for himself that same closeness to his Lord that she had spoken of. Yuri had known that would happen.

Alex was feeling so good he did not even groan when he saw his friend Anatoly Bogorodsk approach.

The man wore a friendly smile, even if his neckless mountain of a figure made it seem on the sinister side. He had the build of a football linebacker but, without that sport in Russia, had turned his muscle to the NKVD. He was a man to be feared, then, on several levels. But for some reason he counted Alex as a friend, often calling him *brother* while giving him an amiable pounding on the back. Alex had treated Anatoly's young son, who had been struck by a car and had been near death. The boy had pulled through more, Alex was certain, by some miracle than by Alex's skill with a scalpel, but no one could tell Anatoly that.

Not that Alex was complaining. One could do worse than having a friend in the secret police.

"Anatoly, whatever brings you all the way here to Kuibyshev?" Alex asked as the agent fell in step with him and they continued to walk together down the hall.

"Official business. As you know, this is now the wartime capital of the Soviet Union." He shook his head as if even he couldn't believe that. "I am already bored to distraction. Glad I'll be returning to Moscow soon."

"I hear we have turned back the Germans in Moscow and will begin an offensive."

"It has already started. How I yearn for the day when we push those butchers back to the Rhine, then burn them and *their* bloody land to ashes!"

Alex cringed because he seldom heard the agent speak with such ferocity. He was a dangerous man, true, but a rather genial one most of the time.

"I am thinking about taking a commission in the Army," Anatoly added. "I could be an officer. I want to kill Germans, not snoop on my own countrymen."

"Is that what brings you to Kuibyshev, Anatoly?" Alex asked with a slight edge to his voice.

"I have several reasons, but I could not come without seeing you. I would have come even if you were not one of my reasons. Let me take you someplace for a meal," said the agent, his tone back to its usual level of good-natured friendliness—for an NKVD agent. "When was the last time we broke bread together? Even with rationing and shortages I think we could find a tolerable café in this village."

"I must be in surgery shortly." Alex paused and decided it would be a good idea to curry this man's friendship. "But I will take you to a place where they have the best cabbage soup in all of Kuibyshev."

"Better than my Vera's?"

"Nothing could match that, my friend, but you will enjoy it."

They took the elevator to the first floor, then Alex led his companion to the hospital dining room where the staff took their meals. It was busy this time of day, close to midday. But they thought nothing of waiting in line for a steaming bowl of soup and a hunk of brown bread. Alex practically lived on this diet, since the hospital had little more to offer and he was, for all practical purposes, living at the hospital. Occasionally there was borsch, but cabbages were, it seemed, more plentiful than beets.

They set their trays of food on a small table that wobbled under the weight of them, making the soup splash over the edge of the bowls. Anatoly's heaving his bulk into a chair didn't help, but he hardly noticed as he picked up his spoon and ladled up the soup. Alex concentrated on the food as well, but he couldn't keep from wondering just what Anatoly wanted. The last time they had seen each other in Moscow, the agent had warned him to stay away from Cameron. Could that be his purpose now? It would not surprise Alex if their few stolen meetings had been discovered by the police. But taking a surreptitious look at the agent over the edge of his spoon, Alex did not think that was it. Nor did he think this was merely a friendly visit.

Alex shook his head. He was becoming as suspicious as the best Russian. Why not a friendly visit? They'd had them in the past. Playing cards together, sharing a meal at Anatoly's home, Alex learning how to play chess from Anatoly's son. Yes, there was a friendship there, one that went beyond merely currying the good graces of the police.

Around a mouthful of cabbage, Anatoly said, "This is good for hospital food. Not good enough to bring me to a hospital for any reason other than to see you, however." He grinned after swallowing. A string of cabbage was stuck between his teeth. "I have some good news for you, Comrade. At least I hope it is still good news."

"What is that? Any good news is welcome these days."

"When the war began, I remember you came to me asking if I could put in a word for you that you might get a commission in the Army and an assignment to a frontline hospital."

Alex had done just that. He'd been caught up in nationalistic zeal as much as anyone. He'd wanted to serve his adopted country. In truth, Russia was more than that. America was more his adopted nation, and returning to Russia had been like returning to the care of one's birth mother. He had never given up his Russian citizenship, though that had been mostly out of respect to his parents rather than to the Soviet Union. When his adopted country had turned on him—no matter that it was his fault—he had found succor and meaning once more in his life through his mother Russia.

It had been surprisingly easy to meld into the flow of life in the Soviet Union. In America he had grown up in a strong Russian community. He'd been steeped in those traditions all his life, and because his parents never learned decent English, he had spoken Russian most of the time and even now could not speak English without an accent and did not think in English. Oddly enough, he had more of an accent than did Yuri or even Anna. Only when he went away for college and medical school did he become immersed in American ways. He may have spent twenty-eight years of his life in America, but he was still Russian. He'd even joined the Communist Party—a monumental mistake he now knew, but when he had returned to Russia four years ago, it had seemed a good idea. Having renounced his faith in God, he had been bitter enough to believe one ideology was just as good as another.

Alex held his spoon midair, hardly noticing the pungent fragrance of cabbage. Why was Anatoly bringing this up now? In June, when the war began, Alex had been turned down for active service. Anatoly thought the reason was a question of loyalty. The police would not want to let anyone suspect get far from the watchful eye of the Kremlin. And though a Russian citizen and a Communist, the fact was that he had spent his entire childhood and early adulthood in America. His position was unusual at best.

"Have you still an interest in this, my friend?" Anatoly asked.

Alex stuffed the spoonful of soup into his mouth, hoping to forestall an immediate answer, for he had no idea what he thought about this matter now. After all that had happened in the last months, he was just the slightest bit surprised to realize that he *was* still a loyal Russian in his heart.

"I will go wherever my country sends me, Anatoly." He meant it.

But there was Cameron. His peculiar status in this country had afforded him the best means possible for any Russian to foster a relationship with a foreigner. Not to mention that his civilian status had made it possible for him to be near her. As a hardworking doctor, he never had cause to feel shame at his lack of military service. He'd really had it all quite nicely.

"I believe this will be possible for you now," said Anatoly.

Alex's throat was dry. "Even when I am still being watched?"

"Bah! The watch is gone, Aleksei. You are as free as any Russian." Anatoly smiled wryly. "You know what I mean, eh? You led my men on a merry chase. Wore them out, you did, so that they would have been happier to man the front lines of battle."

This all but staggered Alex. Dropping his spoon back into the bowl, he stared at the agent. Of course, freedom in Russia was most definitely a relative term, but for him to have achieved even this much . . . it boggled the mind. Yet he still could not prevent a tinge of suspicion from clinging to the edges of his mind.

"Why?" he rasped.

"Do not question. Accept. It may not last, and then where will you be? Gather your rosebuds, as it is said."

"Do you have orders for me?"

"Not exactly. But you are requested to return to Moscow. Will a week be enough time for you to clear your duties here?"

"A week!" He didn't know why it surprised him, since he had never expected to be here long. What shocked him was the regret he immediately felt that he would now only be able to visit Vassily Turkin's home one more time. Then he thought of Cameron—only then. Being parted from her was not the problem. War was a time of partings. They both knew that. The trouble was, just how would things stand between them before they parted?

More desperately than ever, he wanted her to share his faith. And it came to him that if Cameron could but meet the Turkins and the others he'd met at the church meeting, she would drop her defenses.

How could she witness the powerful faith in God he'd experienced last night and not want it for herself?

Alex suddenly saw how everything could so easily fall into place, how all that was dearest to him could finally be in harmony. Drawing Cameron into faith in God wasn't exactly moving a mountain, was it? God certainly was able. Why then did it seem such a great deal to hope for? For one thing, such perfect contentment did not seem very Russian.

QUICKLY CAMERON SHOVED the papers back into her suitcase and snapped shut the clasps. The knock came again at the door of her room.

Her heart was pounding, and she felt like a secret agent who had been caught stealing government documents. But these were her own papers, so she didn't know why she was being secretive about them. Nor did she know why she had told no one here in Russia—not Alex, not Johnny—about her mother's Russian affair. The closest she had come was with Yuri Fedorcenko, but that had been necessary, and even then she had revealed little. Why not tell another? Fear? Shame for her mother? All ridiculous reasons.

The knock came again. She strode to the door and flung it open.

"I don't usually play messenger boy," Johnny Shanahan said without preamble. "But for you, doll, I couldn't refuse." He strode into the room unbidden. His eye immediately caught sight of the suitcase on Cameron's bed. "Going somewhere, sweetheart?"

The man never missed anything!

His observation still caught her unaware. "I . . . uh . . . just finishing unpacking from my trip home."

"I hate unpacking, too. Always put it off. Hey, if you'd like, I'll haul that suitcase upstairs to the storage closet. No sense it crowding you out here."

"Thanks, Johnny, but . . . I . . . have plenty of room." Surely she could lie better than that. Her room, in fact, was little more than a closet itself.

Johnny strode into the room in that manner of his that seemed to take full possession of wherever he happened to be. Plopping down on the only chair, he took a pack of cigarettes from his pocket and lit one up. He indeed had a way about him that dominated his surroundings. He wasn't a particularly handsome man. Only a couple of inches taller than she and wiry in physique, his eyes were too close set, his lips too thin, and his nose too large. Then there was that prominent scar over his right brow, the cleft in his chin, and the high cheekbones. Features all too unconventional to be good looking, yet Cameron had never seen a woman around him who did not nearly swoon or in some way become beguiled by his charm. She had been one of them. Once.

"Come on, doll, what're you hiding from your old buddy?" He took a languid puff on his cigarette.

"What in the world makes you think that? Goodness, you are as suspicious as the NKVD." She shook her head. "You can't be that bored, Johnny."

"Oh, yes, I am!" He jumped up, taking a step toward the bed.

Cameron, purely by reflex, intercepted him, practically throwing herself between him and the suitcase. "Okay," she said with great resignation, "I'll tell you. In there is a ten-page article on an interview I just had with Comrade Stalin."

He laughed. "All right, be that way." He reclaimed his chair. "I know you're lying, 'cause I'm gonna get the first interview with Stalin."

"You are a cocky so-and-so, aren't you?"

He smiled. "You know it, doll. I've had a list of questions prepared for Joe since the first day I got here."

"Doesn't sound like you are all that anxious to leave anymore."

He shrugged, exhaling a frustrated sigh along with a stream of smoke. "I'd go in a heartbeat if I could ever get your father to see it my way. For one thing, Stalin's in Moscow, and I'm here. Fat chance of getting an interview hundreds of miles apart." His eyes skittered toward the suitcase again.

To distract him Cameron asked quickly, "So if you had only one question to ask him, what would it be?"

He thought while he unconsciously fingered the cleft in his chin. "Only one question, eh? Hmm . . . Mr. Stalin, what are you afraid of?"

Now Cameron laughed. Leave it to Johnny to come before the ruler of the largest nation on earth and imply the man had fears, much less ask him to reveal them.

"Why that?" she asked.

"He must be afraid of something, don't you think, to keep the truth so bottled up like he does? I think he must be a very insecure man. Look at the purges of the thirties. He must have been scared to death of something to have killed or imprisoned half his Army officers and even some of his own staff. But it's all the secrets that prove it most to me. Only someone who is truly afraid will behave like that."

Cameron's gaze jerked toward the suitcase then quickly away. She wondered if Johnny had noted the surreptitious movement. He said nothing. She did not think his words were in any way directed at her. But was he right? Was it fear that drove her, as well? Was it stronger than her innate curiosity? But what was she afraid of?

"That's interesting, Johnny," she said weakly, mostly to get her mind off her thoughts.

"So what would you ask him, Hayes?"

"Oh, I don't know. Probably what his favorite color is and which side of the bed he sleeps on," she replied glibly.

Smiling, his eyes said he didn't believe for a minute that she'd make such superficial queries. His faith in her as a journalist made her say, "Johnny, I may want to tell you what's in that suitcase one day. It's a personal family matter, but I sometimes think I should tell someone. I'm just not ready now."

"You afraid, too, sweetheart?" His tone was gentle for him, comforting in a way.

In spite of herself she nodded.

"Well," he said, "I won't butt in again unless you ask. Now, before I forget, I have a message for you." She expected him to take a paper from a pocket, but understanding that, he shook his head. "This is verbal. A certain doctor wants you to join him for dinner at Stroganoff's."

"I wonder why he asked you to tell me?"

"He called me on the phone. Guess he thought it would be safer to call me than you." Crushing out his cigarette in an ashtray, he got briskly to his feet. "Gotta run." He headed to the door, opened it, then paused. "Remember, Hayes, I'm here when you need me." He gave her a meaningful look, eyes only briefly brushing past the suitcase.

She smiled her thanks, wondering if she would ever tell him. And Alex, too. The three of them did seem to share a few secrets. They were her best friends in Russia, probably in the entire world.

Stroganoff's was as unimaginative as its name, but then Kuibyshev offered little better. However, she told herself, the bland menu with poor wines and little meat was not her reason for coming.

Alex was seated at a corner table in the dining room, which would probably seat not more than fifty customers. Now, at the dinner hour, it was a busy place. Mostly foreigners gathered here, and it was a good place for her and Alex to meet because the NKVD always kept watch from the outside. They would have been far too obvious had they entered together.

Alex slipped in first, obviously making certain he had not been followed. It really didn't matter if Cameron had a tail, because it was perfectly natural for her to come and socialize with other foreigners.

She couldn't believe how good it was to see his face. It had been days, and she missed him. Sliding into the chair opposite him and laying her handbag on the table, she reached across the table to grasp his hand. She wanted to kiss him, but that would have drawn attention. Feeling the intense warmth of his large hands would have to suffice.

"I've gone ahead and ordered our usual," he said. "You know how slow the service is here."

Yes, she knew but hardly cared. "The slower the better!"

"Guess I've got medical efficiency ingrained in me, but I will eat slowly." He squeezed her hand. "It is so good to see you. And I have some good news. I am no longer being watched! It will be easier now for us to see each other."

"Alex, that is wonderful! But why now?"

"I'll tell you later. It is part of the other news I have."

"Tell me now; I can't wait."

"It's . . . not as good."

Her fingers tensed in his. "You're leaving, aren't you?"

"I wanted to wait till we'd eaten."

"I couldn't eat. When?"

Just then a waitress came with a pot of tea and two small plates with a salad-like concoction on them. Because of his usual clientele, the owner of Stroganoff's tried to mimic Western dining fare and customs, but usually he fell just short of getting it right. Cameron had never seen such a salad until coming to Russia—a few strings of beets, some grated raw cabbage, and some thinly sliced onions, all covered with a bland vinaigrette. And hardly enough to satisfy a bird. But she had lost her appetite anyway.

"When, Alex?" she persisted when the waitress left.

"Sometimes I wish you'd put your journalistic instincts on hold. Let's just enjoy our meal."

"Could you really enjoy food with this hanging over us?" she asked just a bit caustically.

"I would try. We knew it would happen sooner or later."

"Yes. . . ." She let go of his hand. Nervously she toyed with the brass clasp on her handbag. "Alex, I used to be so tough. Johnny used to call me 'one tough broad.' But since coming to Russia something's happening to me. I don't know . . . I feel like I am losing control of who I am. I feel like life is a tiger and I barely have it grasped by the tail as it is flailing to get away."

"I guess war makes people lose control. I feel it, too."

"Well, I don't like it!" she exclaimed, as if the passion in her tone alone would make it go away. "I used to thrive on adventures and risks. Now . . . I just want . . ." She shook her head. "I am not sure what I want. Tell me that isn't really pathetic!"

"It isn't." He took her hand again and held it firmly. "There is absolutely nothing pathetic about you, Cameron."

"I just want everything to be normal again."

"Cameron . . ." he hesitated, chewing his lip. She didn't like his conflicted expression just then. It wasn't normal. "I often feel the same way, as if I might snap and break. I hold a tiger, too. You know that. But I have found something that helps. Oh, the tiger is still there, swinging all over the place, but I no longer hold it alone—"

"Alex . . ." She knew what he was going to say. In her mind, it was just another problem. Not a solution.

"Confound it, Cameron!" he burst.

That wasn't like him, either. She trembled a bit and didn't know why.

"Would you hear me out at least once? You owe me that much."

"Go on," she said coolly. She slipped her hand from his so he would not feel the tremor in hers.

"Faith in God is not magic, but it's not a placebo, either. It's like firm ground to stand on while chaos swirls all around."

"What good is it, then, if it doesn't take away the chaos?" she asked. He just eyed her silently. He didn't need to tell her how foolish her question was. She well knew. "Okay," she admitted. "I know what you mean. My mother used to talk about that. She would quote Scripture. 'O God our help in ages past, our hope for years to come, our shelter from the stormy blast, and our eternal home.' Don't ask how I remembered that."

"I've heard that before, but it's a song, not a Scripture verse. Still . . . why is it so hard for you to reach out for something that promises that kind of security?"

She laughed, a hard-edged sound, while holding just a hint of bewilderment. "Haven't you been listening to me, Alex? What you are asking is the very height of loss of self-control. I know God. I know what He wants. Everything!"

"But He won't take it. You have to give it to Him."

"I can't." Her regret at those words surprised even her. But she didn't take them back. She couldn't.

"Let's back up a bit, okay?" His hand twitched, and she knew he wanted to hold hers again, but she kept it close to her. "We can take this slowly, one step at a time. You don't have to jump into the lake without getting your toes wet first. You love to sniff out news. Well, here's your chance. All you need to do right now is investigate. You'd be in your element. Ask all the questions you want. What's wrong with that?"

She could think of many problems with his suggestion, but what disturbed her most was that she did not want to ask questions about religion or investigate faith in God. Was she afraid of that, too, then? Afraid of the answers she'd find?

She gave a noncommittal shrug.

"I know where you can start," he went on.

His eyes glinted with that look he got when he was particularly passionate about something. She'd seen it when he had operated on the partisan boy behind German lines.

"I'd like to take you to meet some people I've come to know here in Kuibyshev. They are actually the congregation of a small church."

"What church is that?" An edge of caution continued to lace her tone. "There aren't many here in town. But I have seen some pretty ones." Something was rising up inside her—fear, like the taste of bitter bile.

"It doesn't meet in any building you have seen," he began slowly. He swallowed, and Cameron's insides quaked. "They meet in various homes."

"They must be a small group, then."

"Yes, quite small. A dozen or so."

"Not an Orthodox church?"

"Of course not. I should say it most resembles a Protestant assembly in the States." He paused again before adding, "It is a somewhat clandestine group."

"Clandestine?"

"Despite the freedom of religion now in force," he seemed to be quoting a prepared statement, "there are many believers who continue to operate at a low profile. Otherwise the NKVD would be able to keep track of them; then when or if the winds of freedom change, they would know whom to harass."

"That doesn't sound like trusting, hopeful Christians to me." She knew the words were a mistake the moment they left her mouth.

"Cameron, don't do this!" He drew a steadying breath. "I know this is a difficult time for you. The uncertainties with us, the difficulties with your father, not knowing about your sister . . . I only wish to offer you a means to find comfort."

"What happened to my taking it slowly? Now it appears you are ready to throw me right in the middle of the lions' den."

"I didn't think a few lions would scare you!" he shot back.

"I'm not scared!" she practically shouted, then modified her tone when a few heads nearby turned. "I'm not scared of the things you think I'm scared of."

He just gaped at her gibberish. She was backpedaling desperately. But she didn't care. She suddenly felt as if she had stepped into a snare, as if Alex had trapped her.

"Never mind, Alex. I just don't want to talk about this." He lifted his hand toward her, but she shook her head, then suddenly jumped up.

Before she knew what she was doing, she had snatched her coat from the rack and was striding from the restaurant. She didn't look back, but as the blast of cold outside hit her face, she heard the café door swing open again. Alex strode to her side.

"You can't walk out on me." She could read many meanings into that simple statement. But despite them all, why was *she* the one who felt abandoned?

"That just wasn't the place to discuss this," she said lamely. "But I don't know if there is a place."

He turned to face her, and she backed against the brick wall of the café entryway. They were outside but sheltered on three sides by the alcove.

"Is there no hope for us, then?" he breathed, a puff of icy steam following his plaintive words. "If you are so hardened against something that is important to me?"

"It is obviously more important to you than I am."

"That isn't fair!"

"Isn't it?" A desperation rose inside her. She wanted to run, flee. But at the same time she felt pinned to the wall by his incisive gaze. He seemed to be both drawing her and pushing her at the same time. Her only defense was to lash out. She wasn't afraid! She was no coward!

She continued levelly, as if her own words weren't tearing up her insides, "Alex, by this obsession of yours, you are clearly willing to put our being together at risk." She set accusing eyes upon him. All at once everything coalesced in her. Some logic. Something to grasp. A little control. "You have just been set free by the police. It would be so easy now for us. But you seem to want to throw it away. What if they mistake this little secret church of yours for a concave of spies and fifth columnists?" His eyes twitched just slightly but enough for her to realize he had considered this very thing. "I can't believe it, Alex! You thought of this, yet you went ahead with the meetings. I see now what our relationship means to you."

"You have it wrong, Cameron."

"How so?" Though her tone dared, deep down she hoped he had an acceptable answer.

"They are two separate things. It has nothing—" He stopped

abruptly, then groaned. "Oh, dear God!" He turned away from her.

"Alex, what is it?" She could not help the infusion of sympathy in her voice. The moment before he turned, she had seen something like sharp pain twisting his features.

"They shouldn't be . . ." he murmured. "They can't be."

"What?"

"I love you, Cameron. I can't help that. But I love God, as well. I want Him, no, I *need* Him to be at the core of my life. I have freely given Him everything. Except you. I held you back from Him because I kept thinking I would yet win you over." Facing her again, his expression resembled a devastated village.

"And now you just realized you won't?" Sadness overwhelmed her. And helplessness, too. How easy it would be to fake it. She remembered that Jackie told her Blair had done the same with the man she loved. It hadn't worked. Such deception never does. And Cameron was not one to subject herself thus to anyone. Not even the man she loved.

"I can't make it happen, in any case," he answered. "But what do I do until it does happen, if it does? How can I choose sides? Do you know what is said of a man who serves two masters? He will either hate one and love the other or hold to one and despise the other. I don't want to grow to despise you, Cameron. So . . . I must choose."

Her heart clenched, all anger melting away. She continued to lean against the wall as if it were all that was holding her up.

"We . . . could find a way to make it work." Was she pleading? She didn't care.

"You've seen for yourself the results of that. Each time we are together the tension grows. This is no small thing between us."

"So who will you choose, Alex?" Her voice trembled over the words.

When he hesitated, she wished he had his back turned on her again so she could not see his face and the rejection that was now etched in his wonderful blue eyes. A man like Alex would never choose the mere love of a woman over something as visceral, as soul-deep, as his heart's faith.

"You don't have to answer," she added quickly. "Just go and leave it at that."

His wounded gaze roved over her a moment. He opened his mouth to speak, but no words came. He turned, but still he hesitated, his back toward her, his shoulders bunched under his heavy overcoat. She longed to see his face just once more because she thought—or hoped?—that if she could make eye contact just one more time for one instant, this awful pall would be broken and they would both come to their senses. Yet she did not make a move to do so. Maybe she was a coward after all. Or maybe she was just too proud to appear to be begging for his love.

He let out a long ragged sigh, took a step, then paused. "Cameron . . ."

"No apologies, please." Her defenses wrapped around her like a cold Siberian frost.

"I'll take you home—"

"It's not far. I can manage."

"Then . . . good-bye," he breathed. She saw only a wisp of steam rise before his face.

"Good-bye, Alex." She infused her voice with resolve she hardly felt.

He walked away without a backward glance. It was better that way. He must know it, as well. She was certain she would have crumbled like melting snow had she looked one last time upon the face of the man she knew she loved but realized did not love her enough.

Yet she could not, she would not, compete with God.

Even as she watched him go, however, she felt deep in her soul that it could not possibly be truly over between them. They had known each other less than six months, but it had been the quality of those months that had forged their love. Had it separated them, as well?

Or had this merely been a wartime romance? She'd never thought she would be a victim of that phenomenon. She was above such flights of fancy, such insipid sentimentality. Yet even now, with the ache of his rejection still so fresh, she could not label what she'd had with him as such. She recalled Alex telling her about phantom pains of wounded soldiers, experiencing sensations from a limb even after it had been removed. That surely must be what she was feeling now.

And like those amputees, no matter what she felt, there seemed no way to restore the part of her that had been cut off.

PART II

"Have yourself a merry little Christmas.
Let your heart be light,
From now on, our troubles will be out of sight."

HUGH MARTIN/RALPH BLANE
(*Meet Me in St. Louis,* 1944)

Los Angeles, California
Mid-December 1941

JACKIE WATCHED her fourth graders file past. Each child carried a sack containing a blanket, a pillow, and a few other necessities. This would be stored at school in case the children should be caught there during an air raid.

An air raid!

Such things were inconceivable. This was the United States of America. The last war to have been fought on its soil had to have been the Civil War. But all the coastal states were now on full alert, with invasion plans, blackouts, and even some evacuations.

"This bag is heavy!" groaned a boy as he lugged his bag to the storage room.

"What have you in there, Jimmy?" Jackie asked.

The bag in question bulged far more than the others. Upon inspection, Jackie found several books, a flashlight, tinned food, and other supplies to last for days instead of a few hours.

"My ma told me I should be prepared, Miss Hayes," the ten-year-old said with a shrug.

"But for what?" she said more to herself than to him. She closed up the bag. Who knew, maybe it would all come in handy.

The boy moved ahead with the other children. At the door of the storage room custodians were taking the bags and stowing them. Jackie's master teacher sidled up to her.

"Never thought I'd see the day," the woman said.

Mrs. Brock was only five years older than Jackie and had always made her feel more like a friend than a student. Jackie had been at the school for only a week and would not officially start her student teaching stint until the first of the year, but since her instructors had suggested she go a bit early to meet her colleagues and the children, she was here now. And quite welcome. With all that was happening since the war started—air-raid drills, calming frightened children, preparing identification tags—an extra pair of hands at the school was never rejected.

"My mother said that during the Great War, it hardly felt like war, especially way over here on the West Coast," Jackie said. Though Cecilia had been in Russia during the early part of the war, she had come home shortly before the United States' entry into the conflict.

"The Japanese weren't in it then."

"And I guess the threat is real, though it is hard to imagine the mainland of this country ever being vulnerable."

Mrs. Brock shuddered, then said in low tones so the children could not hear, "Haven't you heard the news? Why, I heard thirty-four Japanese naval vessels were spotted off the coast of Manhattan Beach. I live near there! And there were reports of three Jap destroyers off Palos Verdes Peninsula."

Yes, Jackie had heard those rumors of enemy presence off the coast of Southern California. Her father was a newspaper publisher, after all. But she'd also heard most of those reports were false alarms. The thirty-four vessels turned out to be Terminal Island fishermen waiting for the fog to lift before coming into port.

It might be foolish to completely underestimate the threat to the coast, but it was even worse to blow it up out of proportion. She still winced when she thought of the news that more than a thousand Japanese aliens had been "detained" by the government. True, there had been some German and Italian aliens taken into custody once those countries declared war on the U.S. a few days after Pearl Harbor, but hardly in proportional numbers, she thought.

"I can't wait for Christmas vacation," Mrs. Brock was saying. "Then the responsibility for the children at a time like this will be in their parents' hands. Maybe by the new year it will be all over."

Jackie looked askance at the older teacher. Anyone with sense could not believe that. No doubt that was hopeful thinking on Mrs. Brock's part. Her husband had been among the hordes of men to enlist in the military on December 8. But this war would not—could not—end while Japan had the upper hand, which it most certainly did now.

Confirmed reports from Pearl Harbor of losses had been staggering. Besides extensive damage to the fleet, over two thousand Americans had been killed and over a thousand wounded. The thought of the number of casualties made her blood boil with patriotism. And that was only the beginning. The Japanese had also landed in Guam, Hong Kong, Malaysia, and the Philippines, leaving a trail of destruction. And Blair was there somewhere, no doubt in the middle of it all. Still, for all her heart *hoped*, she could not for a minute believe this war would end anytime soon.

Jackie hung the last of the tinsel on the Christmas tree. Her mother watched from the sofa, a slight smile on her face. They had debated about whether to have a tree this year with Cameron and Blair gone and both stranded in war zones. But a telegram had come at last from Blair saying she was all right. She was in Manila and preparing to evacuate, words that were ominous in themselves, yet they had to take comfort in hearing from her, and it seemed reason to celebrate a little and give in to Keagan's urging to make the best of the Christmas season.

For all his criticism about sentimentality, Keagan was one to enthusiastically celebrate Christmas. The gruff, hard-edged Irishman had always made sure his girls sat on Santa's lap at some department store during the season when they were young. He spent extravagantly on presents, never having to be reminded to do so. He even had several neckties with Christmas designs that he wore during the week preceding the holiday.

"All right! Here goes!" boomed Keagan as Jackie stepped away from the tree. He was crouched down next to the tree by an electrical outlet. He popped the plug into the outlet, and the tree burst into light.

"An air-raid warden is going to give us a citation," Cecilia said.

"Hang them! It's Christmastime," Keagan said, rising and standing next to Jackie to view their handiwork.

Tinsel glittered, along with the gold and silver, red and green glass bulbs hanging from the branches. The lights were shaped like candles in holders, each a different color. At the top was a lighted yellow star.

Jackie smiled and put her arm around her father. "I'm glad you talked us into it," she said. "Goodness, we need some normalcy."

Cecilia rose and joined them. "I suppose so," she sighed. But she did glance toward the windows to assure herself that the blackout shades were in place.

"Now, where's the eggnog?" Keagan asked. "We have to do this right."

That was the family tradition. Two days before Christmas they would all gather to decorate the tree, then have eggnog and cookies. Keagan would always doctor his eggnog with a little whiskey, and Cecilia would always chide him. When the girls had been younger, they would ask for a taste of his, then make funny faces over the awful flavor while Cecilia would again scold her husband for indulging the girls so. It had all been very funny at the time.

"I'll get it, Dad," Jackie said. "You two sit."

Cecilia had a tray laid out in the kitchen, needing only the eggnog from the refrigerator. Jackie put down the cold pitcher she had taken from the icebox and was picking up the tray when a wave of emotion washed over her. Tears sprang to her eyes. Traditions were a double-edged sword, weren't they? She was determined to celebrate the holiday because she knew Blair and Cameron would want to hear all about the doings at home. They wouldn't want to hear how everything was glum and miserable because they were gone and there was a war going on. They would want to hear about all the festivities they were missing and in that way feel part of them.

But it wasn't easy for those holding down the fort at home. The gaping holes of empty places sliced at the heart. Three crystal goblets of eggnog instead of five and empty chairs at the table for Christmas dinner. It would be hardest on Cecilia, but Jackie wondered if she herself would bear it any better. Yet she must, and later she would write to her sisters, hoping the letters would get through.

Jackie would write,

> *Dear sis, what a time we had with the tree this year. Dad had to buy the biggest one on the lot, but then there weren't enough lights to go around. We rummaged through the attic one more time and found another Christmas box in a corner. I think it had been hiding there for years. But it had a working string of lights. Also found the ornaments we each got from Grandpa Atkins when we were babies. Oh, you should have seen how much whiskey Dad put in his eggnog. Or should I say he had a dollop of eggnog in his whiskey? Mother cooked a wonderful turkey dinner. With Helen doing most of the cooking all year, Mom doesn't get much*

practice, but she is still excellent. Her yam casserole was heavenly. We missed you, though, and had a toast to you both. . . .

Brushing sadness from her mind, Jackie picked up the tray and carried it back to the living room. As she set it on the table, Keagan rose and went to the liquor cabinet. There was a kind of resignation in his step, and Jackie had the feeling he'd be having his whiskey for more than just tradition this year. Could it be he missed his older daughters? Was he regretting just a little all the harsh words he had leveled at them before each of them departed? Did he have a tender heart beneath all that surly gristle?

"Did I tell you, Jackie," he said, "that we won't be going to the Rose Bowl this year?"

"I heard that it had been moved, and I figured as much."

"Sticks in my craw that there will be no parade or game this year. First time in twenty-three years. We've gone for the last ten."

"Well, we could go to North Carolina," Jackie replied lightly. No one wanted to do that, of course.

"Maybe if it was UCLA or even Stanford playing, I might consider it. But Oregon State and Duke? I'm not interested in going that far for a game if it isn't with our hometown boys." He uncorked the bottle he held and poured a couple of ounces into his goblet. "Oh well, guess that's a small sacrifice." He sat on the sofa next to his wife.

Jackie handed one of the other goblets to her mother, took one herself, and sat in an upholstered chair. She almost didn't notice that her mother made no comment about the whiskey. She couldn't be blamed. No matter how much they tried, it just wasn't the same.

"Do you think all the precautions are really necessary, Dad?"

Keagan shrugged. "Better than sitting on our tails, twiddling our thumbs. There is some real Japanese activity offshore. I'm certain there are subs patrolling. We have to be alert. But the Japs are for the most part concentrating their efforts on the Far East. On the—" he paused abruptly with a glance at Cecilia. "Anyway, the only way those yellow monkeys can beat us is by a sneak attack."

"Dad, please don't use that language," Jackie said almost without thinking.

"What language?" He squinted at her over the rim of his goblet as he took a drink of the thick white liquid.

"You know . . . yellow . . . monkeys . . . and such." It almost sickened her to repeat the words.

"I could use worse, you know. Anyway, who cares? They are the enemy."

"Not all of them. There are Japanese who are American citizens and completely loyal." Why had she started this? Her stomach twisted, but she could not help herself. She despised all the nasty epithets going around about the Japanese without any consideration to the loyal ones.

"Best not to trust any of them. There is talk about placing a bill before Congress to round 'em all up. The *Journal* will throw its support behind it."

"Dad, you certainly couldn't support such a travesty! And when you say 'all,' you can't mean American citizens."

"Every single one of those slant-eyed devils! There is simply no way to tell the good from the bad."

"But they have rights—"

"Then they shouldn't have bombed our boys in Hawaii and the Philippines." That was Cecilia, speaking softly but with an intensity that revealed both horror and pain.

Then Jackie realized the impossibility of imposing logic upon the subject. Passions were high. Even Cecilia, as even-tempered as anyone Jackie knew, was feeling it. She had a friend whose son had been killed at Pearl Harbor. Her own daughter was still in danger from Japanese attacks on the Philippines. There was no way to reason with that, no way to make people see the difference between an enemy and an innocent who happened to *look* like the enemy.

She let out a ragged breath, resigned to giving up the argument—for now. No sense ruining Christmas. But Keagan swung his shaggy red head around and cast his piercing green eyes upon her.

"Why are you so up in arms about this, young lady?" he demanded.

"I simply want to see justice done."

"That's all, eh?" Squinting, he leaned forward. "You're not still mixed up with those people, are you?"

She hesitated before responding. She'd always planned on lying should the question be put to her. But she could not make herself do that. Not to her parents. Yet she could not tell them about Sam, either. The words just stuck in her throat. She wished she wasn't such a coward.

It was Cecilia who spoke next, her tone even but with the merest hint of a tremor to her words. "Answer your father, Jacqueline."

She wanted so to tell them, "Yes, Mom and Dad, I'm in love with a Japanese man. He's a fine young man. Dad, you would like him. He likes football, too. You'd finally have a son to watch those games with. If only you'd forget his eyes are a little different from yours and mine." She knew their disapproval had as much to do with the shape of his eyes as it did with the war. It had been there long before Pearl Harbor.

But all those brave words were blocked behind a throat that had squeezed tight and a tongue that felt as if it had swelled to twice its size. At the same time, she knew it was too late for words. She had hesitated. They needed to hear nothing else.

Finally she did force something out. "I-I'm sorry." Then she jumped up and fled the room.

As she closed the door of her bedroom behind her, she prayed that no one followed. Maybe she should have left the house, but she knew where she would go, and just then it didn't seem right. She didn't want her being with Sam to always be surrounded by problems.

No one came to her door. She was thankful her father did not storm after her as she felt certain he would. Perhaps he was in too much shock for that. Had he guessed her relationship with "those people" was more than a friendly acquaintance?

Still, she was just a touch disappointed her mother did not come with her usual soothing words of comfort. Even Cecilia had appeared none too pleased by Jackie's hesitation. Maybe she would have no comfort for her daughter. Had Jackie committed the unforgivable sin—the thing even her mother could not absolve?

A great emptiness began to consume Jackie. She laid her head back against a pillow covered with a pretty eyelet sham. All she could think of was sacrifice. Was it worth it? Did she have the heart for it? She never expected to have her father's approval of anyone she might choose to love. She'd always known she would have to live her life without that. But what if her mother's approval should also be withdrawn? What then?

Tears sprang to her eyes. She rolled over and pounded a fist into the pillow. "God, why are you doing this to me? Why bring me a man to love only to force me to have to choose him over my mother? It's not right! It's not fair!"

Another fist slammed into the delicate eyelet. Teardrops splashed onto the cotton surface.

The ringing of the telephone gave her a start. It rang again, and she was going to let someone downstairs pick it up. Then on impulse she lifted the receiver of the phone by her bed just in time to hear her father's voice.

"Hello . . . who is this?" she heard her father boom, none too pleasantly.

A click at the other end of the line was the only response. Her father slammed down his receiver without saying another word. Instinctively Jackie knew who had been at the other end. It had to be. Like an answer to her prayer. An odd answer if it was that.

Keagan put down the telephone receiver and returned to the living room, a perplexed scowl on his brow.

"What's wrong, Keagan?" Cecilia asked.

"Nothing. When I said hello, the line went dead."

"Probably just a wrong number."

"Well, people should be more careful!" He gave a shake of his head, then plopped back into his chair and tried to find his good mood again. Though why a wrong number should so suddenly sour him, he didn't know.

No, it wasn't the telephone at all that had upset him. It was that daughter of his. He knew she was still mixed up with that Jap boy. God help him! He hoped it was only friendship, as she claimed. But even that was bad enough. Still, girls didn't fly to their rooms in a snit over friendships. Keagan knew he should go right up there and . . . what?

She was too old for a good spanking. And all the ranting and raving in the world hadn't kept Cameron and Blair from their foolish pursuits. He knew of no other way to deal with his children. Cecilia's mollycoddling hadn't helped, either. Sure, they liked Cecilia and hated him, but his intent had never been to win a popularity contest. He wanted only to raise decent, proper young ladies who would bring decent, proper sons-in-law into the family. So far, one was in love with a scruffy news hack, though Cecilia had informed him Cameron had lately fallen for a Commie doctor. Bad to worse, as far as he was concerned. Blair was headed for a divorce practically before she'd even had a marriage. And now Jackie.

Helplessly he reached for his glass of eggnog, wishing he could exchange it for a good stiff shot of plain Bushmills. His wife and daughters thought it a great joke how he doused his nog with whiskey. If they only knew. He hated eggnog with a passion and only drank it at Christmas to please them. No one ever gave him credit for all the times he went against his grain to please them.

A little sound from where Cecilia sat made Keagan turn. "What is it?"

"I think you should go up and talk to her."

"I have tried talking to her. The last time I got a heart attack from it—"

"That is a terrible thing to say, Keagan! I hope you have never said as much to Jacqueline." She didn't often stand up to him, and of course he didn't like it when she did, but she was a very appealing woman, especially when her eyes flashed as they were now.

"Of course not!" He gave a "Humph!" under his breath, then drained the rest of the sickening drink.

"Well, I am going to talk to her, then." She scooted to the edge of her seat but hesitated.

"Don't you dare, Cecilia. This is too big an issue for you to undermine me. Do you want her to take up with a Jap?"

"That's not the point."

"What is the point, then?" he demanded, glaring.

"I don't know." Cecilia fumbled with the buttons on her cardigan.

All the fire was gone now, replaced by her usual vapid countenance. He wasn't certain he liked that, either.

"I doubt you'd understand," she added lamely.

"Some silly woman thing, I suppose."

She shrugged and rose. "I'm going to clean up the kitchen."

She must indeed be desperate to get away from him if she was going to do the work the housekeeper could do in the morning.

Before she disappeared, he said in a conciliatory tone, "Listen here, Cecilia, Jackie is a good girl, and she will do the right thing."

"What do you believe to be the right thing, Keagan?"

He snorted at the ire in her voice. So much for trying to offer an olive branch. Firmness was all these women understood. "I am the man of the house, and what I say is right." His narrow gaze dared her to say differently. She only nodded and exited. The fact that she had not argued was further proof he was indeed right.

But he shrugged and rose, as well. He went to the wet bar at the back of the room and poured himself that much-needed shot of whiskey. He noticed the newspapers he had lain there when he'd come home earlier. He took them with the drink and returned to his chair. The *Times*, the *Globe*, and the *Sacramento Bee*. He tried to read the major newspapers daily, but he hadn't had time today what with leaving the office early to do some Christmas shopping and to pick up a few items needed to decorate the tree.

He laid aside the others and stared at the *Globe*. No matter how busy he was, he never missed reading the *Globe*. Every word he read was like ingesting bile, but he made himself do it. He made himself read every article in the news section, and he read Cameron's articles twice. Sometimes even three times. He wasn't ashamed to admit he had cut out each one and had saved them all. Well, he supposed he was ashamed to admit it, since no one, not even his secretary, Molly, knew he did it. He had a small scrapbook he kept in the locked bottom drawer of his desk at the office.

Cameron was a gifted writer. That, also, he had never admitted to a soul. It was no one's business how he felt about his daughter. For one thing, his enemies would find a way to use his pride and even his affection as a weapon against him. Hadn't Max Arnett done that very thing? And what good would it do to tell Cameron? She was the woman she was, the fighter she was, because he had never puffed her up with praise. Had she come to expect praise, she would never have made it in a man's world. And she had truly made it. On her own, too. He was most proud of that. She didn't need him. She didn't need anybody.

Yes, he was proud of her.

As he opened the paper, he saw a figure flash by the living room door.

"Jackie, is that you?" he called.

"Yes, Dad."

"Where are you going?"

"Out."

Keagan gritted his teeth. He wanted to take her by the scruff of her neck and shake some sense into her. But again he was reminded that that would not help. Best to back off for now and see where her own good sense led her. She had a good head on her shoulders. At least two of his daughters had inherited some good old-fashioned horse sense from him. Blair was another case altogether. For the life of him, he'd never be able to figure that one out.

Returning his attention back to the daughter who was opening the front door, he said, with just a touch of irony in his tone, "Well, merry Christmas, then."

14

THEY NO LONGER DARED to meet in any public place. But there was something quite fitting about the end of the back road, with moonlight washing over the top of the adjacent orange grove. It felt sad and romantic all at once.

"How did you know it was me who called?" Sam asked after settling in the front seat of Jackie's car.

Her father's car, actually. And that reminder stabbed at Jackie. Cameron's Ford, which Jackie was using now that Cameron was gone, wouldn't start. It had taken every ounce of gall Jackie had to go back in the house and ask her father to borrow the Cadillac so she could visit some friends. Only an hour had passed since she'd run to her room. Thankfully, he hadn't questioned her, only handed over the keys with a stern admonishment to be home by ten.

"I just had a feeling," she replied to Sam. A feeling bred of need, but she didn't want to say that. It frightened her to need him that much. "Who else would hang up the minute he heard my father's voice?" She smiled to help dispel her fears.

"You should have seen me jump when the phone rang a moment later." He chuckled. "My hand was barely off the receiver."

"Well, at least I wouldn't have had to hang up if anyone else at your house answered. Your family is good about that." Not wishing to discuss that further, she asked, "Why did you call?"

"My uncle's been arrested . . . I guess they call it *detained*."

"No, Sam! On what grounds?"

"He is the president of the Japanese American Association up in Berkeley where he lives. Officials are targeting such leaders, it seems."

"This is terrible! An outrage!"

"It's not a huge surprise. It has happened to others we know, and it was probably just a matter of time."

"What about your father?"

"Nothing yet. My father is a quiet man who keeps pretty much to himself. Though I wouldn't be surprised if just the fact that he is an enemy alien would be reason enough. We just wait for the FBI to come crashing in again, this time to take him away."

"Would they take your mother, too?"

"Who knows what they will do? Probably having the children to care for may spare her. I don't know. . . ." Leaning his head back against the seat, he rolled it back and forth. "None of it makes any sense."

They were both quiet for a long time. Jackie watched his face twitch with tension, just as it did the day she had told him about Pearl Harbor. Like most of the few times they had seen each other since then. Always a crackle of tension in the air. Not between them, but as if it surrounded them, squeezing them. Squeezing the life out of them. Out of what they had together? She did not think so, but the possibility was always there.

As if he had read her mind, he said, "Do you remember when we first met? We had a lot of fun, didn't we? We weren't all glum and serious then. We laughed."

"You told jokes."

"We went to Saturday matinees so our friends wouldn't see us, then made fun of the kiddie shows."

"I was shocked you liked W. C. Fields."

"That was no kiddie show, my little chickadee!" he said in a fine impression of the actor.

She giggled in spite of herself. "My literary giant, my future author of the Great American Novel . . . a W. C. Fields fan! Well, nobody's perfect! But then, I should have expected as much from a man who refuses to eat his vegetables. And you the son of a produce farmer!"

"Makes perfect sense to me. I've had to look at green growing things all my life. And believe me, I have eaten my share of vegetables at home; otherwise I'd have had a perpetually sore bottom. But my father promised me that when I became a man, I could eat what I wanted."

"A fair deal."

"He's a fair man . . . a good man." He shook his head again, then gave a dry, almost bitter, laugh.

Jackie knew he was thinking of the awful and very real possibility of him being dragged from their home.

"Well, we tried, Jackie, to have a little fun again. But we can't really escape the world, not for long."

"Sam, I think my parents know about us." She knew the timing was wrong, but it had to be said eventually.

"Everything?"

"I'm sure they can guess at what I haven't told them. I'm not sure what to do about it."

"What do you want to do?"

A hard edge continued to linger in his tone. She couldn't blame him. But bitterness was the one quality she would never have attributed to him, and it hurt as much as anything else to see it evident in him now.

"I have never expected my father's approval for anything I do. But if I don't have my mother's, I don't know if I can bear that." There. She said it.

"Jackie, if you want to end it now, I will understand."

"Do you think I could that easily? But I am being pulled in so many different directions. We both are, I know."

He nodded. "I have no answers. I pray about it all the time. But one thing I am certain of, we are breaking none of God's laws."

"Except regarding our parents."

"We may have stretched the law a bit there, but I don't think we have broken it." He gave a sharp sigh. "Okay, maybe that's not good enough. But now they know—"

"Your parents know, too?"

"Yes, at least like yours, they suspect. They don't approve, but I am a man, and they can't really stop me. And the way things are in the world at the moment, they don't want to disown me. We need one another as a family, now more than ever. They more or less pretend the problem doesn't exist or will go away soon."

"I don't want to go away," she breathed, knowing the truth of her words above all else. "But I have thought about it."

"I don't suppose your father will pretend I don't exist?" he asked part wryly but part hopefully, as well.

"Never," she said flatly.

"I won't stop believing in miracles."

"Oh, Sam . . ." She lifted a hand and smoothed back a long straight strand of hair that had fallen into his eyes. Letting her gaze study him a moment, she said, "I don't see it . . . I just don't see it."

"What?"

"The thing everyone else sees, the thing they are all so afraid of."

He smiled. No bitterness now in the tilt of his lips, just an expression that was almost crystal clear, pure in a way, free of all the hard edges the world had imposed upon him lately. It made her remember how she had first come to love him and why she loved him still. He had a heart like no other man she had known, complex and uncomplicated all at once. Open was perhaps the best way to describe that special something she found in him. Open to her, open to others, even those who would ill-use him, but especially open to God. He wasn't a man to hide, even from himself.

"It is because you look at me with eyes of love," he said. And when she nodded, he went on, "And it makes me know there is hope for us. We don't have to be victims of the hate going around now."

He snaked an arm around her and drew her close. She laid her head on his shoulder. She could hardly believe she had come to meet him this evening with the intent of ending their relationship. Yet her despair had gripped her to that extent. It was dispersed now for the most part, replaced with the love she felt. She did not understand it, but perhaps she didn't have to.

Headlights swept over their car like searchlights. They both jumped, then jerked apart. Sam gave her an apologetic look, but she just shook her head with sad reassurance. They had *both* jumped.

The engine of the newly arrived vehicle cut off, then a door opened and slammed shut. Sam quickly scrambled from Jackie's car.

"This is private property, don't you know!" came a gruff voice.

Jackie resisted the urge to get out of the car. Best let Sam handle it. He probably knew everyone around there.

"Yes, I know, Mr. Compton," Sam replied.

"You're the Okuda boy, aren't you?"

"Yes, sir, I am."

"What you doing parked up here? Ya got car trouble?"

Jackie saw another light beam in the rearview mirror. It was a flashlight. She kept her eyes forward.

"Ah . . . I see." There was amusement now in the man's tone. "Spooning with a girl, are ya? Well, ya aren't the first to find my grove suitable for that. But with the war and all, a man's gotta be more cautious, ya know. There's rumors flying around all the time of Los Angeles being invaded."

"We'll be leaving," Sam said.

"That'd be best. Your ma would have my hide if she knew I let you get away with it." He chuckled. "You with that Yamishita girl? She's a pretty one, for a Jap."

Jackie heard movement, the crunch of boots in the dirt, a scrambling of feet following that, but she was so intent on looking straight ahead, not letting her curiosity goad her into turning, that the sudden flash of light in her window startled her. Like a deer caught in the headlights of an oncoming truck, she turned and stared right into it.

"What the—!" Compton began, then paused and spit into the dirt. He turned, and Jackie saw Sam was close behind the man. He had obviously tried to intercept him before he could look in the window but had failed.

"You get the blazes off my land!" Compton yelled, no amusement in his tone now. "What kind of filthy goings-on you tryin' to get away with?" He spit again.

"Nothing filthy!" Sam shot back angrily.

"You git! Now! Or I'll call the police. I 'spect this is illegal, it is!"

"I won't have you—"

"Outta here, now! Or I'll run the lot of you dirty Japs out of this community." Compton twisted his neck around to take another look in the window. This time Jackie met his gaze with as much defiance as she could muster. "Looks to me like you're consenting, too. That right?"

She wanted to think of something witty to shoot back, but her throat failed her again. "Yes" was all she could manage.

Compton spit again, barely missing the open window.

"Clear outta here, the both of you!"

Jackie shivered at the venom and revulsion in the man's tone.

Sam pushed passed Compton, making it appear as if he was only trying to get by, but Jackie saw the flash in his eye. He had come as close to really pushing the man as was possible without actually committing the offense. He opened the door, slid onto the seat behind the wheel, and started up the engine. Making no protest that he had taken the driver's seat from her, she just scooted silently over. He maneuvered the vehicle around with a screech of brakes and a grinding of pebbles. He didn't stop or slow until he reached the gates of his family's property.

"This isn't how I wanted the evening to end," he said harshly.

She ran a hand over the curves of his face, as if to smooth out the hard edges. It helped a little. At least some of the tension flowed away.

"Sam, do you think we will have a future together, a *lifetime* together?" she asked tenderly.

"It's what I dream of."

"Then you must know we will always have to face this kind of thing. Part and parcel, as they say. No way around it." It was the first time she considered beyond the *now* with Sam. The first time she knew what a life together would mean.

Nodding, he said, "But I hate that it must be so."

"We'll be able to help each other through it."

"Do you think it is possible? Not the bad part, but the being together always?"

"If that's what God wants, it will be."

"You sound a lot surer than you did up at the grove."

With a faint smile on her lips, she nodded. "Funny, isn't it? I guess that oaf did it. My dad always says adversity makes men wise if not rich. That unreasonable lout made me realize more clearly than ever the right we have to each other under heaven. 'If God be for us, who can be against us?' It just makes sense. Now, I'm not saying that tomorrow I won't be a jumble of confusion again. But right now I feel rather invincible."

He leaned toward her and kissed her cheek. "Maybe there is hope for the evening yet. I had one more reason for calling you, and maybe it is a good time for it after all."

"What is it?"

"Christmas is in two days, and I'm not sure if I'll see you then. We should be with our families. I realize that."

"Your family celebrates Christmas? Aren't your parents Buddhist?"

"My sister Kimi and I are the only Christians in my family, that is true. My brother isn't certain about his faith, and my little sisses are too young to really understand it all. But my parents have always enjoyed all the festivities, if not the message, of the holiday. So we celebrate Christmas after a fashion. I mean, they do. I, as you know, observe it in its fullness. This year, with all that is happening, I doubt we will do much. Anyway, I know you should be with your own family for the holiday."

"I think so, too, and I appreciate your understanding."

He took a small package from his jacket's inside pocket. "I have two gifts for you. The first isn't really a gift. I just want you to know my name is Yoshito, not Sam. Yoshito Samuel Okuda. You can still call me Sam if you like. I have been feeling lately that I cannot deny who I am, and I sometimes think I try to do that when I use my middle name." He gave a dry laugh. "*Try* is too weak a word. Most Nisei, including myself, try to be American with a vengeance, squashing our Japanese parts as much as possible. Even before the war, many of us were downright ashamed of being Japanese. If I were Italian, I could knock a few vowels from my name and have the hope of blending eventually. But I am marked for life—"

She opened her mouth to protest, to somehow reassure him, though she realized she had no way at all to truly sympathize with him. But to feel such shame for what one was—it was heartbreaking.

He spoke again before she could say anything. "The Japanese government is my enemy, too, though many whites, even some Japanese, find that hard to understand." He shifted slightly. Obviously he was still grappling with these matters. "Yet all that is happening is conversely making me more aware of my culture. I feel it would be a disservice to who I am and to my family to lose that. Rotten timing for a cultural awakening, but being the brunt of hatred from people like Mr. Compton makes me see how wrong it is to let them win by hating myself."

"I agree, Sam—Yoshito. I don't want you to be white. I never have wanted that."

He smiled. "Thank you. And I don't want you to be Japanese." But he added with a twinkle in his dark eyes, "That doesn't speak for my mother. And speaking of my mother . . ." he thrust the small package toward her.

Her brow creased at what this might have to do with his mother. But she took the package. It was wrapped in Christmas paper with a silk ribbon, the kind a little girl might wear in her hair, tied around it.

"Go on, open it," he urged when she hesitated.

She slipped off the ribbon and carefully lifted the ends of the paper. Lying in the opened paper was a silk handkerchief. It was pale blue with darker blue embroidered cranes, two of them, in each corner, along with delicate flowers in red, yellow, and blue, and Japanese characters. The edge was crocheted in white lace.

"It's beautiful, Sam!" Fingering the lace, tears suddenly filled her eyes. She didn't know why. Perhaps because she had not brought his present with her. Or perhaps because he had thought of a gift for her in the midst of all that was happening to him and to his family. Perhaps because the gift itself was so perfect. "What do the characters mean?" she asked through trembly lips.

"They are for happiness and long life."

She kissed his lips lightly. "I left your present at home."

"It's all right," he assured.

"This is the first gift we've exchanged," she said, as if he didn't know that, as well. "I'm glad to have something of yours. Something I can look at when you aren't with me. So I can remember."

"Remember what?" A leading question, he must have known.

She grinned and replied, "That I love you."

"What did you get me to help me remember?"

"Nothing special compared to this. A wallet." She gave a disgruntled smirk. "I wanted to give you something wonderful, but I couldn't find anything special enough. So I settled on the wallet."

"I know I'll love it. You get it to me quickly. I need one very much."

"Oh, you!" she gave his arm a playful shove. She knew as well as he that he had very little money these days to put into a wallet. "It's the last thing on earth you need, but thank you for saying so." Pausing a moment, she asked, "Sam, what has this handkerchief to do with your mother?"

"I stole it from her."

"What!"

Now his grin was like that of old—clean and filled with fun. "My mother has dozens of these handkerchiefs that have been sent to her over the years as gifts from relatives in Japan. I had little money to buy you something truly nice, so I asked her if I could have one to give as a gift to a friend. She just looked at me, knowing very well which friend it was for. Finally she shook her head. 'No, Yoshito, your father would not allow me to approve, even in this small way, of what you are doing.' I was crushed to say the least and began thinking I could maybe buy you a bottle of cheap perfume. I turned to go, and Mama called me back. 'Son,' she said, 'do you know how many handkerchiefs I have? Too many to count. I have never been able to keep track of them. If any are missing, I would never even know. Imagine that!' " Sam gave a sheepish shrug. "So do you mind a stolen Christmas gift?"

"I don't think so." Smiling, eyes still moist, she looked again at the lovely gift. "Sam, I think I will like your mother!"

"I know she will like you."

She threw her arms around him then, letting her tears fall on his collar. She wouldn't have dreamed of using her beautiful Japanese handkerchief to wipe them away.

15

Manila, Philippine Islands

THE BOMBING SEEMED never to cease, but when it did, the pall of silence was filled only with the terror of the anticipation of the next attack. Blair wondered why she did not go insane. Her nerves were taut, ready to snap.

She should have left Manila that same day she parted from Gary, but the roads were so clogged that she had decided to give it a day or two. Then she kept hoping Gary would come again or call. She hung on for that.

"I'll leave when I hear from Gary again," she told Claudette and Reverend Sanchez, who both were urging her to go.

The only one not especially anxious to depart was Mateo Sanchez. He seemed to think the longer they delayed the more time he'd have to convince his father to allow him to enlist in the Army. But the reverend was more adamant against this than ever. He had not heard for days from his older son, who was in the Army, and did not know if he was alive or dead.

Blair's bags were packed. One suitcase was filled with tinned food and medical supplies, two others nearly bursting with her and Claudette's clothes. All practical things: sturdy shoes, an extra pair for each, slacks, cotton blouses, a week's worth of undergarments, a supply of toiletries. Heaven only knew how long they would be gone or if they would be anyplace where they could purchase things. Reverend Sanchez had spoken once or twice about the jungle, but Blair had laughingly discounted all such references. She would not be in the jungle except crossing it on roads in the reverend's DeSoto. At the very most it would take her a half a day to reach Silvia in her mountain estate. Then she could just wait out this silly war there. She knew Silvia's place would be comfortable—nothing but the best for that woman.

She simply was not going to listen to or entertain any gloomy suggestions or, as Reverend Sanchez put it, get prepared for "the worst." Goodness sakes! The worst was just having to leave Manila at all. It could not get worse than that.

Instead, Blair clung to the more optimistic rumors. Help was on the way. The United States was sending ships of reinforcements—men, planes, guns. The Japanese would be stopped before they came close to Manila.

Hearing footsteps on the stairs leading up to her apartment, Blair went out to the front room. Claudette had let in Mateo and was ogling the boy with dreamy eyes. Blair was thankful to him for that, at least. When he was around, Claudette forgot all her fears about the war.

"I got the car gassed up, Miss Hayes," he said, laying the DeSoto's keys on the table by the door. "But they only let me have one extra can, and I had to use all of our ration coupons for that."

"I'm sure we'll be fine. There will be gas along the way if we need it."

"Then you have decided where you will be going?" That was Reverend Sanchez, huffing a bit as he lagged after his son on the stairs and came up to the partly opened door.

"To my friend Silvia's. She seemed certain it would be safe there," Blair replied, as if she had given it much thought, when in fact she made that final decision on the spot.

"If that is what you prefer," said Sanchez, mopping his sweaty brow with a big red handkerchief. Though the dry season was upon them, it was still hot and humid. "But if it doesn't work out," Sanchez went on, "the Doyles are good people. I am acquainted with them a little, and they will do well by you. And they are much closer to Manila, on the western side of Mount Santa Rosa, though."

She wasn't surprised he was promoting the missionary family, the one Gary had told her about. She didn't know why they weren't at the top of her list, as well. She had to work out her feelings about God eventually. But she told herself her reluctance regarding the Doyles was just a reticence about going to complete strangers.

"I have the directions Gary gave me," she hedged, "if I need them."

"If you go too far north, Blair," Sanchez said, "you could end up behind enemy lines."

"Only if we don't stop them, but I am sure we will. And Silvia's villa is so secluded no Japs will find it." In truth all she could think of were things Silvia had said in passing about the villa. Cool adobe walls, spacious tiled floors, fountains in front, quite royally appointed. If she must spend the war on this miserable island, that's where she wanted to spend it.

Smiling, she remembered that she was the hostess and her guests were standing in the doorway. "Come in and I'll make something cold to drink." This also politely cut off any further arguments from Reverend Sanchez.

The offer was barely accepted when the air-raid siren droned out in the street. They went to Mrs. Acosta's shelter and found it cramped with people. The landlady was not timid about mentioning this inconvenience, but even she couldn't turn away guests in the middle of an air raid. They listened to her complaints about this and everything else for a good two hours before the all clear sounded. Blair was the first to escape. She was drenched with sweat, since besides being cramped, there was little ventilation. If this was the dry season in the islands, she wondered what the wet season would be like. Arriving as she had in November, she had only caught the tail end of it.

Blair quickly brought out cool papaya juice after they trooped back up to her apartment. She was not the only one to drain her glass in a couple of minutes. Then the phone rang.

She ran to the telephone in the bedroom and grabbed the receiver as if it held the answers to all life's questions. In fact, in the days since parting from Gary, she responded to the ringing telephone every time in this manner. She never stopped hoping she would hear from him.

"Gary!" she said breathlessly into the receiver.

"Yes." No matter how she had hoped, she was shocked it was actually him. "I can't talk long," he went on quickly. "I had to let you know I won't be getting back to Manila." She gasped, but he continued even as she heard another voice in the background urging him to finish his call. "I'm sorry. . . ." She didn't know if he was saying it to her or the other person. "Blair, in a couple days, Manila will be declared an open city. All military personnel will have to evacuate. Do you understand? There will be no more military protection. Theoretically, it also means the Japs have to stop the bombing."

"That's good, isn't it?" she managed to squeeze in when he took a breath.

"The Japanese will move in soon after. You cannot be there when they occupy the city. You'll be an enemy alien. We've talked about this before. You must leave. Now!"

"Will there be a ship or an airplane to take me back to the States?" she asked. All along she had been prepared for a flight to the hills, but she had considered that a temporary situation. Gary made it seem like more now, thus she was certain he meant she would be on her way home to the States.

"Blair . . ." she could hear both frustration and apology as he intoned her name. "There are no boats getting through the Jap blockade now except for small ones reserved for the highest officials. Those can only get safely as far as Corregidor Island. As for planes . . . you must know . . ." The other voice in the background broke in again. "I have to go," Gary said hurriedly. "Remember the things I told you. Listen to Reverend Sanchez. I wish I could do more—hey—!" Suddenly the line went dead.

"Gary!" she shouted into the receiver. Then she let it fall limply to the table, not even bothering to hang it back on the set.

The others in the front room had no doubt heard the conversation, her side, at least, through the beaded curtain. When she returned, they were staring at her expectantly. She just shook her head, then as she slumped into a chair, she told them all Gary had said. They were just as shocked as she.

Reverend Sanchez broke the pall of silence over the group. "There are several hours of daylight left. You must go now."

"Papa," Mateo broke in, "there is still time for me to join the Army—"

"No!" the usually soft-spoken minister said sharply. "I promised Blair you would help her. Do you want me to break my oath?"

Blair knew that wasn't entirely the truth. Reverend Sanchez had asked her to take care of his son in exchange for the loan of his car. But Blair wasn't going to refute his words. She wasn't especially thrilled to have an extra youngster to be responsible for, but if Mateo went off now to join the Army, it might mean the loss of the DeSoto, and she couldn't afford that. Her hope rested on that vehicle getting her as quickly as possible to Silvia's mountain villa.

Obedient son that he was, Mateo just gave a sulky "No, Papa. I will do as you say."

In less than an hour they were making their way through the streets of Manila with Mateo behind the wheel of the DeSoto.

Gary returned to where his unit was bivouacked near the little village of Rosario. He'd managed to slip into the village along with a couple of his comrades to make the call to Blair. They, too, had sweethearts in Manila. Now he had to dig back in and await the coming battle. Waiting was the worst part—they had not been taught that lesson at the Point.

The previous day a Japanese expedition of more than a hundred enemy vessels, escorted by warships, had landed at Lingayen Gulf. Word had reached them that the enemy had hit the beaches to the north all but unopposed. Everyone was heartsick. When the enemy landed, only a few B-17s showed up to harry the landing force, but General Homma, the commander of the Japanese force, was more disrupted by the swell of the sea than by the defending forces.

"We don't have the manpower or matériel to throw at 'em," said Gary's sergeant, Ralph Senger. A farmer's son from South Bend, Indiana, he'd been in the Army for ten years—two tours in the Philippines—and had always been generous in imparting his vast experience to Gary. Gary listened to the man because he knew what he was talking about. He was all one imagined a sergeant to be—more shoulders than neck, thick middle, but all muscle. His booming voice sounded like an idling half-track. His language was saltier than any Gary had ever heard, and in his military life he'd heard some. But Gary liked the man because you always knew where you stood with him.

"Guess it'll be up to us to stop 'em," offered Gary with even less confidence than he felt.

"And we'll give 'em what for!" chimed in a new voice in a deep Texas drawl.

"Hey, Woody!" Gary said. With battle imminent, it was nice to greet another friend. "What're you doing slumming with the infantry?" Though only two weeks since that initial attack on Clark Airfield, it seemed to Gary that he was meeting a friend from an age ago.

"We've been ordered from the airfield to offer reinforcement here. Guess we weren't doing much good tidying up the airbase, since no new planes are likely to come our way." Woody hunkered down on the dirt next to the others. "I had a gander at those troops of yours as I came, and I gotta say them Filipinos sure looked green."

"Yeah, and they're as jittery as a hen in a hornet's nest," said the sergeant. "Most are new recruits, but I got faith in them. They're defending their land, and I know they'll come through."

Gary laughed. "I'm not exactly an old soldier myself."

"And you'll do fine, too," said Woody. "I saw you when Clark was bombed. You got one battle under your belt. It'll get easier."

Gary eyed the man dubiously. He may not have shamed himself at Clark Field, but neither did he believe war became easier. He was far more afraid now than he'd been then simply because now he had an idea of what to expect. He said nothing, however. It didn't help to whine about your fear. He was a soldier; he would fight because that's what he did.

Soon after, the enemy came on in a flood. Had Gary a moment to think about it, he might have run or screamed. The first blast of artillery made him dive instinctively into the dirt. And he wanted to keep his face buried there as explosions ripped apart the humid air over his head. He didn't know what made him scrape the grit from his eyes and raise his head enough to fire his rifle. Not bravery. He knew in those first moments that he wasn't brave, just dogged. He knew how to fire his rifle, so he fired, just by rote.

Until Roxas slammed against his shoulder. The eighteen-year-old youngster's eyes were open wide as if with a profound revelation. But he didn't speak. He couldn't, because a Jap bullet had ripped his throat apart. Fragments of flesh and drops of blood splattered across Gary's face. Gary stared in horror, momentarily frozen, unable to call upon even instinct. He listened to the young man gurgling, drowning in his own blood, and that seemed to make Gary remember who he was. Platoon leader. These boys were counting on him.

"Hang on, José!" Gary fumbled in his belt pack where he had a few first aid supplies, found only a hankie, and tried to stanch the flow of blood. Then, shaking himself further from his shock, he screamed, "Medic!"

The medic came quickly, but Roxas was dead before he got there.

Still the enemy came on, not stopping for a dying teen or a frightened lieutenant. There was not even time to pray, but God gave him the determination to do his job and even to buck up the spirits of his platoon. Besides Roxas, he lost one other man in the first wave—Marcos. He had been shot in the head and died instantly. No one had been able to help the boy, not that they could have done much—they had been too busy fending off the enemy.

Still, in that initial onslaught, Gary's men held their positions, while he'd seen other units break and run. He was proud of them. Some of the Filipinos were smooth-cheeked kids. One had tears on his dirt-stained cheeks, another's hand trembled as he squeezed the trigger of his rifle.

Do I look like that? Gary wondered during a brief lull in the fighting. He wasn't ready to die. He'd grown up learning that Christians had the hope of heaven and eternal life and thus were prepared to meet God. He felt the small bulge in the inside pocket of his fatigue jacket of the New Testament his mother had given him before leaving home. He read it as often as he could. Regardless, he wasn't ready to die—he had more living to do. He hoped that didn't make him less of a Christian. He thought of Blair, the things that still needed settling between them, the life he hoped they could have together. There was just too much left to live for.

A bullet whizzed by his ear. He ducked reflexively only a fraction of a second later. He had to focus. This was no time to worry about life—only about staying alive!

"That one nearly had your name on it, LT," Senger said, only he used a far more colorful phrase.

Gary shook his head, swallowing back the bile rising in his throat.

Captain Smithers crawled up to the rear of their position just then. "We're going to fall back to Rosario," he said. "Slowly, now. Make them Japs pay for every inch you give."

Gary had learned about retreats at West Point, but he had not learned to like them. Especially when he had grown up believing the United States of America was all but invincible. It seemed impossible that a tiny speck of a nation could now be so overwhelming them.

As the captain moved up the line, Gary nodded to Senger to get the men moving. The unit didn't have to be told twice, but they did need to be reminded often to take it easy. Gary was not about to have his unit retreat in a rout.

Night finally descended, but that didn't seem to stop the enemy. Bursts of artillery and rifle fire continued to fill the warm tropical air. As the artillery laid in a cover, the American and Filipino troops continued to fall back. Gary had a hard time keeping his men together. They were hit on their flank by a Jap patrol, and he lost two more men. They cut down most of the enemy patrol but had to swing far into the jungle to avoid the remainder.

The deeper into the jungle they got, the more difficult it was to maintain their bearings, to keep track of which direction the friendly fire was coming from and from which direction the enemy's. But before long the battle sounds seemed far off. Gary feared that the last skirmish had cut him off from the main force. He prayed they were still heading for Rosario and pointed his men toward where he thought the others were. He looked to Senger several times, but even the sergeant seemed bemused.

A quarter of Gary's platoon had been lost so far. But still the remaining ones had not run for it. They were sticking together, though he could tell some feet were itchy to run. He wished his buddy Woody were here now to see just what these guys were made of.

When Gary heard the sounds of tanks, however, he feared the last shred of restraint among the men might cease. He felt his own gut wrench with fear it might be the enemy heading their way.

"Halt!" he said in a voice just above a whisper and, as expected, the sergeant quietly passed the order down the line.

"What do you think, Sarge? Ours or theirs?" Gary asked softly for Senger's ears only.

Senger shook his head. Not often uncertain about anything, he was now. If they were the enemy's, it could be the final straw to throw his men into a panic. They might just scatter through the jungle and become moving targets. Their best bet was to hold still, hide in the brush, and hope they'd be passed by unobserved.

"Sarge, let's get under cover."

The men moved back, but they heard the thundering rattle of the tanks. Eyes bulged with fear; knuckles were white as they gripped rifles.

"Hold!" Gary ordered once they were well hidden.

Intently, he listened. Ours? Theirs?

Then he heard it, that distinctive rattle that had to be a Sherman!

"They're ours," he breathed.

Senger nodded. "Means the road to Rosario isn't too far, 'cause them tanks are no doubt retreating there, too." That was about as close as Senger had ever come to hinting that Gary might be lost. Certainly Gary had not been willing to admit it to himself. He'd kept hoping the road would spring up. But the tanks were an assurance. Pausing, Senger cocked his ear again.

"What's wrong?" Gary asked.

"Dunno, just don't sound right. We better go easy."

Gary continued to keep his men in check as they advanced. There could be Japs anywhere around them. They hadn't met any in the last hour, but that didn't mean they couldn't spring up at any moment behind a coconut tree. He made the platoon creep forward in the direction of the tank sounds. Nevertheless, they were in a jaunty mood as they came within sight of the road and saw the tanks pass and were assured they were friendly.

"Hey, Sarge, were you scared?" asked Ruiz. He was eighteen.

"I been more scared going to the latrine!" Senger replied in what could only be described as a soft boom.

"What about you, LT?" asked Torres.

Gary glanced at the sergeant and knew he couldn't pull off that man's bravado, because he almost believed the sergeant *hadn't* been scared.

"I was ready to upchuck my C rations all over the sergeant's sleeve," admitted Gary with a laugh.

The men laughed, and several others admitted their fear, as well. They had kept their banter to whispers, even the laughter, and Gary let them have a couple moments' release, but then he raised his hand.

"We better keep it down." He looked at the men in the faint light of a quarter moon and was gratified to see some of their earlier tension gone. They'd be battle-hardened veterans in no time. So would he.

Forced to pause on a high ridge overlooking the road because it was lined with rolls of barbed wire, Gary saw, a short distance down the road, the retreating 26th Cavalry. They had been performing great feats that day, often in the forward position of the battle. But they were exhausted now, moving wearily down the narrow road, six hundred mounted troops. The Shermans were already well ahead of them and almost out of sight.

Then Gary heard and soon saw the cause of Senger's earlier unease. Japanese armor was barreling down the road, heading directly for the cavalry! With the banks of the road walling them in, they had no place to go. The Japanese tanks tore through them like a knife through silk. Men and horses scattered, but many were simply crushed beneath the murderous tanks. Tank fire demolished anything else in its way. Gary resisted the urge to fire at the marauding tanks, knowing his rifle wouldn't have done much good. There was not a single grenade left among his men, or he might have risked a pitch or two. All he could do was make sure his men didn't fire and kept their faces in the dirt in case one of the deadly machines saw them and sprayed the ridge with fire. He kept his face buried, too, after the first horrifying moments of the slaughter.

His unit reached Rosario a couple of hours later. They had had to skirt around the road quite a distance to find a way around the barbed wire defenses. At one point they had been pinned down for a half an hour by a Jap machine-gun nest. Two of his men were wounded in the melee, but they had finally managed to flank the machine gunner and take him down.

Trudging into the village with one of the wounded men slung over his shoulder, Gary remembered how earlier that day—or had it been yesterday? He'd lost track of time—he'd been there making a telephone call and haggling with the shop owner about the price of the call. The village was deserted now of nearly all civilians. The Army was digging in here to make another attempt at holding back the onslaught of the enemy.

He heard there were only about a hundred seventy-five of the 26th Cavalry still mounted, with most of the others dead or scattered somewhere. He did not have to listen to the rest of the scuttlebutt to know the defense against the Japanese landings had not gone well. He expected any time now the order would come down for them to retreat into Bataan. The Army would give up the rest of the islands, concentrating itself on the small yet strategically viable peninsula. This had always been the military strategy, but Gary doubted anyone ever thought it would come to that.

He couldn't think of the larger picture now. He had to get his men squared away. The lull in the fighting brought about by the night would not last long. They were assigned a position on the village square and dug in.

ROUTE 3 OUT OF MANILA was a quagmire of both fleeing refugees and the military. Old and new cars, handcarts, horse- or donkey-drawn wagons, and pedestrians all vied for the road in sheer confusion with jeeps, troop trucks, and armored vehicles. Blair began to wonder if they'd ever get out. They had been on the road for two hours and had gone less than ten miles.

Maybe it would have been better to stay in Manila and take her chances with the enemy. But she recalled the shudder in Gary's voice whenever the idea of a Japanese POW camp was mentioned.

The driver of the wagon ahead of them was having problems with his donkey, which was trying desperately to pull the cart that was nearly toppling with the weight of the man's possessions and his family. Mateo, who was driving the DeSoto, tried to edge around the wagon to the right, where there was just enough room on the shoulder of the road to pass. When the backfire of an Army truck made the skittish donkey rear, the loaded wagon lurched one way and then the other with the panicked movements of the animal. For a moment the wagon looked about to crash into the DeSoto. Mateo jerked the steering wheel but overcompensated, sending the car bumping into the ditch.

"Everyone okay?" the boy asked when they came to a stop at the bottom, only a few feet below the road but enough to disable them.

"Y-yes," Blair replied after a quick look in the backseat, where Claudette was sitting. She glanced up at the road and saw the wagon had righted itself without mishap. It would have been far worse for them, with children barely clinging to household goods in the back of the wagon, had they crashed into the ditch.

Blair and company scrambled from the DeSoto. A quick check ensured the tires were intact—a big concern because they only had one spare and tires were extremely hard to come by these days. Mateo started up the stalled engine right away, so that was good, too. The biggest problem—getting out of the ditch—was also remedied quickly.

"Hello there! You need some help?" Glancing up, Blair saw an American corporal and a couple other soldiers standing above them.

Blair's pathetic nod was answer enough.

"Wait here, and we'll tie your car to our truck and have you out in a jiffy," the corporal said.

The truck had to block the road partially to do the job, making those in the stopped vehicles none too happy. Horns honked; people yelled. Blair thought that if people would be more considerate, this would be a far more orderly evacuation. She wouldn't have ended up in the ditch in the first place, and she might even have been close enough to Silvia's by now to anticipate dinner with her friend. As it was, she would be lucky to have breakfast at the villa.

Her spirits lifted a little when the DeSoto was back up on the side of the road. The truck pulled to the side, as well, and the corporal checked out Blair's vehicle, especially looking underneath to make sure it was all right to drive.

Straightening, he brushed off his hands. "Looks good. You were lucky. Where you headed?"

"I have a friend to the north, not far from Tarlac," Blair replied. "I'll wait the war out there, I suppose."

The corporal, a lean fellow only a few inches taller than Blair, scratched his head of disheveled brown hair. "I don't mean to tell you what to do, miss, but the Japs are coming down from the north, and it might be only a matter of days before that area's behind enemy lines."

"They won't get that far." Where her confidence came from, she didn't know.

He merely shrugged. "You'd be better off making for Bataan. We'll make our retreat there, and you'd have the Army to protect you."

"My friend is certain her villa is quite secluded and safe." Had she made the right decision? Did any confidence she might have spring more from her desire for the comforts the villa promised than from practicality?

"Well, if you change your mind, when you get to San Fernando, you can head south on Route 7, then take the road along the coast. You might even be able to get to Mariveles and then to Corregidor."

"All the Army is going to Bataan?"

"Eventually, if we can't stop the Japs."

"Corporal, do you know anyone in the 71st Infantry? That's my husband's outfit. Lieutenant Gary Hobart." Her resolve about Silvia was suddenly weakening. If Gary was going to be in Bataan, she might be able to find him.

"Sorry, miss, don't know the name." He turned and yelled up to his companions, giving them Gary's name. None had heard of him. "That don't mean nothing, miss. There's a lot of men here, be kind of like coming up with a needle in a haystack."

He had meant it as encouragement, but it worked to deflate what hope she had of finding Gary.

"Thank you, Corporal." She also flashed a grateful smile at the other men in the truck. "I appreciate your help."

They reached San Fernando well after dark. Thirty-five miles northwest of Manila, it was situated at a rail junction as well as on the junction of the main road leading into Bataan. A fair-sized town for Luzon, it was crowded with refugees and military personnel. Mateo managed to get them what appeared to be the last hotel room in town. Claudette went to the market area to see if anything was still available that late, while Blair started to unload the DeSoto. As she was unloading the car, a couple of local boys came along and offered to haul their belongings to the room for a couple of pesos. She felt she was doing them a good deed by giving them a way to earn money.

Following the boys into the hotel and up the stairs to the second story, she gave a disheartened stare at the room. It was small for even one person, yet all three of them were going to have to share it. The only window let in none of the slight outside breeze. It had no fan and only one bed, with just enough floor space for a cot to be wedged in for Mateo, and a small corner for their suitcases. She and Claudette would have to share the narrow bed.

Claudette came back empty-handed from the market. Everything was closed, and the hotel served no food because of shortages. Reluctantly Blair opened a couple of tins of sardines, which they put on sliced bread, the only item she had been able to finagle from the hotel manager, and that for one American dollar! Blair was grateful Claudette had insisted on packing a hot plate, kettle, and a few other cooking items. Blair had never considered that they might have to cook for themselves—outdoors or in a hotel room. But even in the heat, she appreciated the hot tea with the meal.

As they prepared for bed, Claudette suddenly became shy, and for good reason with Mateo's bed only a few inches from hers. Blair didn't exactly care for the arrangement, either.

"Do you remember in 'It Happened One Night,' " Claudette said, "how Clark Gable and Claudette Colbert had to share a hotel room?"

"Yes," Blair said. "Clark put up a blanket between the beds."

"He called it the 'walls of Jericho,' " Claudette added with a look at Mateo, who was listening with an odd look on his face.

"What are you looking at me for?" said Mateo, a blush rising to his cheeks. Then the impropriety of their present situation seemed to dawn on him. "There's no room to hang a blanket here!" he protested.

Because he looked ready to flee, Blair suggested, "Mateo, why don't you just step outside while we change and get into bed? Then we'll cover our eyes with our blankets while you undress."

Claudette mildly protested this, and Blair was certain she much preferred the romantic notion of the blanket in the movie, but Mateo had run out before she could do more than utter a single argument. Blair's plan worked well, and everyone's modesty was spared.

Blair tossed and turned all night. Her mind, waking and sleeping, was tormented with decisions that must be made. Settling the problem of the sleeping arrangements was simple by comparison to all that faced her. That day she had spoken to other soldiers on the road besides the corporal, and all had given her basically the same advice. What was worse, none had known Gary. One fellow she talked to was also in the 71st, but he, too, did not know Gary.

There was bombing in the north. She could hear the sounds, though the town where they were was not touched. Still, Silvia's villa dangled before her temptingly. For so long she had looked upon it as near salvation. Now she was flooded with uncertainty. Shortly before dawn it occurred to her to pray about the matter. She didn't know if God would listen to her prayers, but it was worth a try. So she asked for divine direction just before she slipped into a deep sleep.

She awoke oddly refreshed—she hadn't asked God for that extra boon, but she wasn't about to complain, especially when she felt sure for the first time about what to do next. The pull of Gary and Corregidor proved stronger than the lure of the comforts of Silvia's villa. She couldn't say if this was an answer to her awkward prayer last night, but it certainly was further confirmed when Claudette and Mateo heartily agreed to the new decision. She thought in Mateo's case he agreed because he thought this direction would take him closer to the Army.

Loading up the DeSoto after a breakfast that was a repeat of the previous night's dinner—bread, sardines, and tea—Blair took the wheel, and they headed down Route 7. There was still quite a jam of traffic. At one point the road was bombed out, forcing them to take a detour that nearly got them lost. But they reached the little village of Layac by noon. This place was less to speak of than San Fernando had been, consisting of a couple of dirt streets lined with a few adobe structures but mostly nipa shacks. These were the houses most common to the countryside, though Blair had seen some in the suburbs of the larger towns. They were raised on bamboo stilts, with sides and roofs made from the broad fronds of the nipa palm. They made the village appear typical of the romantic view one might have of the tropics.

At the market she and her entourage purchased onions and turnips, the only fresh vegetables to be found, and a few papayas. They ate the papayas for lunch. In a shop window Blair saw a faded paper Santa Claus and only then remembered that tomorrow would be Christmas Eve. On impulse, while Mateo and Claudette were wandering around the village, Blair went into the shop, a small pharmacy, and did a little Christmas shopping.

Back on the road the going was not as intense as it had been, or perhaps Blair was just growing more used to it all. With Mateo driving, she took some time to appreciate the tropical scenery. She saw there was more to be seen than the presence of the military. Beautiful bushes of white and pink hibiscus colored the lush foliage. Bird-of-paradise, bougainvillea, too, added splashes of color to the verdant green. Reverend Sanchez had always spoken so ominously of the jungle, but she thought a stroll among those lovely plants would be very nice sometime. She forgot all about that, however, when steam started rising from the DeSoto's hood.

"Mateo, what's that?"

He was already braking and pulling over. Getting out and lifting the hood only confirmed the obvious. The steaming and hissing radiator was nearly empty.

"I checked the water this morning," he said. "Must be a leak."

"Can we drive like that?"

"Of course not!" he replied testily.

She didn't think he was angry at her; rather, he was most likely taking responsibility for the mishap himself.

"I'm sorry, Miss Hayes." Her dismissive wave and encouraging smile did little to dispel the grimace on the boy's face. He got their jug of water from the backseat. "This might be enough water to get us to the next village, where maybe someone can fix it."

Billows of steam were rising from the hood of the vehicle again when they hobbled into the village of Hermosa. It did not look promising that they'd find what they needed for the car here, where there were only a few shops besides a tiny city hall with a post office. Thus Blair's surprise when they found a gas station. There was no gas to be had, but the mechanic, covered with grease from head to toe, who came out of a garage was nearly assailed with a kiss from Blair. She stopped just short of that and was glad she did when he scratched his dirty hair after looking at the DeSoto and pronounced his grim diagnosis. At least he spoke English, and Blair could deal with the man without Mateo or Claudette translating.

"You need a new radiator, miss," he said, then after a quick look at Claudette and Mateo, he added, "or is it Mrs.?"

With an offended sniff—how dare he think she might be old enough to have children the ages of her two companions!—she said, "*Miss* Hayes." Or should she have said *Mrs.*? After all, she was married even if she didn't quite feel it. Why was life so complicated?

He leaned over the engine and pointed. "See, rusty."

Blair did not even attempt to look. She stood well back of the opened hood, as if fearing the exposed engine might leap out and grab her in its dirty, greasy paws—she felt much the same about the mechanic, notwithstanding her initial impulse to kiss him. At any rate, she was happy to let Mateo hover under the hood with the mechanic and do whatever it was men did in such circumstances.

"How long will it take to put in a new radiator?" she asked.

The greasy man chuckled. "New radiator? Ha ha. There's a war, you know."

"An old one, then?"

A smirk still on his face, he shook his head.

"Can it be fixed?" she asked, her hope plummeting.

"Can you patch it?" Mateo asked, with just a slight tinge of superiority to his tone. He certainly must have realized she knew nothing about automobiles.

Slowly the mechanic nodded. "You got money?"

"Yes," she answered. "I'll give you ten American dollars to fix it." She probably had answered too quickly, if that was the meaning of the aghast looks from both Mateo and Claudette. She just didn't want to fiddle with Filipino bartering just then. She was hot, tired, and hungry—papaya didn't satisfy for long. As an appeasement to her young companions' scandalized looks, she added, "I'll pay when it's fixed. Now, is there someplace to stay here?"

He pointed out a house at the end of the street, not a hotel, as there wasn't one in the town. But the mechanic said the people there would put them up for the night. It was another nipa building, but larger and a bit more affluent—if a grass hut could ever truly be affluent—and appeared more sturdy than many others she had seen.

It was hot work hauling their luggage down the road from the gas station, and there was not a single child around for Blair to *help* by giving them the job. Because she was exhausted, she was glad the residents of the house spoke Tagalog, thus Mateo had to do all the talking and bartering for rooms.

"Only one room again," Mateo said of his conversation with Mr. Padilla. "One dollar per night. We provide our own food, but we can use their kitchen to cook."

"That sounds fair. Tell him we'll take it."

Blair was too tired to think of cooking that night, so she doled out more from the suitcase of supplies. At least they were lightening that load, which she was having to haul around far more than she had intended when she packed it back in Manila.

The DeSoto was not done in the morning; in fact, it didn't look as if it had been touched.

"Tomorrow," the mechanic promised.

In a way Blair was glad for the respite. Maybe if she remained in one place for a while, Gary might find her. She used the time to do laundry at the town pump. Claudette had volunteered to do the task, but Blair felt it wasn't right to make the girl do her usual maid's work when Blair could no longer pay her. She determined that work should be divided equally among the three of them. And she thought it might be a nice distraction to visit the pump, which was the village's only source of water and seemed the spot for such activity. About a half dozen village women were already there with washtubs and piles of dirty clothes. Here, also, seemed the place where the women gathered to gossip. She couldn't understand any of it, since they spoke Tagalog, but there was something so normal in it all that she appreciated it anyway. These women had been coming here for years, all their lives, and even war didn't change that. Maybe war didn't have to change everything.

"No, no!" said one of the women, tugging the cotton blouse from Blair, who had been holding it by two fingers and swishing it halfheartedly in the water as if afraid to get her hands wet. "Like this." The woman, who was about as old as Blair's mother, took the garment and manipulated it expertly in the soapy water in Blair's pail. The few words of English she spoke were thickly accented.

Blair couldn't see the difference in technique except that the woman had approached the job far more aggressively, soaking her hands completely in the water. As a result of years of this approach, the woman's hands were wrinkled and dry, almost leathery, with nails blunt and rough. To be congenial, Blair smiled her appreciation and tried it the woman's way, but she shuddered inwardly at the work, especially when she chipped one of her fingernails. For the first time since leaving Manila, a seed of thought was planted in her mind. Maybe doing laundry at a pump wasn't all she was going to have to learn before she reached her destination. She glanced at her slim white hands, with nails neatly manicured and covered with a fresh coat of Cherry Jubilee nail polish. She considered paying the woman to do her laundry. It would only cost a couple of pesos. But the trip was already taking days longer than anticipated, and she was going to have to start conserving her limited funds. How she hated to budget money!

After the laundry was hung to dry, Blair and Claudette went to the open-air market to forage for food. This market was larger than others they had encountered, with a more varied selection of goods. They had picked out some carrots, more onions, and a few potatoes, when Mateo came running up to them.

"Miss Hayes, I talked to some soldiers who might know Lieutenant Hobart," he panted.

"Oh, really?" she nearly dropped the potatoes she was holding as she thrust them toward Claudette. "Claudette, see if you can find some chicken to go with this." Giving Claudette money, she hurried after Mateo.

All the villages they had passed through were heavily populated with soldiers, and she always asked about Gary. But lately she had grown discouraged at the negative responses she received and had nearly given up finding him.

Three soldiers, one American and two Filipinos, stood outside the local cantina with glasses of warm beer in hand. Blair knew it was warm because cold drinks were next to impossible to find.

"Are you in the 71st?" Blair asked breathlessly, coming to a stop before them.

"Naw," said a lanky towheaded lieutenant. "I'm a grounded flyboy myself. Lieutenant Woodburn," he added in a southern accent. "But this young fella here mentioned a Lieutenant Hobart, and I know a Gary Hobart."

"That's him! That's my husband!" In her excitement she forgot she hadn't been using the term *husband*. But how else was she to logically express her interest in the man? "In the 71st, right?"

"Yep. That's gotta be him."

"Where is he? Is he all right?"

"Last I saw of him was a couple days ago north of here near Rosario. That's a spell of miles from here. His unit was pushing back, so I doubt he's near there any longer. But he was fit as could be when I saw him."

That was something, she supposed. "You haven't seen him since?"

"Naw. But all the troops are withdrawing into Bataan, so it's a sure bet he's somewhere around here now. I haven't seen him, though, I'm sorry to say. He's a fine man, your husband."

She smiled but couldn't keep it up for long. She'd been too hopeful when she ran from the market. She'd thought perhaps she might be taken to Gary right then. Now she was right where she had started. On the maps Bataan seemed a tiny place, hardly worth all the attention upon it lately. But it might as well have been the size of the state of California when trying to find one soldier among thousands.

Thanking the lieutenant, she ambled back to the house. She let Claudette finish the shopping on her own. It was too hot to go inside, so she sat on the front step. She felt like weeping. So that Mateo wouldn't see her break down, she sent him to get the laundry, which surely must be dry in this heat.

Ten minutes later she was wiping away the last of her tears when Claudette returned from the market. In one arm she carried a basket with the fresh produce she had purchased. In the other she held a cage-like crate from which a squawking sound could be heard.

"What's that, Claudette?" she asked, nodding toward the crate. Peering through the wooden slats, she saw something move.

"A chicken, Miss Blair."

"A chicken! What in the world do you have that for?" Blair did not hide the ire she felt.

"You said to get chicken. This is all I could find."

"And I suppose you know how to turn that . . . creature into stew?"

"I buy—" Claudette thrust the crate toward Blair. "You kill."

Blair laughed dryly. "I don't even know how to *cook* a chicken, much less kill it. You're the cook."

"I have cooked lots of chicken, but it never started out like this. Even in the orphanage when I cooked, it was butchered first." Claudette might have been a street urchin when Blair found her and a very savvy one at that, but she was nevertheless a city urchin, not a country one.

Just then Mateo ambled up to them. The two women turned expectant eyes upon him.

"What?" he said a touch defensively at their pointed looks.

"Here, Mateo." Blair held the crate out to him. "Surely you must know how to make this critter into dinner." She didn't know why she would assume that, since he was from the city as well, but she figured he wouldn't want to appear ignorant in front of Claudette. It was cruel of her, she knew, to take advantage of his young male ego, but she counted it necessary.

He rolled his eyes. "I have never been with such helpless women." Then he jogged off toward the garage down the street. In a few minutes he returned with a machete.

"Where did you get that?" Blair stared incredulously at the huge, lethal-looking instrument.

"My father packed it in the trunk of the DeSoto. He said just a precaution should we need it in the jungle."

Now Blair rolled her eyes. "He would!"

Mateo opened the crate and reached in for the chicken. He pulled it out, gripping its scrawny neck, and took it to a stump that looked as if it had been used in the past for this very purpose. Ignoring the animal's squawks and the frantic flapping of its wings, and looking as if he'd done this countless times, Mateo raised the machete.

"Wait! Stop!" Blair yelled. "Don't kill it."

"What? You want to boil it alive?"

"No!" Blair gave a shudder. "But . . ." She gazed at the pathetic creature. "It's just a lot different when you've looked dinner in the eyes before eating it. I can't do it."

"Go in the house, and you won't have to look," suggested Mateo.

Claudette added, "I can make a nice *vegetable* stew, and there's some Spam in the suitcase I can throw in. It'll be really tasty."

Mateo lowered the machete and, without thinking, let go of the chicken. The reprieved animal, showing no gratitude at all, quickly scurried away, forcing Mateo to scramble all over the yard after it, diving into the dirt, dust and feathers flying everywhere. Blair and Claudette were laughing too hard to help him. Finally he caught the ungrateful beast and stuck it back in the crate.

"I'm not letting it go," he said. "We might get hungry enough yet, and she cost good money."

"Let's call it Mae West," Claudette said.

"Our little chickadee," added Blair dryly, realizing this was just another mouth to feed, another creature to be responsible for.

Mateo gave a loud "Harrumph!" He knew as well as Blair that they would never be able to eat a chicken with a name.

She didn't care. It felt rather good, in the midst of war, to spare a life for a change.

17

DECEMBER 25, 1941. Christmas Day. It was like no Christmas Blair had ever spent before.

In the morning for breakfast they had bananas for a change, tea, and the last of the loaf of bread purchased two days ago. Then Blair surprised her traveling companions by presenting Christmas presents. They were a little chagrined they had nothing for her, but she told them emphatically that just having friends to spend Christmas with was gift enough.

Her gifts were hardly worth the "oohs" and "ahhs" they received. She had bought wide-brimmed straw hats for each of them, including herself. Mateo's had a blue kerchief tied around the crown, Claudette's had a red one, and Blair's was green. Hers and Claudette's were fixed in such a way that the band around the hat also tied around their chins. They were the most practical thing she could justify spending money for. The more time she spent in the blazing tropical sun, the more she realized just how practical such an item would be.

Naturally the DeSoto still was not fixed. She couldn't very well expect Pedro, the mechanic, to work on Christmas. So they spent the morning lolling about, more thankful than ever for hats to ward off the sun. The Padilla family, their landlords, invited them to join them for Christmas dinner later that day.

Soldiers continued to pass through town. Mateo and Blair mingled among them as much as possible. The Americans were pleased when they saw an American woman among the villagers and often engaged her in conversation. They talked about home for the most part, obviously wanting to avoid talking about the war, and Blair had no problem with that. Talk of war was simply too depressing. The men were from Kansas and New York and Texas, and they were all homesick on Christmas Day. Most had been in the Philippines longer than she, so she brought the most current news from the States. They listened eagerly about the latest movies and songs and celebrity gossip, all of which Blair was far better versed in than politics, sports, and such. But it was news from home, so they weren't particular.

Around noon truckloads of wounded came through. Blair learned a field hospital was being set up just outside the village. These were men who had engaged in the fighting in the north and were now being evacuated into Bataan. She hated to think Gary might be among them, but practicality made her walk down to the site. She found everything in mayhem there, as they were in the process of setting up the place, which made her search difficult. She tried to look among the wounded, but a doctor told her to either help or get out of the way. She chose the latter, since the idea of tending sick men, some bloody and dirty, appalled her. She'd return later, when things calmed down a little and all the wounded were tucked neatly into beds and their wounds did not show so horribly.

She tried to make the best of Christmas dinner. The Padillas were a genial group. Blair couldn't understand ninety percent of what they said, but she enjoyed their company anyway. There were easily a dozen of them gathered around the big table they'd set up in the living room. It was the only room in the house big enough for the table, which was actually two pieces of plywood on a couple of sawhorses that Mrs. Padilla had covered with bedsheets.

When Blair had Claudette ask if they could bring anything, Mrs. Padilla had eyed Mae West covetously. Instead, Blair contributed all three remaining cans of green beans, a treat appreciated by her hosts as much as the chicken would have been, especially when Blair included all their fresh produce and a hunk of goat cheese she'd found at the market. The main course was a delicious chicken stew, made from the Padillas' stock of chickens. Blair enjoyed it. She had no problem eating a chicken as long as she hadn't met it personally beforehand.

Oddly, the dinner with the Padillas brought to Blair melancholy memories of her family rather than thoughts of Gary. Yes, she missed Gary, but she had never spent a holiday with him, so they had no shared stock of memories. The holiday memories with her family might not be all joyous—certainly her parents and sisters had never experienced the near raucous conviviality the Padillas shared together. But, such as they were, they were her only Christmas memories, and they weren't all bad.

Decorating the tree . . . would her family have a tree this year? Or was it the height of arrogance on her part to think her absence might make them forego family traditions? Cameron was gone, too, at least as far as Blair knew. Blair could almost taste her mother's eggnog. The Padillas had none of that, nor did they have a tree. But that eggnog . . . she remembered the time she had sneaked a measure of her father's whiskey into hers, and how both she and her father had become quite tipsy. It was one of the few times she recalled enjoying her father's company. Maybe that's why she had taken to drinking alcohol so much in later years. Unfortunately, all the alcohol in the world never brought a repeat of that singularly pleasant time.

Suddenly Blair remembered something else. Shortly before leaving the States she had seen a wonderful hat in a shop window that she thought would be perfect for Jackie. She'd bought the hat and hid it away in the closet of her old room at her parents' house with the intention of giving it to her sister for Christmas. Goodness, the hat must still be there. It very likely would be out of style by the time Blair had a chance to give it to Jackie.

She shook the depressing thought from her mind. The war wouldn't be that long. It couldn't! Just that morning on the radio there had been a message from the States: "Hang on, Bataan! Help is on the way!"

Surely she would be home before the spring fashion season.

After dinner she felt an urge to write a letter home. A couple of handwritten pages filled with lies about how everything was all right—to keep her family from worrying. She told them about Claudette and Mateo and how enjoyable they were. She mentioned the incident with Mae West mainly because she had run out of innocuous things to fill the last page with. She wished them a merry Christmas and said she was sure she'd be home soon. Then she walked to the post office and dropped the letter in the box. Turning back down the street she ran into Pedro, the mechanic.

"Merry Christmas, Pedro," she said, making a point not to say a word about the DeSoto. It was Christmas, after all.

"Same to you, miss. Are you mailing a letter?"

"Yes, to my family in the States."

He laughed.

"What's so funny about that?" she asked, a touch indignant at his demeaning tone.

"There is no mail leaving the islands, miss. Not for days now, I think."

Feeling the fool, she just shrugged and walked on. She supposed her letter would now sit in that box for the duration of the war. Not long, she fervently hoped. Would her family know she was all right? She had sent a telegram to Jackie a few days before she left Manila. That would have to do.

Blair wandered back down to the field hospital. The place was more orderly now. In fact Blair was rather surprised at how quickly they had put it into shape. There were several tents spread out in a meadow, a flag with a red cross flying over the center on a tall flagpole. Doctors and medics and even some female nurses were moving purposely about the compound, all busy about their work, even on that holiday. One of the medics pointed out the tents where the patients were, and Blair headed to the first of these. She would go through them all if she had to, looking for Gary.

In the tent the men were just finishing Christmas dinner. Along with C rations they'd had roast pork. Apparently one of the Filipino medics had gone hunting and returned with a Christmas present of a fat wild boar. Blair had thought merely to circulate quickly among the beds, then go to the next tent. But that plan turned out not to be so easy. These men were no different from those soldiers she'd met on the road or in passing through the village. The Americans wanted to talk about home, and it was deemed a particular treat to do so with a pretty American girl. Some tried to flirt with her, but none of the men were rude or off-putting in their attempts. Blair, used to such attention, might have even been a touch offended if they had ignored her.

For her part, she felt far more awkward with their wounds than with their wolf whistles and winks and appreciative grins. She could hardly look any of them in the eye, though neither could she look at their wounds if they showed above the bedcovers. She made a point to keep her eyes on their faces, unless their heads were bandaged or battered. Then she was in real trouble. Arms and legs in casts, bandages around heads were the least of it. Missing arms and legs bothered her the most. The sight of blood seeping through bandages sickened her, though she managed to keep down her Christmas dinner. At least she was actress enough to hide the repulsion she felt—cramming it behind a glib smile, a joke, or a bantering comment.

Until one of the nurses had the audacity to ask for her help.

"Could you give me a hand?" the woman asked mildly enough, as if any ambulatory person in the ward was fair game.

Blair would have felt foolish refusing.

"I've got to change this dressing," the nurse said. "Just lift the leg a bit so I can get it off."

The leg in question was really a stump below the patient's knee. Blair looked at the bloody bandage, then up at the nurse.

"Go ahead," the woman said. "It won't bite."

Easy for her to say; she'd probably seen countless such sights. Blair sucked in a shaky breath and, touching the stump with only her fingertips, lifted it about two inches from the bed.

"A little more," said the nurse.

Blair's head felt woozy, but she obeyed, swearing to herself she would never go near a hospital again, even if it meant never finding Gary. Then the nurse started unwrapping the old bandage. Blair's jaw dropped open, gaping more and more as the bandage came off. When the last strip fell off, her head was absolutely spinning. She'd never seen such an awful sight! Red, raw, bloody, with bits of pus clinging to slightly blackened areas. Then the limb twitched. It was the most grotesque thing Blair had ever seen. Her stomach heaved. Without a thought, she dropped the limb and raced from the tent.

Barely outside, she lost most of her dinner.

"You okay?" called a passing soldier.

She just glared at him, and the man had the good sense to mind his own business. Another wave of nausea hit her. It splattered on her shoes and clothes on its way to the ground. True, the shoes were only sneakers and the clothes were sturdy cotton, but now she was going to have to do laundry again. If this kept up, her hands were really going to be as leathery as that woman's at the pump. It occurred to her that worrying over laundry kept her mind off what had caused her to be sick in the first place, but that only made her think of it again. Her stomach roiled.

Ten minutes later she was sitting on the ground, leaning shakily against the side of the tent. She'd used the hem of her skirt to wipe away excess moisture from her lips but could still taste bile in her mouth. The nurse she had been helping came up to her.

"Here's some water so you can rinse out your mouth," she said. Blair took the glass, eyeing the woman, though there was little gratitude in her gaze. She did manage a brief assessment of the nurse, as if seeing her for the first time, and indeed, she had been far more focused on the horrible wound at the time to see anything else. The nurse was Blair's age, perhaps even younger. She was pretty, with dark hair. Her nose was a bit on the large side, emphasized by eyeglasses that had large black-rimmed frames.

Taking the water, Blair just grimaced at the nurse. She wasn't about to thank this person who had caused her such embarrassment. She did, however, use the water as suggested, then took a swallow, as well. It seemed her stomach was ready to accept it now.

The nurse hunkered down on the ground next to Blair. "I'm sorry for making you do that. I wasn't thinking. I thought that if you were there, you were ready to help."

Blair wanted to maintain her sour attitude; after all, the nurse did not deserve a quick reprieve. Yet the woman's apology was so sincere Blair found it difficult to browbeat her, especially when she knew she was mostly just angry at herself, at her own weakness.

The nurse grinned and said, "My name's Alice Wharton. I'm a Navy lieutenant."

"I'm Blair Hayes. I was mostly there to look for someone."

"Who's that?"

"My . . . Lieutenant Gary Hobart. He's in the 71st."

"Your boyfriend, I assume."

"Well, sort of. My fiancé, I guess . . ."

"Hmm . . . sounds complicated." Alice smiled, and all Blair's remaining ire toward the woman fell away. She even began to feel a kind of camaraderie toward the nurse that she seldom found with other women. "I've had about three fiancés since I arrived here," Alice went on. "The other girls say I'm fickle, but I don't know . . . I just don't want to make a mistake. Anyway, now I'm worried about all three."

"You don't know where they are?"

Alice shook her head. "One was on the *California* in Manila Bay. I think the ship got away okay. One is stationed on Mindanao Island.

And the other is fighting in the north, I think. I dread every new patient that comes in, fearing the face might be familiar. Oh, what am I saying? I dread them all, familiar or not. Goodness, I hate to see these fine men all shot up."

"Then why in heaven's name are you a nurse?"

"What else is there for a girl to do if she doesn't want to get married right away? I didn't want to teach school. I wanted to travel and have some adventure. Well, I'm getting adventure now, in spades!" She laughed, not bitterly at all, just a clear, good-natured laugh. "Nursing suits me, though."

"Obviously it doesn't suit me, not that I would ever have considered it, not in a million years!" She laughed, too, though her laughter did hold just a touch of bitterness, as she considered the choices she *had* made in life had not been much better. Then Blair realized her words might have been offensive to her companion. "I'm sorry. I didn't mean—"

"Never mind that," Alice said dismissively. "We do what we do, that's all. It was pretty brave of you coming here to look for your Gary, considering."

Blair felt ashamed, Alice calling *her* brave! This woman was in the middle of the war by choice, while Blair was doing what she could to run from it. Why, she couldn't even look a wounded man in the eye!

"Say," Alice continued, "what's your fella look like? I can keep an eye out for him." When Blair gave a description, the nurse whistled. "He sounds dreamy. No wonder you're looking for him."

They talked for a few more minutes, then Alice wiggled to her feet. "I have to get back to work."

"Thanks so much for stopping, Alice. Maybe someday I can help you with another bandage." Blair rose, too, though her knees were still a bit wobbly.

"Why don't you just stick to flitting around the wards, giving the boys a pretty face to take their minds off their misery. That's just as important, you know, as medicine and bandages."

"You are too generous. Well, at least I can finish my search. I have one more tent to check."

"Let's talk again later."

Blair and Alice went off in different directions. Blair had to put more resolve in her steps than she would have admitted to Alice in order to get to that last tent.

Once inside, a quick glance around told her the search would be as fruitless here as previously. But she thought of what Alice said and this time made a point of moving around the cots visiting with the men.

"Hey! I know you!" one of the men called from a couple of beds away. "You were one of the singers at the Casa Mañana, weren't you?"

"Yes, I was," Blair replied. "Not for very long, though, before the war started."

"I went there every night I could get leave just to hear you," the man said. "Mel, don't you remember her?" Another man nearby agreed.

Blair blushed a bit. It was nice to be remembered and in such a positive way. Yet what must these men think of her, knowing she had been a nightclub singer? She knew she told Gary and others it didn't have to be a sordid job, yet many believed it was anyway. Oddly, though, none of the men in the tent seemed to respond to her any differently.

"Could you sing something for us, Miss Hayes?" asked the first soldier, Steve.

Mel offered, "You sang the best rendition of 'Over the Rainbow' I ever heard. Sing that."

Blair, feeling as melancholy as she was already feeling that day, had no desire to sing that of all songs. She was longing for a better place too much to wish for the sad reminder of the song. She expected the men there were feeling the same way.

"I've got a better idea," she suggested with all the enthusiasm she could muster. "Why don't I sing some Christmas carols? You can join me if you want."

Blair knew quite a few carols. That had been another family tradition, gathering around the piano to sing on Christmas Eve. She or her mother would play the piano, though usually it was Blair at the keyboard after she'd had lessons and became more proficient than her mother.

After she sang "Joy to the World," Claudette and Mateo poked their heads into the tent. "Is everything all right?" she asked them.

"Sure," Claudette answered. "We just . . . thought we'd keep you company."

Blair grinned a welcome, though she felt a little bad she'd gone off and left them. She had mentioned she was going to the hospital again that day but had forgotten they might be feeling holiday blues as well and not want to be alone. Aside from that, pleasure welled up in her that they had sought *her* out for companionship. The idea choked her up just a little. To offset that she launched into a rousing chorus of "Jingle Bells." Then followed with "Away in a Manger," "What Child Is This?" and many others. Some she sang alone, and others she was accompanied by her audience.

Finally, one of the men requested "O Holy Night." It happened to be her favorite. They left her to solo on that one. And a cappella, as well. She wasn't sure she could pull off that more complicated song, but the first words were barely out of her mouth before she became so caught up in it that she forgot her uncertainty.

"O holy night, the stars are brightly shining, it is the night of the dear Savior's birth. . . ."

Somewhere in the distance, there were sounds of bombing. Of course, the Japanese did not celebrate Christmas. Bursts of ack-acks mingled with the explosions, a glaring reminder that war was only a short distance away.

"Long lay the world in sin and error pining, till He appeared and the soul felt its worth. . . ."

Blair's eyes roved over the faces surrounding her, and amazingly, she saw only faces, not blood, missing limbs, or other horrors. Only bright, rapt faces, filled with . . . was it hope? Was it peace? Though only God himself knew just how far away peace was.

"A thrill of hope the weary world rejoices, for yonder breaks a new and glorious morn."

She remembered hearing somewhere—probably during one of her visits to church with either Jackie or Gary—that peace was different for God than it was for men. With Him peace was not merely the absence of war; in fact, it wasn't even the opposite of war. God's peace went beyond that, something like peace in the midst of chaos, though she could not fully understand what that meant. But, oh, let it be so! If that were true, God, then surely anything was possible.

"Fall on your knees! Oh, hear the angel voices! O night divine! O night when Christ was born! O night divine!"

Claudette snaked an arm around Blair's waist, and Mateo drew near, as well. The men seemed to draw near with their eyes. As never before in her life Blair felt a strange kind of contentment. She would have been hard-pressed to explain it. Perhaps it was best that she didn't try. However, the word *peace* kept flitting across the edges of her mind. She couldn't quite grasp it, but she knew it was gift enough that at least some of its odd aftereffects showered over her.

18

Kuibyshev, Soviet Union

CAMERON EXITED the cable office and immediately tore open the missive in her hand.

BELIEVE BLAIR ALL RIGHT STOP JACKIE RECEIVED CABLE FROM HER YESTERDAY STOP BLAIR CANNOT LEAVE COUNTRY BECAUSE OF JAP BLOCKADE STOP WILL KEEP YOU INFORMED STOP LOVE MOTHER.

Cameron let out a breath as though she had been holding it since that first cable two weeks ago. In a way she had. Since then she had begun to feel her entire life was in suspension. She had not a drop of Russian blood in her, but often lately she felt steeped in Russian doom and gloom. All that had happened between her and Alex had in no way detracted from her worry over Blair. Both had been equal weights pulling her down. She had always been a cynic, but to be such a gloomy one was too much even for her.

She determined she was going to grasp her mother's words as an offer of hope. She needed that desperately right now.

Cameron went to the hotel common room, hoping even at that late hour of the evening to find someone to share her news with. Again she felt that "phantom" ache of not having Alex be that person. But he was gone in more ways than emotionally. He'd left for Moscow a week ago. He had not called her to say good-bye, though she didn't know why she would have expected that.

It was over between them.

And she wasn't going to turn into a maudlin, simpering female over it! She'd always guarded her independence carefully. Now she had it back, and she should celebrate. This was exactly why she had fended off romantic involvements in the first place and why she was going to guard herself even more closely in the future. Sure, Alex was a handsome, exciting man, but enough so for her to give up the sweet life she had carved for herself before he stumbled into it? No, and of that she was certain. She was too much her own woman to give a man like Alex the things she was certain he needed. He was probably far better suited to her sister Jackie, anyway. Hmm . . . maybe she should find a way to fix them up. They could babble together about religion until the cows came home.

Bitterness. That was worse than melancholy. What she wanted was indifference. Unfortunately, she could not even lie to herself that she was there yet.

In the common room she was pleased to find Shanahan seated at a table smoking one of his Lucky Strikes, the perennial glass of vodka before him.

"Cameron, sweetheart! Just in time to share a toast with me!" He had a grin on his face that reached into his eyes. It held only a touch of his usual sardonic light.

"What have you found to celebrate, Shanahan?" she asked.

"You haven't heard about the communiqué, then?"

She shook her head. Despite the encouraging word from home, she had managed to work herself back into a sour mood.

"Aw, out of sorts, doll?" How could a man as shallow as Johnny pick up so quickly on her mood? "Well, this should perk you up." He paused for effect, sucked in a draw on his cigarette, knowing the longer he took the more tormenting it would be for her. He seemed a little deflated when she didn't needle him with her usual curiosity. "It's just this: our friends at the Narkomindel are issuing us correspondents an all-expense paid vacation to—" he gave a verbal drumroll—"Moscow!" Arching a brow, he grinned.

It was momentous news, and so as not to drag him down to where she was, she forced a smile. "At last!" she said. "When?"

"Tomorrow morning."

"Don't you love it? For months we've been begging for such a trip and our requests have been mired in red tape—then voila! With only a few hours' notice, we are off." She slid into the chair opposite him. "Of course it is coincidentally just a day after the Russians claimed victory in the Battle of Moscow."

"Well, you should know by now they ain't gonna let us see an actual battle. But this should be interesting nonetheless. Moscow! It's actually like going home, though I hate to admit it." He jumped up. "Let me get you something to drink. Self-serve tonight."

"I'm okay."

Reseating himself, his brow creased. "You really okay?"

She was moved by the genuine concern in his tone. "I am. In fact, I just got some good news from home." She pushed the cable toward him. "My family heard from Blair, and she is okay."

Scanning the cable, he said, "That's great. Takes a load off you, I'm sure."

"Well, she is still trapped in the Philippines, and the situation there is not very encouraging." Goodness, she *was* becoming Russian! Finding the downside to every boon.

"She'll be okay. And when she gets out, you can write a book for her about all her adventures."

"Blair would like that. Something highly dramatic that could be turned into a screenplay." Cameron chuckled. "Hey, Shanahan, I am suddenly hungry. How about taking me to dinner?"

"Okay, doll, I'll take you out on the town. We'll paint this dreary iceberg red—ugh! On second thought, let's paint it any color *but* red!"

Laughing, they retrieved their coats, then linked arms and exited the hotel. Stroganoff's was the only café open at that late hour. Cameron hadn't been there since that night with Alex, and upon entering she felt a pricking in her chest. She made a quick, if not completely successful, attempt to brush aside the errant sensation. Alex was gone. She was with Johnny, just like old times. How often in the last week had she longed for old times? But she knew it would never be the same between her and Johnny. He was just a dear friend now, and she didn't feel she wanted to fall into his arms even on the rebound. She needed a friend now far more than a lover.

Seated at a tiny table in the corner of the nearly vacant restaurant, they leaned back in their chairs, settling in for a long meal. Russian service was notoriously slow, but Cameron was not in a hurry. Yes, they would have an early morning tomorrow and she would need to pack before that, but she did not care. For once, she just wanted a few hours to pretend life was good again.

They talked about trivial things for a while, and Cameron enjoyed it.

"Do you remember Donald Farr?" Johnny asked as their salad was served.

"Yes, of course. I broke the story on his shady dealings last year. That does seem ages ago." Donald Farr was the wealthy California industrialist whom she had exposed for dabbling in some questionable government contracts. Her articles had prompted a Senate hearing. But then Farr and his high-priced lawyers had managed to get him exonerated.

"He's back in the news," Johnny said.

"I hope they've finally locked him up."

"No, but Harry Landis thought you'd like to know. Told me to pass it on to you. Farr was just awarded a multimillion dollar arms contract."

"That's what I like to see—sniveling lowlifes getting their due," she grated sarcastically.

"There's bound to be a lot of his ilk profiting from this war. I guess in a way, so are we."

"It's hardly the same. At least we are honest about it. Aren't we?" A shadow of doubt gave her a twinge. Shouldn't she be fighting harder against Soviet censors? Had she grown complacent? She had not even felt guilty about Oleg Gorbenko in a long time.

"We try, anyway." He impaled a limp cucumber on his fork, examined it distastefully, then let it drop back into his dish. "I wonder if it would be hugely different as a U.S. Army correspondent. There'd still be censorship."

"Have you changed your mind about a transfer, then?"

"Censorship or no, I'd still rather be in a real war zone. But that ain't gonna happen. Your father wants me here. Landis wants me here. So here I stay."

Their dinner arrived, a chicken concoction the chef called Chicken Kiev. Cameron doubted any Kievian had ever seen the like, but it was popular with the American clientele.

"Shanahan, I have a confession to make," she said rather sheepishly. "I'm glad that transfer hasn't come through. It would be pretty dull around here without you."

"It couldn't get much duller, sweetheart." He speared a piece of tough chicken and studied it a moment before continuing. "I've had it up to here"—he tapped his chin with the back of his free hand—"with these Soviets, and I use the term *Soviets* pointedly instead of Russians. It might have been different if we'd been allowed to see some regular Russian citizens, not to mention a couple of important officials. If we'd been *allowed* to do anything!" He popped the chicken in his mouth and chewed.

"It has been frustrating, though we have had some incredible moments."

"Yeah, but only moments. I will say, though, it has been fun having you tagging after me, Hayes."

"I was never tagging after you!" she countered, but her tone lacked the usual acerbity such a comment would normally have prompted.

He smiled, and it was a good impression of his rakish, devilish smile. But Cameron knew John Shanahan was not the same man as the one she'd fallen for in Los Angeles. But then, neither was she the same woman.

As if reading her mind, he said, "When you showed up in Europe—was it really less than a year ago?" He shook his head. "Seems longer. Anyway, when I saw you in Rome, I wasn't certain you'd make it. You were such a kid."

"Thanks, Shanahan, for not saying that until now."

"Is this the first time I've said it? I must be slipping." Another grin appeared that could have melted snow and might even sear through her newly bolstered protective barrier.

"So do you think I'll make it now?" She supposed she would never stop needing his approbation.

"You've grown up—"

"*Aged*, I'd say."

"Naw, just matured. You've come into your own, as they say. And you have seasoned beautifully." Glancing away, he fiddled with his wineglass, obviously reluctant to continue. But he drew a breath and did so. "I respect you, Cameron—as a colleague and as an equal." For once, there was absolute sincerity in his tone.

Moisture sprang into Cameron's eyes as she realized just how much his words meant to her. She remembered painfully how she had failed to elicit such praise from her father, yet coming from Johnny, it meant nearly as much.

"Don't get all blubbery on me," he said quickly.

"I have never gotten blubbery in my life!" she protested with affront.

He laughed. "You're a rotten liar, sweetheart."

"Am I ever going to get you to quit calling me that?"

"Not as long as I can get a rise from you with it." Chuckling, he added, "It has been one of my dearest sources of entertainment here."

She had a strange sense, as they both seemed to speak in the past tense, that they were ending a phase. In a way, since the Japanese attack on Pearl Harbor, the whole world was ending a phase and beginning a new one, though none could guess what that new road would hold.

Unable to resist the gesture, she reached across the table and took his hand in hers. "You sound like you're going to leave after all."

"Just practicing. But I'll confess something to you now. I have a feeling one of my greatest regrets in life will be letting you get away."

He was serious. She thought of all he'd meant to her and knew she might regret it, too. But she realized anew that there was no going back. She said nothing, too moved to speak.

"You gotta patch things up with the doc, Hayes. You and he really had something."

That might well have been his most shocking remark of the evening. Her eyes bulged with surprise, but when her balance returned, she shook her head.

"No," she said, "there's not a chance for us anymore. We just had too many differences."

"Opposites attract, you know."

No matter how hard she tried, she couldn't hide her regret on that front, but still she shook her head again.

"What'd you two fight about, anyway?" Shanahan asked. She'd told him about her and Alex, briefly and casually, a few days ago when he had wondered why the doctor hadn't been around lately. Funny that he hadn't probed her for reasons then. She wished he hadn't done so now because she wasn't certain what to say.

"Well, he . . . that is, I—he was . . ." Her voice trailed away. What had it been all about? She wrinkled her nose. "I don't know . . . I mean, it sounds silly when I try to put it into words."

"That's the way most lovers' spats are," he said with that superior air of his.

"It was serious, Johnny."

"More so than the good that was between you?"

"I was scared," she admitted.

"So was he, I'll wager."

She stared at him, nodding with wonder.

"Look, Cameron, no one can blame you for being scared. This is all new to you, isn't it? I mean, how many experiences have you had with men? First your old man—that'd confuse anyone. Then you had me, a no-account cad. No wonder a relationship with a decent guy like the doc sets you on edge. What you have to realize is you're good enough for him. What am I saying? You're more than good enough. You're the best thing that ever happened to that man. No kidding!"

"Goodness!" she said, swallowing back a lump in her throat. "I don't know what to think." She especially didn't want to think about the spark of hope Johnny's words threatened to ignite in her. What if there was something left to be salvaged between her and Alex?

The risk of being wrong, however, seemed much too great. Wasn't it? She didn't know if she could open herself up to it again.

Letting her lip curl up into a sly smile, she said, "I forgot you are a consummate liar, Shanahan."

"I'm crushed!" He gave a mock expression of great chagrin. "Well, to prove you wrong, I didn't lie about taking you out on this poor excuse for a town. So let's get outta here."

"You mean this greasy-spoon café isn't going to be the extent of it?"

He grinned that old grin of his. "I know where there's some dancing." He sprang to his feet and grabbed her hand. "Come on."

Dancing on a grim Russian winter night? Maybe there was some hope after all.

19

CAMERON HAD BEEN on some miserable rides since the war began, but she was certain none could equal the one she took the next morning in a Soviet-made DC-3. The takeoff was from an icy, windy runway. Snow leaked into the cabin from a shabbily constructed gun turret, as did the cold and the wind. The only heat on the plane was generated from a couple bottles of vodka being passed among the thirteen passengers, most of whom were journalists.

"Get out of my way!" gasped Levinson as he lurched toward the pot in the stern of the aircraft. He left most of his stomach contents behind before resuming his seat on the hard bench where the others huddled together, mostly for warmth but also for that camaraderie evoked by mutual misery.

Cameron felt frozen to that bench. The cold was so bad she had stopped shivering long since and was simply paralyzed, except for her mouth, which insisted on trembling fiercely. The icy chill penetrated her clothes and the piles of wool blankets heaped over all the passengers. She felt as if her very bones were frozen. The others were in little better condition. No one moved except for regular trips to the pot to expel stomach contents, generated by the incessant turbulence.

"My ticket on this iceberg cost way too much!" groaned Shanahan. Even he, whom Cameron thought could take any physical abuse, was green around the gills.

"Ticket?" queried their NKVD agent with a cocked brow. He and his cohort were the only ones on the plane who appeared unscathed by the flight. But then, Soviet secret police were barely human. "There was no charge for the flight," he deadpanned, and Cameron could detect little mockery in his tone.

Shanahan gave the man a sour look as he lifted the bottle of vodka to his lips.

"H-how m-much l-longer?" Cameron asked, completely unable to control the chattering of her teeth.

"Only three or so more hours," said the agent. Was that a barely concealed grin on his thin, taut lips? Certainly there was an evil gleam in the man's eyes.

Everyone groaned and passed the bottle once again.

The five-hour flight from Kuibyshev to Moscow pushed through endless foul weather. Near Moscow, visibility dropped with the temperature. Cameron clamped her eyes shut as the plane circled for a landing. Only once did she venture to open them, and that proved a major mistake. The plane had dropped below the thick clouds and fog and was skimming treetops, appearing to be hurtling itself toward the buildings of Moscow's suburbs.

It did nothing for the passengers' plummeting sense of well-being when one of the crew members came into the passenger cabin and climbed on a crate so as to watch through the gun turret for enemy aircraft. Cameron thought it might have been a blessing to get shot down rather than simply crashing ingloriously into a chimney or one of the trains moving beneath them.

Miraculously, they landed in one piece, but Cameron knew it would take a couple of days for her body to recover from the abuse of that ride. Aside from that, she was thrilled to be back in the capital and surprised by the crowds of pedestrians in the streets. Half the city's population had been evacuated, but many had remained for its defense. A jubilant mood greeted her. These people had faced a city's worst fear—an enemy driving upon them who had swept through most of Europe and half of Russia unbeaten. But these Muscovites had stopped the enemy, literally within miles of their city. Victory was theirs.

Pabyeda! The Russian cry of victory was bandied about freely in these exuberant days.

Otherwise the city seemed little changed from when she had left it over two months ago. She heard the Bolshoi Theater had been bombed, and she was certain there had been many other casualties, both brick and mortar and human, but it was still Moscow. Red

Square and the Kremlin stood proudly, unscathed.

After only a day to settle back into the Metropole Hotel and thaw out, the group of intrepid journalists were herded into stout Russian ZIS-101 vehicles, which were far more comfortable than the M-1s they had used for the last trip to the Front and were more like limousines in appearance. Their destination was Kashira, about a hundred miles south of Moscow. The outward trip took two days, and Cameron experienced firsthand what the Germans must have endured in their advance on Moscow.

Late that first afternoon, one of the vehicles in their convoy bounded off the road into a snowbank, much like many abandoned vehicles she'd seen that day—often with swastikas, but not a few with red stars painted on their doors, as well. While the Russian drivers held a confab about how to remedy the situation, Nikolai Palgunov trundled all the journalists up the snow-covered bank, followed by a short hike to a small log building, or *izba*, as the Russians called it, on the edge of a tiny village nearly hidden from view. Amazingly, this village appeared untouched by the war, unlike other villages and towns they had passed that had been almost entirely burned to the ground.

As if the Russian press chief were some kind of magician, the building turned out to be a restaurant! Cameron wondered when was the last time this place in the middle of a war zone had entertained customers. But a decent meal was eked out nonetheless. Hot borsch, followed by a potato and meatball concoction and thick slabs of brown bread, with hot tea to warm up their frozen bodies. And, of course, Palgunov also managed to produce bottles of liquor from what seemed to be his never-ending supply.

Cameron would have been content to spend the night in that cozy house, now that she had a full belly and warm feet. But Palgunov was intent on reaching Kashira that night.

Jed Donovan was of Cameron's mind. "There are enough beds in this house to accommodate us for the night," he suggested.

"I don't mind the floor," Shanahan said.

"We are on a schedule," insisted Palgunov.

Everyone burst out laughing at that. When was a schedule *ever* kept in Russia?

"There is a back road lined with telegraph poles that we can easily follow," said the press chief firmly. "Those who were in the disabled car will divide among the other cars. We will be to our destination in no time."

Two things about that statement worried Cameron. "Back road" sounded risky. Even main roads in Russia were substandard. But worse was the phrase "in no time." She knew they were in for a long night.

Picking their way from telegraph pole to telegraph pole with their vehicle headlights might have worked even as darkness fell had not the weather turned on them. In a matter of minutes after they set out, snow and wind began to cascade from the heavens. Visibility fell to zero, and the headlights were worthless.

Cameron imagined the invading Germans, and no doubt Russians, too, had been mired in such weather during the Battle of Moscow, with blizzards pounding them, rendering even tanks all but worthless. She could picture men plowing through a snowstorm, fingers nearly frozen around the triggers of rifles made useless by the cold. Others talked of the problems of fielding equipment in snowbanks and blizzards, but Cameron could not shake the image of *men* from her mind. Rumor had it that German soldiers had but one winter coat between a half dozen soldiers. Hitler apparently had ordered shipments of weapons and ammunition to take precedence over clothing for his army.

Cameron was not surprised when another of their vehicles slid off the icy road. The driver churned up half the bank before giving up the effort to extract his car.

It seemed they were all alone in the whole world. Only snow swirled around them, with darkness clinging as if it, too, wanted companionship. Where only a few days before a battle had raged, now there seemed to be a vast emptiness. As they resigned themselves to spending the night in the cars, darkness closed in on them as never before.

Wolves howled in the distance.

"I remember interviewing a Montana rancher once," said Ed Reed of the *Chicago Daily News*. He was crammed into one of the cars with Cameron, Shanahan, Levinson, Barton, Palgunov, an NKVD guard, and the driver. "He told me he'd been stranded once on a mountainside with a broken leg. He made a campfire, and in the night a pack of wolves came down the mountain, but they stopped just outside the glow of his fire. There were five of them, and they hunkered down not a stone's throw from the rancher and stayed there all night. He kept the fire going as if his life depended upon it, but an hour or so before sunrise he ran out of wood. He was so tired and weak that before the fire died out, he dropped off to sleep. When he woke, it was daylight, the fire was dead—and the wolves were gone. They never came near him!"

"Come on, Ed," laughed Shanahan, "surely you can come up with a better ghost story than that!"

Levinson tried to peer out the frosty car window. "Well, wolves can't tear through steel. We're safe in here. Aren't we?"

"I'm more worried about freezing to death," Cameron said, "than of wolves." The snow had stopped falling, but the temperature hadn't.

"We can remedy that by pooling our collective body heat," smirked Shanahan with a suggestive lift of his brow.

Cameron punched him in the shoulder. "I'll take my chances with the blizzard first rather than with you human wolves."

Palgunov tried to bolster spirits with a box of chocolates and more of his liquor supply. Still, the men couldn't resist the opportunity to regale their companions with more spooky stories. But Cameron thought what must have taken place in the surrounding countryside in the previous days had to have been far more harrowing than any stories they could conjure up. They might be stranded, but at least they didn't have to worry about an attack on top of it—well, not much, at least. Palgunov did mention casually that there were still frequent reports of Germans lost behind the lines who still had a taste for drawing blood. If the press chief was admitting anything, it must truly be a danger.

In the morning a Red Army truck came along and pulled out their stranded vehicle, and they continued on their way.

The reality of the horrors Cameron had only imagined the night before greeted them vividly in the cold, pale light of day. In one field lay hundreds of mired panzers, a pathetic remnant of the mighty German war machine. Smaller snow-covered mounds were scattered among the tanks, and despite all her imaginings, it was still a shock to realize those mounds were the frozen bodies of the panzer crews who had not been able to escape the blizzard that had trapped them. "General Winter," as it was called by both the Germans and Russians, had stopped this division as effectively as any human general's battle strategy.

More frozen bodies along the way gave the effect of a wax museum. Some of these men—yes, *men*, she reminded herself grimly—were draped over stalled vehicles, almost as if just resting from the rigors of war. Others nearly gave the illusion of being in the midst of some action. It appeared that even at the very end they had retained a hope to fight on.

Cameron's stomach churned. A breakfast of more chocolates and lukewarm strong tea from a thermos had not set well. But she gripped the door handle and stilled herself to tough it out. From the looks on some of the men's faces in the car, they were in no better shape than she.

Several figures suddenly loomed up in the road ahead. Cameron could barely make them out through the half-circle etched in the icy windshield by the wipers. For a moment her heart boomed an extra beat. They might be German stragglers. But as they came closer, she saw there were children in the group.

The driver would have sped—or rather crawled—past them, but Cameron tried to intercede. "Wait!" she said.

"No. No. We must go on," Palgunov said.

"Come on, Nikki," Shanahan said. No one ever called the press chief Nikki to his face, though all the reporters used the name in private. Palgunov was too shocked at this breech of protocol to respond, and Johnny went on quickly. "They might have some good stories for us, and you know very well nothing will get printed that you don't approve of anyway."

Everyone clamored so loudly the man finally relented. He did indeed know he had complete control. The ZIS pulled over, the driver honking his horn to alert the pedestrians.

Cameron was the first one to bound from the vehicle. There were about ten people in the group; several were children. A teenaged boy was pulling a sled loaded with household goods. Two toddlers sat on top of the bundles in the sled. There were also three women and a bent old man with the group. With shock, Cameron saw one of the women was barefoot, while the other two and the man had little better covering their feet. All were clothed shabbily with several layers, as if they wore every item of clothing they owned.

Cameron called to their interpreter, who also was the driver of one of their vehicles, and asked him to introduce her to the refugees, for indeed, they could not be anything else.

"We are returning to our village," said one of the women, a pretty, buxom gal of about thirty, whose rosy cheeks and nose looked becoming on her broad Slavic face. Cameron realized the "roses" had to be because the poor thing was freezing. "We've been told the Fascists are gone now."

"When the Germans came, they made us leave our homes," put in the thin barefoot woman who looked to be fifty. Her rosy cheeks merely emphasized her sunken, weary eyes. "We escaped to the forest and hid there until we learned it was safe to return. My six-month-old baby died there." Cameron realized the woman must be a lot younger than fifty.

"They wanted to know if we were Communists," said the buxom woman. "I think they would have killed us if we had been Party members."

"Those miserable Fascists told us Moscow had fallen," the old man interjected. Spitting into the snow, he added, "Liars!"

A defeatist lethargy mixed so incongruously with defiance in the three speakers that Cameron's head spun. That they had been beaten down was obvious. Cameron's vivid imagination could not even begin to picture what hardships they had suffered while trying to exist in the forest with little food and no warm clothes and a battle raging around them. Yet they were now trudging back to their homes, or what was left of them. She had no doubt they would rebuild, that they would fight again if the tide turned in the war.

Cameron wanted to take them all into the warmth and comfort of the cars, but even if she had offered and Palgunov had allowed it, she knew they would not come. They belonged in their village.

Near their destination the convoy of journalists stopped at another log house, the headquarters of General Ragozin. The general was not there, but the officers present welcomed the foreigners.

Another fine meal was laid out for them, and afterward several of the officers, their tongues loosened by rich food and Palgunov's special "stash," talked freely of the war. It helped that the press chief had fallen dead asleep in one of the soft chairs and that one of the officers spoke passable English, thus eliminating the need for the NKVD interpreter.

"Some say General Winter stopped the Fascist barbarians. I say, fah!" boasted Colonel Barsak, a tank commander. A broad face, creased and dark with small sharp eyes, and his stout muscular frame made him look something like the vehicles he commanded. "It was the mighty T-34 that won us victory." The English-speaking lieutenant translated.

"That's the new tank you Ruskies just developed, isn't it?" asked Donovan.

"A marvel of modern invention! We made—how is it you Americans say?—mincemeat out of the German panzers. Our seventy-six millimeter guns could cripple a panzer with one shot." He grinned, showing teeth and hardened mirth. Cameron wondered how many he had destroyed in that way. Probably hundreds.

"What do your T-34s have that the panzers don't?" Cameron asked.

"First, sloping armor that makes German shells slide off it, like my hand slides through my wife's silk curls." Another grin, a bit softer this time. "And then, a wider track. We can climb a slope faster than the panzers can turn a turret. We run circles around them. Ha! Those arrogant panzer divisions finally met their match."

"Tell them about the telephone call," said one of the officers.

Barsak smiled rather dreamily, as if a pleasant memory had been evoked. Then he shook his head. "No, they will not believe it."

"We'll believe anything these days," encouraged Shanahan.

Hesitating only a moment longer, Barsak went on. "Okay, but remember this is the truth, because it happened to me personally. It was during the worst of the battle in November. I was at headquarters to receive orders from General Ragozin. He was busy and his clerk was busy, so I picked up the telephone when it rang. A voice said, 'Stalin here. Are you holding?' Then of course I recognized the voice, though I'd only heard it giving speeches on the radio. I have faced divisions of panzers with a steadier hand! I nearly dropped the receiver." Barsak chuckled, slightly embarrassed, slightly amused at his humor. " 'Yes, Comrade Stalin, we are holding,' I said, and my voice did not falter at all, I am proud to say. 'Who am I speaking to?' he asked. 'I am Colonel Vassily Barsak, Comrade Stalin.' He said, 'Good, Colonel. Keep holding on. Russia is behind you. I am behind you.' Then he cut off. I have heard he made other calls like this. And we did hang on, because we knew our Little Father was still in Moscow."

Shanahan whistled, impressed. He was not alone. Cameron knew Stalin to be a brutal, ruthless man. Yet the man also knew how to be the Little Father to his people. It was impressive.

A renewed storm forced them to turn back after leaving General Ragozin's headquarters. After another night on the road, they arrived back in Moscow by the next afternoon.

NOT SINCE THE INVASION *of the Mongol Hordes in the thirteenth century has the landscape of Russia been so devastated by war,* Cameron wrote of her visit to the Front. *The retreating Wehrmacht left little in their wake. The razing of towns and villages was accompanied by robbing and looting. Thousands of civilians were left homeless in the dead of winter, with few possessions and little food. This reporter entered one burned-out village and with her own eyes saw a gallows from which hung the bodies of several Russian partisans, left to freeze in the biting wind. This was Nazi justice for a conquered land. In the past the Russians have hated their German enemy, but now this reporter senses that hatred has penetrated to a depth that is frightening to observe. It has the effect now to raise the nationalistic spirit of the Russian people to a frenzied pitch. One can only wonder what will be the plight of the enemy should the Red Army ever cross the Danube.*

Cameron lifted her fingers from the keys of her Underwood. What a way to spend Christmas! But it had been by choice. She had made an appearance at an embassy Christmas party given by the few that still manned the Moscow American embassy. But feeling out of sorts with the holiday mood, she had made excuses and left long before it ended. It seemed far more apropos that she spend the supposedly joyous holiday seated before her typewriter.

But were there not happy stories to tell? Earlier in the day she'd visited a couple of hospitals, ostensibly to search for some such stories—good human interest stuff her readers would want to hear during the holidays. She'd avoided thus far seeking out Alex but wasn't surprised when her steps led her to his hospital. She learned he was no longer there. He'd been commissioned in the Army and was somewhere on assignment. The news shocked her, worried her, and relieved her all at once. Mostly, though, she was just fearful for him. The fool man! Hadn't he been doing enough already, working day and night in this hospital patching up the wounded? No. He just wouldn't be satisfied unless he was at the Front.

Surely she had not had anything to do with that decision. Nevertheless, with a sick feeling in her stomach, she had tried to distract herself by going to the children's ward of the hospital. Not the best path to take when one needed cheering. Surprisingly, it was not as depressing as she would have thought it might be to spend a Christmas afternoon with sick children.

She arrived in time to catch a small holiday program the hospital staff was presenting to their young patients. A tree had been installed in the corner, though no one called it a *Christmas* tree. In fact, the whole event was instead referred to as a Winter Festival. This was a state hospital, after all, and despite the broadening of religious freedom, many still held to old Communist forms.

Father Christmas even made an appearance. They called him Father Winter, but he looked every bit like the Santa Claus Cameron had grown up with. Fancy red velvet coat, high black boots, and even a long white beard marked the man for what he was. He wasn't fat—few in Russia were these days—but he was as jolly as any St. Nick Cameron had ever seen. And patriotic, too. A proper Party man he was!

Laughing, he told the children stories of the heroism of his partisans—his version of elves, Cameron supposed—and of his merry band of guerrillas who found time to make presents for the children even while killing Fascists and making Russia safe. Even Cameron laughed when he began capering around the tree, more like Bacchus than St. Nick, singing rousing military ditties and reciting propaganda slogans Cameron had seen on posters plastered on walls in the city.

Each child was given a ribbon with a likeness of Stalin and the word *Pabyeda!* down its length that they could pin to their hospital gowns. They seemed thrilled with the present, but Cameron was still glad she had thought to bring a bag of candy she had purchased at the foreign commissary. If they were thrilled with a likeness of their Little Father, they were ecstatic with the candy. It made Cameron feel good, really good.

Shortly before the new year, Cameron had a visit that truly bolstered her spirits. Sophia came to see her. The moment she saw her friend's face, she threw her arms around the girl as if she were another sister.

"Come in. I can't believe this! I would have called you, but I thought you were in the Army. Let me take your coat. Sit down. Do you want some tea?" Cameron was babbling, even bubbling a bit, she supposed.

Just seeing Sophia Gorbenko, that she was alive and well, was good enough. But truth be told, Cameron was growing tired of the company of men. She had never in her life had many women friends and was realizing suddenly how very valuable they were. Before Cameron and Sophia had parted two months ago—Sophia to join a women's battalion as a sort of penance for the Oleg escape attempt and Cameron because of the evacuation—a friendship had been on the verge of developing, though spoiled somewhat by the troubles with Oleg. Perhaps Cameron was assuming too much now, but her need for a friend was so great she wanted to hope it was so.

Sophia laid her coat, hat, and gloves on the bed, then sat at the end of the sofa. "I would love some tea."

Cameron filled a kettle from the bathroom and set it on the hot plate on the sitting room table—of course, the sitting room was just a corner of the larger area that held a desk, bed, sofa, lamp tables, and such, but it was palatial compared to the room in Kuibyshev.

"Can you believe I went off and left my old hot plate and kettle in Kuibyshev? I had a time finding replacements here."

Sophia laughed, as she, too, must have remembered the shopping excursion they had taken together to find a hot plate shortly after she had been assigned as Cameron's interpreter. It had been more like a treasure hunt.

"It is so good to see you, Miss Hayes. You have been here a week, I heard. I have only been back a few days myself."

"Will you be here long?" Cameron asked, barely able to restrain the hopefulness in her voice.

"As long as you need me—or, I suppose, as long as I am permitted by the Narkomindel." Sophia allowed herself a wry smile.

Though it had been a short time since they had last seen each other, Cameron was certain her young friend looked years older in her eyes. They held a depth of experience that had not been there before.

"Then you will be working for me again? I didn't want to hope. Perhaps they will let you return to Kuibyshev with me." Cameron was suddenly choked up, and her lip trembled slightly, but she bit it hard as she took the steaming kettle from the hot plate and filled a teapot with the boiling water.

"There is a desperate need for interpreters and less of a need for me in the field now," Sophia said as Cameron brought the pot and cups to the table in front of the sofa. "Though I am happy to be home again, I would be also happy to accompany you when you return to Kuibyshev."

"Is your family well?" Cameron asked after seating herself on the sofa next to her guest. "I saw your father once in Kuibyshev, and he gave me a brief report." She restrained herself from asking the other question haunting her thoughts. Sophia might have news of Alex, since he was a close family friend. Yet to ask would only open the issue of their failed relationship, and she was not ready to discuss that.

"Nothing has changed very much," Sophia responded. "I thank God my brother and sister have not been harmed in the war. I have not seen Oleg."

It might well be that all was status quo with Sophia's family, but the more she spoke, the more convinced Cameron became that Sophia was not the same person.

"Was it bad for you, Sophia, in the Women's Brigade?"

"No more than it was for our brave boys." There was now a poise in her speaking that had not been present before. She no longer wore the look of a nervous puppy dog. "I am embarrassed to say that I had never before done a great deal of manual labor. For that reason alone, I thought I might break during those first days. We were put to work digging trenches around the city. I have heard the women ended up digging at least a hundred miles of trenches!" She said it proudly.

Almost without thinking, Cameron grasped the young woman's hands. Yes, they had seen much hard labor. Dotted with blisters, some barely turned to calluses, they were dry and still reddened from the abuse they had taken. Nothing at all was left of the fragile pale hands that had typed copies of articles for Cameron and answered her phone.

"Oh, Sophia!" She cradled the hands in hers. "Tell me about it."

Sophia's eyes misted over, revealing there was still some of the little child left that Cameron remembered. She suddenly was reminded of the peasants she had met on the trip to Kashira and the strange mix of defiance and vulnerability in them. It wasn't really as if they were evolving from weakness to strength or the other way around even. In some peculiar way, they were possessed at the same time by both. Frailty, vulnerability, pluck, courage, and defiance mixed within each of them, as it was with Sophia. They looked as if they might crumble at a mere touch—or carry the world on their shoulders.

"Will you write about it?" Sophia asked.

"Do you want me to?"

"I think so. I know it will never pass the censors, but perhaps one day the story of the bravery I witnessed will be told. It should be. I was not brave myself. I was scared all the time. We worked always beneath the threat of attack by air and many times were strafed. Once in such a strafing, ten women I was working with were killed or wounded. Though I was spared, we all lived daily in fear of such attacks. Let me tell you about Aniya. . . ."

For the next hour Sophia poured out the tale of her work on the front lines of the Battle of Moscow. She made no protest when Cameron grabbed a pad and pencil and jotted down notes. It might never reach publication, but it was an account worthy of saving in some way.

Finally, her cheeks moist with freely shed tears, Sophia took a breath and came to an end—she had spent enough emotion for the time and needed a rest. "Cameron," she breathed, "we saved Moscow, but the cost was very heavy!"

Cameron almost smiled when Sophia finally used her given name. How many times in the past had she tried to get her to do so? Yet now it just seemed natural. No longer was there any sense of an employer-employee relationship between Cameron and Sophia. In fact, Cameron had an odd sense that Sophia could easily become the mentor in the relationship, the protector. She certainly projected an emotional balance that Cameron seriously lacked at the moment. Yes, Cameron was able to acknowledge her own basic inner shortcomings. Oh, she was still going to deny it publicly, but within herself there would always be a part of her that would know the steel in her was not impervious. It could bend. Perhaps it could break.

She could very well learn much from Sophia.

It was this sense of closeness she felt toward the young woman and the sense of her own frailty that enabled her to ask the question she had told herself she wouldn't.

"Sophia, have you . . . heard from Alex?"

"I hoped it wasn't true, what my father told me, that you and Alex had parted company."

"It is true. I saw him last in Kuibyshev a couple weeks ago." She could hardly speak without choking up. It was so hard to admit, especially when she had come to fear their problems had been all her fault. "I tried to see him at the hospital here, and that's when I learned he was in the Army. What was he thinking? The crazy dope!"

Sophia's lips curved into a sympathetic smile. "The war makes us all do crazy things, I suppose."

"Does it ever! Like falling in love."

"Then you do love each other?"

Cameron shrugged, then gave a noncommittal answer. "What does it matter? We had too many differences. It couldn't have worked."

Sophia nodded with just a hint of wizened superiority. She knew everything, no doubt, but had the grace not to browbeat Cameron with it.

"That is too bad. You seemed so right together."

"Do you have any idea where he is?" Cameron asked, despising herself for her curiosity but feeling she couldn't help it.

"I am sorry, I do not." She truly did seem upset that she had no information, but then, as if to make up for that, she added, "But I am sure he will write to my father. When he does, I will tell you."

"No . . . a clean break . . . that's what is best." Her tone held not a particle of resolve.

"What happened between you, Cameron? If I may ask?"

"Like I said—"

"What differences?"

The girl must know the answer to her question, but she was trying to be delicate about it.

"Okay, it was religion. There! Are you happy?" Cameron stopped with a gasp at her harsh tone. Sophia was in no way deserving of such, even if she held the same faith as Alex. "I'm sorry, Sophia. There's no call to lash out at you."

"No, but I can understand. Alex and I share the same faith in God."

"Do you want more tea?" Nervously Cameron jumped up, even after Sophia declined. Grabbing the pot, she took it to the kettle, refilled it with the still hot water, and brought it back to the table. She made no move to replenish her own cup when she returned to her seat. She had no interest in tea. With a bitter laugh, Cameron said, "I have heard God has a sense of humor. He must have split a rib when he put Alex and me together. At first we were on quite equal footing, both ambivalent, or at least cynical, about God. Then, just as I was able to make a commitment of love to Alex—and Sophia, it was not an easy thing for me to make myself so . . . so . . ."

"Vulnerable, Cameron?"

"Yes! What a fool I was. And how much more of a fool I felt when Alex suddenly *got religion*, spoiling it all."

"So this rift between you all stems from your differences about faith?"

"I don't know . . . I guess that's what it came down to. He felt he had to choose between me and God. Well, some slim chance I have against the Almighty!" Pausing, she sucked in a steadying breath, shocked at her openness, shocked at the ire welling up in her. She'd thought she'd gotten over that. Threading her fingers through her hair, she cast an imploring gaze at her friend. No doubt about it, now Sophia was indeed the mentor. "I don't really understand it, Sophia. You and I are friends—I feel it now more than ever before. Yet I don't hear you saying you must choose between me and God."

"I don't feel the need."

"What's that supposed to mean?"

"I do not believe God expects that of me—"

"Oh? But He might one day, eh?" Cameron said sharply. "In that case, I don't want your friendship. Not if it is conditional." Sophia's wide eyes grew even more so, filled now with hurt and self-blame. "Sophia, I am sorry!" Cameron relented, grasping her friend's hard, rough hands.

"I will not stop being your friend," Sophia replied with such assurance it somewhat eased Cameron's heart. "God will not make me do that, I am sure."

"But why did he make Alex do it?"

"All I can think is that there is something far deeper between a man and a woman who wish a committed relationship and are building toward marriage, as I expect you and Alex were. 'One mind, one spirit, one flesh.' Those are the words Oleg and I spoke in our marriage vows. Two are made one, Cameron. Can you really be so when his deepest desire is to please God and yours is . . . different?"

Ignoring the little hesitation in Sophia's words, Cameron shook her head.

Like a lost little girl, Cameron asked, "Do you think he stopped loving me?"

"I don't think so. I think the sacrifice of choosing God over you must ache like an open wound to a man like Alex."

"Oh!" Tears erupted from Cameron's eyes, tears of pity for Alex, of all things. But she very nearly did feel his pain. Indeed, she *did* feel it.

Sophia gathered Cameron into her arms. Cameron remembered when Sophia had comforted her weeping husband in much the same way—he a dark, sinewy storm cloud. Cameron felt much like how he must have felt then. The delicate flower consoling a veritable horse. A strong flower, a pitiful horse!

Finally, when Cameron's tears were spent, Sophia asked softly, "Have you considered what you will do about your faith, Cameron?"

"I can't do anything. I can't lose control of myself like that. If I did, I fear I'd die inside. Crack like a too ripe melon." She refused to see the incongruity of her words as she wept in a frail girl's arms.

With neither rebuke nor irony, her tone as soft as the brush of a flower's petal, Sophia murmured, "You are crumbling just a little now, aren't you?"

Cameron gaped at the younger woman. A harsh response rose, but before it reached her lips, she found herself nodding. "That's what God wants, isn't it? He wants to break me."

"No, Cameron. God is not like that. He heals and restores. The Great Physician He is, not the Great Breaker. If you break, it is because you choose to."

"I'm more confused than ever, Sophia!"

"Good! That, I don't think God minds, as long as your confusion leads you to work things out. That's all you can do, anyway. Find answers to your questions, your confusion."

"Alex wanted me to do that."

"That is where you are at your best, Cameron. Searching, asking questions. Getting answers."

"Well, I'll think about it, then."

"Exactly!"

Sophia gave Cameron another hug, then insisted that they not waste the rest of the tea. She poured them both another cup.

PART III

"The newspapers give so much space to the great crusade to rescue England that they have little left for events in other quarters. Thus there is not much in them about the doings of the Jap infidels in the Far East, though there is good reason to suspect that something unpleasant is afoot there."

H. L. MENCKEN
January 1941

21

January 1942
Bataan, the Philippine Islands

THE YEAR 1941 passed away with little fanfare. Blair hoped 1942 would be a better year.

The withdrawal of the American and Filipino forces into Bataan continued now in earnest. Bombings by the Japanese had been stepped up, and the northernmost areas of Bataan seemed a particular target in an attempt to cut off retreating troops. A village not far from Hermosa had been completely destroyed. Many residents of Hermosa had taken that as a sign to evacuate. The field hospital was also ordered to move south.

"You're welcome to join us," Alice told Blair.

"I don't want to abandon my car," Blair told the nurse. "It should be fixed soon. I've got to wait for it."

Blair knew that wasn't the entire reason for her reluctance to move. In the last few days she had known a small respite in the little village and a contentment in the lazy existence the place had offered. She was enjoying the meals with the Padillas and the gossip sessions at the village pump, where Blair was learning to speak a little Tagalog as well as do her laundry. Then there were her visits to the hospital, singing to the men, writing letters home for them—even if they could not be mailed, the act of doing so was a comfort to them. She also helped with other nonthreatening jobs like serving meals and cutting hair, a task she only just discovered she had a small talent for. Alice was careful to protect her from anything more harrowing than that.

No wonder she had not spent much time nagging Pedro about his slow service. She was certain the DeSoto could have been done days ago if she had pressured him. But the foremost reason for her tarrying was that, in the back of her mind, she hoped somehow word of her presence in Hermosa would get around—everyone talked about the efficiency of the "bamboo telegraph." Maybe it would finally reach Gary that she was there and he would come to her.

But as in the past, it was the war that finally decided her fate.

Shortly after the new year, the bombs came so close to the village that the Padillas and most of the others who had remained decided to make good on their talk of evacuation. Blair found it hard to bid these people good-bye, but the evacuation also spurred Pedro into action, and within hours of the others' departure, he had the DeSoto done.

"You have no more troubles with this car now, miss," he assured.

As Blair paid him, she asked, "Are you leaving, too?"

He jerked his head toward the garage where a beat-up old truck sat piled with household goods and several children. His wife, a dull-eyed, plain-looking woman, was seated in the front seat. For some reason Blair was surprised the lazy mechanic had such a huge family. "We are leaving this minute. You must leave, too, miss."

"Yes, as soon as we get packed up."

But since it was already noon, she decided it wouldn't hurt to have a final meal in the Padilla house, even if the place was empty and rather lonely with the family gone.

"We will go soon, Miss Hayes?" Mateo asked, a slight urgency to his voice.

"Yes, Miss Blair," put in Claudette, "we don't want to stay in a deserted village."

In her present mood Blair grated more than usual at their use of *miss*. It had always irritated her to no end, making her feel old and horribly responsible. But she knew they were anxious now, so she held her tongue. Instead she assured, "I know. We'll go as soon as we eat and pack." Her response held impatience, she knew. They must realize it wasn't entirely directed at them.

After they finished their lunch, she and Claudette cleaned up the dishes while Mateo loaded up the DeSoto.

"Miss Hayes! Come quick!" yelled Mateo from outside.

Blair dropped the dish towel she was holding and ran out, Claudette close on her heels. Reaching the porch, she paused when she saw the boy pointing at an Army truck rumbling down the dirt road. Didn't he know that not everyone was as obsessed with the Army as he? She started to turn back to the house as the truck came to a stop and the passenger door opened. A khaki-clad figure emerged. Her hand gripped the porch rail. His visored hat shadowed his face for a brief moment, and Blair held her breath. How many times in the last week had she made the mistake of running to meet a complete stranger? She could not bear another disappointment. Not now when she was close to breaking inside.

The soldier slammed the door shut and, straightening to his full height, turned toward her. The sun wiped away the shadows, but still Blair could not believe it was true.

"Thought I'd get a better welcome than this," he said with a grin.

"Lieutenant Hobart, it is finally you!" said Mateo, striding up to him.

Gary placed a hand on the boy's shoulder as they continued to walk toward the house. His eyes, however, remained on his wife. Blair opened her mouth to speak, but her heart felt wedged in her throat, cutting off speech.

"Aren't you going to say anything?" Gary prompted her.

"She just can't believe it is really you, Lieutenant Hobart. She's been looking for you every day," said Mateo.

"Really?"

Was he truly surprised to hear that? What else would she do?

Claudette gave Blair a sharp elbow jab in the ribs. "Miss Blair, say something!"

"Hi, Claudette," said Gary. "How are you? Is she mad at me or something?"

"No . . . I'm not . . . mad," Blair finally said. "It's just that—" But that's all she could manage before a torrent of tears assailed her.

He took the steps of the porch two at a time and had his arms around her in a moment. "There . . . there," he murmured.

He held her thus for some time, taking his attention from her only once to wave the truck on. Out of the corner of her tear-filled eyes, she saw another man jump from the truck before it left but paid it little more mind than that. Gary was here. She didn't care about anything else. This time it was surely to rescue her and not leave her again. He'd even sent the truck away, so that must truly mean he meant to stay with her.

Her tears quieted eventually, and she found her voice. "I can't believe you are really here! How did you know I was here, or is it just chance you found me?"

"I'd heard stories of a pale-haired goddess who could sing like an angel. I knew it must be you." Brushing back a strand of her damp hair, he smiled. He was still the most handsome man she'd ever seen, yet his appearance was definitely tarnished at the moment with his face streaked with grime that was hardly distinguishable from the several days' growth of beard. There was a bruise over his left eye and a raw scrape over the opposite cheek. And the intensity of his obsidian eyes, which she had always loved, held a deeper edge, a pained weariness that even his smile could not fully dispel.

Trying to ignore those eyes, which at the moment she found more disquieting than enchanting, she smiled. "I had hoped you would find me."

As if he truly was weary, he slid down to sit on the top step, taking her hand and pulling her beside him. Claudette leaned on the rail, her chin resting in her hand, while Mateo squatted down on the dirt at the bottom step. For the first time Blair realized they had been hoping and looking for Gary almost as much as she had. And though she wanted to be alone with him now, she didn't have the heart to shoo them away. The other man, a Filipino dressed in the civilian clothes of a farmer, sat on the nearby stump—the one for chopping wood and sometimes even chickens.

"Is he with you?" Blair asked, eyeing the stranger more closely.

Nodding, Gary called to the man. "Juan, these are the people I was telling you about."

Juan gave a nod in reply, his lips quirking into a brief smile, not exactly friendly, more indulgent and polite. He was a short man, not much taller than Mateo, but husky, though he seemed more muscular than fat. Blair had always found it difficult to judge age on Filipinos, but she'd guess his to be about forty. His dark hair and moustache had no gray in them, and his swarthy skin was barely lined, yet there was maturity in and around his eyes, which were dark and unsmiling.

"I've hired Juan as a guide," Gary went on. "He says he knows the hill country as well as any."

"We are just about all packed, Gary, and can leave as soon as we finish. The DeSoto is running well."

"First, do you have anything to eat?" Gary asked. "Our rations have been pretty short." His stomach rumbled just then as if to prove his words.

"I'll get something, Miss Blair," offered Claudette as she turned and scurried toward the house.

"How is the war going?" asked Blair.

"The Japanese have occupied Manila—"

"Oh, no!"

"It was inevitable." He sighed, then turned to eye her with those weary, intense eyes. "Why didn't you go to the Doyles'? I thought you'd be safe with them by now."

"I thought that with the Army retreating to Bataan, it would be safer here. And I thought I could eventually get to Mariveles and then to Corregidor."

"Blair—"

"But now that you're here, we are safe."

He was silent for a time, and feeling awkward over the lull, Blair tried to fill it with talk of her travels since Manila.

He said nothing the entire time, and just as he was about to speak, Claudette returned with a tray. She gave him a sardine sandwich, some fruit, and a mug of cold tea, then she took the same to Juan. Blair was impressed at the girl's thoughtfulness in remembering the stranger. Blair herself had already forgotten about the man.

Nothing was said as Gary devoured the food. Blair wondered when he'd last had a decent meal. Surely supplies were not that low. It must just be that he had been too busy to eat. But he cleaned up every morsel, even licking the crumbs and sardine juice from his fingers. With a finger still in his mouth, he suddenly seemed to realize what he must look like. He gave an apologetic grimace. "My mother would whop me for eating like that." Still, he licked the finger clean. "Your supplies are holding up, then?" he asked.

"We have enough for several days if we can find fresh fruit and vegetables to augment them. I heard there is a nice market in Balanga. We should go right through it. The Padillas, the folks who own this house, left us a couple loaves of bread."

"And then there's Mae West," Mateo said with a wry smirk.

"Mae West?" asked Gary.

"Our *pet*," said Blair pointedly.

"A chicken who is getting fatter than any of us and who is one peck away from our dinner table," countered Mateo.

"I'll eat you first," rejoined Blair. "Mateo and Mae West don't get along," she said to Gary. "I think Mateo is jealous because Mae West is cuter and faster than he is."

Mateo chuckled dryly, then picked up a twig from the dirt and tossed it at Blair. She ducked and it missed her, but she retaliated by attempting to give Mateo's foot a kick. She had to stretch too far to reach it and nearly slid down the steps into the dirt herself. Mateo laughed as she caught herself and scooted back into place beside Gary. She giggled, as well. Gary looked at both of them, a bit astonished, either at the fact that they seemed to be acting like brother and older sister or simply at hearing such silliness in the middle of a deserted village with a war booming just over the near horizon.

"Well, that's good to hear about your supplies," he said after a moment, "because the military has little to spare. Still, you better cut back on your intake. You can't count on finding markets, and I don't expect you'll be much good at hunting."

"You can hunt, Gary," Blair said.

"Yes, but—"

"We are going south with you." It was not a question.

"I want you to go to the Doyles', Blair." And that was a statement, as well. Not a request. "And I cannot go with you. That's why I brought Juan."

"You're leaving me again!"

"Don't say it like that."

"Well, that's the truth, isn't it?"

"We have been through this before." The weariness deepened in him. For a moment, he looked almost old and weighted down by a heavy burden. Her!

"I know you have your duty. That's fine, but I see no reason why we can't go with you. I am your wife. You have a certain duty to me, too."

With exaggerated patience and pointedly ignoring her final statement, he said, "Listen to me, Blair. There is going to be a lot of heavy fighting around here for a while. It isn't safe for you to be here. You've seen yourself that the bombing has been stepped up. The enemy isn't just going to let us have Bataan. We will have to fight to keep it, and even then . . ." Pausing, he glanced from her to Claudette and Mateo, then back to her.

"What, Gary?" she demanded. "I want to know. I need to know why you must desert me again."

"Desert!" His face reddened, noticeable even beneath all the grime. He seemed about to retort a response, then stopped, took a breath, and replied with a forced calm. "We're going to fight to keep this bit of land, but it doesn't look good now for success. We have no air support. The Japs are superior to us in every way. At best we can only hope to harry them a little, keep them busy and give the U.S. a chance to arm for this war."

"And to send us help."

"Maybe that, too." She wished he'd sounded more hopeful. "But we must be prepared for the worst. And for you, that means going to the Doyles' place. I have heard they are planning to hold out at the mission as long as possible. They also have some enclaves secluded farther back in the hills that they have used as religious retreats. You will be safer there than anywhere else on the island. That's what you are going to do, Blair." He swung his head around to take in the two young people. "You two will go with her. I am not going to argue about it."

As if he hadn't heard that final sentence, Mateo said, "I will be seventeen next month. I'm going to join the Army."

Gary jumped up, strode to the boy, and towering over his seated figure, stared down at him. His expression was dark, even more so than could be accounted for by dirt and stubbly beard. Blair knew he would never harm the boy, but he certainly *looked* as if he might.

"You will do no such thing!" he intoned in a sternly quiet voice that had far more force than a shout. "You haven't got your father's permission, for one thing. And for another, Blair and Claudette need you. You will not be a coward and desert them—!" He stopped suddenly, too late realizing his poor choice of words.

Blair chose his slip to drive her point home. "And what about you, Gary? You are deserting me—us."

"That's different, and you know it!" He did nearly shout this time. But a small twitch in the corner of his eye indicated his own ambivalence about what he was doing. "I'm AWOL right now," he barked. "They'll probably throw me into the brig if they can find one to lock me up in around here. I could even be shot for desertion, since this is war." As if all the fatigue of days finally crashed in on him, he sank down on the bottom step, letting his head drop into his hands.

Blair regretted her words—as usual too late. When was she ever going to learn to think of others besides herself, or failing that, just learn to think before she spoke? One would think she'd learn from her past mistakes. Heaven only knew, she tried! But always her fears got the better of her. She did care about other people. She was scared witless for Gary. She didn't want to consider all the danger he was in. She supposed she was just too weak to put him over herself. Maybe if she was the Christian woman Gary wanted . . . But all she could do was try harder.

She slid down the steps until she was beside him again. She put her arm around his shoulders as far as she could reach. He tensed at her touch. She knew she deserved it.

"I'm sorry," she murmured.

"I don't know what more you want," he said, head still down, words muffled. "I'm here, at great risk. I brought someone to take care of you. I'm doing all I can do, maybe more than many men would do under the circumstances."

She winced at his words, despite their truth. She had deceived him in perhaps the worst way a woman could. She had used him terribly, even if her motives hadn't been exactly evil. Yet she could sense the hurt was still deep in him. Regardless, he had always been gentle with her, kind, at times even loving. He'd never thrown into her face what she had done, not as much as he could have. He'd truly tried to accept her repentance. She had a lot of nerve to keep making demands of him.

With a self-deprecating sigh, she said, "I expect too much, I know."

"If laying down my life for you would help, I would do it, Blair," he said with a ragged sigh. "I don't care what you did to me in the past. Believe me when I say I am not holding back from you because of that, but I am divided. I have no choice. I think I can do more to help you by fighting this war, by keeping the enemy from overrunning this island and everyone on it. Maybe you have every right to expect more from me. I just don't know anymore."

"I'm sure you know what the right thing to do is better than I do. I have never known." Gently, she stroked his shoulder. The muscles there were tight, bunched up like knots. Her heart ached for him. She'd been so focused on herself she hadn't even asked how he was. She hadn't even thought what it must be like for him to be fighting battles. Yet she had seen the pain of it in his eyes, and she felt it now in his body.

He seemed to accept her words as they were, which she meant as an apology seasoned with some understanding, as well, even if she didn't come right out and say either. At any rate, he seemed too tired to press the matter. And she was certainly too ashamed of herself to encourage further discussion of the matter. They sat in silence for several minutes. She changed her gentle stroking into a massage, and his soft groans sounded appreciative. It wasn't much, but at least it was a small thing she could do for him.

Claudette and Mateo wandered off. Juan continued to sit on the stump like a stump himself, silent, patient, unmoving.

With great reluctance Gary finally inched to his feet. "I have to get back, or I *will* get locked up. Can you drive me? We're only four or five miles down the road."

"Of course."

"After that you should leave this village as soon as you return to pick up the kids and Juan. There'll still be hours of daylight."

They were mostly quiet on the drive to where his unit was bivouacked. He told her a bit more about the war, more general information than his own part in it. She told more about her adventures in Hermosa. They never spoke of personal matters, never a mention of the uncertainties hanging between them. There wasn't time for any resolutions, so why torture themselves?

At their destination he only kissed her lightly on the cheek before jumping from the car. She didn't know what she had expected. Maybe she did expect too much. But she held her tongue and silently watched him go. Nevertheless, she wept the whole time on the drive back to Hermosa.

Maybe that's why she was so testy with her companions the rest of the day. It didn't help when they chose a particularly sensitive topic of conversation not long after they started their drive away from the village.

"Miss Blair," Claudette asked, "are you and Lieutenant Hobart really married?"

"Sort of," she mumbled in reply, barely restraining a groan. She'd never seen the point of telling anyone the truth. It was easier and far less humiliating to let them believe she and Gary were just dating or at best engaged. "It's a long story," she added in response to their confused looks.

"Then I am wrong in calling you Miss Hayes?" asked Mateo.

"I don't care what you call me."

"You want me to call you Mrs. Hobart?" He persisted, not realizing the dangerous ground he had stepped upon.

"No! Not that . . . oh, call me anything except that or Miss Hayes or Miss Blair. Anything but that, please! You make me sound like some plantation mistress or something." This had been a thorn in her flesh since the beginning of their journey—really, since taking in Claudette. Now it was like a scapegoat for everything else troubling her. She glared at both of the youngsters and tossed in a glare toward Juan, as well, who was sitting silently behind the wheel of the DeSoto and who as yet had called her nothing at all, hardly sparing a single word for her. "You are not my servants or my slaves, for goodness' sake!" she added, giving her head a toss. She was mad, even furious, but not at any of them, not even at Gary. Just mad at life. Mostly at herself. "Just call me Blair. That goes for all of you. Do you hear me, Claudette? Blair. Nothing else!"

A squeaky, contrite "Yes . . . Blair" from Claudette made Blair want to crumble. When was she, Blair, going to learn to think of others? Feeling her own remorse, she would have hugged the girl if she hadn't been in the backseat. Then Claudette reached a hand over the back of the seat and patted Blair's shoulder. Blair gave her a trembly smile at the tender, well-meant gesture. Of everyone in the vehicle, Claudette best understood the confusion of names. She understood loss, too, and being hurt by those who were supposed to love her.

22

"ARE WE GOING to drive after dark?" Blair asked, noting that the afternoon shadows had definitely lengthened. Perhaps Juan did know the roads well enough to drive at night, and now that Blair was on her way, she wanted to get to their destination as quickly as possible.

"No, we stop soon," Juan said in clipped tones. The man seemed to believe speech cost pesos and thus spared it as much as possible.

"Then we won't get to the mission tonight?"

"Tomorrow."

"It seems so deserted up here that I wouldn't have thought a village was near." Indeed, since leaving Hermosa that afternoon, they had climbed steadily into the hills, encountering thick jungle and little else. The dirt road had narrowed, and all seemed far less civilized. The DeSoto bounced over rocks and slapped into tree branches. There had been no sign at all of human habitation, not even an occasional nipa shack. "Well, I could use a bath but will be happy if we find an inn or something, even if it just has beds and some food."

Juan glanced askance at her but remained silent behind the steering wheel.

Several minutes later he eased the car to a stop and opened his door, climbing out.

"Juan, do you really think we should take the time for a rest stop? It is almost dark," she said.

"Wait here," he said, then headed down a footpath into the jungle.

Blair said nothing, thinking he really did have to make a "rest" stop. She still wondered how there could possibly be a village near.

Usually before coming to a village one passed through "suburbs," even if they consisted of just a couple of huts or barns. Shaking her head, a small twist grew in her stomach.

Five minutes later Juan returned. "Get your belongings and follow me."

"Follow you where?" A reasonable question, she thought.

"A place to stay."

"In there?" She stared toward the jungle.

"Come."

He didn't wait for an answer but strode down the narrow footpath. Mateo and Claudette had gotten out of the car and were now hurrying after Juan. Blair said nothing about the fact that their suitcases were left behind. Best to see this so-called place to stay first, then come back for their things. With an irritated shrug, she headed after the others. She was surprised to come upon a clearing with a hut in the middle of it. This was a true bamboo hut, not the sturdier stilted structures she'd seen in and around villages. It looked as if a stout breeze would topple it. She thought ruefully of the *Three Little Pigs*. Juan began to look more and more like a big bad wolf.

"You expect us to stay here?" she asked in measured tones. No sense in venting until the facts were known. But it was more than obvious the place had been deserted for some time.

"I hoped it was still here." Juan seemed quite pleased with himself as he went up to the door and pushed it open.

Everyone else crowded around him, peering into the dark interior. It could not be larger than a hundred square feet. Even in the gathering darkness, Blair could see it was filthy inside, probably having housed only animals for the past decade. As she wondered what kind of animals, she heard a sound, then to her horror saw a varmint scurry across the rough plank floor. It paused only long enough for its beady eyes to glint in the dull light. A rat!

She jumped back. "Forget that!" She shuddered. "Gary told you to take care of us. Well, this isn't my idea of being taken care of. You find us a village right now! And it better have an inn and beds—I'll forgo running water if I have to!"

Juan chuckled. "No villages up here. You lucky to have shelter. Very nice, too. If it rains you stay dry, yes?"

"I am not sleeping with rats!"

He turned from the hut and walked to a grassy space in the clearing. "You can make a good bed here." He patted the grass.

"I have never in my life slept out of doors, and I don't intend to start now." Spinning around so hard it made her a bit dizzy, she stomped back to the car.

She and Claudette ended up spending the night in the car. Mateo, who no doubt had to prove his virility, and Juan stayed in the cabin. When morning came, she refused to admit they looked far more refreshed than she and Claudette. Blair had not slept well curled up like a pretzel on the front seat with door handles poking her shoulders and her hip bumping the gearshift each time she wanted to turn.

After a scanty breakfast of bread and bananas that Juan cut from a nearby tree—he was good for something after all—they set out again. The road became worse, with much winding and steep drops on one side of the narrow passage. Juan mentioned a couple of times the possibility of abandoning the car, but Blair would not hear of it. They did not see a soul until about noon, when they nearly drove right past some people sitting on the side of the road. Blair pointed them out, not for any altruistic reasons, but rather she hoped they might direct them to a decent village. Vain hopes died hard with Blair, but it was difficult to accept they were in the middle of nowhere.

Juan slammed on the brakes, and the three refugees scrambled up a slope to the car. Their greetings were in a dialect that did not sound like the Tagalog Blair had grown accustomed to hearing. Claudette said it was Ilocano, but she could only recognize it, not speak it. Juan, however, was able to converse with the three. While he did so, Blair looked them over. The woman looked about thirty-five, rather plump but pretty with nut brown skin and black kinky hair. Her eyes were black and small in relation to her round face. They were hard eyes, perhaps merely shrewd, except when she happened to glance at her young companions, two boys about the same ages as Mateo and Claudette. By the slightly softened looks the woman gave the boys, Blair was certain they must be her sons. The older boy was as tall as his mother, solidly built and quite handsome, at least enough for Claudette to take her eyes off Mateo for a couple of moments. The younger was scrawny by comparison, with a face too thin to be handsome. Blair wondered if he'd lost in the fight for food each day. More likely he had some sort of intestinal parasite.

After a few moments of chatter back and forth with the strangers, Juan turned to Blair. "This is Quinta and her sons, Aurelio and

Sancho. They, too, are heading for the hills and would like to ride with us."

Blair hadn't expected that, and she thought they were cramped enough in the car. But she couldn't very well turn away fellow refugees after all the help she had received in her own flight from the enemy. So she nodded, and quickly, as if they feared she might soon change her mind, they squeezed into the car, the two boys in back with Claudette, Mateo, and Mae West, and Quinta in front. Juan loaded their few belongings, three small knapsacks, into the trunk.

The woman jabbered away after they started moving. Juan, probably out of politeness, translated for a few minutes, but when Quinta seemed as if she could talk nonstop, he soon fell silent, all but ignoring her. She kept talking for a while, mostly to Blair, who kept trying to tell her she didn't understand. Finally the woman gave it up, either being too tired or too frustrated to continue. In the backseat all was silent. Quinta's sons made no attempt to converse with Mateo or Claudette.

When the sun started to drop toward the west, Juan said, "We will stop for the night soon."

"I thought we would get to the mission today," Blair said, trying to make the edge in her tone as soft as possible. She really didn't want to be querulous.

"The road is worse than I thought."

Indeed, in many places they had crept at a snail's pace over washed-out areas and had even had to stop to clear away fallen trees and brush. The road looked as if it hadn't been used in some time, perhaps since the last monsoon had swept through a few months ago. At one point they had been forced to take a detour. Blair had feared Juan might be lost, though she hadn't said anything. He was their only hope, so she did not want to accept his possible failure.

Juan miraculously found another cabin. From what Blair could drag out of him, these huts were way stations for the workers in the lumber camps higher in the mountains and were built at appropriate intervals for their night stops on trips up and down the mountain. She asked why they didn't keep the road in better repair, and he said the camps had been abandoned a couple of years ago. The mission was on the western slopes of the mountain, and the missionaries apparently used a different road in order to travel into Manila.

There was still enough daylight for Blair to inspect this hut thoroughly, and finding no critters in the place, she decided it would be better than being crunched in the car for another night. At any rate, she was becoming resigned to her fate.

There were blankets in the car, and Blair laid them on the rough, dirty floor as meager padding and to cover some of the filth. It was so hot they needed no covers, but Blair refused to lie on that floor unprotected. It would be cramped with seven of them in there, and Blair hoped Quinta and her sons would politely opt to sleep outside. After all, they had been sleeping in the open before. But Blair gave up that hope when Quinta brought in their packs and pulled small, thin blankets from them and laid them out—near the door, Blair noted with some satisfaction. At least they wouldn't climb over her, nestled as she was in a back corner, if they had to get up during the night. They worked out the problem of modesty by sleeping fully clothed. Claudette placed herself on the other side of Blair, as far away from the boys as possible.

Though otherwise poorly supplied, Quinta did have mosquito netting, an item Blair had failed to pack. But even had she thought of it, she probably wouldn't have included it, instead expecting inns along the way would provide such for guests. When she left Manila, she'd had no concept of what might lie ahead. Even Reverend Sanchez, with all his talk of the jungle, must have thought the same thing about inns, because Mateo had no netting, either, nor did Juan. But this was the dry season, so mosquitoes should not pose a serious problem.

Unfortunately Quinta had no food in those packs. And she made no pretense in her envious stares at Blair's suitcase, which, though now only little more than half full, was still a treasure trove of tinned meat, beans, and even a box of crackers that weren't holding up well in the humidity but would be edible if they were desperate.

Blair set Mateo to building a fire. She would have a cooked meal tonight. She didn't care if she had to share it with half of Luzon, though she did so grudgingly. She wanted to be the kind of person who was generous, giving, caring for the less fortunate. She knew that was the kind of woman Gary idealized. But she had to look out for herself and those she was responsible for, so she didn't think she was making an excuse when she told herself that giving to Quinta and her boys was taking food from the mouths of Blair's charges.

Nevertheless, she felt guilty for her greed when Juan, who had gone off alone without a word of explanation, came back in an hour with meat of some sort. She pointedly thought of it as *meat*, not *animal*. Juan had been thoughtful enough to clean the thing before bringing it in, so it looked very much like what might come from a butcher, especially since Blair averted her eyes from it as much as she could until it was cooked. When it was boiling in a pot of water over the fire, it smelled so much like chicken soup, she let it go at that.

She found herself wondering what her mother and sisters would think of her cooking over an open fire, eating wild meat, sleeping in a hut on the bare ground. They would not believe it. She didn't believe it, and she was doing it!

After dinner Claudette came and sat by her near the fire. It wasn't cold, but the fire lent a bit of comfort to the dark night. Juan was showing the boys how to make a fishing rod. Quinta sat across the fire, her knees hugged to her chest, staring into the flames and quiet for a change, even a bit sullen.

"Will they be with us long?" Claudette asked.

Instinctively Blair glanced toward Quinta, but the woman ignored them. Blair hoped she really did not understand English, but spoke softly anyway. "I hope not. But there's really no place else for them to go."

"You are so kind, Blair."

Blair did a double take at that, then chuckled. "It is not kindness, Claudette; it is just having no choice."

"I don't like them. Aurelio is cute, but I don't like the way he looks at me. His eyes are mean, like he might enjoy pulling wings off flies." She also spoke in low tones.

"I just hope it's not far to that mission."

"Is it true you never slept outdoors?"

Blair laughed. "Never in my life! Once I stayed in a three-star hotel—that was about as close to this as I have come."

Claudette laughed. "I used to sleep in alleys a lot in Manila. I suppose that counts. But this, I think, is better. It's very pretty here."

Blair studied her friend. Claudette seldom spoke of her life before coming to live with Blair, and Blair, sensing it a delicate subject, did not often ask about it. Everyone had their secrets, things better left hidden in their hearts. Yet Claudette had such a good attitude about the hardships she'd experienced. She always tried to look for the good in things. Blair wanted to aspire to that. In her distaste for this rough life they had been forced to live lately, she'd forgotten how beautiful the jungle could be.

"Claudette, you have made this flight of ours tolerable. I don't know what I'd do if I didn't have a friend like you with me."

"Thank you. I feel the same way." Claudette paused before adding, "My parents left me on the doorstep of the orphanage when I was a baby. I never had anybody, Blair, until you. I guess you aren't old enough to be my mother, but maybe an older sister, if you don't mind."

"I like that idea very much. Do you mind going to the mission? I never really asked you."

"Well, Lieutenant Hobart was the one who didn't ask!" Claudette said with mock indignation. "But I suppose he had good reason. And I don't mind much. They tried to make me into a Catholic at the orphanage. But it never took. The sisters meant well, but when they talked about God being a loving father, I didn't get it. What was to keep Him from abandoning me just like my own father did? I figured I was better off on my own."

"We all need someone," sighed Blair, "but I understand what you mean. Goodness! If I pictured God to be like *my* father, I'd run in the opposite direction. And I have been doing just that most of my life. But I have seen many good, decent people of faith who make me wonder. Gary, for one, and Reverend Sanchez. I'll bet those nuns who took care of you were decent, too."

"Yes, they were mostly, except when they blistered my bottom. But I usually deserved it. If God isn't like my father, Blair, how will I ever know what He is really like?"

"I don't know. I'm looking myself. Maybe we'll find out at the mission."

"Do you think they'll preach at us?"

"I hope not!" Blair shuddered at that thought. She'd be in a fine pickle if that were the case and she were stuck there for the duration of the war. Then a bright thought occurred to her. "Gary speaks highly of them, so they can't be all bad. But I don't want to be preached at. If I find God, I want to find Him for myself. I don't want to be pushed into anything." Her tone ended with a stubborn note she just now realized she felt. She had not given much thought to actually being at this mission. Now there was suddenly something else to worry about.

Despite those disquieting thoughts, she slept soundly that night. But she woke with a start at the sound of commotion in the hut.

"They're gone!" Mateo shouted.

"What? Mateo, keep it down. It's still early," she mumbled.

"No, wake up. They're gone. So is the car."

Everyone was up now and talking at once—everyone but the three strangers. They were nowhere to be seen. The open cabin door revealed that Mateo was right about the car, too.

"That can't be!" Blair stared in disbelief.

"It's my fault!" groaned Juan, the first time the man had shown any emotion since Blair had met him. "I should have set a watch last night but . . . who would have thought? A woman and two children . . ."

Well, Aurelio was certainly no child. And Quinta . . . no, there really had been no way of knowing they had been up to no good.

"Maybe they have just taken the car to find a market," Blair suggested, but even she could hear the naïveté in her words.

"The question is, do we go after them?" Mateo asked.

"No," Juan said. "They most likely went back down the mountain because it would be a faster escape for them. But whichever way they went, we would never catch them on foot."

Only then did their true plight sink in. They were on foot now. And everything they owned had been in the car.

"Mae West!" cried Claudette. "She was still in the backseat."

"No . . . not Mae West!" Blair sank down on the step of the hut as reality hit her. She began to cry, as if she were weeping for the chicken—and in part she was because she knew exactly what someone like Quinta would do to a helpless chicken.

Claudette sat beside her and let her tears fall, as well. Mateo just stood and helplessly watched. Juan stood by for a few moments, then walked away. Maybe he would desert them, too. He was little more than a stranger, even if Gary had hired him. Blair was truly on her own now. What was she supposed to do? She didn't even know in what direction the mission was if she *could* tell one direction from the other. Suddenly complete panic gripped her. She jumped up.

"Juan!" she yelled, running this way and that. "Juan! Please don't leave us! Juan!"

With a brisk rustling of leaves, the man reappeared.

"Where did you go?" Blair accosted him. "I thought—"

"I was looking for food. I still have this." He held up his knife, which he had used to catch dinner last night. "And in their haste, our guests forgot to take that." He pointed to the pot that was still sitting in the dead embers of the fire.

Blair sniffed noisily and wiped a hand across her damp eyes. "Well, next time would you please let someone know what you are up to?"

"I am sorry."

"Will . . . will you continue to guide us?" That was hard to ask, but despite her fear she had to know.

"Of course. Lieutenant Hobart paid me to get you to the mission. He is fighting for my country, so the least I can do for him is this."

"Why aren't you in the Army, Juan?"

"I am too old. But after I get you safe to the mission, I will try again. I am sure they will take me now."

She decided he must be older than he looked, but more important, he would not abandon them. Still, even with someone obviously savvy about the jungle—though he hadn't been savvy enough to set a watch last night—how were they to go on?

This question plagued her as Juan went off to continue his hunting expedition. She tried to distract herself by taking stock of what they had left. It was as good a time as any to adopt some of Claudette's positive attitude. As it turned out, both Juan and Mateo had taken their packs into the hut last night and had used them as pillows, so the thieves had not been able to take them. Blair did not feel bold enough to inventory Juan's belongings, but Mateo emptied his pack, revealing two extra shirts, a pocket knife, and a Bible, which surprised Blair because he hardly ever talked about religion, even though his father was a minister. He also had a flashlight, though the batteries were almost dead, a toothbrush, some rope, and a canteen. This was quite a cache, considering he'd also had a suitcase in the car.

"I was a Boy Scout, you know," he explained defensively. "I wanted to be prepared in case we had to hike."

"I wish I would have thought to have a small day pack," Blair said, "that I could have also used as a pillow. I'd have some lipstick now, and a toothbrush, and some clean underthings."

"And some extra food," said Claudette.

"At least we are not completely destitute." Blair turned her back on Mateo, quickly reached into her blouse, and when she turned around, she held out a roll of cash. "A hundred dollars. I thought it would be safer with me than in the suitcase."

They spent the next hour rolling up the blankets and figuring out how to strap them to their backs with Mateo's rope. Only Blair and Claudette would need to do this, as both Mateo's and Juan's packs had straps for a bedroll. When Juan returned with another of his nameless meats, the others were in better spirits. They were further encouraged when he dumped out his pack. He had the kind of useful things a man would think of: a spare set of clothes, a canteen, a rope, and such. But an item at the bottom caused mixed feelings in Blair. He pulled out an Army-issue revolver with spare ammunition. He said Gary had given it to him. Had Gary expected them to be in the kind of danger that would require a gun? Or was it simply for hunting? She was relieved the thieves had not gotten hold of it.

Those concerns aside, Blair tried to put herself in a proper mindset for what lay ahead. They were going to have to hike through the jungle, but it couldn't be too much farther to the mission. This would be an adventure. Like Tarzan. True, Blair had never been much of a Tarzan fan, but that dreamy-looking Johnny Weissmuller was well worth sitting through the movie once or twice. And if Maureen O'Sullivan could survive in the jungle, so could Blair. True, O'Sullivan had Tarzan, while all Blair had was a sixteen-year-old boy and a forty-plus farmer, but maybe together they might add up to one Tarzan.

In any case, she certainly did not give a single thought to Reverend Sanchez's ominous words about the jungle as they set out after eating breakfast. The squeal of monkeys in the trees, the fragrance of jasmine and other tropical flowers in the air, even the faint breeze to dispel some of the heat did indeed make it seem more like a movie than a true life adventure, and certainly far from a nightmare.

23

IT RAINED within the hour—not a shower but a real downpour.

"I thought this was the dry season," muttered Blair, scraping moisture from her eyes so she could see to take the next step.

"Only by comparison to the wet season," said Mateo, who was bringing up the rear of the group directly behind Blair.

The fact that the rain stopped in a half hour and in another hour the heat had dried their clothes helped Blair's plummeting attitude only a little. The sense of adventure she had tried to cultivate at the beginning of the day was wearing thinner with each miserable step. The heat and humidity were only part of it. Mud and flying insects—once she nearly swallowed one!—combined with sore feet and little hope for much to eat at midday to make her want to scream.

Claudette, who was walking ahead of Blair, let a wet branch swing back and slap Blair in the face. It knocked off her straw hat, another item "Ma Barker" and her clan had deemed not worth taking. But as Blair stooped to retrieve the hat, her foot slipped on a muddy incline, and she fell flat on her face, mud and dirt splattering her.

She cursed, not caring that she was supposed to be setting a good example for the young people in her care. She hated being an example! She certainly had never agreed to be one. Had she known that was a requirement, she might not have signed up for the job—had there been a choice in the first place!

What really mattered was that there was no hope of a bath at the end of the day's hike. No bath and no dinner. Certainly Juan's luck with hunting could not last forever. With these grim thoughts, she was surprised to look up from where she was sprawled in the mud and see a hand thrust out at her.

"Thank you, Mateo," she said, taking the proffered hand, though she still had to struggle to her feet on the slippery ground, trying at the same time not to pull him down with her. She gave him a grateful smile after she had gained her feet.

He burst out laughing. But when she wrenched her hand from his with a scowl, he added contritely, "I'm sorry, Blair. You got mud all over your face."

"Hurry up back there!" came Juan's voice several feet ahead. "We must not become separated."

"Then slow down a little," snapped Blair as she scurried forward. Juan had paused at the top of a rise and was gazing upward. Without seeing what had caught his interest in the sky, she stopped in front of him and planted her muddy hands on her hips. "Why do we have to take this cursed path, anyway? Don't tell me it's a shortcut. I doubt there has ever been a human being through here. I see no reason why we shouldn't go along the road. We might even catch a ride."

He pointed, and then she saw a plane winging overhead. Its wing dipped, and she saw the red circle painted on its side. Anyone who had lived through the bombing of Manila could readily recognize a Jap Zero.

Still, she didn't understand the significance. She already knew the Japs had air superiority. "What of it? They can't see us, can they?"

"They are too far away, but it is a concern. Follow me," he replied.

How she hated it when he wouldn't explain things, but he was already moving forward, not giving her a chance to argue. She and the others trudged after him as he veered slightly off the rough path they had been on. He scaled a cliff—well, it was only a few feet up from the path, but it was wet and slippery, and he had to give everyone a hand up. Blair was hopelessly filthy by then. Her beige slacks and white blouse were the color of tropical clay, as were her white deck shoes. But she forgot all that when she went to stand beside Juan.

She hadn't realized they had climbed so high since leaving Hermosa. And that extra boost up the low hill had served to bring them up onto a knoll that gave a spectacular panoramic view of the valley they had left behind. She recalled hearing Bataan had some mountainous peaks over four thousand feet, and gazing out into the distance, she saw some of those peaks rising above where they now stood. She gave an impressed "Ah!"

"Look over there." Juan pointed toward the east. Blair only knew it was the east because the lowering sun was in the opposite direction. "Hermosa is down there. I fear the Japs have it now. I haven't seen any enemy aircraft in this area until today, which tells me a lot."

Blair gasped as she swung her gaze around. Details were vague from that distance, but she could just barely make out signs of a village.

Everyone groaned. Claudette took Blair's hand in a pincer grip.

An odd feeling overcame Blair. She had been in Hermosa two days ago. Now the Japs were there, stalking through the very buildings she had walked by. She wouldn't be surprised if they had set up headquarters in the Padillas' house, one of the largest in the village. Something even more disturbing occurred to her. She had yet to see an actual Japanese invader. She supposed she should be glad her only contact with them was a distant aircraft, yet it made it all no less intangible. It was as if all these days she had been running from a shadow.

There were still practical considerations. "All the more reason to take the road," Blair persisted. "We can get away that much faster."

Juan shook his head. "We must assume the enemy will be patrolling the road now, or soon. I have seen other aircraft, but I didn't want to worry you."

"Juan, I thought we were clear about this. I want you to talk to me. I want to know what is going on."

"I will try, but you must learn to trust."

She eyed him carefully. He was all but a stranger, and it seemed lately she was indeed having to trust strangers. No use fighting it. The question was, could she trust her own instincts? "I will try, Juan. But I'm not so good at that. I mean, look what happened with Ma Barker."

"Who?" He blinked as if questioning her sanity.

"Quinta. Anyway, I didn't do so good there."

"Neither did I," he admitted, and his humble words seemed a difficult exercise for him. "We must do the best we can and learn from our mistakes."

"Yes, good idea. I have one more question. How far to the mission?"

"If we had driven," Juan said, "we might have reached it by now. But if it is any comfort, we might also have had to abandon the car because the road is worse than the last time I was here. Unfortunately it is not bad enough to hold up military vehicles. From here, I guess the mission is about twenty miles. We have climbed as high as we must, and now the way will mostly be downhill."

Blair had no concept of how long it might take to walk twenty miles. She wasn't even certain how long it might take to walk a mile. She supposed she had walked that far before, but surely it had been broken up with stops in shops and such. Yes, she had been shopping in London once and had covered several miles in a day on foot, except there had been a couple of taxi rides, too. That's when she had found that exquisite angora sweater, in a shade that made it look like opals, with cultured pearls beaded into the neckline.

She gave her head a shake. That line of thinking wasn't helping at all. If she was of a mind to think of the positive, she supposed it was positive that they could cover a mile here much faster without the distractions of shops and tearooms. Perhaps they could cover a mile in an hour, even in this heat. She did the math in her head. Twenty miles . . . twenty hours. How many hours of daylight? Why, if they didn't dally, they might reach the mission tomorrow.

"Well, what are we hanging about for?" she urged. "We might get to the mission tomorrow."

"What makes you think that?" Juan asked. "You will kill yourself at such a pace. Two days is more reasonable. The jungle is thick, and the trail is often steep."

"Two days!" Her groans were joined by Claudette's and even Mateo's.

"The trail will not always be clear, and we must stop to find food and water. You must be patient."

She didn't tell him she had never learned much patience in her life. Two days! Of course, she wasn't all that anxious to get to the mission, but two more days of this wilderness! How could she survive? Then glancing at Claudette and Mateo, she knew she must be strong for them. They were both fairly mature for teens, far more than she had been at that age, but they were still depending on her. She could feel it, especially from Claudette, whose hand was still gripped viselike around hers. If she gave up, they might also.

She took a breath. "Well, then, let's go." Her voice lacked the enthusiasm of a few moments ago when she thought the journey would only be hours instead of days.

As they trudged onward, she again forgot how beautiful the jungle was, for her feet kept tangling in the lush underbrush, which Juan called creeper ferns. In one place they came upon a banyan tree, and Blair remembered when she and Gary had sat under one in Manila and she'd thought what a romantic and lovely tree it was. Now her foot twisted in one of its exposed roots, and she fell, scraping her hands and knees, tearing a hole in one pant leg. Maureen O'Sullivan had never been covered with mud and scrapes. Blair glanced at her hands. They were hopeless now, the nails chipped beyond repair. She was going to look a sight for meeting Gary's friends if they ever did reach the mission!

When it rained again, she muttered and sputtered and complained, never noticing how it was cooling her sweaty skin and washing off some of the grime. The only boon of the day was that Juan managed to find a dry spot for them to spend the night. Not a cabin. Goodness! She never thought she'd come to appreciate one of those rat-infested structures. Now they merely spread their blankets out over the ground. A few barely ripe bananas were all they had for dinner. Mosquitoes plagued them that night despite the fact that Juan told them the insects were usually worse at lower elevations. Yet he admitted that Bataan was one of the worst areas in the world for breeding mosquitoes.

Morning brought no great epiphanies. Just more of the same. Jungle, rain, mud, and heat.

Then the unthinkable happened.

Blair had been lagging, as usual, with Mateo bringing up the rear closely behind her. He had tried to urge her on, probably frustrated that she forced him to move slowly, but he felt responsible to hold the rear position. They both realized at the same moment that they had lost sight of Claudette and Juan. Not only that, but they could not even hear them breaking through the thick foliage.

"Juan! Claudette!" they both yelled.

When there was no immediate response, they ran forward in a panic, continuing to yell their companions' names.

Finally a response came. "Hurry up!" That was Juan.

Blair wanted to hug him when he came into sight. "Must you go so fast?" she demanded instead.

"I thought you were anxious to reach our destination," he countered. As he spoke, his gaze swept over the group. "Where is Claudette?"

Blair's head swiveled around. Claudette was nowhere to be seen. Now real panic seized her, like none she had known before. Spinning around, she began to run back along the path they had just taken, shouting the girl's name. She'd taken only a few steps when Juan raced up beside her and grabbed her arm.

"Stop!" he ordered. It was no shout, no cry, just a simple calm command. There was no panic in him. "We will lose you, as well."

He swung his gaze around to take in Mateo. Only then did Blair note the wild, frightened look on Mateo's face. He was just as scared as she.

Juan continued. "We must stay together, else you might be lost forever in this jungle. There is not enough sunlight penetrating the foliage to tell direction unless you have some experience."

Blair had hardly noticed that fact. The heat had penetrated, as had the rain, but now when she glanced up, she saw a roof of thick foliage overhead. She could see no sky at all. Then Juan's words truly sank in. "Lost forever. . . ."

"Claudette!" she let out a shuddering, helpless cry.

For fifteen minutes they searched within a wide radius of where each last remembered seeing Claudette. The terrible thing was that no one could definitely say when he had last noticed her. Blair had to admit that she had been dwelling on her own misery far too much to take note of others, even poor Claudette. Some friend she was! Again she was faced with the awful reality that her repentance was too late. And even then, what she thought about most was how unfit she was for anyone to rely on. But she hadn't *asked* to be relied upon. She'd never wanted this. She was no example and certainly no leader. Leave that to worthy women like Cameron and Jackie. Oh, how perfect Jackie would be here. She would inspire and comfort. She most definitely would not have lost one of her charges! This only proved God had quite a warped sense of humor to put a no-account fool like her in charge. What had He been thinking?

"Arrgh!" she suddenly groaned. There she was again, thinking of herself.

She had to concentrate on finding Claudette. She cried Claudette's name several times but only received the cackle of monkey chatter in response.

Claudette, where are you?

A monkey tittered merrily.

Wait! That was not a merry sound. It was a whimper. Blair stopped dead still and signaled her companions to be quiet, as well.

There it came again. "B-Blair . . ."

"Claudette!" Blair yelled. Looking around frantically, she still could not make out the direction from which the sound had come.

Juan, however, went right to it. He strode to where the tangled ground sloped down. Blair ran to his side, but his arm shot out in restraint. She saw then that the slope was quite muddy. Another step and she might have slid right down into the pit beside her friend.

"Claudette, honey, we're here," Blair called. "We'll get you." The use of *we* was certainly stretching it. If Blair tried to help, she'd probably just get the poor girl in even deeper. It registered with her that Claudette had called her name in her distress. But that fact only heaped more misery upon Blair.

Juan had to knot together both his and Mateo's lengths of rope before he had enough to reach Claudette. Within a few minutes they had tugged her out of the pit. The first thing Claudette did was run into Blair's arms. Blair found herself crying, not from happiness at rescuing her friend but because she was so unworthy of the girl's grateful affections. Claudette gave Juan and Mateo thankful hugs, too, but that did not change the fact that she had first sought Blair.

"We must stay together," Juan said after they were all calmed and settled. When Blair opened her mouth to protest, he added, "I will go slower. It is my fault what happened. Blair, you will go first from now on and set the pace. I'll stay close enough to give directions."

Blair wanted to protest, because this plan made her seem the leader, but it made too much sense to do otherwise. Instead, she agreed and added, "Maybe we can stop for a few minutes and rest."

"That is a good idea," Juan agreed, much to her surprise.

They found a small clearing and sat on the ground in a tight circle. There was nothing at hand to eat, and no one had the energy at the moment to forage. It seemed enough just to be together. Blair knew she wasn't the only one affected by the incident. They all now realized how important they had become to one another. Moreover, it had become more apparent than ever that this was no Sunday stroll. There were more dangers in the jungle than discomforts. It had taken only a twinkling for Claudette to slip into the deep pit. And only by the grace of God it had not been deeper and she had escaped with only a few scrapes. That they had found her and she had escaped was a real miracle.

After about a half hour Juan jumped up, signaling the end of their rest. They all scrambled to their feet, rested and ready to continue. A renewed sense of camaraderie had them chattering with one another almost like the monkeys.

Suddenly Juan raised a hand and hissed, "Hush!"

Amazingly, they all obeyed instantly. Even Blair. With sharp hand motions, he silently directed them to move out of the clearing where they had been sitting. He prodded them until they were well off the path and wedged in behind a thick tangle of brush and trees and vines.

"A truck," he finally explained in the barest of whispers.

Blair strained to hear. Maybe it was someone to rescue them. She didn't want to think of the alternative. Moments passed, and she heard nothing more. If it had been a truck it probably had gone on. But if it had stopped, when would they know if it was safe to show themselves? The thought of missing a rescue was almost as bad as the fear of being captured by the enemy. The next sound she heard was not a motor at all. The faint rustling of leaves drifted to her ears, then followed voices. Not English. Not Tagalog. That was clear. There were at least eighty-seven dialects of the Filipino language, but she would have bet her last tube of lipstick, if she'd had any at all, that what she now heard wasn't any of those.

She'd heard her family's gardener speak like this on a few occasions. But she had never paid much attention to the man, since he was only a gardener, nor had she paid attention to the busboy at the country club or the fellow at the flower stand she sometimes patronized on Sunset Avenue. Whoever would have thought one day it might matter? Whoever thought that one day she would be crouched in a foreign jungle straining to hear that foreign tongue or that her life might depend on it.

Indeed, she'd seldom heard that language before, the gardener, busboy, and florist notwithstanding, but she knew the guttural male voices in the jungle were speaking Japanese.

She couldn't help a gasp when the reality hit her. Juan threw her a look as sharp as the belt knife he now gripped in his hand. Fleetingly she wondered why he wasn't holding his pistol, but she had enough sense to save her questions for later. She clamped her mouth shut.

In a moment two men broke through into the clearing where she had only five minutes before been sitting. They were conversing and looking all about. Had they heard them? Had they heard the shouts during the search for Claudette? Surely if they had been so close, they must have. But it had been at least a half hour since the search had ended. And if the motor Juan had heard had come from their truck, they couldn't have heard anything of the search. There might be hope this was only a coincidence. Blair braced herself for capture anyway.

With her nearly mesmerized gaze pinned upon the men, it dawned on Blair that this was her first glimpse of a Japanese soldier. They both bore the small stature so typical of that race, but they were no less menacing, armed to the teeth as they were. Ammunition bandoleers crossed their chests, grenades hung from their trouser belts, and rifles hugged their shoulders. At least they weren't holding weapons, which seemed a good sign. Their faces were shadowed beneath visored caps and turned away from Blair's view. She was glad she couldn't see their faces clearly. The last thing on earth she wanted was to look into the eyes of her enemy.

Suddenly one of the men began to yell and shout and dance around the clearing. The other drew and fired his pistol twice at the ground. Then he burst out laughing as he bent to pick up something from the ground. The first man now yelled at the second man and then ran from the clearing. The second man dropped what he had been holding and jogged after his companion, still chuckling. Blair hadn't a clue what had transpired, but it apparently had distracted the two from their search—if a search it had been. And it might well have saved her neck and that of her companions.

No one argued when Juan motioned for them to keep still long after the soldiers had departed. They waited like statues for nearly half an hour. Once Blair was certain she had heard the sound of an engine. The road could not be too far away. But even when Juan said they could move, she was reluctant. What if there were more Japs out there? How could they be certain they were safe?

Would she ever be safe again?

But Juan was already in the clearing. For his age the man was incredibly spry. It took Blair some long moments before she could work all the kinks from her cramped body. When she got to the clearing, Juan was holding the same thing the second Japanese soldier had held—a bright green ropelike object about three feet long.

"Rice cobra," Juan said.

"A snake!" Blair shuddered as if the thing were still alive. Trembling, she cowered away from it.

"Very poisonous," Juan said as casually as if he were pointing out a rare flower. "But it saved our lives. We can be thankful that Jap was as fond of snakes as you seem to be, Blair."

They never did discover what the soldiers had been up to. Juan thought they must be a patrol from the road, which he confirmed was less than a quarter of a mile away. He did not think it possible they had heard their search shouts. And it was sheer luck that the snake had materialized when it did. Blair tried to be thankful about the snake but failed. She was keenly aware of the fact that the snake had been hiding in the grass right where she had been sitting before the Japs came.

In the time since they had been on foot in the jungle, she'd had a nebulous notion of critters and creeping things around. More than nebulous, actually. She'd seen some harmless geckos and of course the rats. Flies and mosquitoes were a constant nuisance. They all had caused her skin to crawl at the mere sight of them. But seeing that snake had a horrible, almost paralyzing, effect on her. There *were* creatures in the jungle—dangerous, poisonous ones.

Only one thing now drove her to continue the trek. She focused entirely on the destination, on the end to this shattering nightmare. Concentrating on their goal didn't prevent her heart from stopping every time she heard a rustling in the grass, nor did it help her to sleep at night knowing there was absolutely nothing to prevent any awful creature from slithering over her exposed body. But keeping the mission in mind did give her a trickle of stamina, perhaps even courage, to put one foot in front of the other.

She was never going to watch *Tarzan* again. It was just a bunch of Hollywood malarkey!

24

THROUGH THE GLITTERING HAZE of another downpour the following morning, Blair caught her first glimpse of the mission—a small cluster of buildings, mostly nipa houses raised on stilts, though one house, also raised off the ground, was a frame structure. There was a stone building with a cross at the peak of the shingled roof that indicated it was the church. Blair wondered where all that stone had come from, and even from the distance of a quarter mile away, she could tell great care had gone into the building.

Claudette came up beside her and spoke with a touch of awe, perhaps a little apprehension, too, in her voice. "It doesn't look so bad. I mean, it kind of looks inviting."

Blair just nodded. For so long the mission had loomed as the great salvation, at least from her physical discomforts. Always in her mind she'd thought, "When we get to the mission . . ." Now that it lay before her, her heart was thudding with no small amount of apprehension. She'd never been afraid to meet new people in the past, but she had to admit a reluctance now. She was thrusting herself and three others upon strangers at a time when the last thing these people needed was more beings to be responsible for.

"Where is everyone?" she asked no one in particular.

"They would not be out in this rain," Juan answered.

She almost laughed at the fact that she hadn't thought of this. She'd become so accustomed to the rain, she hardly noticed it anymore. Suddenly she was acutely aware that she was going to have to meet Gary's friends looking like a bedraggled stray puppy, wet to the skin, hair hanging in limp strands, no makeup, tattered clothes.

With a shrug she hoped adequately hid her self-consciousness, she led her entourage down the hill. She slipped and slid in the mud half the way, and from the sounds behind her, her companions weren't doing much better. In an impulsive moment, she just let go and broke into a run. May as well make a truly dramatic entrance. She was an actress, after all.

When two figures stepped into her path some fifty feet ahead, she tried to make an abrupt stop and ended up with her feet flying out from under her and skidding nearly to their feet on her bottom. She looked up to see two Filipino men staring down at her. One was young, probably only a few years older than Mateo, and the other was perhaps ten or more years older than Juan. She gave them a lopsided smile, not knowing what else to do to spare her dignity.

"I'm here to visit the Doyles," she said.

Just then her friends jogged up to her. Juan gave her a hand and pulled her to her feet. The two strangers said nothing but looked the new arrivals over carefully.

"I don't think they speak English," Blair said to Juan.

The older man then spoke. "We speak English. We are patrolling this area. I did not think you were Japanese, since you made so much noise, but we must be careful."

"Yes, of course." Blair noted neither man was armed and wondered what they would have done if indeed she had been Japanese. Nevertheless she tried to choose her words carefully. Maybe it wasn't entirely too late to make a good impression. "We have come to seek refuge at the mission. My husband, Gary Hobart, is a friend of Reverend and Mrs. Doyle."

"I know Lieutenant Hobart. Follow us, if you please."

In a few minutes they were among the buildings. At closer range they looked quite snug and sturdy. A couple of the houses had colorful curtains hanging at the windows, and there were potted plants about, and colorful boughs of bougainvillea draped the nipa roofs and the eaves of the houses. The scene could have made a picture postcard.

The two men led Blair and company up the steps of the frame house. She noted many potted plants in particular on this porch, lush, well-tended plants, along with a glider-style loveseat and a few lawn chairs. She latched on to these things because they were indications of a friendly place.

The older man knocked on the door. "Reverend Doyle, it is Ruberto. We have visitors."

In a moment the door swung open. A white woman of about forty years gazed through the screen door. She was taller than Blair by an inch or two, slender and handsome, if not pretty. Her straight hair was mousy brown with a few strands of gray mingled in, which did not improve the color. It was pulled straight back into a ponytail, tied at the nape of her neck, and a straight row of bangs fanned across her forehead. The screen somewhat softened the woman's rather sharp features—a long nose, long, narrow chin, and deep-set eyes. She was not pretty and perhaps not even handsome, but she was a striking woman. Blair saw that in the first glance, though she couldn't quite put a finger on exactly what made this woman so.

Blair smiled as warmly as she could. She sensed immediately that this was a woman whose good side she wanted to be on. "I'm Blair . . . Hobart." Maybe she could manage to hide, or at least downplay, her mixed-up life.

"Gary's wife?" The woman's voice was deep and resonant though not musical, more like an orator's.

All Blair could think in that moment was, *She knows*. This woman, this stranger, knew all about her and Gary. She wanted to crawl into a deep hole. How could Gary spill his life out to this person? Goodness, he wouldn't even talk to Blair about it all.

"Yes," Blair squeaked, hating the crack in her voice that sounded like guilt.

"Come in." The words did not exactly lack welcome. Perhaps *cool* was the best word to describe the tone. "Dominador," the woman said to the younger man, "please go down to the spring and get Reverend Doyle. Tell him we have guests, and please make sure he knows they are *friendly* guests. Ruberto, from what you said when you knocked, I might have thought you had the Japanese Army behind you. Of course I looked out the window, so I knew better."

Both men apologized for causing the scare, then trooped back down the steps. Blair detected no fear at all in the woman, if she had indeed been afraid of Japanese visitors. She had almost attributed the woman's odd reception to fear but immediately realized that could not be so. This woman did not scare easily. Well, Blair was not going to judge the woman so quickly. Everyone had off moments. Still, she had hoped for a warmer welcome, the kind one might expect when coming to a Christian mission.

Inside, Blair took in a comfortable, neatly kept living room. She saw electric lamps and even a ceiling fan, but none were operating at the moment, and the room was dim and warm. Wicker furnishings were mixed in with wooden tables, an upholstered sofa, and a large overstuffed chair. A few framed pictures of tropical scenes hung on the walls. Blair thought they were original watercolors and quite well done, though she was no art connoisseur. Potted plants filled the room with greenery, and a slightly worn circular rag carpet nearly covered the entire floor. Everything, the furnishings at least, was a bit worn.

As Blair's eyes adjusted to the dim light, she saw two girls were also in the room. One, a slender, pretty girl with auburn hair, was about Blair's age or a couple of years younger. She was seated in the big chair, a book in hand. The other girl was more Claudette's age. She was seated on the bench at the mahogany upright piano, turned away from the piano now to observe the newcomers. She had brown hair like her mother's—Blair assumed these were the woman's daughters because there were many similarities between them. The younger girl also had her mother's sharp features, but her large brown eyes seemed to soften them.

"I am Meg Doyle," the woman said. "My daughters"—she held out a hand to indicate the girls. "Patience is the older, and Hope is the baby." As the girls stood in polite recognition of the guests, Meg Doyle added, "Girls, this is Blair Hobart, Lieutenant Hobart's wife."

"Hello. Nice to meet you." Both girls had more warmth in their greetings than Blair had felt thus far.

"I'm happy to meet you, too. Let me introduce my friends. This is Claudette, my first and dearest friend in the Philippines. This is Mateo Sanchez, whose father is a minister of a church in Manila." She didn't know why she added that last, perhaps in order to give herself some credibility. It must mean something if a minister would leave his son in her care. "And finally, this is Juan. . . ." She suddenly realized she did not know Juan's last name.

"Juan Torres," he supplied, with a hint of a bow toward Mrs. Doyle.

"Juan has been our guide," added Blair. "I don't know what we would have done without him."

"Please be seated," Mrs. Doyle said.

There were enough seats for everyone, but Patience vacated the big chair and offered it to Blair, who protested that her wet clothes would ruin it. Patience glanced at her mother, who gave a curt nod, and then the girl insisted Blair take the chair anyway. Patience sat in a straight-backed wooden chair. Blair supposed there must be a family rule about the guests receiving the best and she was too tired to protest further. She could hardly remember when she had sat in something so comfortable. After everyone was settled, there followed several moments of silence. Mrs. Doyle sat in a wicker chair with her hands folded in her lap. She didn't appear awkward at all. In fact, Blair could not picture her any way but totally self-composed. But why didn't she say anything? It seemed only right that as hostess she would say something to set her guests at ease.

As if reading Blair's thoughts, Mrs. Doyle finally spoke. "As soon as my husband arrives, you can tell us what brought you here. That way you won't have to repeat yourself."

"Yes, that does seem the practical thing," Blair said. "I do want to thank you again." She wasn't certain if she had anything to thank her for yet besides letting them into the house, so she stopped at that. Nothing had been said about spending the night, and Blair was reticent to bring it up.

Another long silence. Then to Blair's horror, her stomach gurgled loudly. Well, she hadn't eaten all day and precious little before that. Yet she felt somehow this was yet another black mark against her.

"Mother," Patience said, "shall I get refreshments for our guests?" Was there just the tiniest bit of censure in her tone? Impossible! No one could have the nerve to remonstrate, even in Patience's mild tones, the formidable woman seated so primly opposite Blair.

"Yes, Patience," said Mrs. Doyle in even tones. "I am remiss. Please forgive me. Reverend Doyle is taking longer than I thought."

"Shall I give you a hand?" asked Hope.

"Thank you, that would be nice," Patience said kindly to her sister.

Blair had never heard such polite girls. Was this a show for guests? Or did their mother just have them trained well? She could believe both. The girls went through an open doorway at the left of the living room. Blair could see cabinets and a stove in there.

More moments of silence followed. Blair prayed the girls would hurry so at least they would have chitchat about the tea, or whatever, to occupy them. The only sound in the room was the rain drumming on the roof. And an occasional growling stomach, from her friends, as well.

Then the door burst open. "Whewee! Is it ever coming down. If I didn't know better, I'd start building me an ark."

The newcomer gave his rain slicker and hat a shake onto the porch before hanging them up on a hall tree in the house. He was not notably tall but was built rather like an ox, thick sturdy shoulders, narrow in the waist, with arms and legs like battering rams. Blair thought of a blacksmith rather than a minister when she first glimpsed the man who must be Reverend Doyle.

"What's this about visitors?" he went on without a pause. "I can't remember the last time we had visitors. A month at least, don't you think, Meg, honey?"

"Before the Emergency," his wife replied.

Blair wondered at the term *honey*, but the reverend did seem sincere with the endearment.

Reverend Doyle strode into the room, his cheerful gaze taking in the visitors. "Well, it don't rain but it pours!" He laughed at the irony of his words. "Maybe I'll get me a decent attendance for the church service Sunday after all. But you are all welcome here at the mission, even if you don't want to come to church. Look at you all!"

And that he did, his gaze sweeping the guests once more, his bright blue eyes twinkling with laughter and, Blair was certain, pleasure. She nearly basked in that look, much of her tension falling away. Perhaps they would let her stay.

"Now, y'all introduce yourselves." After they did, he went on. "You can call me Reverend Doyle if you like, but I don't mind being called Conway, either." He paused with a quick glance toward his wife. Blair noted the woman's mouth had tightened. "Oops!" laughed Reverend Doyle. "Meg likes a little more formality than I do. That's what comes of mixing a Minnesota farm girl with a Texas cowboy. I guess the young ones ought to stick with *Reverend*, but Juan and Blair, you gotta call me Conway. I just don't hear my given name enough anymore. Now, Blair, whatever brings you to the Philippines? And how is Gary?"

At that moment the girls reappeared, each carrying a heavily laden tray. Reverend Doyle went to them and put an arm around each. "Ain't these the best girls you ever did see. And the prettiest—though

I gotta admit our female guests are close competition in the beauty department."

"I hope we can be friends instead of competitors," Blair said. She'd spent most of her life competing with other beautiful women and didn't want that to happen again.

"I think there is plenty of room in this house for more lovely girls," said Doyle.

"It is *inward* beauty that we value," Meg Doyle said coolly.

Another silence followed in which even Reverend Doyle momentarily lost his verbal stride, then he laughed again. "And I am married to a woman with a definite corner on the inward beauty department and the outward, as well. Not to mention that she is the wisest woman I know." He sat on the arm of Meg's chair, put an arm around her, and kissed the top of her head. She actually looked briefly flustered. Then the chair arm creaked dangerously with the man's weight, and he jumped up and took a seat on the sofa beside Mateo and Claudette. "Girls, bring on that grub. Our guests look like they haven't seen a morsel in a spell."

Blair tried to be dainty about the food on the trays, and she noted the same from Claudette and Mateo. Even Juan was behaving politely detached. Besides a pot of tea, there were dishes of fruit and several kinds of cookies. Blair thought she could devour everything in sight by herself. But she took one cookie, an oatmeal raisin, and nibbled on it with sips of tea while Reverend Doyle kept up a steady stream of conversation, mostly one-sided except for scattered comments from the others. He talked about a problem with the spring, a leak in the roof of the church, and other things mostly of interest to his family. He tried to ask questions about the war and Blair's travels, but it seemed her mouth was always full, even with her attempts at politeness. The same was true of her traveling companions. Finally the dishes of food on the tray were empty, and Blair did not recall seeing any of the Doyles eating a thing!

To cover her embarrassment over what must seem to them outright gluttony, she launched into an account of their experiences since leaving Manila. She hoped the Doyles would feel some sympathy for them. Blair was not the chattering sort, so her account was prompted along by questions from Reverend Doyle and even a few from the girls. Mrs. Doyle spoke little. Claudette was also silent, as was Juan, but Mateo offered some small input. The Doyles were especially interested in war news, but they referred to it only as the Emergency, at least Meg and the girls did. Since the fall of Manila they had heard nothing, because the radio broadcasts had been cut off by the invading Japanese.

"All our people here at the mission, except Ruberto and Dominador, left not long after it started," said Doyle.

"That surprises me, Reverend Doyle," Blair said, trying to hide her apprehension at hearing this. "I would think this would be the safest place for them. That's why Gary suggested we come here."

"There's no accounting for what some folks will do in wartime. Most left just wanting to be closer to family, some going deeper into the hills, while others joined family in Manila. The majority of our ministry is to the hill people, and once they get to their mountain villages and enclaves, the Japanese will never be able to find them. But don't you worry; I believe the mission is safe."

He glanced again at his wife, and a look passed between them that Blair could not define, but she was certain it contained past tensions.

"We are prepared to evacuate to a retreat we have deeper in the hills if it becomes necessary."

"You should know, Reverend Doyle," put in Juan, "that the Japanese have probably occupied as far south as Hermosa, which no doubt means other coastal villages, at least on the east, will soon fall. We also encountered an enemy patrol on the road about fifteen miles from here."

"Then perhaps the time is nearer than I thought," said Doyle thoughtfully, his ebullience fading momentarily.

He questioned Juan further. An hour passed. Blair's head jerked as she caught herself dosing. It was only eleven in the morning, but she'd hardly slept at all the previous two nights. Claudette's head was lying against the back of the sofa where she sat, and she was sound asleep. Mateo's eyes appeared heavy, and he looked as if he was straining to remain alert. Blair was having the same problem but was determined not to be rude. She didn't think she'd last much longer, though.

Finally Mrs. Doyle spared them further strain. "Conway, I believe our guests are fatigued."

"Well, I am an insensitive lout, now, aren't I?" he exclaimed. "Guess I am just starved for information. Meg, honey, how about let's find accommodations for our guests? You are welcome to stay here as long as you wish."

Meg Doyle stood and took command of the situation. "Conway,

will you show Juan and Mateo to the house where Ruberto and Dominador stay? You'll be quite comfortable there, I am sure." As the two in question rose with Reverend Doyle and headed outside, Mrs. Doyle turned her attention to Blair. The woman was very polite, and Blair sensed no reluctance at all in her. But she was still cool. "Blair, you and Claudette may have rooms in one of the huts that is now vacant if you wish. Or you may stay in the spare room here in our house."

Blair was too tired to wade through all the implications of that choice. It might be construed as standoffish if she opted for the vacant house, or she might be assuming too much to accept a room with the family if it had been offered only in politeness. She did not want to offend these people, especially the formidable Meg Doyle. She glanced at Claudette, hoping to get some clue from her, but she was still asleep.

Patience Doyle came quickly to Blair's rescue. "Oh, do please stay in our home. I would so like a chance to get to know you better."

"Yes, please do," Hope added.

The stark sincerity in the girls' words was a shock to Blair, so accustomed she had been to the phony Hollywood scene. She also sensed in the Doyle girls a need for companionship from females their own age. She wondered how long since they'd had such. In either case, she could not refuse. In fact, she didn't want to refuse. She wasn't anxious to be in close contact with Meg Doyle, but Patience and Hope were another matter.

"That is so kind of you," Blair said. "I would like that very much. And so would Claudette, I'm sure."

"Let's get you settled, then," said Mrs. Doyle. "We'll wake Claudette after the bed is made up."

While Hope cleared away the tea things and Mrs. Doyle went to get linens for the bed, Blair followed Patience down a hallway to the spare room. They passed a room with a closed door that Patience indicated was her parents', then another room with an open door that belonged to Patience and Hope. This room had two beds and was pink and frilly. The spare room was at the very back and was simply furnished with one double-sized bed, a nightstand, dresser, and another rag carpet. Patience apologized that there was only one bed but said another bed would be moved in after Blair and Claudette had had a chance to rest. Blair assured Patience that the bed would be glorious, even shared.

Mrs. Doyle came a few moments later, her arms piled with linens.

"Patience, why don't you show Blair the bathroom so she can wash up a bit. Then find her some of your things she can wear. You two are about the same size."

The bathroom had running water but no hot water. Patience explained that since the Emergency they had to conserve the diesel fuel that ran the generator. "Mother lets us have a hot bath once a week," added Patience. "It's cold 'bird baths,' as Papa calls them, in between. I'll see you get a hot bath tomorrow."

"In this heat, the cool water will feel fine."

When Blair returned to the spare room, washed up and clad only in the housecoat loaned to her by Patience, she found the bed made and turned down, showing crisp, clean white sheets. Folded neatly across the foot of the bed was a beautiful quilt. It had several large pink poppylike flowers and green leaves sewn to a muslin background. It was old, but Blair instinctively knew it was precious. She'd never been one to appreciate old things, but she was certain Mrs. Doyle had chosen her best quilt for her guests. Blair wondered again at this woman, so reserved, perhaps even stern, and definitely cool, yet putting forth her best even for unexpected company.

There also was a neatly folded stack of clothes on the bed. A pretty pink short-sleeved sweater—thankfully Blair liked pink as much as her hosts—a beige linen skirt, dark brown slacks, bobby socks, and slightly worn Oxfords. Also an assortment of underclothes. Despite the few scuffs on the shoes, all was obviously from Patience's best clothes, not her castoffs. A white lawn nightgown was also lying there.

Blair felt strange about going to bed at noon. True, she was often wont to *wake* at noon, but to go to bed at that time and sleep through the day seemed rather lazy. But she was tired.

After knocking at the door, Patience poked in her head. "You sleep as long as you need to, Blair. You have a lot of catching up to do. If you wake up in the night and are hungry, just help yourself in the kitchen."

"Thank you," Blair said, abashed at such open hospitality. Whatever kind of person Mrs. Doyle was, she had somehow taught her girls well. "And thank you for the clothes. But don't you have something . . . uh . . . older? These are too nice—"

"Now, I won't hear of that! Don't you know what joy I have in giving such? This is the most fun I've had in months."

Just then Claudette and Hope came to the door. Claudette looked clean and scrubbed and was wearing a white nightgown, the twin to Blair's. She also had a bundle of clothes, apparently from Hope, in her arms. Her eyes were still droopy, and it almost looked as if Hope were holding her up.

Once Claudette was guided to the bed and folded her body snugly inside the covers, the Doyle girls left. Blair put away the borrowed clothes except for the nightgown, which she slipped over her head. When she crawled into bed, she was certain she would not be able to sleep at that hour no matter how tired she was.

"Claudette, do you think. . . ?" A snore from her friend indicated she would not be responding to conversation.

Blair closed off the mosquito netting, then laid her head against the feather pillow and pulled the sheet up to her chin. It was too warm for any other covers, but she liked the sense of security the sheet seemed to afford. But it wasn't just the sheet, it was everything that made her feel secure, safe at last. And comfortable. Goodness! She had been longing—indeed, thinking of little else!—for days now. And it felt so good. Yet something nagged at her, threatening her contentment.

Was it a touch of guilt? Did she really deserve all this? She'd been selfish so often, always realizing her fault too late. Maybe she would learn something from Patience and Hope, who seemed so giving and caring. Failing that, maybe Meg Doyle would teach her a thing or two. That thought gave Blair a little shiver as her eyes finally drooped and sleep overtook her.

PART IV

"Nothing can hurt us now.
What we have can't be destroyed.
That's our victory—our victory over the dark."

BETTE DAVIS
(*Dark Victory,* 1939)

25

Leningrad, Soviet Union
February 1942

LENINGRAD, LACED BY CANALS and bedecked with bridges like a queen with her jewels, was surely the most beautiful city in the world. Alex did not think it was mere prejudice that made him believe it so. Nevertheless, he prepared himself to not expect too much when he saw it next. For months now the city had been under unceasing bombardment by the Germans.

The truck Alex was riding in skidded on the ice. A crate fell toward him, grazing his shoulder before he caught it and shoved it back amongst the others filling the back of the transport. They had already made it halfway across Lake Ladoga on the ice road, though the going was slow. Skidding was the least of their worries. Twice the truck convoy had been strafed by patrolling German bombers, which their Red Air Force fighter escort was unable to keep at bay. The enemy had made most attempts to aid the beleaguered city extremely hazardous.

Alex still could not believe that three million people had been trapped in the city when the German blockade had begun in September. The civilians had simply underestimated the danger until it was too late. Oddly enough, in October Moscow had seemed in far worse peril, and a considerable shipment of guns and ammunition had been sent to the capital from Leningrad munitions factories.

"Captain Rostovscikov." One of Alex's companions in the back of the truck called to him. Now in the Red Army, Alex used his full Russian surname—the name the Army insisted on using. "Have something to eat. It will be at least two hours until we get there."

"Thank you, Corporal." Alex took the slices of bread and cheese the young man held out to him, which were placed on an old newspaper that served as a plate. The sight of the paper gave Alex a twinge of melancholy. It was always hard to shake fleeting thoughts of Cameron. At the moment he certainly didn't need that on top of what he was about to face. As a distraction he conversed with his companion. "Corporal Pleskov, have you ever been really hungry?"

"No, not truly."

The boy had probably been a baby at the time of the great famine in the early twenties—if he had been born at all.

"There were a couple of times at the Front," Pleskov continued, "when we were too busy to eat. Once we were pinned down for two days—" Stopping suddenly, he gave a dismissive shake of his head. "It is nothing compared to what those in Leningrad experienced this winter. I was born in Leningrad."

"I didn't know that, Pleskov. Your family . . ."

"We moved to Moscow a few years ago. They are safe, but I still have friends in Leningrad."

"I, too, was born there," Alex said. "I left when I was two. Still . . ."

"We are all Russians," Pleskov finished for him, as if nothing more needed to be said.

More than twenty-five years in America, yet Alex knew he was still more Russian than anything. In America, except for his years away at college, he'd been raised in a tight Russian ghetto in Chicago. He'd actually been proud recently when he had received his Red Army commission and had been issued his uniform a few weeks ago. Well, he was still a Party member, he thought ironically. That had nothing to do with it, of course. There were many who hated Stalin yet were still fighting and dying for Russia.

"What do you think we will find there, Captain?" asked the young soldier. He didn't have to say he meant in Leningrad.

"A lot of courageous people—starving and half dead but still very brave."

"I think you are right." The boy smiled sadly. "The Fascist butcher, Hitler, thought he could storm the city and take it quickly. He has to satisfy himself with a siege that is being weakened even as we drive."

"The blockade is not broken," said Alex with pessimism so typically Russian, "even with this road across the ice. Our relief will only help the citizens withstand a long siege."

Alex chewed on his bread and cheese, thinking about the rumor he had heard from a wounded general he'd treated recently. At the beginning of the German offensive against Leningrad, the Wehrmacht had been issued orders directly from Hitler's headquarters that the city should be completely obliterated. Hitler did not want the burden of feeding millions of prisoners, nor did he wish his Army to be exposed to mines and other booby traps they were sure to encounter upon entering the city should they capture it. There was small comfort in the fact that the Fuhrer would be disappointed in his original goal. The devastation he did leave, however, was certainly just short of oblivion, especially for the tens of thousands who had already perished from starvation.

For months all attempts by the Russians to reach the city had been rebuffed. Before winter set in, boats attempting to cross the lake had been bombed by the vigilant German Air Force. By October Lake Ladoga had been made unnavigable by ice, and it had not been expected to be hard enough for safe crossing by land vehicles until late November or early December. Before the ice was properly thick, however, the Russians had attempted to ferry supplies across in horse-drawn carts and small trucks, but only small loads could be delivered, and even at that many fell through the ice. But before they could make even those tenuous attempts to use the frozen lake road, the Russians had to surmount the problem of capturing German-held railheads to the ports on the lake so that goods could even be brought that close. This was not achieved until December 9. Still, railheads and roads continued to be harried by the Germans.

Alex's convoy was among the first of any sizable proportions to reach the city. They arrived in the midst of an air raid. As bombs shook the earth, Alex feared the truckloads of supplies would be destroyed in the bombardment before reaching their final destination. This air raid was as bad as the worst of the bombings of Moscow. But he had to remind himself that here it had been going on for months, with hardly a pause.

The convoy reached a warehouse intact, and Alex waited while the matériel was sorted and medical supplies were gathered in one place. His main task was to oversee the distribution of the medical provisions. He also had an important shipment of antityphoid serum. The winter freeze had caused many pipes to burst, forcing residents to carry water directly from the Neva and the many canals in the city.

This water was far from safe to drink, and epidemics were feared, especially during the thaw. Spring would bring another source for disease when thousands of corpses that had not been properly buried in the winter would thaw and have to be dealt with.

Alex tried to think about these things clinically. As he was driven by truck through the Leningrad streets later that day to make his deliveries, he made a mental list of the various medical tasks he must address during his visits to several hospitals. He would have two days to visit as many hospitals as possible and to ensure stations were installed for administering the antityphoid injections. But it was difficult to be scientific when he looked out the truck windows and saw living skeletons shuffling along the sidewalks. Seeing a figure lying in a doorway, he made the driver stop so he could give medical aid. But the body was cold with death and probably had been so for quite a while. After two more such futile stops, he finally made himself fight the urge. He breathed a prayer of great relief when they reached the first hospital. It couldn't possibly be worse there.

Dr. Scerba greeted him at the People's Hospital—it had been Holy Cross before the Revolution. It was located on an island he remembered as Petersburg Side, an industrial area of the city that had been hit hard by bombs. Alex had glimpsed the Peter and Paul Fortress from the bridge as they crossed onto the island. He could not hold history over human lives, but he did murmur a brief prayer that the historic places such as the Fortress and the Hermitage, which represented so much of the Russian national soul, would be spared. He'd already heard that Tsarskoe Selo, some fifteen miles from the city, a beautiful palatial compound that had once been the primary residence of Tsar Nicholas II, had been burned and gutted by the enemy.

"My good Captain Doctor Rostovscikov," Scerba said, "you are a welcome sight."

Dr. Scerba was about sixty years old and several inches shorter than Alex. Even in the best of times he had probably been of a diminutive stature. Now the man looked like a bag of bones. His neatly trimmed white goatee and moustache stood out starkly against his cadaverous face.

"I wish I could have come sooner" was all Alex could say.

"Shall I show you about?"

Huge sections of the hospital had been bombed out, and it was not nearly as crowded as Alex had expected it to be.

"Our census is actually up lately, though it may not appear that way," Scerba explained. "But during the worst of it, there was so little we could do, and those who needed us most did not have the strength to come. And why should they bother? Why not die in their own homes rather than travel miles or even blocks to die in a hospital?"

"What of the wounded?"

"Without nourishment, they died quickly. We were . . . simply helpless."

"They needed food, not medicine," said a woman who joined them. "Please excuse my intrusion but—"

"No, no, Dr. Belostan," Scerba said quickly. "I was remiss in not calling you to greet our guest. This, Dr. Rostovscikov, is my assistant chief of staff, Vera Belostan. She is one of the finest physicians I have had the honor of working with."

"I know that quite well," said Alex with a smile at the woman. "I met Dr. Belostan at a medical conference before the war."

"I did not know if you would remember," she replied with a hint of modesty.

But the Vera Belostan Alex had met in Yalta in 1940 had definitely not been the modest sort, at least in her opinion of herself and her medical skills. He supposed that might have extended to her looks, as well. She had been quite beautiful then—nearly as tall as he, swanlike in grace and physique, luminous golden hair framing smooth fair skin, large gray eyes, and high, well-defined cheekbones. Yes, she had been quite lovely, and she had carried herself as if she knew it and expected others, especially men, to notice.

She was skin and bones now. The swan had more of the appearance of a starved hawk. Her hair hung lank and dull, her eyes lacked spark, and her skin was like parchment ready to crack at a touch.

"To be honest, Vera, I—"

She laughed, but the tone of it was only an empty form of the real thing. "Don't apologize, Alex, we have all turned into wraiths. Do you mind if I join you and Dr. Scerba on the tour?"

"I have a better idea," said Scerba. "Since you two seem to know each other and perhaps would like a small reunion, why don't you, Dr. Belostan, finish the tour with our guest?"

"But, Dr. Scerba," Alex said, just barely repressing the sudden panic he felt. He tried to think of a reason for the elder doctor to remain but could not. "I . . . well, if you are certain."

"I will see you when you finish, and we will talk more then." At that Scerba scurried away.

"Are you still afraid of me, Alex?" Vera Belostan asked when they were alone.

"Afraid?" Was that a slight squeak in his voice? He swallowed in a vain attempt to moisten his dry mouth.

That week in Yalta stirred in his memory. Balmy summer breezes, the sparkling seaside, the fragrance of flowers in the air—it had been the perfect setting for romance. It needed only a charming, intelligent, beautiful woman and a man far from home desperately trying to recover from a deep trauma. They had been drawn together quickly and were nearly inseparable that week. At some point he'd realized she was not the woman for him. She was too perfect, too refined, too charming, too beautiful. Not exactly shallow, she was so cool as to quell any passion in her character. Yet he'd allowed the relationship to stretch out through the week because he had enjoyed the distraction of her company. He'd always felt guilty about that. When she expressed interest in extending the relationship beyond the conference, he'd backed away, letting her down gently, he thought.

"That must have been it, Alex," she persisted. "Why else would you have run from me so quickly after I expressed an interest in having more than a friendship with you?" She arched a brow, and her old arrogance still tinged her voice.

"I wasn't ready for anything like that then." That was the truth. Back then he still believed quite firmly he would never marry and subject a woman to the uncertainties of being tied to an ex–drug addict. Back then he'd still been able to taste the allure of the pills that had so recently enslaved him. "Besides, your career was tied to Leningrad and mine to Moscow."

"I don't hold it against you, Alex." Even half starved, she held her head as high as if she were a queen. "I wasn't really ready, either, to tie myself to one man. I don't know why I even suggested it. You just . . . have quite a devastating effect on women."

He laughed outright at that.

"And that's exactly why." She smiled. "You have no clue at all of your charisma." She gave her head a shake, momentarily all swan. "Let's continue that tour."

There wasn't much of interest to see in the hospital, so he used the time instead to question her about the ordeal of the winter.

"You cannot believe what starving people will do to survive," she said as they walked through the hospital corridors. "I do not believe any of the stories about cannibalism, but you will not find a dog or cat left in the city. The rat population has been diminished, as well. Vaseline and hair oil are consumed, and even glue is scraped off the back of wallpaper and boiled into a soup. That delicacy I have tasted myself, and I can tell you there is no hope of it gaining popularity after the war."

"It sounds beyond imagination" was all he could think to say.

"My personal favorite was sheep's gut jelly." She smiled grimly. "Some resourceful person found a thousand tons of sheep guts frozen in a warehouse. They boiled it down to a jelly, but it was so disgusting they tried to camouflage the wretched flavor with cloves. As horrid as the stuff was, you won't find any of that left, either. Despite everything, the only thing the hospital was good for was to hand out vitamins, until we ran out of those. I have become an expert on treating scurvy ulcers."

"What of crime and antisocial behavior? I have heard amazing stories of courage, but there must have been some discord."

"In a city of millions there are always bad apples, but on the whole the citizens refrained from riots and protests. Partly, I am sure, because of harsh penalties but largely from sheer patriotism. Ration card fraud was big in the first month or two. I heard of one woman who was in possession of a batch of those who was executed. The Germans also airdropped forged cards to cause confusion.

"But, Alex, scarcity of food is only part of it. By November fuel shortages were severe, and heat and electricity were reserved only for the most essential uses—factories, of course, and some government institutions. Our hospital ran at a minimum."

Alex glanced toward his companion, marveling again at the incredible pride in her bearing. He could not fault her for it now. He knew it had likely been the key source of her survival. Such must certainly be the reason also why one starving person crumbled and surrendered to death while another fought it.

She gave a dry laugh. "You look at me as if you don't believe me."

"I believe. I simply cannot fathom it."

"Alex, I would like nothing more than to escape this place for a few minutes. Would you take me someplace?"

"Where is there to go?"

"Surprisingly enough, Leningrad has not dried up completely. Socially, in fact, it boasted many theatrical performances through even the worst of our ordeal. Starving actors, barely able to hobble across the stage, did what they could to keep up morale. Still, I realize it is all horribly dismal out there, but some fresh air at least would be nice."

When he nodded, she took the lead—a most natural thing for her to do in any case—and led them through several corridors to an exit. Outside, the air was frigid. She had fetched her coat—a shabby thing, making Alex recall she had been particularly fastidious about her appearance before. Regardless of the heavy wool coat, she linked her arm around Alex's and walked quite close to him.

The sky overhead was a pale winter blue with no ominous clouds in sight. The ground was icy, and they had to step with care. Snow had piled up in high drifts against the buildings and little effort had been made in clearing it away except in narrow paths to allow for minimal traversing.

Vera sighed, almost, Alex thought, a sigh of contentment. He didn't want to think what that meant or if he was in any way the cause of that particular sigh. Perhaps, as she said, he was generally oblivious regarding his effect on women. Johnny Shanahan had once made a similar observation, he recalled. But nevertheless, he wasn't a total fool. He'd noted a hunger in Vera's eyes that had little to do with her empty belly.

They walked for a few minutes until the wind began gusting around them.

"I live nearby," she said. "Shall we get in out of this?"

Two blocks away they paused before an apartment building. The street they were on had amazingly been left fairly unscathed by the bombing. The building itself was rather nice, and Alex recalled this area was one of the nicer districts in the city, an affluent enclave apart from the factories on this particular island. Vera always had impeccable taste.

Inside, the building felt little warmer than the frosty air outside. Alex exhaled white puffs of steam as they climbed two flights of stairs. She unlocked the door to her apartment and let him into a clean room, almost pristine by comparison to the extensive rubble Alex had thus far witnessed in the city. But it was stark in décor. An upholstered sofa, a couple table lamps sitting on the floor, a few knickknacks, framed pictures, and photographs on the walls.

"I fear I must be a poor hostess," she said apologetically. "I have no refreshments to serve. Only the sofa to offer as a seat. Anything I owned made of wood was burned long ago for fuel. But at least we can sit and try to be comfortable."

She took her own advice and sat on the sofa, patting a place beside her for Alex. He sat quite a bit farther away from where she had intended.

"I was right. You are still afraid." She smiled. "But I suppose I am not the desirable woman I once was."

"It is not that . . ."

Unabashed, she scooted close to him and turned to face him, her knee touching his leg. She laid her hand on his arm. "You don't know, Alex, what it is like to be close to a man with some flesh on his bones, a man who is whole and healthy." She gazed with frank admiration at him, making no attempt at all to mask her desire. Then she chuckled bitterly. "I doubt I have the stamina to do anything more than admire you, but . . ." She gave a vague shrug to complete her thought. The sigh she breathed now was more hollow than contented. "And for that man to be you, of all men . . . something stirs in me that has not stirred in an age."

"Yalta was a long time ago."

"I think I would sell my soul to feel your arms around me again, to feel for just a few moments that I'm not truly the animal I have lived like for the past months."

He knew what she wanted. It wasn't love or sex but rather intimacy, that basic need of all humans. At least that is why he could not refuse her, why he did offer his arms to her. She came to him with an appreciative murmur, followed by a whimpering sob.

"I'm sorry," she said. "I don't mean to cry."

"I understand."

He was as a brother offering comfort to a needy sister. He let her lay her head against his chest and quietly release her emotion. He patted her hair, wondering if a proper diet would restore it to its former silky sheen. He also wondered how many others were in need of a mere embrace.

It took him completely off guard when she lifted her head and pressed her lips against his. Despite her previous denial, she still did have a spark of passion within her starved body. With a startled gasp, he jerked his head away. Her stamina indeed was apparently suddenly revived. "Vera, I can only give you an embrace."

"I want more, Alex. Please . . . I have been alone for so long. . . ."

He licked his lips, an ache rising from the pit of his stomach. "I can't."

"I don't care if it is out of pity. I am so empty inside."

"I'm sorry. . . ."

"If it is not fear, then, Alex, you are in love with someone else, aren't you?" She laughed. "Oh yes, now I remember. You were always so noble and pure."

"You laughed at me even then, I think."

"Not so you could see. I admired you a little, too, that I could not corrupt you." She pushed slightly away from him and tilted her head so she could gaze directly into his eyes. "I envy that woman who owns your love. I never did, and I know now I never could. Not even your pity."

"You don't want my pity, Vera, or anyone's." He grasped her shoulders with his hands, squaring them as if to remind her of the pride he knew was in her. "You are beautiful, strong, and brave. If you are empty inside, it is only because you have forgotten who you are, what you have survived."

"Next you will be telling me to snap out of it."

A smile slanted his lips. "I might!"

"Seeing you threw me off balance, I suppose. It made me remember I am a woman and not just a paragon of *strength*." She slurred that final word with a touch of disdain. "But I suppose you are right, this is not the time to forget. There is still a war ahead."

"Will you remain in Leningrad? Some residents will now be able to be evacuated."

"Of course I will stay! I may be a lot of things, but I am not a quitter. Besides, the worst is over."

"I hope so."

She patted his cheek affectionately, then rose briskly. "Let's get back to the hospital. Old Scerba will wonder what happened to us."

As they reentered the hospital ten minutes later, Vera paused at the door. "Thank you, Alex, for making me remember what is important. I think I will be able to face what lies ahead."

"Of course you will."

"I am still terribly jealous of the girl who has your heart!" She swung into the building, her shoulders and back straight, her pride intact once again.

Later he borrowed a jeep—the American variety, a product of FDR's lend-lease program—and drove across town to the district where his mother had lived. He had a difficult time finding the street because all directional signs had been removed. There had been a lot of bombing in the area, but he managed to locate a couple of landmarks his mother had mentioned, and he was fairly certain he had found the right house.

He did not approach it any closer than across the street. It was empty now, and he doubted he'd need a key to get in. But even if he'd had his mother's key, he knew, after thirty years, it would no longer work. Many people had lived in the house since then, especially after it had been converted into an apartment house. The locks had no doubt been changed many times. It certainly no longer belonged to his mother now that all buildings were the property of the state.

The key was merely symbolic.

A fist seemed to grip his heart as he thought of that symbol. Cameron must still have the key if she had not thrown it far away—no, she would never do that. But she hadn't given it back to him, either. Was it still on that chain around her neck? Perhaps that was hoping too much.

He thought of Vera. Even she had known he was not a free man. He'd walked away from Cameron—or she had walked away from him; he wasn't quite certain which was true. Well, he had done the physical walking. But not in his heart. He did still love her, and even kissing another woman would have been unfaithfulness to that love. He had no desire to do so, anyway. He wanted only Cameron. That tough, independent, rough-tongued, tender, vulnerable reporter. She had turned his life upside down and inside out. She had made him feel alive again, so alive, in fact, he'd been compelled to connect with the true source of life, his God. Without Cameron he might never have had the courage to open himself up again to the love of a woman or the love of God. What irony!

But it made him hope that God was not finished with them yet. Cameron held the key in more ways than one. She was still very much a part of him, and she would remain so until—he wasn't certain until when. He prayed constantly that God would make him aware of the time when it came. He only knew it was not now, and for that reason he turned from his mother's house. He would not step inside until Cameron was at his side.

26

BEFORE THE END of the year, the correspondents were flown back to Kuibyshev. Cameron was glad to put Moscow behind her for now. For some reason memories of Alex were sharper there, and she didn't need that. She must move on.

If only Kuibyshev could offer more diversion. But the press department must have taken some pity on the bored journalists, because during the next weeks they were shuttled around to various fronts and given tours of farms and factories and such in the region of Kuibyshev.

Cameron threw herself obsessively into her work. The dogged determination she displayed was not unlike that of the country she wrote about. *Pabyeda,* or victory, in Moscow did not lift the German threat to the rest of the country. The citizens of Leningrad, still under siege, were starving to death. Although a supply route across the frozen Lake Ladoga had been established, it was going to take much time to catch up with the food needs of the besieged city. Even as they starved, they still had to put up a military defense and face daily shelling. Cameron made several attempts to obtain permission to visit the city, but still no foreigners were allowed in.

On one especially dull afternoon, with shadows already starting to stretch across her hotel room and not yet even three o'clock, she turned to a new diversion. Sitting on her bed, she brought out the packet from her mother and the one Dr. Fedorcenko had smuggled out of the prison. Opening them, she spread the contents out on the coarse cotton bedspread. Only once or twice had she glanced briefly at them since they had come into her possession. Her natural curiosity had for once in her life been overshadowed by her fear.

She still did not know what to do about Semyon Luban. She'd heard Colonel Boris Tiulenev, one of her father's friends from the old days, now had an office in Kuibyshev, but she had refrained from contacting him again. And he certainly had not sought her out. He must surely have forgotten her rather vague inquiry months ago regarding that matter.

With a resigned sigh, she took up the packet of letters her mother had given her. They were stacked in chronological order, the first dated December 24, 1916. The envelope, yellowed now with age, was plain and not addressed. There was no salutation on the first page of the letter. It was handwritten in English in neat, precise printing.

> *Forgive me for taking so long to write. I have only now worked out a way to communicate. This first letter I have arranged to be carried out of the country by the hand of one I can trust. Thus, I can be somewhat freer in what I say. The regular post cannot be trusted, but I pray a means to send future letters will arise. I cannot promise they will be frequent, but I will try to be faithful in this. The one who carries this letter (I will not put a name in writing) lives in America and is willing to act as a go-between for our correspondence. He will exchange all pertinent contact information with you when he delivers this to you.*
>
> *I must admit I debated about whether to write at all. I would understand if you did not wish to communicate. You must go on with your life. Yet I know you well enough to believe you may want some idea of the well-being of our mutual gift. If you do not, I will not press the issue. I will respect your wishes, knowing full well how difficult it is for you.*
>
> *Tonight is Christmas Eve, the first He will experience.*

Cameron noted throughout the letters Semyon was referred to as He with a capital *H*.

> *I have bought a small tree and a few ornaments.*

Cameron thought her mother had mentioned Yakov was Jewish, so she wondered at him celebrating the Christian holiday. Was he a Jewish Christian like Oleg? She would have to ask her mother about this sometime.

> *He is, of course, too young to fully appreciate the holiday, but*

his large brown eyes are quite fascinated with the tinsel and bright bulbs on the tree. When He is near, He tries to reach for them, but I have placed the tree on a table so He cannot pull them down. He is a very alert child and is already crawling. I have made the acquaintance of a couple of females who are mothers, and they have been very helpful to me. One has told me He is quite advanced to be crawling at this age. Her son did not start to crawl until he was nine months old. (I think she is a little jealous!)

Is this hard for you? I am so unsure of how to proceed. I have bought a small camera. Quite an amazing contraption that takes what are called snapshots with great ease. Shall I send a photograph? I pray I hear from you at least once to know of your wishes. Things here are very chaotic. The war is going poorly, and the government is shaky. I try not to involve myself in politics. All I need in life are my books, my God, and now the dear gift God has given me, the gift you also gave me. Yet because of the political situation, mail delivery is uncertain.

I pray then that this and all correspondence goes with God. Happy Christmas to you.

There was no signature at the end, and Cameron thought about the risks on many levels that these letters represented. Beyond that, what impressed her more than anything was the verbal picture the letter gave of the man who had written it. Just the act of opening the letter with the word *forgive* said volumes. He was a man of deep sensitivities. She could easily picture him fussing over the Christmas tree or talking with lady friends about child rearing. The love he felt for his child was the clearest image of all.

Cameron tried not to make the obvious comparisons between this man and her father. She tried not to think of her father at all, because no matter what she felt about Keagan, she could not shake the tiny particle of disloyalty she felt in having these letters in her possession, much less in reading them. Nevertheless, she carefully folded the letter in her hand, replaced it in its envelope, then opened the next. She read each letter slowly and carefully and with the same care replaced each in its envelope. She drew from them much the same picture of the writer, Yakov Luban. A tender, sensitive man. A man who loved his son. After he apparently received permission from Cecilia to continue the communication, he freely shared news of the child. He told amusing antidotes and detailed accounts of Semyon's various growth milestones.

Today He took his first step, and I knew I must write. He took the step, tottered, and fell on his bottom. It took some coaxing to get him to try again a few minutes later. I fear I bribed him with a cookie. But it worked, and He walked all the way across the room. I will say one of my lady friends thinks I give him too many cookies and He is too fat. But another says in this time of war and hardships, I should feel blessed to have a fat child. I agree. Russia is falling apart at the seams. We have a provisional government now that the tsar has abdicated, and there are shortages of nearly all goods. But have no fear. He is healthy and happy. By the way, here is the photograph I promised of him on his first birthday.

There were seven letters in all from December 1916 to March 1920. Cameron recalled her mother saying that was the last time she heard from Yakov. That final letter for the most part had the same tone as the previous ones, all focused on Semyon, and if there were any other references, they were included because they related to the child in some way. None of the letters had any reference to Yakov and Cecilia's relationship, nor to anything personal about Yakov unless it directly related to the child. Until that final letter. Perhaps he was trying to prepare Cecilia for the worst.

I do not wish to burden you with my troubles, but I thought you would like to know I have lost my bookstore. A year ago, it came under state control. The new Bolshevik government wishes to make Russia a true Socialist state, whatever that is! Thus private ownership is greatly limited. Since I did not own the building where my store is located, only the inventory, it came into the possession of the state. My store at first was not touched, and I continued to operate much as before. But perhaps as the government became more stabilized, they had time to scrutinize areas previously left alone. The Cheka, or secret police, are it seems on the hunt for subversive material and have found such in my store. Most Western literature to them is subversive, so what must they think of an English bookstore!

I tell you this news so you are aware that I must move. If you recall, my apartment was above the store. I have a little savings, so we should be all right for a while. I cannot say where I am going, for obvious reasons. He continues healthy and content. He is almost four years old. You will see in the enclosed photograph He has lost most of his baby fat and is quite a handsome boy, if I do say so! He is most articulate, with a large vocabulary for a child his age. I am debating as to whether it is too early to teach him English. I plan to do so eventually, but the child experts I speak to think it might be confusing to him. I think I will start with just a word or two and see how He does. Yet, I must be careful because I do not want Comrade Lenin to think my little one is subversive!

Feeling drained, Cameron set aside the letter, rose from the bed, and went to the table where she kept a hot plate. There she fixed a pot of tea, poured herself a cup, and returned to the bed. Staring down at the items scattered around her, she sipped the hot brew. It proved calming and also warming, which she appreciated because the radiator in the room was not functioning again. Returning her attention to the task before her, she glanced down at the letters. She knew she was going to want to read them once more, but first she picked up the photographs. There were three. One of Semyon at a year, another of him at two being held by his father, and the last at three years of age, actually nearer to four, since it had been taken only two months before his fourth birthday.

If Cameron had entertained even the smallest inkling that this child might be Keagan's, this photograph of Semyon and Luban together dispelled that notion. Perhaps that had been his intent in including himself in the photo when he had so refrained in his letters from speaking of himself. Other than the fact that Yakov's hair was brown and Semyon's several shades lighter, they both had a look about them that indicated a close blood relationship. It showed even in the poor quality of early photographs. Another thing quite clear was that Semyon was an adorable child. He had such a mop of thick curls that Cameron immediately thought of Shirley Temple. But Semyon was all boy, even more apparent in the last photo in which his curls had been cut short. She thought he had a slightly impish look on his otherwise cherubic face, as if he might be a touch spoiled.

Cameron smiled, a sudden knot rising in her throat, but she didn't let tears escape. Still, emotions tugged hard at her as she reminded herself that he was no longer an impish three-year-old. He was now nearly twenty-six. A full-grown man—if he was alive. And for that reason, if not a hundred others, she could not—would not!—allow herself to become attached.

Yet, he was her brother. . . .

She shook her head firmly. No, he is a face in a photograph, a few words on paper. He is not real. It cannot be possible that he is alive.

Then why even continue this process? Why bother? It was not logical.

But she would. She knew that. She just would not become attached.

Setting her half-empty cup of tea on the bedside table, she resumed her place on the bed, surrounded by the remnants of a life—of two lives, really. She took up the packet from the prison. It contained a book and a single letter that was tucked inside the book. First, she focused her attention on the book. It must be important for Yakov to have kept it in prison. It was written in Russian, but she was able to decipher the title with the use of her dictionary and her growing knowledge of the language. A book of fairy tales by Pushkin. An odd book for a man to have in prison.

Then as Cameron leafed through the pages, she saw on the title page a handwritten inscription. She'd have Sophia verify her translation later, but she was almost certain it said, "To Semyon on your first birthday, May 10, 1917."

No wonder he'd kept it with him. A reminder of his son. And it was then, of course, that the weight of what she had known since she had spoken to Dr. Fedorcenko fully bore upon her. Father and son had been separated when Yakov had gone to prison. How long had the separation been? Dr. Fedorcenko had mentioned that Yakov Luban had been in the gulag for nearly twenty years. He would have been arrested around 1922. Semyon would have been six years old.

A picture invaded Cameron's mind of a young child being wrenched from his father's arms by cruel Cheka agents. A terribly traumatic experience for a child, a heartrending loss for a man whose world was that child. Still, Cameron could not know if the child had been alive even then. Hardly a comfort. She would almost rather think of Semyon as dead than thinking of that sweet impish face twisted by such pain.

Cameron took a breath. "All right, Cameron!" she said out loud. "If you are going to do this, you *must* remain detached! You will be useless to anyone if you turn maudlin every minute. You are on the track of a story. That's all."

Only a little fortified by this pep talk, she took the letter from the book. It also was in Russian, and even with her dictionary it would take forever for her to translate it if she could at all. Her grasp of Russian was growing but still was not that proficient. She glanced at her wristwatch. Only four o'clock. Sophia would not be here until nine for Lozovsky's press conference.

Cameron whiled away the rest of the afternoon by finishing a couple dispatches. Then she went to dinner. She lingered afterwards, discussing war news with the other journalists. None of it was good, especially from the Far East. Hong Kong had fallen at Christmas, Singapore only two weeks ago, and the latest news was that MacArthur had been ordered to leave the Philippines. Cameron's sister was, as far as she knew, still stranded on those embattled islands. How much longer could they stand against the Japanese?

When Cameron saw Sophia come into the hotel, she raced into the lobby and nearly pounced on the young woman.

"I wish they would let you have a room in the hotel," Cameron groused. "I'll bet they could squeeze a cot into my room—"

"Only yesterday you called your room a closet," Sophia said with a bemused look on her face. "Is something wrong, Cameron?"

"No, I just have need of you, and you know how impatient I can get." With a firm hand on Sophia's elbow, she steered her toward the stairs. "We have some time before the press conference. Would you come up to my room and give me a hand with something?"

She'd had no doubt her friend would agree. Cameron had waited a long time to finally investigate the legacy of Semyon and Yakov Luban. But now that she had broken through the barriers of her reticence, she was anxious to plow ahead. She had to make up for every moment she had dallied before.

In her room, barely giving Sophia a chance to remove her coat, gloves, and hat, Cameron explained what she wanted. She tried to keep it simple, but if Sophia was to get involved at all, it was only right she have some idea of what it was all about. The girl had enough troubles of her own. Translating a letter wasn't going to get her arrested, but if she knew Sophia, she would want to help in other ways. And in the future Cameron might need her help, as an interpreter if nothing else.

"I will be happy to do this," Sophia said. "And please feel free to call on me whenever you have need. I wish I did not live in another building so you would not have to wait for me."

Cameron laughed. "My mother always told me, 'Patience builds character.' "

Cameron got Yakov's letter from the packet, and they sat at the table—Cameron had finally persuaded the hotel staff to get her a second chair so she and her interpreter didn't have to use the bed for their work.

Cameron asked Sophia to later write out a translation, but for now she translated as she read aloud.

"November 1923

"Dear Yakov,

"I am permitted to send you a letter because a certain matter has arisen. I have tried to be faithful in the charge you gave me before your arrest. I am your brother, and even though you moved far away to Petrograd and we were never close, I took your request seriously. I have tried to care for your son fairly and faithfully. My wife dotes on him nearly as much as on our own four children. But these are hard times. I can barely put food into the mouths of my own children. Our baby, in fact, recently died of starvation. I do not say your child robs food from my children, yet surely you must understand that I must put them above all. Even at that I would never leave little Semyon destitute. I have found a good home for him. They are a well-to-do couple, I am told, who have lost their only child, a six-year-old boy. To help heal the woman's grief, they are willing to take your boy to replace theirs. I do not know who they are, as they wish to remain anonymous. The government agent who has arranged this assures me they will care for the boy well.

"Forgive me, Yakov, but I must do this thing. We are heartbroken, but it must be done.

"Your brother, Leo."

As Sophia finished, Cameron found it harder than ever to maintain her detached attitude, but she forced herself. Cool logic was the only thing that would aid her in her search. But logic only told her now that Semyon Luban was yet another step farther out of reach. At least she knew he had been alive in 1923. Alive and forced to endure another separation. An anonymous well-to-do couple. This matter was coming to resemble a puzzle. She had another piece, but it didn't help at all.

"Are you sure there is nothing more said of the couple who took the child?" Cameron asked futilely.

"I see nothing." As if to appease Cameron, Sophia turned the pages of the letter over. They both knew she'd find nothing.

Cameron tossed down the envelope she had been holding. "I don't know why I expected anything. I should have known it was a lost cause when I found out Yakov had been in prison for twenty years."

"I wonder why he was sent to prison," Sophia mused.

Cameron could tell by the intense look on her face that she was getting drawn into the mystery. "Would knowing matter?"

"I suppose not, but you mentioned he was a good man, a good father, hardly the criminal type."

"Yes." Cameron picked up the stack of letters to her mother. "And he mentions in his letters that he is not political. Yet I recall your father mentioned he was a political prisoner."

"That can mean anything in Russia. There are a hundred ways a person can fall afoul of the government besides politics and crime." Sophia eyed the letters in Cameron's hand.

"Would you like to read these, Sophia?"

"I would like to, but are you sure? It seems such a private matter."

"You couldn't get much more private than what I've told you already." Cameron laid her hand on her friend's arm. "You are the only person I have ever told. Perhaps the only person besides my mother and me who knows. It truly feels good to have shared this secret with a friend."

"I am honored, Cameron." Sophia started to reach for the bundle of letters, but her hand stopped in midair. Instead of taking the letters Cameron held out for her, she picked up the envelope that had held the letter from Yakov's brother. "I did not notice this before," she said. "The envelope has writing, though not an address as if for mailing. It says, 'To Yakov Luban, Slobodskoi Prison, Kirov.' Under that is, 'From Leo Luban, Vdovin, Russia.' But Russia is crossed out and, in another hand, is written, 'Union of Soviet Socialist Republics.' " Sophia smiled. "No doubt a Soviet bureaucrat was offended by the old usage."

But Cameron hardly heard Sophia's final sentences. "Sophia, Vdovin—that must be the village where Leo is from." Her heart raced. "I have something! I finally have something!" She jumped up and nearly danced a jig. "Have you heard of this place?"

"No, I am sorry. It could be anywhere."

"I don't care. I'm going to find it. I'm going to go there!"

27

VDOVIN WAS AN OBSCURE VILLAGE, certainly not one on the average atlas. Cameron thoroughly pored through a couple that were in the press room's research department, actually a shelf of about a dozen books, most collecting dust because they were so useless to the journalists.

Cameron pursued the search for a couple of weeks, but it was Sophia who stumbled upon the possible locale of the village as she was at her usual task of reading the daily newspapers. An article in *Pravda* focused on the success of factory evacuations from German-occupied zones. In fact, from July 1941 to at least December, some fifteen hundred factories had been moved, quite literally "lock, stock, and barrel" into the eastern regions of the country. One of these regions was Sverdlovsk, the capital of the Ural territory.

"Listen to this, Cameron," Sophia said and began reading from the paper. " 'In the Sverdlovsk Steel Works three workers have received special commendation this month for surpassing quotas.' They list the three names," she added, "but only one is of importance, 'Pavel Mokasov of Vdovin.' "

"Oh . . . goodness! That's it, isn't it? Dare I hope it says more?" Cameron said.

"It doesn't. I am sorry. And I suppose it could mean anything, not necessarily that the village is near Sverdlovsk. Many thousands of workers were evacuated far from their homes along with the factories."

"There is only one way to find out." Cameron jumped up, then quickly sat down. She had to think this through. "I need to contact my source in the State Planning Commission. Only I can't be too direct."

"It would be harmless enough for you merely to say you want to follow up on this article."

"That would be a good approach." Cameron sighed. She didn't like to raise the touchy issue of Oleg. "But my friend Colonel Tiulenev may have been the one who informed on you and your family. Remember I unwisely spoke to him after Oleg's arrest? I still believe Tiulenev is a good man, but even if he slipped accidentally, there is now a seed of doubt."

"I still don't see why you cannot use this article."

"He's a cagey old coot. Besides, if I do find out Vdovin is near Sverdlovsk, I doubt they will arrange a trip there for me just to interview some commendation winners. And if I have already asked about Vdovin, he might make a connection when I ask to visit the region. Or maybe I am just too paranoid for my own good."

"I would suggest you continue to try finding out on your own the location of the village. At least you have a specific region you can make a more thorough search of. After you find it, use your contact to arrange the visit. If it is near Sverdlovsk, there are an abundance of draws there that would warrant a tour."

The certainty in Sophia's tone was encouraging to Cameron. "Such as?" she asked.

"Well, for one, even before the war it was an industrial center, the home of Uralmash, a huge industrial complex. Also, I recall reading in the newspaper that, because of its proximity to mining regions of the Urals, a good portion of the Geological Institute was moved there after the war started."

"I think we are in business, Sophia!"

"There is one more significance to the city." Sophia paused as if for effect. "Before the Revolution it was called Ekaterinburg. It was there that the last tsar of Russia and his family were executed."

"You'd think because of the industry alone, they would have taken us there already."

"It is several hundred miles from here. But at least the region is not in a war zone."

After another day of exhaustive research—made a little easier now that they had a specific place in mind on which to concentrate—they located Vdovin, and it was near Sverdlovsk. The problem still remained as to how to finagle a visit there. To ask directly for anything in this country was always a great risk.

"I cannot let Uncle Boris suspect anything," Cameron said.

"There is a particular Scripture," Sophia replied, "that Russian believers are fond of. It goes, 'Behold, I send you forth as sheep in the midst of wolves: be ye therefore wise as serpents, and harmless as doves.' "

"That's in the Bible?" Cameron asked rather incredulously.

"Yes, in the book of Matthew."

"Well, I'll be. I never thought Christianity could be so practical."

A hint of a smile twitched Sophia's lips. Cameron thought she was fighting back a huge grin. Sophia always walked softly when spiritual matters were broached between them, but she never backed off from them. To her credit, she seldom brought up the topic herself, but rather it usually just naturally slipped into the conversation, as now. Cameron never felt her friend was in a conspiracy to entrap her.

"Extremely practical," Sophia said. "You will not be disappointed when you become a believer."

"When?" Cameron arched a brow, she hoped in a good-natured gesture.

Sophia blushed anyway. "Well . . . I hope . . . you do not take offense. . . . It is only that I wish so—"

Growing a bit embarrassed herself, Cameron cut in gently, "I was only joking. Who knows what will happen."

"In Moscow you thought you might look into it further. . . ?"

"I was sidetracked somewhat. Maybe when I get this Vdovin business settled . . ." She really had intended to give religion more thought, and she still might. Perhaps when she had time, she would take a look at the Bible Jackie had sneaked into her suitcase.

"Well, then," Sophia said briskly, "shall I give this Colonel Tiulenev a call?"

"I better do that since I have been the only one to contact him in the past. But you can find the number and ring it for me."

As Cameron waited for the tedious process of making a telephone call through the hotel switchboard—indeed, any phone call in Russia!—she considered just how she would handle Uncle Boris. "Wise as a serpent" was a good start. But she wouldn't forget the "harmless" part, which she took to mean a dose of subtlety.

"Colonel, thank you so much for seeing me," she said the next day when she was received into Tiulenev's Kuibyshev office, which appeared to be a transported replica of his Moscow office. She gave him one of her most winning smiles.

His response was full of warmth, and she questioned her suspicions. Still, even with the best intentions he might have inadvertently let something sensitive slip.

"I am always happy to visit with you, Camrushka. How have you found your stay in Kuibyshev?"

"Not as stimulating as Moscow. The Narkomindel tries to keep us occupied, but . . ." she gave a shrug to complete her thought. "I have, however, discovered something that might prove a nice diversion. My editor, who is quite a rock hound—"

"Rock hound?"

"Yes, one interested in geology and such. He asked if I could do an article on Russia's mining industry. I have discovered that the Geological Institute has been relocated to Sverdlovsk. While looking into this, I also learned this city is the site of Uralmash and some historically significant sites. It would be a grand place to visit."

"It is rather far from here. Such a visit could take several days."

"Oh, Colonel! We have nothing but time on our hands here. Even the war offers little diversion, it being in winter mode."

"I will see what I can do. But you realize such an extensive tour cannot be arranged for you alone. The other journalists must almost definitely be included."

"I suppose if it must be." She gave a resigned sigh. Actually, she wanted it that way. She would need the cover of others in order to more easily slip away. To the colonel she added, "It might even make me a bit of a hero to them."

Tiulenev made a couple of phone calls right there, and before Cameron left his office, she had assurance a tour of Sverdlovsk would be arranged.

That night Cameron opened a Bible, something she hadn't done since she was in fourth grade and her Sunday school class gave out awards for memorizing Scripture. Because she had so recently returned home from Russia, she had desperately wanted to impress her classmates. But she had been completely frustrated because she simply could not concentrate enough to commit anything to memory, especially all those strange, incomprehensible biblical words.

She wondered if her motives now were just as skewed as they had been then. She fully realized she was doing it because she'd been so successful with Uncle Boris and felt that maybe she owed God this gesture, since advice from the Bible had been vaguely involved in her good fortune. She probably would have been just as successful without Sophia's serpent-dove advice. But . . . she gave a shrug, not really knowing how to complete the thought.

As she opened the book, she recalled something else from Sunday school. She'd heard that children, new Christians, and such should begin reading the Bible at the New Testament. Now she wondered why that was. She well knew the Old Testament could be tedious. But something in her suddenly rebelled. Maybe they were trying to trick her by sucking in the unsuspecting with the gentler words of the New Testament before pounding them with the "laws" and the "prophets."

"Humph!" she grunted as she opened the book to Genesis. "I certainly can take anything. I don't need milk toast to start."

She fell asleep halfway through the book of Genesis and was a modicum humbler the next night, but for some reason she was no less determined. Everyone—well, Alex and Sophia—had told her to research Christianity. Now that she had started, she wasn't going to be easily discouraged. That was her nature. A puppy with her teeth in her master's cuff, she wasn't about to let go until she had some answers. It helped that she had something to prove to herself after falling asleep the night before completely befuddled by the little she had thus far read.

This time she flipped to Matthew and, after a tedious genealogy, was pleased to find the Christmas story. She felt on familiar ground. She could do this.

Do what? a small voice murmured in her head.

Read the Bible, that's all. Research. Nothing more.

She sensed her defensiveness. But why shouldn't she be a little so? Religion had seemed so ineffective in her mother's life. It had also torn Alex from her. That alone should make her run from it.

Excuses, said that same voice.

"Be quiet!" she muttered out loud.

Maybe they were excuses. She could not deny there were some forceful arguments in support of religion. Jackie had always been a solid, admirable person. And Anna Yevnovona, Sophia's grandmother, was the kind of strong woman that Cameron would be proud to emulate. And Sophia. And Alex . . . Even as Cameron thought of him she knew he was one of the reasons why she must do this research. They had said it was over between them, but her heart was certainly not finished with him yet. Nearly every day she thought of things she wanted to talk to him about. Even last night before she fell asleep her reading in Genesis had raised several questions and she'd wondered what Alex would think about them.

There were many good reasons for her to do this thing. She could indeed wait until her mind was free of the search for Semyon. But something told her that was the coward's way out. She had never in her life looked for a way out of anything. She wouldn't now.

She let her gaze drop to the open book in her lap.

Now the birth of Jesus Christ was on this wise: When as his mother Mary was espoused to Joseph, before they came together, she was found with child. . . .

Cameron did not soon fall asleep that night. She finished the entire book of Matthew. Then she lay awake, her mind buzzing with thoughts and questions.

28

QUICKLY THE PLANNING of the trip to Vdovin took on the proportions of organizing a major military offensive. The largest hurdle to surmount was that of language. As was the norm for such trips arranged by the Narkomindel, the journalists would not be able to take their own interpreters. The press department would instead provide their people for the job.

Even if Cameron could have arranged for Sophia to be one of those, she would have been too easily missed slipping away from the group, and two of them could not have left without somebody taking notice. But there was no question of her using any interpreter she could not trust implicitly. Cameron thought about feigning a broken arm and insisting that the special circumstance required her to bring her own secretary to take notes and such. But that idea was laden with far too many pitfalls to work. Sophia suggested that she write a letter in Russian explaining the circumstances that Cameron could show to the family in Vdovin she hoped to locate. But the chances of these people accepting a foreigner were slim, if any, and even if they did, the process of them writing out answers to Cameron's questions was too laborious. Besides, what if such a letter fell into the wrong hands?

It was not until a week before the planned trip that Cameron figured out the best approach.

"Sophia, could you get to Vdovin on your own? You could request a few days off while you are not needed by me to visit an aunt in Vdovin."

"They may check into that," Sophia said. The two of them had been using this process, questioning back and forth, to eliminate the many other harebrained schemes they had considered. "They might want a name."

"You can give them the name of the fellow in the article—Pavel Mokasov, wasn't it? I doubt any of them saw that obscure article, and they aren't going to speak personally to the man. I really doubt they will check at all."

"No, even they will not waste the time." Sophia screwed up her face as if thinking intently. "But what if. . . ?" She shook her head. "Cameron, I can't think of any problems besides that—at least any major ones!"

"There must be." Even if the idea was Cameron's, she could not believe it wasn't as bad as all the rest.

Sophia laughed. "So Russian of you, Cameron! But not always is there a bad side to things."

"So you travel to the village and meet me there. Then all I have to do is figure out a way to slip away from Sverdlovsk unnoticed. I checked a map, and it is ten miles away. I'll need transportation—" She cut off abruptly and gave a grim laugh. "Goodness! I keep thinking of weaving tangled webs. And I keep seeing myself hanging by my thumbs in the middle of that web. Is it really worth all this? Who knows if I will find Leo Luban still there after all these years. He could be dead, his family moved long ago. There's no way to check ahead of time. If I do find him, even with you along, who says he will speak to me? And he could well not know a thing beyond what is in the letter. There are simply too many uncertainties for all the risk."

"So you will give up?"

Cameron saw no guile in Sophia's statement, yet she could not have said anything that would cement Cameron's resolve more firmly. Give up? Never! And Sophia, guileless or not, knew that facet of her personality well.

"Not on your life. The thought never crossed my mind." She gave Sophia a smirk just in case the girl's words had been a prod.

Sophia smiled back innocently.

They spent some time ironing out all the details. Cameron realized she would need a confidant among the journalists, but she did not approach Johnny until the Narkomindel gave Sophia permission to visit Vdovin, along with official travel papers. Johnny did not give the request a second thought. He loved a bit of intrigue.

Cameron had seen some dismal places in her travels, especially in the Soviet Union, but Sverdlovsk had to rate quite high among those. This was no doubt partly due to its rapid growth during the first of Stalin's five-year plans. Before the Great War, Sverdlovsk had a population of seventy-five thousand, but by the mid-thirties it had exploded to five hundred thousand. Now, with the wartime evacuation of factories, it had burgeoned to one million. Buildings were bleak and utilitarian. Parks, picturesque historic buildings, and broad aesthetic avenues were conspicuously absent from this city. Set in a pretty part of the Urals with lakes and woods and meadows of grazing cattle, this smoke-spewing monstrosity was like a scar on the landscape.

The hotel housing the journalists during their stay was aptly named Sovietskaya and seemed to represent the most unimaginative, austere aspects of modern Soviet culture. But Cameron hadn't come to this city to enjoy its amenities, had it any. However, she was going to miss the first planned excursion of the trip, an all-day tour of several factories in the Uralmash complex. But she had decided to set her plan in motion early in case there were delays. She'd begun the ruse on the plane ride from Kuibyshev by casually mentioned physical complaints.

"Does anyone else feel warm?" She'd unbuttoned her coat for

effect. Like most Soviet planes theirs was far from warm, and she expected the chorus of denials she received. Fanning herself, she'd remarked, "It must be me."

At the hotel that first evening upon their arrival, she dragged about as if all activity was an effort. She barely touched her dinner. Johnny and the others were solicitous toward her. Cameron feared Johnny was laying it on too thickly, since his doting went quite against character. But by morning no one doubted Johnny when he announced that Cameron had a fever and wasn't going to be able to join the group for the day's tour. Nikolai Palgunov looked in on her, and she grunted and groaned her regrets.

"I think if I just sleep today, I'll be right as rain tomorrow," she sighed.

"Shall I send for a doctor?"

"Oh, no. I think it's just a touch of ague," she replied, hoping the man didn't note her sudden surge of panic upon realizing she hadn't taken this offer into account. Who would have thought old bureaucratic Palgunov would have been so concerned?

Johnny, who had accompanied Palgunov, added, "I've given her an aspirin and a sleeping powder. She just needs to rest."

Palgunov had no reason to suspect otherwise and left it at that.

A half hour after she was certain the entourage had departed, Cameron dressed in some very Russian-looking clothes Sophia had found for her before leaving Kuibyshev—a drab brown wool skirt, brown-and-black striped cotton long-sleeved blouse, a brown sweater over that, thick black stockings, and scuffed oxford-style shoes. A black wool coat went over that and a pale pink wool scarf over her head. All was old, ill fitting, and unfashionable. She thought she should blend in well.

Before leaving her hotel room she placed a couple of pillows under her covers just in case anyone looked in. Taking for granted there would be some NKVD spies in the hotel, she took great pains not to be seen as she exited her room and the hotel. Getting out of the city would be even more difficult.

A few innocently fashioned questions the night before to the Intourist officials who were directing the tour had given her the location of the bus station. Once there that morning, she learned there were no buses to Vdovin. But she was able to take a bus that got her close to the road out of Sverdlovsk that went to the village. From there she would try to hitch a ride. Walking the ten miles was not an option, because she had to get back to the hotel by nightfall. Johnny would do what he could to fend off any visits to her room, but even Johnny could do only so much.

Glancing at her watch, she saw it was already nearly eleven. Another worry was Sophia. Today was the planned rendezvous, but Sophia was supposed to have arrived at the village yesterday. Had she found a place to stay? They had discovered there was a small hotel in the village but could not make arrangements for lodgings ahead of time. Sophia said she would "go on faith" that there would be a vacant room.

Cameron beat her gloved hands together to fend off the cold. Her friend was placing much faith indeed in her God, because one could not survive this cold sleeping on the street.

Cameron nearly froze, though the exercise of walking kept the cold at bay somewhat. She tried to wave down several vehicles without luck, choosing only those that did not look in any way official. After she had walked two miles, a small flatbed truck stopped. It was loaded with sacks of something in back. In the cab four passengers were already seated.

Cameron took out a slip of paper Sophia had written for just such a circumstance. She gave it to the driver with a questioning smile on her face.

The paper read: *I am Sophia. I am a deaf mute. I need a ride to Vdovin. Thank you very much.*

The driver looked at the paper with a blank expression. Cameron groaned inwardly as she realized the man could not read. He handed the paper to the woman next to him. She read it to him, and they talked afterwards, with some input from the other passengers. Finally the driver nodded.

He spoke in Russian, but Cameron had enough grasp of the language now to decipher his words. "We weren't going that far, but we will take you there anyway."

She shrugged and scratched her head as if she didn't understand. He nodded, adding loudly, "Yes, we take you!"

Appearing to understand his gesture, not his words, she nodded in response, grinning.

"Get in back," he said.

She squinted, as if trying to understand. He said loudly, "Back!"

and pointed. She nodded then and scurried around to the back and climbed up with the sacks. The truck rumbled into motion just as she realized the sacks were not grain or seed, as she had imagined. They were sacks of fertilizer! She asked herself again if it was all worth it. Then and there she uttered a prayer that it would be.

Vdovin was a village of several unpaved streets and perhaps a few hundred inhabitants. The structures were mostly of wood, some nicely framed, others rather ramshackle, and no particular order to the location of these. Flimsy lath fences surrounded some yards, and the ground was covered with snow, though its brownish hue lacked the pristine look of fresh snow. Somehow, even in March, there was the sense that mud lay not far beneath the snow, and in some places where the snow was especially dirty, it was more than merely a sense. There was nothing quaint about this village, yet despite that it had a homey look. Though some buildings were coarse, unpainted wood, others were painted cheerily, one green, one yellow, another with a blue door. The paint was chipped and peeling, but nonetheless the village was inviting.

Cameron picked out the hotel quickly. It was one of the few brick structures in the village but was not large. It looked to house about ten guests. Oh, please let Sophia be in there warming herself by a cozy fire!

The building looked more like a house than a hotel. She felt strange walking right in until she saw a little handwritten sign above the door: *Fkhadit!* Come in. She grasped the door latch, turned it, and stepped into a dimly lit foyer. Though warm inside, she saw no hearth with a fire but quickly recalled that most country homes had large brick stoves for heat. These were often low with a bed on top of them.

"Hello!" she called in Russian.

In a few moments a woman came into the front room. She was stout, round-faced, and middle-aged, with obviously dyed red hair. She wore bright red lipstick that was applied fuller than her actual lips, and had dark, thin penciled eyebrows. Otherwise, her clothing and bearing said "farm wife," as did her friendly smile.

At this point Cameron had decided it would be difficult to maintain the ruse that she was Russian, so she said in her accented Russian that she was looking for a guest named Sophia Gorbenko. She was quite proud of her progress with the Russian language until the woman replied with a fast-paced gibberish, of which Cameron could understand none. It was one thing speaking a language and quite another hearing it from an expert. Cameron shrugged her confusion. The innkeeper then simply said Sophia's room number and pointed to the stairs.

Cameron found the room, and when her friend answered her knock, she was so glad to see Sophia she flung her arms around her. She realized then just how stressful her journey from Sverdlovsk, alone with no interpreter, had been. It brought to mind her first day in Moscow when she had been alone during the air raid. But she realized this excursion was far easier than her first, because she had learned a great deal since that day.

Sophia had not been idle during the time since her arrival in Vdovin last night. She had located the Luban family. Only a daughter of Leo Luban remained—her brothers were all in the Army. But finding her had taken some detective work because she was married now with another name. Sophia had also laid the groundwork for Cameron to visit by informing the young woman of Cameron's desire to speak with her. Marfa Elichin had been leery upon first hearing the suggestion of socializing with a foreigner, but Sophia had finally won her over.

"Not knowing when you would arrive," Sophia said, "I could not make a definite appointment, but she said she would be home all day. She is expecting a baby and so has a leave from her job at a factory in Sverdlovsk."

"Let's go, then." Cameron's stomach chose just then to rumble.

"When was the last time you ate, Cameron?"

"I don't know. Lunch yesterday, I guess. Remember, I couldn't eat because I was supposed to be sick." She glanced at her wristwatch and saw it was nearly one in the afternoon.

"Well, you will eat now, or you will be sick for real. It's past the inn's time for lunch, but I am sure the innkeeper will have leftovers."

It was nearer to two o'clock before Cameron and Sophia walked down the street to the Elichin house. It was one of the poorer structures in the village, not painted, and it appeared as if a good wind might topple it. The lath fence was indeed toppled in some places, and the gate hung on only one hinge. But when Cameron took a breath and knocked on the door, she thought that it at least felt sturdy enough.

The woman who answered was, according to Sophia, in her mid-twenties. But like so many Russian women, especially country women, she looked older. Her dark hair was pinned up rather haphazardly with several bobby pins. Her flowered cotton housedress was faded, as was the wool shawl wrapped around her shoulders. Cameron was no expert, but she guessed Marfa was within only a month or two of giving birth. Her smile was tentative but genuine. Two toddler-aged children were peeking out from behind her dress.

The house was poor in every way but neat and tidy. Marfa motioned them to follow her into the kitchen, explaining to Sophia that it was warmest there. They sat at a small table, small because the kitchen itself was small and cramped. A rough bench on one side of the table was up against a wall, and here Marfa directed Cameron and Sophia to sit. A chair on the opposite side of the table left only a narrow path to move about the rest of the room, especially pushed out as it was to accommodate Marfa's bulk.

Cameron wanted to get right to her interview, but the young woman, being a good hostess, insisted on fixing tea. While she cut up slices of plain brown bread—obviously all she had to offer with the tea—her children literally clung to her apron strings.

At last the time came for talk.

"You say you know my father?" Marfa asked in Russian with Sophia translating. The woman's younger child, about two years old, sat on her lap trying to grab at everything on the table, so Marfa's words were constantly punctuated with "No, no, Ilya," or with Ilya's protests. The other child, a three-year-old girl named Anya, sat on the floor at Marfa's feet, munching quietly on a slice of bread and playing with a faded rubber ball.

"I never met the man, but his brother is an acquaintance of my family, and I am trying to find his son, Semyon."

"I remember Semyon a little, but I was only four when he came to live here."

"What do you remember about him?"

Marfa leaned an elbow on the table and rested her chin in her hand. She was silent as if considering the question. "Sophia says he is your brother."

Cameron shot a surprised glance at Sophia, who responded with a mildly stricken look. Her eyes held apology. They hadn't really discussed what to tell the Luban family. Cameron had been keeping this secret for so long she wasn't sure what to make of the fact that yet another knew it. But what could be the harm? Marfa did not look like an informer. Wouldn't it be better if she knew the truth? Any other approach might make the woman too suspicious to talk, and justly so.

"Yes, he is," Cameron replied in an amazingly steady voice. He was her brother! She had a brother. She was perhaps drawing close to finding him. The idea of it still amazed her. "It is a long story how it came to be, Marfa, but he is my mother's son, and she had to give him up when she returned to the States."

"Is my uncle Yakov, then, the father?"

"Yes . . ." She was about to say, "as far as I know," but changed her mind. She, too, had to accept the truth.

"I don't remember my uncle," Marfa went on. "Everything I know is from what my mother spoke of later when I was old enough to understand. I wish you could talk to my mother, but both of my parents have passed on. But Semyon was only a year or so older than I, and we played together. But even most of those memories are from what I heard later. He only lived with us for two years. Mama told me that my two older brothers tended to bully the younger of us children. Once when they were picking on me, I started to cry and Semyon jumped on Petyr and fought him for me. Mind, Petyr is two years older than Semyon and was always a husky boy. My cousin was very protective of me, more like an older brother than my blood brothers. But Semyon was like that. He came home from school more than once with bruises on his face from fighting. And the fights always started because he was trying to protect someone or because he was fighting for something he believed in. Oh, he was murder on cheaters! He would not abide cheating." A slight smile bent her lips. The memories of Semyon seemed, for the most part, to be pleasant ones for her.

"It must have been hard for him to lose his father."

"Oh, yes. My mama said they were very close. Maybe that was why Semyon fought so much." Marfa paused. Anya started to cry because her ball had rolled out of reach. Marfa began to heave her bulk to her feet, but Sophia jumped up instead and went after the ball. Marfa gave her a grateful smile before continuing. "I remember he got a bad cut on the end of his eyebrow from a fight. That's when the teacher called my parents to school. They were considering expelling him."

"But he couldn't have been more than seven years old!" Cameron knew nothing about child rearing, but that did seem harsh punishment for a child that age.

"Not long after that my baby brother died, and then Semyon was sent away. I remember thinking I better be good or I might be sent away, too." Marfa smiled slightly, as if at a child's fancies. "Later, of course, Mama explained that the reason Semyon went away was so he could live with a rich family who could afford to take care of him. We were very poor."

"Do you know anything about that family, Marfa?" Cameron had a difficult time voicing this crucial question. Everything hinged on that point.

"I knew you would want to know that." Marfa sighed, and the sound was none too encouraging. "They were very firm about not having their identity known. I know they were not from Vdovin, for it would have been easy to pick them out then. I always asked if I could go visit Semyon, and finally, when I was old enough to understand, my mama told me that his new family lived far away and that it was best for Semyon to have a whole new life with them."

"Far away. . . ?"

"I am afraid, Miss Hayes, that far away could mean only a hundred miles away, especially then, when few people traveled far from home. Or it could mean a thousand, you see."

Cameron tried to accept that she had run into a dead end. At least she had learned a little more about Semyon Luban, but she wasn't satisfied. She had to learn more.

"Marfa, who arranged the adoption?" Cameron leaned forward, ready to be shot down again or to be given new hope.

"Just a minute." Marfa rose and left the kitchen.

Cameron exchanged glances with Sophia. Her friend smiled with hope gleaming in her eyes. Cameron tried to grasp on to that. If Marfa had documents . . .

When Marfa returned she indeed did have a paper. She laid it before Cameron. "This is all we have. The only memory left of Semyon." Her lower lip trembled. "We have no photographs because we could never afford them."

Before Cameron gave her attention to the paper, Marfa's words raised another important question. "What happened to Yakov's things when he was arrested? He had a camera and must have had many photographs."

"All I know is that Uncle Yakov showed up here one night completely empty-handed except for Semyon in his arms. I remember being awakened in the night. Later Mama told me that Uncle Yakov had had to leave Leningrad in a hurry, barely escaping the police, I think. He came here and begged my papa to take his son—you must understand, it was a great risk for my father to take the child of someone in trouble with the police. But the police were after my uncle, and if he was caught, he wanted to know Semyon was in good hands."

"Do you know why the police were after Yakov?"

"He was suspected of distributing subversive materials." Marfa leaned forward and added in a conspiratorial tone, "Mama thought they were religious tracts."

"He was Jewish, wasn't he?"

"He and my father were about a quarter Jewish, but their family practiced the Russian Orthodox faith in tsarist times. My father was not much for religious matters at any time and especially not after the Revolution. But Uncle Yakov . . . my papa said he was far too religious. It caused a rift between the brothers. But Yakov was quiet about his faith until the last few years before his arrest. I am not sure if the problems with the police were because of his faith, but my mama always thought the difficulties strengthened his faith and made him more open about it. And that brought more police persecution upon him."

"His arrest was for neither political nor criminal reasons?" That was Sophia. Her eyes were glittering with interest. When Cameron glanced at her, she gave a slightly embarrassed shrug. "I wondered after reading the letters," she merely added.

So Yakov Luban was a religious fanatic? Cameron mused. She didn't know what to make of *that*. Instead, she returned to safer ground. "Your uncle came here that night all the way from Leningrad?"

"I don't think so. He had been moving around quite a bit, eluding the police. I'm not sure where he had been before coming to us. It was 1921 when he came to us, in the spring—I remember because we were celebrating my brother's name day. Maybe that's why he never liked Semyon much, because his day was ruined."

"I had assumed Yakov was arrested nearer to 1922."

"Yes, my mother later told me he had been a fugitive for months after he left Semyon and before his arrest."

"You are certain he left none of his possessions with you?"

"Do you think I would hide them from you?" Marfa asked, and

Cameron noted the effrontery of her tone even before the translation.

"I'm sorry. I didn't mean it that way."

"I know it is important." Marfa shook her head with her own apology.

"Uncle Yakov only stayed with us that one night for a couple of hours so we would not get into trouble. I suppose running from the police forced him to leave all his possessions behind."

"That's too bad. . . ." Not only because it left Cameron with no new clues, but mostly she felt a deep sadness over a life so thoroughly destroyed, nothing left but a few pieces of papers, three photographs, and a book. Cameron wished she had one of those photos with her now to give to Marfa. She knew the woman would have treasured it.

Cameron then focused on the document before her. Though quite simple, it appeared official; at least it bore an official-looking seal. Cameron passed it to Sophia.

"It simply states," she said, "that Leo Luban, completely of his own accord, does give over to the State for care and fosterage one Semyon Luban, a seven-year-old child. It is signed by Leo Luban and Comrade Vasily Zharenov, of the Council of People's Commissars, Ural Region."

"A name . . ." Cameron breathed. She knew what a thin shred of hope that was, but still, it was another piece to the puzzle.

"I wish I had more," Marfa said.

"You have been a tremendous help. I thank you so much!" Cameron grasped the woman's hands and wanted to smile but found sudden emotion allowed her lips only to twitch.

Marfa understood. She squeezed Cameron's hands warmly. Then when Cameron slipped her hands away and slid the adoption document toward her, she shook her head.

"No, Miss Hayes. You keep it," Marfa said. "Maybe it will help you."

"I couldn't. It's all you have—"

"Please take. And when you find him, maybe you will tell him he has a cousin who still loves him, yes?"

All Cameron could do was nod. Tears clogged off any other response.

After that they chatted a while longer as they finished their tea. Cameron enjoyed hearing more stories of Semyon's childhood. When it was time to leave, Marfa arranged a ride for them back to

Sverdlovsk with a neighbor who had a vehicle. Sophia went, as well, and would spend another night in the city, out of sight of the journalists, of course, before returning to Kuibyshev.

Back in her hotel room, well ahead of the other journalists, Cameron looked once more at the adoption paper. Even if it meant extending her "illness," she would try to track down that name while in Sverdlovsk. But mostly she thought of a scrappy little boy, fighting for righteous causes. She was liking him—her brother!—more and more.

THE BOY HANDED the packet to the tall young man.

"Thank you." The young man glanced at the packet now in his hand, then his eyes flickered to the delivery boy. "Is there something else?"

"I am going to Major Simonov's office next if you have anything you wish me to take."

"No . . ." the young man said slowly, then glanced again at the packet. "Not yet."

The boy left, and the young man took one more look at the packet marked only with his surname, Tveritinov. Then he turned from the door. He was surrounded by clutter in a small room containing two drafting tables with high stools at each and another desk with a telephone and other office paraphernalia arrayed on top. Against the walls of the room were shelves full of a vast variety of items, some even relating to the work occurring in the room—paints, brushes, art papers, a wide selection of pencils and rulers. It was, in fact, very well supplied. The work that went on in this room was important.

"What have you got there, Semyon?" asked the other person in the room, a man a few years older, shorter, and stockier than the younger man. He wore thick spectacles over pale eyes.

Semyon lifted his gaze. He'd nearly forgotten he was not alone. "Nothing."

"You don't look like it is nothing."

"Well . . . it is everything, really." Semyon Tveritinov strode to the drafting tables, which were side by side to take advantage of the light that came from a large window over the tables, now with its black-out shade lifted, and also from a pole lamp standing between the tables. Semyon sat on his stool, then opened the envelope. He withdrew about a dozen eight-by-ten-inch photographs. Thus far he'd been hesitant, but now, with a dogged resolve, he quickly shuffled through the photographs. Grunting, he dropped the stack on the table. "They're terrible."

"Let me see." The second man reached for them.

"No, Dmitri!" Semyon laid a hand protectively on the photos. Then he shrugged resignedly. "All right, look." He shoved them across the table.

Dmitri looked through the photos, taking more time with them than his companion had. When he finished, he handed them back. "They are not bad. How long have you been at this? A few months?"

"These are my best work, Dmitri. I planned to show these to Major Simonov." He rubbed his chin, covered with a dark shadow of a day's growth of beard. In contrast to what one might expect of a man with a head of light caramel-colored hair, he'd developed a good thick beard at sixteen and since then could never make it to the next morning without the need to shave. Luckily, he was usually too busy to care. "Look at this one." He shoved a photo in front of his friend's face. "The woman is out of focus. I had intended her to be the subject of the picture." The photo showed a queue of shoppers before a bakery. "I wanted to show the dogged determination of the Russian people in supporting the war effort by waiting patiently for goods. You should have seen the look on this woman's face. Pure heroism."

"It is still good if you don't know what your intent was. But take a better look at the next photograph. You were going too quickly, I think, to really see."

It was of women removing shell casings from a furnace.

"It should be closer up—"

"Ah! You are too critical of yourself, Semyon."

"I wanted them to be perfect."

"Do you think every shot a combat photographer takes in the middle of gunfire and bombs is going to be perfect?" Dmitri shook his head in answer to his own question. Then he asked another. "Are you certain you want to do this?"

"Why do you think I have been working so hard to train myself in photography? So that I can sit in this office in Moscow all day drawing propaganda posters?" Semyon swept his hand over the drafting table, littered with rulers and pens and paper.

"It is an important job," argued Dmitri.

"I want to be at the Front."

"Well, of course, so do I. But this is where the motherland wants me." Dmitri's face was dead serious for a moment, then a smile slipped across his lips. "I certainly can't complain that I am not getting shot at."

"Maybe you'd feel differently if you were here because your parents wished a safe job for you."

Semyon raked a hand through his thick hair. The light curls were unruly again, in desperate need of a haircut. He thought about it now because the curls made him look young, like a boy coddled by his mother. His dark eyes flashed as he denied to himself that that was true. But he well knew his father would never have prevented him from joining a frontline unit had it been entirely up to him. But they had both been completely stymied at Semyon's mother's tears when he had attempted to enlist at the start of the war. He was, after all, her only child, and she had already lost a son years ago.

"You should feel lucky you have an important father," offered Dmitri. He was of peasant stock and had worked hard for a position in the Communist Party's Administration of Propaganda and Agitation, or UPA.

All Semyon had done to gain this position had been to win an art contest years ago while in the Young Pioneers. He rued that day still! His artistic skills had been rudimentary at best—he thought they still were—but the sentiment of his entry had captured the judges' attention. The words "Be Vigilant!" had been emblazoned over a picture of a Young Pioneer tearing a smiling theatrical mask off an evil anti-Party villain. After the success of the contest, his parents had encouraged him in this talent, eventually enrolling him in the Frunze Institute of Moscow, a school for political training.

He'd been fairly content to follow this path. After all, until coming to live with his adopted parents, his life had been full of disruptions and strife. His parents had told him so, and he believed them. He'd had nightmares as a boy that also supported what his parents had said. He recalled little of his life before coming to live with his adoptive parents. It was as if a fuzzy curtain had been drawn between the two lives. Sometimes it would flutter and let out a shadowed glimpse of the past, never enough, but maybe too much, because he thought the nightmares sprang from these shadows. His father said it was well he could not remember clearly. Semyon hoped that was true, though it was odd at times to feel as if a chunk of his life was missing.

This did not trouble him often, because in his new home his parents had lavished upon him love and care and stability. No wonder he seldom referred to his parents as "adoptive." They were his real parents. He had no memory of any others and in truth wanted no other memories. His life had truly begun the day he entered the Tveritinov home.

Yes, his present course had not been a bad one—he did indeed have a talent for disseminating propaganda! But the war changed everything. Now he just wanted to be in the thick of it, not drawing posters and designing pamphlets. He'd dabbled a bit in photography at the Institute and enjoyed it, but his other studies had left little time for that diversion. Yet with a war on, he saw the camera, not the brush, as the best way to get to the Front, since he couldn't defy his mother outright by joining a regular military unit. But she didn't understand the mission of a war correspondent and could easily be led to think he was in no direct danger.

He was certain his father would support him should he win an assignment as a combat photographer. The man might even put a word in for him. Stanislav Tveritinov was an important man, the deputy to Nikita Khrushchev, who was the Supreme Political Commissar of the Red Army. Not exactly frontline soldiers, Khrushchev and his staff performed the vital task of circulating among various fronts, ensuring that Comrade Stalin's orders were carried out. They were in effect watchdogs, guarding the loyalty and obedience of officers and Party members. As such, Semyon's father had been quite torn in assenting to his wife's wishes. The loyalty of a man in his position might be questioned if his own son was not on the front lines of the war.

"I do not deny my good fortune, Dmitri." Semyon picked up the stack of photos, tapped them briskly on the table to straighten them before replacing them in the envelope. "But still I do not belong here, not now."

"Then you will take the photographs to Simonov?"

"They will have to be good enough."

"You will defy your parents?"

"Not really. I will still be in the UPA. But I must go where I am assigned, eh? Even my mother realizes that. A small deception only."

"I'll miss working with you, Semyon." Dmitri added with a wry grin, "I won't, however, miss all those bullets!"

"Perhaps I should question *your* loyalty to the motherland," Semyon said, partly in jest.

Dmitri laughed but cut it off as a hint of doubt crept into his eyes. "You wouldn't?"

"Only yesterday you made a questionable reference to Comrade Stalin, wondering if we could be certain that he had been in the Kremlin during the glorious Battle of Moscow. I thought to let it pass out of friendship. But—"

"You couldn't, Semyon!" gasped Dmitri, his face having gone more pale than usual. "It was a careless comment. But we do know he was not in the Kremlin during the worst of it but rather was in a bunker in a Metro station."

"Such remarks imply cowardice in our leader."

"I was only clarifying a known fact, and you well know that."

"I don't plan to inform on you, Dmitri." Semyon fastened a gaze on his friend, part entreaty, part warning. "But guard your tongue in the future. We, above all, in this department, must be unsullied in our loyalty to our country, to the Party, and especially to our leader."

Semyon rose, tucked the packet of photographs under his arm, and exited the workroom. His previous self-doubts were gradually falling away as he reminded himself once more of what his goals truly were. He did not want to be at the Front for glory and adventure—well, not entirely. He believed with all his heart that it was from there that he could truly serve his country. Not by carrying a rifle and killing Germans, though he would if he had to, but rather in the way his talents were best suited—capturing images of battle that would inspire a nation to victory. His mechanical skills as a photographer were not perfect, but his passion for his country and the mighty Communist system that sustained it would go far in overshadowing any mechanical flaws. There was no flaw in his fidelity.

30

Los Angeles, California
February 1942

EVEN IN THE EVENING LIGHT—moonlight only with blackout in force—Sam saw the sign in the barbershop window. "Free shaves for Japs. Not responsible for accidents."

He'd seen such sentiments before, but still he winced. He did not, however, point it out to his companions, three Japanese friends with whom he had just been to the movies. No sense in spoiling the evening. They were trying to have a good time, beginning with their choice of the movie, *Hold That Ghost* with Abbott and Costello. They had roared with laughter despite the fact that upon entering the theater they had slipped into the back row so as not to cause a stir. All of them had felt the sting of rejection in public places—even before the war. They usually did what they could to avoid causing themselves embarrassment.

They were walking to a nearby coffee shop for a snack, a place they knew would accept them because a Japanese man ran it. As they walked, Charlie and YoYo were reenacting one of the goofball scenes from the movie, which they had seen several times before this evening's viewing. Actually YoYo, a nickname for Yosuke, who was a bit on the stout side, was doing quite a good impression of Lou Costello.

"I said go outside, Furdy," mimicked Charlie in his best Bud Abbott growl.

"I don't wanna," whined YoYo's Costello. "It's too dark, and I don't wanna go out there all by myself with no one to talk to." He gave a shudder like the actor had in the spooky haunted house.

"Why don't you talk to yourself?" asked Charlie's Bud.

"I give too many stupid answers," came the Costello response.

Everyone laughed at the performance, but Sam noted the final member of the group was more reserved in her amusement. Even during the movie Emi had appeared as if her mind was elsewhere. As well it might be. Her father, a manager of a large Japanese import-export firm and a prominent leader in the Japanese community, had been arrested—though the FBI called it *detained*—shortly after the attack on Pearl Harbor, along with many leaders, including Sam's uncle in Berkeley. Most were Issei, though there was no real distinction between them and Nisei by government officials—it was only happenstance that the Issei, being first generation, were older and had risen to dominance in the Japanese community. With the bank accounts of all Issei frozen, it was causing a hardship on all, but with Emi it was probably worse because she had always lived a very prosperous lifestyle.

Sam didn't think that was entirely her problem tonight. Maybe he would find a chance to talk to her alone. These were his best friends from high school. Charlie and YoYo were also at UCLA with him. But Sam knew those two would not be interested in offering emotional support to Emi. It simply would have embarrassed them. Well, he wasn't completely comfortable with it, either, but being a year older than all of them, he had always acted as a sort of big brother, a role that came naturally to him. His mother had always told him that starting school a year late because of a childhood bout of scarlet fever would turn out good. Maybe this was why he was a bit more mature and a little better at offering support to his friends.

They reached the café and quickly found a table. The place wasn't very busy—most Japanese establishments weren't these days.

"I don't need a menu," Charlie said when the waitress held them out to the group. "I want a hamburger and a Coke. Everything on it."

"Only ice on our Cokes," the waitress said with a smirk.

Everyone laughed. The waitress was white, but the manager of the restaurant was Japanese, so they felt at ease here. Even the waitress laughed.

"What a wiseacre!" gibed Charlie. "Ha ha. You know what I mean."

"Anyone else need a menu?" asked the waitress.

No, they had been to that particular coffee shop many times and almost always ordered the same things. Charlie always had everything on his burger. YoYo had everything on a burger and also French fries and a slab of apple pie. Emi ordered a burger, hold the mayo. Sam's hamburger was hold the lettuce, tomato, and pickle, but extra mayo. They all, of course, drank Coca-Cola.

"You know, Sam," Emi said as they waited for their food, "I'm glad you decided to come out with us tonight. We hardly ever see you."

"So much has been happening," Sam said vaguely. He'd not told any of them about Jackie, though he supposed they had heard rumors via the grapevine. "Anyway," he added to deflect the attention from him, "if you had decided to go to UCLA, we'd see more of you."

"To my parents' great dismay," she said, "I never had any interest in school."

"She just wants to get married," said YoYo in that teasing way more suited to high school kids than to the near-adults they were.

"Some say college is the best place to meet a husband," Sam said.

"Only clowns like you three," she said with a laugh that seemed to Sam to be a little hollow. "What has been keeping you so busy, Sam?"

Just then their food arrived, and the question was lost in the flurry that followed, but Sam knew Emi wouldn't let it go. He also knew he should tell his friends. It wasn't a huge secret. But he knew Jackie was handling the situation in the same way. They weren't hiding, but then again, they were. Hiding in a world that encompassed only their love, a safe world with just the two of them. It wasn't embarrassment or shame that drove them into that world, merely a desire for peace.

But the world was at war.

"My mother is packing," YoYo was saying. "Can you believe that? I keep telling her she is being overly cautious. No one is going to make us leave."

"Don't be so certain, Yo," Emi said. "They took my father without a trial, a warrant, or any legal stuff. You've heard the rumors, too, haven't you, Sam?"

Sam blinked. How had the conversation turned to this topic? The world situation must be bad indeed if even his fun-loving friends were talking about it.

"Yeah, I guess so," he said, trying to focus.

"Well, my uncle says if they can arrest my father like they did, they can do anything."

"I have heard rumors about this since the war started, and nothing has happened," Charlie said. "Can't we talk about something else?"

"Yeah," Sam said, "we were supposed to have fun tonight, and we only have an hour left before curfew."

That was an unwise remark if he'd intended to lift the spirits of his friends. They all just groaned at yet another injustice, an eight o'clock curfew for all Japanese.

Making another attempt to redeem the situation, or perhaps escape from it, Sam jumped up and headed toward the jukebox. His budget was tight, stretched already to the limit by the movie and now dinner, but he supposed another nickel would be well spent if it took everyone's minds off their troubles. Some Andrews Sisters ought to do it. He picked "Scrub Me, Mama, With a Boogie Beat."

Leaning against the jukebox, tapping his foot to the tune, Sam watched Emi approach. He hoped she wasn't going to ask him to dance, but she should know better. He'd never been much of a dancer.

"Sam, have you been avoiding me?" Her voice was soft, and the music was loud enough so that no one else could hear.

Panic gripped Sam. There had always been an unspoken rule among this group of friends that they were friends first and foremost. Emi dated many other boys but had never shown an inclination in that way toward the three guys. They were like brothers and sister, and all content with that. Now Sam feared something had changed. He was hardly relieved, however, when Emi's next words dispelled that fear.

"Are you ashamed of having a white girlfriend?" she asked.

Gulping, he felt heat rise above his collar. "Gosh, Emi, why would you say that?"

"That's why you have been avoiding us, isn't it?"

"I don't—"

She gave her head a shake. "This is beneath you, Sam."

"What?" He tried to act innocent, but he knew what she meant, and he knew if he was indeed embarrassed by his relationship with Jackie, it *was* beneath him or anyone for that matter. But that made it no less difficult to talk about.

"No matter how YoYo or anyone tries to deny it, our world is changing," she said, her intense words a strange counterpoint to the toe-tapping beat of the Andrews Sisters' tune. "I knew the day they took away my father that nothing would be the same again. I saw that sign on the barbershop before we came here. You saw it, too, I know. It made you sick, didn't it? Well, something has got to give, and I think it will be us Japanese."

Sam knew it, too, and nodded. But he said, "I don't see what that has to do with . . . anything."

"Sam, are you serious about this white girl?"

"Don't lecture me, Emi!"

"I'm not!" She sounded a little offended. "I . . . I . . . just need to know what you are going to do . . . about it." Her trembling voice surprised him. If it wasn't because she was romantically interested in him, then what?

He was silent for a long time. The music now pounded against his head like an anvil, and he wanted to shut it off, but of course, there was no way to get back his nickel.

"Sam . . ." She chewed her lower lip before going on, "I don't want to embarrass you. I . . . you are the only one I think I can talk to."

"About what, Emi?" He was really confused now.

"I don't know anyone else with a white . . . friend."

That was true enough. The Japanese Nisei did everything possible to be American, yet few ventured beyond their race for romance or even for social outlet. He didn't know anyone . . . except—

"Emi, what do you mean, 'anyone else'?"

She continued to chew on her lip. It was trembling again. "There is this boy. We met at the grocery store where I work."

"Oh, Emi." His tone was full of sympathy.

"He's shipping out in a week."

"He's in the Army?"

"Navy." Her eyes glistened with tears. "He wanted to marry me, he really did, but that's pretty hard the way things are. We . . . we married each other in spirit." Sam gaped at this tearful confession, not knowing what to say. She went on. "Now . . . I'm in trouble." She swiped away a tear that slipped from her eye and pointedly kept her back to their friends at the table.

Her devastation was obvious, but Sam's own knees suddenly felt weak. He could only think, "There but for the grace of God go I." But Emi was a Christian, too. Yet he knew how easy it must have been for her to get caught in the place she was now. How many times had he wanted to fling aside his moral convictions in the face of the gross unfairness of society? He knew beyond doubt there was nothing wrong in God's eyes with loving one of another race. Yet society had made it a crime. So was it not a law that could be broken? He'd asked the question a million times and had no answer.

"Emi, do your parents know?"

She dismally shook her head. "I am so afraid to tell them. And with Dad gone, I don't know if Mom could stand something like this." She took a handkerchief from her pocket and blew her nose. "I know we weren't really married, no matter how much we tried to believe we were. I thought if maybe we could somehow really get married—that's why I wanted to talk to you."

"I don't know what to say." Sam realized that even now he had not come out clearly confessing—what an awful way of phrasing it!—his relationship with Jackie.

But Emi was too desperate to let it go at that. "You and she must have talked about it. Haven't you thought of a way—?"

Just then the music stopped. As abruptly as a slap, they were surrounded by silence. The only response he gave her was a quick shake of his head.

"Hey, you two!" called YoYo. "What's going on?"

"Yeah, is there something you aren't telling us?" taunted Charlie.

It was all in good fun even if very poorly timed. Without responding and with a sour look on his face, Sam went back to the table and took out his wallet—the very one Jackie had given him less than two months ago for Christmas. "It's getting late," he said, taking out his share of the bill. "We better go."

Charlie and YoYo exchanged befuddled looks, but one glance at Emi's reddened eyes told them not to argue. They also knew better than to taunt their two solemn friends again. Everyone was silent on the way home. Sam was driving, and he took Emi home first. She got out of the car but paused before heading up the walkway to her house.

"You've got a right to happiness, Sam. Take it. But . . . don't mess up like I did." She turned, but Sam reached out of the window and grasped her arm.

"You gonna be okay?"

She just shrugged and gave a twitch of her head. Then she turned quickly and walked away.

As he pulled into the street, Charlie and YoYo both asked, "What was that all about?"

"Nothing," said Sam shortly.

"You two aren't—"

"No!" Sam practically shouted. He knew his friends didn't deserve his ire. They wouldn't know he was mostly angry at himself for his inability to help Emi. He supposed he was a little angry at the world, too.

"I'm sorry," he said to his friends. "Emi's just got a problem." No need to tell them he had a problem, too. A huge problem. But like Emi, he feared he must keep it to himself.

When Sam got home, his family was in the living room listening to the Lux Radio Theater. He didn't feel like company and went into the kitchen, poured himself a glass of milk, and got a handful of his mother's sugar cookies from the tin canister. He didn't know how he could be hungry now after the coffee shop, but he hadn't finished his hamburger. Dunking a cookie into the milk, he tried not to think of the forty-five cents wasted on that meal. He'd spent seventy-five cents altogether for the evening's entertainment—seventy-five cents he could hardly spare—and now wished he hadn't gone. Maybe if he had been able to help Emi it might have been worth it. But how could he help her when he couldn't even help himself?

Yes, he'd thought many times about the things he and Emi had discussed. He'd prayed about them, as well. He had also thought often of ending his relationship with Jackie. But how could it end without them both being hurt? And if they pursued their relationship, could they truly be happy with the world against them?

But he loved her. Again he asked himself, why Jacqueline? Why not a girl like Emi? A Japanese girl. It wasn't that there weren't many nice girls of his own race that he could have loved. But he didn't love Emi or Seiko or Mitsue. He loved Jacqueline. For some reason he could not explain, she completed him.

Why, God? Should I thank you or curse you for it? No! Never that. She is a gift from you. That's all I know.

That is all I know.

"Yoshito."

Sam's head jerked up, almost guiltily, as he heard his mother's voice from the doorway.

"Hi, Mama." He smiled wanly, hoping to cover the hated sense of guilt assailing him.

"Why didn't you join us at the radio? The show is good tonight."

"I don't know. I just wasn't in the mood." He wished his mother would speak English. He felt even worse now speaking Japanese, when for the entire evening until a few moments ago he'd felt so American. It emphasized his inner conflicts. He thought about answering her in English, but in their family that was taken as a sign of disrespect.

"You didn't have a good time with your friends?" She sat at the table with him. "You want some more cookies? There's oatmeal in the other canister."

"No . . . I'm all right."

"You don't look all right, Yoshito." She reached out and laid a hand on his forehead. "No fever."

"YoYo said his mother is packing," he answered, knowing his words were a smokescreen to cover the truth. "She is certain there will be an evacuation."

"It could happen. I have packed up my best china. Joan Fenton says she will store whatever can fit into their basement."

"Mama! Not you, too!" Momentarily Sam was removed from his own problems. His mother was not one to panic. There must truly be some basis to the rumors. But that thought just made his problems crash in on him again. He hadn't considered that he and Jackie could be torn apart by outside forces—he had in fact considered it, but not specifically like this.

"I think it is best to be prepared for anything."

He picked up another cookie and stared at it. Anything? "Mama, how did you know Papa was the man you were supposed to marry?"

She didn't even blink at the question, especially seeming to come out of the blue as it had. "You know our parents matched us. Your father was already in America. So we wrote letters to each other for about a year. Even though our match was arranged, we still had the final choice in the end."

"You only had letters to go on?"

"Your father does not talk much, but he can write fine letters." She smiled dreamily.

"But how did you know? You must have been certain to have traveled all that way to marry a man you'd never met."

"When I wrote your father near the end of the year and told him I was ready to come to America and marry him, he wrote back quickly." She chuckled at the memory. "He said he had to tell me he wasn't at all like his letters. He said his tongue was slower than his hand. I knew that already. I had met him before when we had been children, and I remembered that he didn't talk much even then. So I wrote back to him and asked him if he meant the things in his letters or if they were lies. He said, 'Of course I meant them.' He promised me he would never lie to me. I could tell from his letters that he was a man who knew what he was about. He wrote about dreams but not like a dreamer. He knew what he would do and had no doubt he would do it. I cannot explain it, Yoshito. I just knew he was the right man for me. In here." She thumped her chest in the vicinity of her heart.

Could it truly be that simple?

"Yoshito, you will know." Her gaze was full of its own *knowing*. Sam had never spoken of Jackie to his parents, but like his friends, he had no doubt they knew. He was certain they had not confronted the issue because they hoped if they ignored it, it would go away.

"I . . . I think I do know, Mama." He licked his lips and didn't know what he'd say if she pressed for more information.

"Then you must follow what is in your heart."

"Even if it—" He was cut off by her fingers pressed against his lips.

"Yoshito, you also are a man who knows what he is about. You have never been a thoughtless, frivolous boy. Your papa and I are very proud of you and trust you to do what is right."

"If only I could know what is right," he groaned.

She thumped *his* chest. "Your heart tells you what is right."

"But, Mama, you don't understand—"

"I understand. And I know it will not be easy for any of us. But if I was in your place, I would not hesitate." Hoshi Okuda gave her son's cheek a sympathetic pat.

His eyes bulged, and his jaw fell open.

When he regained some of his composure, he managed to barely squeak another question. "Then I have your blessing?"

"Your father and I have discussed this. We will not stand in your way."

He thought it was a terribly evasive answer. But he was wise enough not to press the issue.

"Now, I think your papa would like some oatmeal cookies. Come and listen to the rest of the program with us."

"I'll be right along," he said.

She retrieved a canister from the counter, then returned to the living room. He sat a moment longer. He'd never felt more out of balance in his life. He had his parents' blessing? Well, not exactly, but he had *something*. And what was even more remarkable was that he had not even had to tell them about Jackie. Still, all his problems were far from solved. There were uncounted other hurdles to surmount.

Two events, occurring almost simultaneously, propelled him closer than ever to making a decision. The first took place on February 19, when Executive Order 9066 was signed by President Roosevelt. No doubt spurred by the stunning Japanese victories in the Pacific and the rampant paranoia that followed on the West Coast, the order allowed, under the flimsy disguise of 'military necessity,' for the evacuation from designated areas of any persons the authorities believed necessary for general safety. The word *Japanese* was carefully avoided in the order, but everyone knew that's who it was directed at.

But the second event was the one that struck Sam truly close to home. He heard the news from his sister that Emi Tanaka had committed suicide.

31

SAM BRAKED HIS CAR to a stop in the driveway, but for some reason he could not tear his hands off the steering wheel to open the door and get out. Perhaps that was just as well because he wasn't certain, even if he'd been able to grasp the door handle, that he'd be able to make his legs work. His knees felt like jelly.

He wouldn't be in this predicament if Jackie had accepted his first solution to their problem. But when he had brought it up the day after receiving the shocking news about Emi, she had nearly hit the roof—except there was no roof because they had been outside walking in the place they liked on the college campus. The sky, however, did have the appearance of a low ceiling. Gray and heavy, it looked as though Los Angeles would finally get some winter weather.

"That is the most ridiculous thing I have ever heard, Yoshito Okuda!" she had retorted. She hadn't yelled, but she had managed to put a great deal of passion in her soft tone.

"I think it is for the best." When he had rehearsed this discussion by himself, his responses had come out far more intelligently than that.

"You think breaking up is for the best? For whom, may I ask?"

"Jackie, listen to me—"

"No! I won't." She started walking fast, and he had to jog to catch up. She didn't slow her pace but did wait to speak until he was beside her again. "What you just asked tells me that you must not truly love me. Maybe you never did."

"You know that's not true!" he panted. He grabbed her arm to get her to slow. A passerby stared at them, and he dropped his hand, thinking of the injustice that he couldn't even put a hand on his girlfriend's arm without feeling he might be arrested for the gesture. Jackie slowed and turned a gaze upon him so full of confusion and beseeching that he wanted only to hold her. But he kept his arms at his sides and kept walking. He should never have met her at school. They needed to be alone, though maybe that wasn't a good idea, either, the way he was feeling all tangled up inside.

They walked in silence for quite a while. Sam's suggestion of breaking up had seemed to him so logical, so rational—until now, until he was with Jackie, near her, feeling her love and her hurt.

"Sam," she said after several minutes, "what brought this on?"

He didn't want to talk about Emi. The litany kept pounding in his brain, *There but for the grace . . .* But where was the grace in Emi's case? Life was too fragile, and God's will too confusing. Jackie might be fragile, too. And if something like that happened to her because of him— The mere thought was like a fist gripping his insides.

"Sam, what?" she persisted.

Before he knew it, because it was so right to share his heart with Jackie, he spilled out everything about Emi.

"Oh, Sam!" Her eyes embraced him even if her arms couldn't do so there on a public pathway.

"I don't know what else we can do, Jackie," he said miserably.

"You don't think something like that can happen to us?" The utter incredulity of her tone surprised him.

"Haven't you thought about it? Not the suicide part—however, if it could happen to Emi, then we are all vulnerable to it! More, though, the other part. Being . . . together. Sometimes what they did, a marriage in the spirit, does seem the only way."

"I've thought of it, Sam." Her voice was rock steady.

"Jackie!" It utterly horrified him that she sounded so willing. "I know you better than that."

"It's not wrong to *think* about something," she recanted, "and you must admit it is tempting."

"That's what I mean. Too tempting. But it ends up a trap that doesn't solve a thing. Not for you and me, when our convictions are not only what we are as individual Christians but what brought us together as a couple."

"And so your answer is that we simply break up? Ignore our love? Go our separate ways as if there had never been anything between us?"

It did sound stupid stated in that way. "What else?"

"We could get married. I mean, for real."

His jaw gaped. This was the third time in less than a week a female had thrown him off balance. First Emi, then his mother's amazing words. And now this. He didn't like the feeling. He liked even less the way these women were usually right.

To counter that unwelcome sensation, he laughed. "Now, there's an easy solution. Why didn't I think of it?"

"I'm serious, Sam."

Again that rock-steady tone that really should scare him.

"Why shouldn't we do what any couple has a perfect right to do in our situation? I refuse to bow to unholy social rules."

"My parents did give us their blessing," he said softly. His words surprised even him because he still wasn't certain he could accept Jackie's simple solution.

"What!"

"They refused to speak of you directly," he explained, trying to recapture his equilibrium, "but in their way, they did. Mom said that she and Dad would not stand in our way." He ran his tongue over his suddenly parched lips. What was he saying? Where was this headed?

"If we were looking for a miracle, Sam, that is definitely one."

"That's not all we need."

"No . . ."

He knew she was thinking of her parents, as was he. "If we do this thing . . ." he said, and suddenly he knew they would. Somehow. "We must do it right. No marriage in spirit, no children out of wedlock, and no secrets."

She nodded, then said with just a touch of amusement, "Only one problem—you still haven't proposed to me."

"No, I haven't." Now his tone was rock steady, and he couldn't figure out why, because his next words were the most frightening he'd ever spoken. "First, I will ask your father for your hand."

She stopped dead still. Obviously she just that moment realized what "no secrets" meant, what "doing it right" meant. All her previous confidence appeared to flee.

"M-maybe we should wait," she sputtered. "K-keep on the way we are. There's time." But they both knew there wasn't time. At any moment he could be dragged away from his home, maybe imprisoned, more likely "relocated" somewhere else. She gave her head a firm shake. "What am I saying? It is the only way, isn't it?"

"The only way for us, Jackie." Now he felt steady, sure. Maybe that was the way it should be with couples. When one was weak, the other was strong so that one was always there to support the other.

But now, sitting in his car in front of the Hayes home, he wondered where that previous moment of strength had gone. He needed Jackie beside him now, but they had decided it was best if he just dropped by on a Sunday afternoon when they knew her father would be home. Jackie said that to warn her parents ahead of time would only make the confrontation more difficult. They wanted to do it right, but they didn't want to shoot themselves in the foot from the very beginning.

Sam peeled his fingers from the steering wheel, knowing now exactly what the prophet Daniel had felt like when he was put into the lions' den. God had been with Daniel through it, and Sam was certain God was with him now. He just didn't *feel* God's presence at the moment.

He knew it had to be God who gave him the power to open the car door, to kick his rubbery legs out and propel them up to the fancy oak door of the house. And only God's strength could have gotten him to lift his leaden arm and ring the doorbell.

When he croaked, "Oh, God!" it was the most heartfelt prayer he had ever prayed.

He knew immediately that the woman who answered the door was

Jackie's mother, though he'd never met her. She had Jackie's eyes, wide-set, soft brown, and pretty. Her gray-streaked brown hair was pulled up into a bun, with soft wisps of stray hair falling about her ears. It gave her a frail look. But Sam trembled inside anyway.

"I . . . I am here . . . that is, I was hoping to see Mr. and Mrs. Hayes." His voice squeaked like an adolescent's. She was probably wondering what a salesman was doing on her doorstep on a Sunday afternoon—a Jap one at that!

"I am Mrs. Hayes." Her tone was refined and poised but with a hint of questioning. "May I ask your business?"

"Well, I—" His mind went blank. He could not remember a single word of what he had rehearsed. What had he decided to say at this point? "I'm . . . a friend of your daughter's, that is, of Jacqueline's." At least he remembered that Mrs. Hayes preferred Jackie's given name over her nickname.

"Mom, who is that at the door?" came Jackie's voice. Relief washed over Sam. She had known exactly when he had planned to come and must know he had arrived. She had come to rescue him. He conjured a prayer of thanks, not the first he knew he would silently utter that day. She gave him a covert wink as she came up behind her mother's shoulder. "Oh, Sam. How nice to see you. Mom, this is a friend of mine from school." Her voice sounded so natural.

"But he asked to see your father and me," Mrs. Hayes said.

"Well, he—" Jackie began.

"I wanted to meet Jacqueline's parents . . . since we are friends, you know." Sam was pleased that his voice was finally steady. He knew he was drawing a lot of that from Jackie's presence.

"Well . . . ah . . ." Mrs. Hayes stammered slightly with uncertainty. Had she already guessed what this was all about?

"Do come in, Sam," Jackie said. "It is okay if Sam visits with us, isn't it, Mom?"

"Of course . . ." Misgiving resonated in the woman's tone, but her inbred sense of hospitality won out. She stood back for the guest.

Sam had no trouble restraining a sigh of relief. The biggest lion was still waiting.

Sam followed Jackie, with Mrs. Hayes bringing up the rear, to the living room. If Sam hadn't had so many other things to fret over, he might have felt daunted just by the wealth of the house itself. Jackie never behaved as if she was rich, so he had never given it much thought. Thank goodness he didn't have time to think about it now.

As he came to the living room doorway, actually an arched entry without doors, he saw Keagan Hayes seated facing them. Sam's knees felt wobbly again. The man *was* a lion. His mane of red hair was so fierce-looking that one hardly noticed the strands of gray making an unsuccessful attempt to soften it. Sam didn't know if lions had green eyes, but if they did, they would surely look like the ones now leveled at him. Truly at him alone! And in that moment when their gazes met, Sam felt certain those eyes saw everything in an instant. They put together the Japanese boy, the rumors, everything. They might even know why that Japanese boy was now invading the lions' den. Like any sane man in such a situation, Sam had the strongest urge to flee. He didn't know why he kept standing there.

"Dad, this is a friend of mine from school, Sam Okuda." Jackie didn't use Sam's given name, and for that he was grateful. It had worried him that she might, because she had a habit of using that name at the oddest times. Right now he wanted to be as American as possible.

For a wonder—a true wonder!—the lion did not snarl and attack. Rather, a nearly palpable restraint encompassed the man. He did not smile a welcome. His eyes flashed from Sam to Jackie then back to Sam. He did not rise, and he most especially did not extend his huge paw for a gentleman's handshake.

"A friend from school?" Mr. Keagan Hayes said. He managed to infuse those simple words with accusation and menace.

"Daddy, please." Jackie's earlier aplomb was weakening. "We would just like to visit."

When Mr. Hayes opened his mouth, Sam forced himself to forget the stupid "lion" analogy.

But Mrs. Hayes stepped forward and spoke. "Please sit down, Mr. Okuda. We would be pleased to visit with you." She shot a glance at her husband that Sam was not supposed to see. It had pleading in it but something else, too. Menace? Like a lioness protecting her cub? Sam knew from Jackie that Mrs. Hayes, since the war, had indicated no love for the Japanese. But perhaps love for her child was stronger than any hatred for an enemy. Sam hoped it was so, anyway.

Sam followed Jackie to the sofa and sat down on the very edge. Jackie sat about a foot away from him, pointedly not touching him. He resisted the strong urge to look at her. He tried to think of something to say, some nice innocuous conversation starter, but his mind again was blank and his mouth dry.

"Sam was majoring in English at UCLA," Jackie said. "He graduated in June and is working on his master's degree. He wants to be a writer, Daddy."

"Actually, I hope to teach English in high school—" Oh, great, his first words were to contradict the man's daughter! He added quickly, "I want to be a writer, too, but only after I have a steady income."

Mr. Hayes cocked a brow, as well he might, since Sam's statement was certainly that of a prospective suitor.

"A teacher," said Mrs. Hayes. "A wonderful aspiration. As I am sure you know, Jacqueline wants to be a teacher, as well. She is wonderful with children. She has been teaching Sunday school since she was thirteen."

"Yes, I know," Sam said. "She's helped with the children at my church when she's visited—" Panic gripped him. Had he said too much? He suddenly realized he hadn't really thought out how far this meeting would go. How much of their relationship should he reveal at this juncture? Was this the time he should bring up the subject of marriage? It might be best to wait for another visit for that.

"Your church?" Mr. Hayes fairly jumped into the sudden silence. "Do you mean my daughter has been attending a Buddhist church?"

"No, Daddy," Jackie said quickly. "Sam is a Christian. I have visited his church once or twice."

Hayes sat forward in his chair, eyes cutting between Sam and Jackie like a blade. "Let's cut the bull—"

"Daddy!"

"Keagan!"

Both women exclaimed in unison.

"What is the meaning of this little visit?" Mr. Hayes persisted, though he eased up a bit on the sharp edge to his tone. "You are here to 'meet the parents,' aren't you? Well, I can—"

"Yes, sir, I am," Sam cut in, shocked at his effrontery at doing so, but he kept going. "At this point in my relationship with Jackie, I feel it would be wrong to continue to carry on without your meeting me."

"At what point?" Hayes's voice rose for the first time. "Carry on? Carry on what?" He leaped to his feet. "There is nothing to carry on. Do you understand? Now get out!"

"Keagan, you are being rude!" Mrs. Hayes's voice was sharp. "I will not abide rudeness to our company."

Hayes's head snapped around, and he gaped at his wife. Sam gaped as well. For the fourth time a woman's words astonished him. He'd heard many times from Jackie how meek her mother was.

"Please sit down, Keagan, and let's discuss this like civilized human beings," the woman said smoothly.

"Do you understand what is going on, Cecilia?" asked Hayes.

"I believe I am beginning to. This is no casual visit, is it, Jacqueline?"

"We didn't mean to deceive you, Mom . . . Dad," said Jackie. "We just didn't know the best way to approach you, that's all."

Sam gathered courage from the amazing young woman beside him, though he still dared not look at her. "We feel very strongly that we should do this right. 'This' being—" Sudden fear caught in his throat. But he forced out the word. "Marriage."

Hayes choked out a laugh. "Over my dead body!"

"Please, Daddy!"

"I am not going to talk further about it. It is the most ridiculous thing I have ever heard. The discussion is over!" Hayes took a step toward Sam.

Sam rose. He didn't know if it was to look the man in the eye or to make a fast retreat.

"Jackie and I love each other," he heard himself say, but he sounded odd, far away, like a voice in a tunnel. "I love your daughter, Mr. Hayes. No matter what you do to me now, that will never change. We feel we have a right to that love and to the commitment of marriage that such love requires. But we don't want to defy you."

"You will have to if you think this is going one step further!" boomed Hayes. "If my daughter marries you, she will be disowned by her family. Do you want that?"

"No, I don't."

"I've heard enough," Mrs. Hayes said with a glance at her husband. She was on her feet now. She turned to Sam. "Sam—may I call you Sam? Do you mind ending our visit now?" It was a polite request. "I think it is time for a private family discussion."

"Of course." Sam certainly couldn't argue with the woman. Besides, he had the distinct impression she was on his side.

"We'll have you back again soon," she said cordially, as if this was a completely routine visit. Though Sam doubted such a return visit would ever happen, he found the woman's tone oddly comforting.

"Mother?" Jackie's voice trembled over the word.

"Sam understands that there are some things a family has to discuss alone," her mother said. "Now be a good girl and walk Sam to the door. But don't be long."

Jackie walked him not only to the door but out onto the front porch. She closed the door behind them. In the next instant all that had been holding Sam up seemed to dissolve. He slumped against the wood framing of the house. Jackie gathered him into her arms. A new panic tried to grip him as he gave a quick glance around to see if they could be observed from the house. Then suddenly he didn't care. He needed to be held by her.

"You were so brave!" she murmured.

"I was scared to death."

"I know," she said, kissing him.

"Now what?"

"I'm not sure." She kissed him again, and he did not have the reserve of strength to stop her, no matter who was looking. "But I think it will be all right. I think my parents liked you."

He nearly choked, then burst out laughing, then choked again. "I-I g-guess because they didn't kill me?"

"We must think positively." She gave him one more kiss, then gently pushed away. "I have to go now, but I'll call you. And Sam, I love you."

He nodded dumbly and somehow made the trek to his car.

Sucking in a deep breath through clenched teeth, Jackie reentered the house. How easy it was to say everything would be all right. Easy even to believe it. That didn't mean the road wasn't going to be rough along the way.

Her parents were both seated again in the living room. Both were silent. The kind of silence that crackled and vibrated. The silence gave her goose bumps. And she knew it wouldn't last. No matter what her parents said, she was not going to let herself forget the amazing courage Sam had displayed. Nor would she forget the feel of his strong arms around her. Only then would she be able to fully convey to her parents the kind of love they felt for each other.

"Your mother thinks this will have a happy ending," Keagan said without preamble.

Jackie shot a glance at her mother for confirmation. But Cecilia's eyes were focused on her husband, almost fastened upon him, as if she dare not let go for a moment lest she lose whatever hold she had on him.

"Your young man showed a great deal of courage today, Jacqueline," Cecilia said.

"That's the kind of man he is," Jackie replied. "One of the finest people I know."

"I'm not going to listen to this!" growled Keagan. "Courageous. Fine. Bah! I don't care about any of that. I will see you cut off, Jackie. I will see him arrested—"

"Shut up, Keagan!" Cecilia burst out, then she gasped at her outrageously uncivilized words. But she didn't recant them.

Keagan sputtered, unable to form a coherent response to the shocking words.

Jackie felt she had to say something. "We don't want to cause discord. We want more than anything for you, for our parents if no one else, to accept us."

"How do his parents feel?" asked Cecilia.

"Much the same as you and Dad, I think. But they said they trust his judgment and won't stand in his way."

"I don't care what a bunch of Jap malcontents think!" bellowed Keagan.

"Don't talk like that, Keagan!" Cecilia demanded.

"And I have had it with your nerve, woman!" Keagan swung a fiery gaze at his wife, apparently having regained his stride. "You have a lot of gall speaking to me like that."

"Yes, I do, because this is important." Her cheeks were actually colored a deep hue of pink that Jackie was certain had nothing to do with embarrassment. "I should have stood up to you with Cameron and Blair, but now I finally draw the line."

"So you approve of having your daughter marry a Jap and having little Jap grandbabies?" he sneered.

"No, I don't." Cecilia's gaze jerked briefly toward Jackie with a hint of apology in it. "Not really. I've felt outrage and even some hatred over the Japanese bombing of Pearl Harbor, especially the bombing of the Philippine Islands and the terrible position that has put our Blair in. But I will not succumb to the irrational attitude that every Jap is bad, because that is no more true than every German is bad or every Italian—or that every American is good. But all that aside, I will not stand in the way of Jacqueline's happiness. If this young man were some sleazy sort . . . well, I might. But he is obviously an exemplary man, a man of honor. The kind of man I myself might have chosen for my daughter."

"Well, she can just find herself a *white* man of honor," Keagan declared as he rose to his feet. "She is not marrying a Jap. I will disown—"

"You will not!" Cecilia nearly shouted as she, too, stood. Jackie was certain she had never heard her mother raise her voice so. "You have pushed two of our daughters away, but by all that is sacred, you will not do it again." She glared at him, eye to eye, nose to nose, as much as her shorter stature would allow.

"I have spoken!" Keagan started to stride from the room, but Cecilia stepped in his way.

Like a wall. Like a wall of fire.

"*I* have spoken, Keagan Hayes!" she barked. "Jacqueline will marry Sam Okuda if she wishes, with our support—with the support of *both* her parents. And you, Keagan, will not leave this room until you admit that was the most courageous young man you have ever seen."

"I will not!" He tried to move around her, but she blocked him again.

"Yes, you will!"

He met her with silence. Though Jackie was proud of her mother, she was certain she had pushed the man too far, over the edge surely. She feared Keagan might actually strike her mother. And for all the fights Jackie had witnessed between them, he had never before resorted to physical violence. Jackie prayed this would not be the first time. She prayed, against all logic, that somehow this confrontation would end peacefully or at least with an armed truce.

"Okay. He was courageous," Keagan mumbled softly but no less distinctly.

Jackie would have been less shocked if there *had* been a physical blow.

Then, as if the woman had no fear, Cecilia pressed further. "And you will support Jackie because you trust *her* judgment."

Keagan's jaw worked furiously, a great battle waging inside him. His mouth opened and closed soundlessly. Finally he merely nodded.

Jackie, for one, wasn't going to expect more than that from the man. She ran to him and threw her arms around him. "Thank you, Daddy!"

32

KEAGAN RETREATED to his study. *Retreated*. That was indeed the perfect word.

He'd been completely overwhelmed by the military might of a single flimsy, frail woman! He, a man who had never in his life backed down from a fight. What was happening to him? Had his bum heart robbed him of his manhood?

Had he truly given his approval, however tacit, of the marriage of his daughter to a Jap? Well, he had been pushed into a corner by that stubborn woman he had married. Shaking his head, he still could not believe she had physically barred his way, yelled at him. Told him to shut up!

No wonder he had conceded. He had simply been in shock. He could take his words back, though that would be another first for him—withdrawing one of his edicts. Better than letting his daughter ruin herself and likely the whole family in the process. Cecilia and Jackie spoke of romance and courage, but they had no concept of the realities of their society. Keagan personally knew of a family at the country club whose daughter had defiled herself with a Negro man. The whole family had been ousted from the club.

Yes, he could retract the approval. But he wouldn't, and he knew why. Cecilia's words of love and courage and Jackie's happiness were bunk, as far as he was concerned, at least insofar as they had swayed him. But she had made one point that had jabbed into a painfully insecure wound. The fact that he had pushed Cameron and Blair away. Not intentionally, of course, and in Blair's case she had largely asked for it. Both girls had hurt him, Cameron by working for the enemy, and Blair by making a fool of him after he walked her down the aisle for her marriage.

But he had to ask himself what kind of father was he if he had two estranged daughters and was on the verge of estranging the last. He had never claimed to be perfect, but something must have gone terribly wrong for it to have come to this. Maybe he had been a little too hard on them at times. Maybe he had expected too much of them. They were, after all, only girls.

Keagan shifted uncomfortably in his desk chair, thoroughly disliking the trend of his thoughts. He was not going to start second-guessing himself. What was done was done. Imagine him apologizing to Cameron for being too hard on her for going to work for the *Globe*! Why, if he lowered himself with a smarmy plea for forgiveness, she would lose all respect for him.

The past was done. Bum heart or no, he wasn't going to start sniveling about it. But perhaps there would be no harm in reevaluating the future. Making up a bit for the past by doing things differently in the future. Nothing drastic, but for starters not being so hard. Maybe a word of encouragement once in a while. He didn't have to become a gushy fool. Giving in to Jackie was a start, though it was a horrible place to start, and he cringed inside over the idea of her marrying a Jap. Yet even though Cecilia had forced the admission from him, he wouldn't have said it if he hadn't truly believed the young man had showed a lot of nerve standing up to him as he had. The boy's desire to receive the parents' blessing proved this Jap boy was probably a man of honor, as well. And Keagan respected that in a man, in any man.

Besides, he had recently spoken to the state's attorney general, Earl Warren, and he had it on the best authority that very soon all the Japs on the West Coast would be evacuated. There was talk of placing them in internment camps for the duration of the war. That should handily put a wrench into Jackie's marriage plans.

A soft knock on the door diverted Keagan's attention from his thoughts.

"Come in," he said.

"There you are, Keagan," Cecilia said, stepping into the study and closing the door behind her.

"And where else would I be? It is the only place where I can find some respite from a bunch of lunatic women!"

Smiling gently, Cecilia came around the desk and stood by him. He should have stood, as was the polite thing to do when a woman entered a room, but at the moment he didn't feel much like being a gentleman toward this wild woman.

"You did the right thing, Keagan," she said. "I am proud of you."

"Bah! Proud of what? Sending my baby daughter into the pit of hades? I don't think you realize what she will face if she marries that . . . man."

Not immediately responding, Cecilia bent over, kissed his forehead, then went around the desk and sat in an adjacent chair. Finally, with a bend to her lips she said, "I realize I am terribly sheltered, but I do have an idea of what Jackie will face. It won't be easy for them."

"But they will have their love to see them through!" he sneered.

"Much more than that, dear. They have their faith in God."

"God, eh?" Leaning back in his chair, fingers steepled and tapping his chin, he saw a new argument that might sway his wife. "What if it is true, what the majority of people believe, that mingling the races is unholy, against the natural way of things?"

"I'm not going to debate that with you," she replied with a coy grin. "You always win debates with me no matter what is right or wrong. All I know is that I just had a talk with Jacqueline, and she has assured me that she and Sam are committed to God and trust Him in all things. That's all I care about."

Keagan knew, despite what his wife said, that he didn't have a chance competing against God. He didn't hold with much of the religious mumbo jumbo Cecilia spouted, but he wasn't a complete heathen, and he supposed it was something that the boy wasn't, either. What was done was done. He would let nature take its course.

"So what do you want, Cecilia?"

"I just wanted to thank you."

He gave a grunt.

Cecilia continued, "Jackie said they want to take Friday off school, leave Thursday—"

"Leave?"

"You must know they can't marry here in California. Sam has

looked into it and feels Albuquerque would be the best place."

"Albuquerque!"

"They don't expect us to come. They want us to suffer as little social stigma from this as possible. I have to agree with them on this, though it will be hard not to attend my baby's wedding. They want to protect us, you see."

Keagan scrubbed a hand through his mop of hair. "This entire situation is insane. A week? What's their hurry?"

"The president signed something recently that will probably cause the Japanese on the West Coast to be evacuated. Soon. Surely you must know—" She stopped, leveling her wide-set, soft eyes at him. She was still quite a lovely woman, even now when a flash of anger marred those eyes. "Of course you knew! Were you hoping that would happen and put a stop to their plans? Oh, Keagan! Is that why you conceded?"

He shrugged. "I conceded because you backed me up against a wall. But even you must see that would be the best solution to this insanity. I won't stand in their way, but you must see the sense in them waiting until things settle down. If they marry now and the Japanese are evacuated, what will they do? Will Jackie go with him?"

"Go where? Do you know?" Her question was as sharp and incisive as something their oldest daughter might utter.

"There is talk . . . of camps."

"Concentration camps!" she breathed, aghast. "Like Hitler has in Germany?"

"I'm sure they will be far more civilized than that."

"I don't care if they are country clubs! It is wrong."

He had never seen his wife like this. Such passion, such fire. He didn't know whether to spit nails or smile in appreciation. "Regardless, do you want Jackie in such a place? That's what it could come to," he added, sensibly enough.

"I will not believe such a thing can happen, not in this country. Sam is a citizen. They will never do this to American citizens."

Keagan nodded noncommittally. From what he'd gathered in his conversation with the attorney general, the powers that be weren't really distinguishing much between alien Japs and citizen Japs. General DeWitt, the head of the Western Defense Command, probably said it for many with his statement, "A Jap's a Jap!"

When he glanced toward his wife, he thought the stricken look on her face was a far cry from the fiery one that had blazed upon it a few minutes ago. He suddenly felt great sympathy for her. She was torn between happiness for her daughter and the harsh realities of life. He would never admit it out loud, but he could sympathize with her in every way. The twists of life were rotten. He wanted Jackie to be happy, too, but he didn't think she would be the way she was going. Still, he was not such a brute that he hadn't seen the look on her face of pure love for her man. He'd seen it wasn't schoolgirl hogwash, either. Pure love, real love, such as he himself had never truly experienced, but at least he could recognize it in another, especially in his own daughter.

On impulse—what in heaven's name was happening to him!—he rose, went to his wife, and took Cecilia's hands in his.

"I wish I could be more comfort to you now, Cecilia," he murmured gently. He could hardly believe it was he speaking. "You know as well as I that I am dismally deficient in such matters. But I wish . . . things in our family had turned out differently."

"You do, Keagan?" Were her eyes glassed over with moisture?

"I am not one for regrets, but . . ."

"You don't have to say more. I understand." She turned her hand so she could squeeze his. "I only hope, Keagan, that we can weather ours together."

"What else would we do?"

"So true, dear!" She swiped a hand across her eyes. "That's really why I came here, to thank you for standing with me concerning Jackie. We did right there, I know it. Everything may seem black at the moment, but it doesn't change that what we did was for the best."

"I will trust you on that, Cecilia."

She blinked, surprised, no doubt. Well, he wasn't a complete buffoon. He didn't have to be right *all* the time! Today Cecilia had proved that she was more than a lovely piece of fluff, that she was a force to be reckoned with. And he rather liked that.

33

THE TRAIN RIDE had been long, at least in relative terms, but being nearly two days exclusively with the man she loved had been glorious for Jackie. It might have been perfect if they hadn't been subjected to the stares and derisively muttered comments of other passengers. Jackie wished they had spent the extra money on a private compartment, but their finances were limited. Her parents had given her some money, but Sam, not unreasonably, was reluctant to accept too much help from them. More than that, she and Sam had decided it would not be proper to be alone in a compartment, even chastely, the night before their wedding.

So they had endured the regular seats, the stares, the comments. They had been extremely circumspect in their behavior, but just sitting together, obviously *being* together, was bad enough to many.

They arrived in Albuquerque, New Mexico, on a crisp, cool morning on Friday, March 6. The sky was clear and blue, not a cloud in sight. An ideal day for a wedding.

They took a taxi from the train station directly to the courthouse. They were tired, since they'd slept little on the hard seats. Nevertheless, there was no sense in waiting. Their return tickets were for tomorrow morning. They were going to have to spend one night in the New Mexico town, and they intended to do so as husband and wife.

Just thinking of those words made Jackie tingle all over. She was ready to be Sam's wife. She knew what it meant, that it might not be easy for them to be together. She had no fear about that. Well, none that she couldn't give over to God. If she quaked at all over what was about to happen, it was just at the idea of being married. Was she ready? Could she be a good wife? She was twenty-one now, an adult. But sometimes she still felt like a kid.

Stepping from the taxi, she looked up at the building where she would embark upon a new life, then she glanced at the man at her side. A Japanese man. Never had she tried to pretend he was white. She clearly saw his physical differences, but unlike so many in their society, that was not all she saw. His character, his spirit, his sense of humor—these drew her love, but she realized they could not be separated from his culture or his race, which had nurtured much of who he was. She thought of this now because she was marrying the whole man. She did not want to forget that.

She knew he felt the same way about her. They were not racists, but they were both aware of race. How could they not be when everyone threw it constantly into their faces? But to them it was not a stumbling block. It was a gift.

"Well," he said ruefully, "are you ready to give up your freedom?"

"Ball and chain time, eh?"

"Never has a man gone more cheerfully into the abyss!" He grinned. "As long as we're together, I don't mind falling forever."

"I feel more like I am flying . . . very high!"

"Soaring! I like that much better than falling." He took her hand in his. "Then you have no doubts?"

"None."

"Neither do I. It's strange, isn't it? Oh, I worry about whether I'll be a good husband, you know, the usual stuff. But I have no doubts about the rightness of this." He gently tugged her hand. "Let's go."

The clerk looked as though he was going to refuse to give them a license. He had no right, since New Mexico was a state that had no laws against interracial marriage. In the end Jackie was sure adherence to the letter of the law, his commitment to that alone, was what spurred the man to give them the form after he had carefully scrutinized their birth certificates and blood test results, which they'd had done in California. He passed the paper under the window without comment.

Jackie smiled at him. Nothing was going to ruin this moment for her. "Thank you so much!" she chirruped cheerfully.

The easiest next step would have been to have a justice of the peace perform a marriage ceremony for them, but they had both agreed they wanted a minister, even if they couldn't have the ceremony in a church. But they went to two churches in town and were turned away. One minister offered the lame excuse that he was too busy. The other clearly refused to marry a Japanese man and a white girl. Next they tried a Catholic church that was near the second Protestant church, but of course the priest declined on the grounds that they were not Catholic. Jackie's cheerful attitude began to wane.

They stopped at a café for lunch. Neither was hungry, but they wanted a place to sit. Jackie's feet were sore. She had worn a new suit for her wedding, a jade green wool with a hip-length jacket. The felt hat with the turned-back brim matched the suit, as did the shoes. But the shoes were new, and she hadn't had time to break them in. She had thought about wearing white but felt any kind of wedding gown seemed inappropriate for a courthouse or a minister's office, and she had not found any practical suit in white that she liked. Besides, she felt that if she was going to spend money on a new suit, it should be something she could wear again. She had to learn to watch her budget. Someday Sam would make a good living teaching high school and writing, but for now they must be careful.

Sam ordered the blue plate special—roast beef, mashed potatoes, and green beans—but he asked the waitress if he could substitute corn for the green beans. She was none too happy about this and said that *if* she could do it, it would cost extra. But the woman's unpleasant attitude had begun before Sam's request. Jackie's stomach churned, and she ordered only a bowl of vegetable soup. They both had coffee. After getting nothing but catnaps on the train, they were both exhausted and needed the caffeine.

The waitress brought their food. She sloshed the soup onto the table, a splash barely missing Jackie's suit. Sam's dish had green beans, not corn, and the beans were dumped all over everything, so he had to pick them out of potatoes and gravy before he could eat. He was no doubt accustomed to such abuse, and he raised no complaint to the waitress. Experience had taught him not to make a scene over such matters. He did joke to Jackie that he might be nearly a married man, but he still couldn't eat anything green. The joke was hollow, though. He was obviously trying not to let the waitress's behavior get to him, but it was, compounded, of course, by the rejections from the churches.

They finished their food, found a telephone book to get the address of another church, then went on their way. Jackie could feel Sam's discouragement.

"Jackie," he said after yet another taxi passed them by when Sam had clearly waved, "doesn't that license say we are married?"

"I suppose so."

"I mean really married?"

"Well, there are places for a minister to sign and for witnesses. What are you saying?"

"Nothing . . . just a crazy thought that maybe we don't need to bother with any kind of ceremony, that the license might be enough. But we need those signatures. I guess it won't be legal without them."

The thought of foregoing a ceremony had crossed her mind, as well. But even if the license alone did make it legal, they were both determined to speak their vows before God, to do it right, at least what seemed right in their eyes. Jackie refused to let society rob them of their convictions.

Sam took the paper with the address from his pocket. "That waitress said the church was off the next street—if she wasn't lying just for fun." They started walking, but he stopped. "Wait! I knew something was missing."

"What are you talking about, Sam?"

Saying nothing, he practically dragged her across the street, against the signal so that a couple of cars honked at them. On the other side of the street, he paused before a florist shop.

"Oh, Sam!" Her throat clogged with emotion, and she could say no more.

"You've got to have a wedding bouquet. I'm such a lug for not thinking about it." Before he opened the door of the shop, he paused. "I also haven't told you how beautiful you look. I am a lug. How do you put up with me?"

"Because I love you, you lug!"

He chuckled, pleased by her reply. "I know you probably always dreamed of a silk wedding gown with one of those train things and lots of lace and all. A huge church with flowers everywhere and all your friends—"

"Stop it, Sam!" she chided. "This is what I want. You and a green suit and a place in a minister's study. I need no more. You must believe that."

"I do. It's just that every now and then I need to be reminded."

"It's been hard, but we will do this thing, and no one will rob us of our happiness, no matter how hard they try!" Smiling, she linked her arm around his and defiantly kissed him on the cheek. "There! Albuquerque, take that!"

She chose white lilies. The clerk smiled as he put them into a bouquet and tied it with a ribbon that matched her suit—he had spent much effort finding the right color, a shade lighter so it made a nice contrast. He looked to be of Mexican descent, and he didn't seem to notice that the couple buying wedding flowers was mixed. Jackie hoped their fortunes were changing.

Buoyed by this, they found the church, a little white building on a side street. There was a parsonage next door, but they went to the main church entrance first. The door was ajar so they went inside. A small narthex led to the sanctuary, which was equally small. Jackie guessed it could not seat more than a hundred people, if that. A man was sweeping the worn wood floor around the altar. He was dressed in a plaid flannel shirt and khaki dungarees.

"Excuse me," Sam said in a quiet voice that suited the inside of a church.

The man stopped his work. "Yes, may I help you?"

"We were looking for the minister."

The man smiled, a pleasant smile it was. He was a tall, lanky fellow, about fifty, with brown hair and thick spectacles over small pale eyes. The smile danced in his eyes even as the corners crinkled.

"I know I don't look much like a minister, but you have found him." He strode toward them. When he was near, he set his broom aside and reached out a hand to Sam. "I am Peter Billingsly, reverend and sometimes janitor."

Sam clasped the extended hand. Jackie could almost feel a tingle of energy between the two men. She felt something on her own, as well, the sense of finding a kindred soul. She looked into this man's eyes and knew he was a friend. She whispered a prayer of thanksgiving.

"My name is Sam Okuda, and this is . . . my fiancée, Jackie Hayes." He paused. Perhaps even despite the obvious warmth of the man, he was waiting to be shot down.

"Glad to meet you both."

"You are?" Sam's impromptu response made a crooked smile slant his lips. "I'm sorry, sir, we haven't sensed that from many people today."

Reverend Billingsly shook his head. "That is very sad. What may I do for you?"

Sam took a breath. "Well, sir, we . . . we are from California, but we are here to get married. We have a license." He finished in a rush, as if he wanted to get the words out before the rejection came this time.

"I see . . ." The minister drew out the words. Clearly he saw a great deal. "Why don't you come with me to my study and we can talk."

"Talk?"

"Yes, if you don't mind. I like to get to know the people I marry. Normally I have a few counseling sessions with them, as well."

"Reverend Billingsly," Jackie put in quickly, "we would be willing to do that, but we have to be back to California by Monday."

"Let's talk for a few minutes," Billingsly said. "I really must be certain you meet my main criteria for marriage—that you love each other and that you love God."

They talked well into the afternoon. Later, Billingsly said he had pretty much sized them up in the first two minutes and knew they met his standards, but the rest of the time he had just enjoyed talking to them. Jackie felt the same way, and the time had gone so fast she hardly noticed two hours had passed. Sam had relaxed, as well, and Jackie thought that must have been part of the reason the minister had visited so long with them. By the time they left the study, they had made a friend for life.

"I'll go change into something more suitable for a wedding," Reverend Billingsly said.

"You look fine to us," Sam said.

Jackie could tell he had enjoyed the conversation with the minister, but no one could blame him for being anxious to get on with the ceremony.

Billingsly laughed. "I know it has been a long day for you, son, and you are anxious, but we can take a few minutes to do it right. I gathered from our discussion that that is important to you. I also need to scare up a couple of witnesses. My wife will do for one. Her sister lives nearby, and I'm sure she will consent to come. We'll go to the parsonage now, and Edith can fix you some tea while you wait. It won't be long before we head to the sanctuary."

"The sanctuary?" breathed Jackie, hardly willing to believe it. "We can get married there?"

"Of course."

An hour later, the small party gathered at the freshly swept altar of the sanctuary. The reverend was in his best suit; his wife, Edith, and her sister, Evelyn, were also dressed in their finest. Jackie wanted to cry for joy at how the sisters were turning her wedding into an occasion. Edith played the wedding march on the piano and insisted that Jackie walk down the aisle. She thought then of Blair's wedding and how their father had walked her down the aisle. It might have saddened her to make her own way alone, but oddly it didn't because she knew that had she asked, her father would have come.

Evelyn had a camera and took pictures, promising to send them to Jackie when they were developed. Jackie never dreamed she would have this much of a wedding. She certainly hadn't wanted it or needed it. She hadn't even asked God for it. Yet only God would give a girl the desires of her heart, even when she hadn't known they were her desires.

"Take hands, and face one another, then repeat after me," Reverend Billingsly said when they came to the time of speaking vows.

Sam's hands were steady and dry; hers were trembling a bit.

They each spoke the vows in turn.

"I, Yoshito Samuel Okuda, do take thee, Jacqueline Marie Hayes, for my wife. . . ." Somehow he imbued each word of the traditional vow with the depth of its truth. He did not falter over a single one. He sounded as if he had been ready his entire life to make this vow to her.

She wanted to be just as steady. She wanted him to know how each word came from that part of her heart that belonged entirely to him.

"I, Jacqueline Marie Hayes, take thee, Sam . . . I mean, Yoshito Samuel Okuda, to be my wedded husband, to have and to hold from this day forward, for better or worse, for richer or poorer, in sickness and in health, to love and to cherish till death do us part, according to God's holy ordinance, and thereto I plight thee my troth."

After that, they exchanged rings, simple gold bands they had purchased in California. Then it was over. Evelyn, bless her, threw rice at them when they stepped on the front steps of the church. Then she snapped more pictures, and Jackie insisted that she take a picture of the reverend and the two women. But Evelyn wouldn't let Jackie throw her bouquet.

"We're both old married ladies, so you keep it for a memento," Evelyn said.

"And this, too," said Edith, handing Jackie a small wrapped package. "I give one to every couple Peter marries. It's just a small wedding album where you can put the photos and tell about the wedding. Luckily, I keep a couple of spares."

Sudden tears welled in Jackie's eyes, and she hugged each woman. "Thanks to you, I will have wonderful things to put into this."

Jackie would keep the memories in her heart until the time she would be able to record them in the album. She kept them especially close after several hotels refused to give her and Sam a room for the night. And when they ended up in a dirty, squalid place near the train station, for which they paid twice its worth, she hardly noticed. Torn sheets, cockroaches, sticky floor—all faded in the bliss of being united in heart and soul with the man she loved, the man who God, in His unfathomable grace, had given her.

PART V

"The duty and the necessity of resisting Japanese aggression to the last transcends in importance any other obligation now facing us in the Philippines. . . . I therefore give you this most difficult mission in full understanding of the desperate situation to which you may shortly be reduced."

FRANKLIN D. ROOSEVELT
TO GENERAL DOUGLAS MACARTHUR FEBRUARY 1942
(*The Fall of the Philippines* by Louis Morton)

34

The Philippines
March 1942

BLAIR HELD OUT HER HANDS. They looked like those of an old washerwoman. Since coming to the mission she had begun to feel like Cinderella but without the hope of a happy ending. The only difference, she had to admit, was that *everyone* worked at the mission. Meg Doyle saw to that!

Still, Blair felt that she was receiving a special dose. From the first she'd suspected Mrs. Doyle had it in for her. Maybe Blair had asked for it a little, but the woman had backed her into a corner seemingly from the first.

"All the women take turns cooking," Mrs. Doyle had said a couple of days after Blair's arrival. She and her companions had been given some time to recover from their ordeal in the jungle, but now it was time to join the flow of mission life. "You can cook, can't you?"

The way that question was asked, almost assuming that the flighty girl who had deceived a fine man like Gary could not possibly have any redeeming qualities, made Blair rear up defensively.

"Of course I can cook," she lied, giving a covert look to Claudette for her to support the lie. Dear girl that she was, Claudette kept her mouth shut.

"All right, tomorrow morning you can work with Hope on breakfast. We eat here at seven, so you need to be up by six."

Blair felt rather smug. She thought Mrs. Doyle was hoping to trip her up with the early hour in the morning. But since leaving Manila, Blair's sleeping habits had changed, not by choice or design but because on her travels there had been nothing to do at night to keep her up, so she went to bed early and naturally rose early in the morning. Six would be no problem at all.

The problems began with the actual preparation of the meal. Hope, at fourteen, was quite proficient in the kitchen—well, she would have to be with such a terror for a mother! But she was not much of teacher, even if she had thought Blair might need instruction. Rather, she assumed Blair knew what she was doing.

Hope simply said, "Why don't you make the coffee, and I'll make the pancakes."

Blair agreed readily to the suggestion. She couldn't have made a pancake to save her life. But she thought any idiot could fix a pot of coffee. It wasn't Blair's fault that a spider intruded upon the scene. She hated even ordinary spiders, but this one was bigger than a large coin. She forced herself not to scream. She did have *some* self-respect, especially in front of a child. Anyway, the creature was way at the other end of the room, and if it got close, she'd do something. But the idea of squashing it was every bit as loathsome as having it creep nearby. Nevertheless, she kept her eye on it but in the process lost count of how many scoops of coffee she had put into the pot. She decided the amount looked right, so she put it on to boil. The spider turned around and headed out the door.

When the coffee was served with Hope's light, delicious pancakes, everyone around the table made faces but politely kept quiet. Everyone except Meg Doyle. She fairly hit the roof.

"I cannot believe such irresponsibility in an adult woman," she said when she learned Blair had prepared the offensive brew. It was strong enough to tarnish silver—thank goodness the Doyles had only stainless steel for utensils. "We believe in being good stewards of God's bounty, but now in the Emergency it is more important than ever!" She wasn't yelling. It was more of a stern lecture. Blair cowered beneath the woman's words, hating herself for it, and nearly hating the woman, as well, for humiliating her so. "Every bit of food at this mission," Mrs. Doyle continued, "is precious, and who knows when we can get more. Coffee especially!" She shook her head, full of disappointment. "I truly thought better of you."

"She didn't do it on purpose, Meg," offered Reverend Doyle. "I reckon we can water down the coffee and save some for tomorrow."

"I am mostly disturbed that she appears to have lied to me," Mrs. Doyle said. "*Can* you cook, girl?"

Blair was furious. Being grilled like a criminal. She was a guest, wasn't she? She didn't have to take this.

"Excuse me?" Blair arched a brow at the woman. "You have no right to call me a liar."

"Now, let's everyone calm down," said the reverend. He focused a slightly reproachful eye at his wife. "Meg, Blair is a guest. I agree, we all have to pull our weight here, but you do need to ease up a bit, don't you think, honey?" His smile, mingled with the look of reproach, was quite canny really. Masterful, Blair thought. He knew how to handle his wife. She liked the man, even though she was certain that look was about to swing around toward her. It did. "Blair, the last thing on earth we want to do here is embarrass you. You can be frank with us. No one is going to adversely judge you if your skills are . . . uh . . . different from what we are accustomed to." The quirk of his lips was disarming.

"Well, I can't cook," Blair admitted grudgingly.

"Now, there you go, Meg," said Reverend Doyle, as if that solved everything. "After breakfast why don't you two put your heads together and see what Blair would like to do around here to help out. You do want to lend a hand where you can, don't you, Blair?"

"Of course I do. I'm not lazy." She cast Meg Doyle a sidelong glance that dared the woman to refute that final statement.

The reverend was a good mediator, but he was still a bit naïve if he thought Blair and Meg could put their heads together in any kind of friendly confabulation.

Later that morning they managed to talk and work out a plan of chores for Blair, but it was in a stiff, forced fashion. Neither liked the other, that was clear. And Reverend Doyle was truly naïve if he thought his wife wasn't judging Blair. Blair had felt it from the beginning, though Mrs. Doyle no doubt leveled it with the kind of womanly subtlety that men often missed.

In the end, chores were heaped on Blair. Oh, she had agreed to them when she and Mrs. Doyle had "put their heads together." But she hadn't really had much choice. To do otherwise would have just confirmed all the woman's negative opinions about Blair.

What truly amazed Blair was how the woman could come up with so many tasks, keeping everyone at the mission, not just Blair, busy working from dawn till supper. Blair did much of the sweeping and dusting. Meg Doyle had a perfectly good electric vacuum, but because of the fuel shortage due to the war, they were conserving use of electricity. Why use the Electrolux when Blair was around with strong arms perfectly capable of wielding a broom?

Meg loved to say, "Idle hands are the devil's playground."

After Mrs. Doyle had intoned that maxim one too many times, Blair asked for a Bible, much to everyone's pleasure, and asked Patience to show her how to use a concordance. Then Blair used these tools to prove that particular saying wasn't in the Bible. Mrs. Doyle was not happy about Blair's discovery or that she had frittered away precious time to make it, but she only mumbled something about insolence that she thought Blair could not hear.

Despite the tensions with Mrs. Doyle, Blair did find pleasure in getting to know Patience and Hope. Meg Doyle, whom Blair thought of as Mrs. Nazi, did allow her minions some freedom in the evenings before bedtime, which was strictly enforced to occur at ten after an equally strictly enforced half hour of quiet time—this quiet time was used by the family for personal Bible reading and prayer, though guests were not expected to read or pray but only "quietly reflect," as Mrs. Doyle put it.

The "free" time was even more limited, as it took place after Mrs. Doyle monopolized the hour following dinner with a devotional. Blair still didn't know why Reverend Doyle seldom delivered these devotionals. She thought his would be far more entertaining than Mrs. Doyle's dour presentations.

Following the devotional there was usually an hour or two free, during which Blair, Claudette, and the two sisters would often go into one another's bedrooms and chat. Once, they gave each other manicures, which Blair desperately needed. Patience shared her only bottle of pale pink nail polish. Mrs. Doyle would not let her daughters have any darker polish, and Patience said she'd had to beg for the light one.

The Doyle girls, for all their strict religious upbringing, were rather easygoing. They never preached at Blair and Claudette. Mostly they just talked "girl talk"—clothes, boys, movies. The girls were not allowed to go to movies, but even in the remote islands, they knew a little about Hollywood and were eager to hear Blair talk about the stars. They were also fascinated with the subject of boys. Blair, of course, was the most experienced of the four, but she never spoke of, or even hinted at, the more risqué aspects of her experience. She appreciated their innocence and was embarrassed by her own lack of such innocence, despising that shady part of her own life so thoroughly that she would never vaunt it.

The younger ones did have more ingenuous questions, the kind one might find answers to in an Andy Hardy movie.

"How do you let a boy know you are interested?"

"What should you do if a boy tries to get fresh?"

"Have you ever called a boy before he called you?"

Actually, most of these questions were academic for Hope and Patience. Dominador was the only boy around who was even close to their age, and he had a girlfriend in a village down the mountain. When the girls went to school, it had been to a girls' boarding school in Manila. Now, of course, with the war on, there were no more trips to Manila. But there was a boys' school near the girls', and there had been dances and such. Meg Doyle disapproved of most types of dancing but permitted sedate forms of the activity, such as the waltz, because Reverend Doyle didn't see the harm.

During these talks Blair also learned more about the interactions at the mission. When they were discussing dancing, Blair asked, "Don't your parents agree on everything?"

"I don't think so," Patience replied and then giggled. "They try not to let us see, but when their voices rise, it's hard not to hear. Papa says if two people agree on every little thing, one of them isn't necessary."

"They didn't even agree on our names," Hope said.

"Who won?" asked Claudette, who always had a great interest in people's names.

Blair knew the answer to the question before Hope replied, "Mother, of course!" She grinned.

"It must be hard to have to live up to such names," said Blair. She didn't add that she would have been horrified to have such a name. But she did say, "I thought I had it bad being given a boy's name. But to be named for a virtue!"

"I know. It's awful, but you get used to it," said Patience. "Even I did, and I think I got the worst of it. Patience, really!"

"I guess it's not so bad that I got to choose my own name," Claudette said.

"I don't know that," said Blair. "You have never said what your given name is."

"Because it's awful."

"It can't be worse than our names," Hope said.

"Come on, you have to tell us," said Patience.

"Okay, but you must promise you will never use it. What else is the use of being an orphan and getting to choose your own name?" She gave each one a searching look, and after they had each nodded in turn, she said with a sour look on her face, "Aquilina! Ugh!"

"Do you know what that means in Spanish?" asked Patience.

"Yes, I know some Spanish. It means eagle. Isn't that stupid?"

Blair rather thought it was prettier than Claudette Colbert and a lot less silly, but she loved Claudette and would never voice such an opinion.

"It's a great name, Claudette." Patience's tone was infused with sincerity. "Eagles are symbolic and beautiful. Listen to this, it's something I memorized years ago and never forgot. 'They that wait upon the Lord shall renew their strength; they shall mount up with wings as eagles; they shall run, and not be weary; and they shall walk, and not faint.' " She smiled, and there might have been just a touch of envy in her eyes—a nice kind of envy.

"What's that from?" Blair asked.

"Isaiah 40:31," said Patience with a pleased smile that she remembered the reference. "From the Bible," she added.

"Oh." Blair had hoped it was from something safe like Shakespeare. Part of her might be searching for God, but another part was still uncomfortable with the topic.

Claudette didn't seem to mind. "Maybe later you can show me exactly where it is. I didn't think the Bible had such good things in it."

This was usually how their little chats turned to religious matters—innocently, subtly, never in a heavy-handed way. Blair and Claudette were open vessels. Oh, Mrs. Doyle could easily put Blair off Christianity, but she told herself there were bad apples in every basket. But even as she thought such a thing about "Mrs. Nazi," the woman would turn around and do something totally contradictory.

Like the day she had called to Blair from the back door of the kitchen.

"Blair, would you like to help me fix the stew for dinner?"

Blair had been outside beating rugs—her most hated of all chores, because even with the many days of rain, there was still more dust in the mission compound than Blair thought could be possible. And it all sank into the rugs or clung to the furniture inside the house. When Mrs. Doyle called, Blair gave a quick glance around. Surely the woman was addressing someone else. Her voice was too pleasant to be directed at Blair.

"Well, I—" But Blair didn't know how to respond. Could it be a trick question? Did Blair really have a choice?

"I guess after what I said about your cooking soon after you arrived," said the woman, "I can understand if you don't want to. But I was thinking maybe you might want to learn, that's all."

"You want to teach me how to cook?" Still, suspicion rose in Blair's tone.

"Just stew to start."

"I'm rather a mess right now, with the dust and all." Blair thought they would both be relieved if she declined. The woman was probably just asking because her husband had pressured her into making a concession.

"I'll take down the rug," Mrs. Doyle offered. "You go in and wash up, and we'll meet in the kitchen."

This did not sound like a person who was looking for an escape from an odious duty. Still, Blair remained uncomfortable with the situation even after she met the woman in the kitchen a few minutes later. Mrs. Doyle smiled and handed Blair an apron. That friendly smile looked just a tad bizarre on the woman's austere face. Not that she never smiled, it was just that when she did, she never seemed quite at ease with the gesture.

"Your man Juan is quite a wonder," Mrs. Doyle said conversationally. "He went hunting today and came home with two plump rabbits. Conway was never much of a hand with hunting."

"I wish we could do more to help with the supply situation," Blair offered. "I know they must be getting low."

"God will provide."

"Still—"

"You mustn't feel bad about eating, Blair."

"But because of me you have four extra mouths to feed."

Meg lifted the lid from a large pot bubbling on the stove. "We do not begrudge any of you a morsel," she said with conviction. "God brought you to us, and He will provide. It is as simple as that."

"Do you really think God brought *me* here, Mrs. Doyle?" Blair eyed the woman, not exactly baiting her. She was curious only.

"I do indeed," Meg said simply. There was an air about her that seemed to hint she wanted to say more but was restraining herself.

Finally, after a moment's pause, she added, "I have been simmering those rabbits for several hours."

"In what?" Blair asked, glad that her earlier curiosity had led nowhere.

"I put them in the pot and covered them with water and added some seasonings—a bay leaf, salt, pepper. Oh, and an onion. Conway likes his food simple, or I might have put in some rosemary, too."

"Then what?"

"Now we will cut up some vegetables—these are the last of my carrots. But we have more onions and turnips and plenty of bamboo shoots." She chuckled softly. "I wonder what my mother would say if she saw me putting bamboo shoots into stew."

"I guess you have learned many exotic ways living here . . . how long has it been?" Blair took a knife as she spoke and began to cut the carrots Mrs. Doyle handed her. She thought four or five pieces from a carrot should do.

With a slightly amused smile on her face, Mrs. Doyle said, "You have to scrub them clean first." Blair sensed the woman was trying hard to be patient, but it was also obvious she was shocked at how ignorant a young woman could be about such a simple task. "Then cut them into about half-inch slices."

Scrubbing the carrot as vigorously as she could under the tap of running water, Blair edged the conversation back to the previous track. Best to keep talking about Mrs. Doyle so she didn't have to talk about herself—or Gary. "So how long have you been at the mission?"

"Ten years. Hope was three—no, as a matter of fact, she had her fourth birthday two weeks after we arrived. We had no cake, no candles. Goodness, I was depressed—" Mrs. Doyle stopped abruptly, with a quick glance at Blair, then almost as if it was an apology, she explained, "I was young. My faith in God was not as steady as it should have been."

Blair wondered why the woman felt she had to excuse her remark. Was it not all right to be depressed if you were a Christian? Did one have to be perfect? Blair knew many claiming to be Christians certainly weren't. Did that mean they weren't as good Christians as the more perfect ones? But she didn't dare pose any of these questions to Mrs. Doyle. They might be having a pleasant few moments, but she wasn't about to purposely fire the woman up about religion.

"Shall I do the onion?" Blair asked innocuously as she finished the carrots.

"Yes, why don't you."

After brief instruction on the proper technique for peeling and cutting an onion, Mrs. Doyle was quiet for a time, yet she again had that look on her long angular face that indicated she wanted to say more. Blair hoped she didn't. She nearly sagged with relief when the conversation returned to cooking.

"We'll let the vegetables simmer with the meat until about a half hour before dinner," Mrs. Doyle said. "But there should be at least an hour for the vegetables to cook and their flavors to mix in, so longer wouldn't hurt. Then I'll thicken the broth."

"How?"

"All I have is flour, so I will use that. Cornstarch works as well. You don't want to dump the flour directly into the hot broth, because you'll get lumps if you do so. First, put about a half cup into a bowl with some water and make a paste like a thick cream. Then gradually add it to the broth. I'll let you do it when the time comes."

"Thank you, Mrs. Doyle, I really appreciate this." Blair gave a tentative smile. "You must wonder about a woman who can't even make decent coffee."

"I have forgotten all about that incident, Blair." She appeared affronted that it had been mentioned. "Gary did mention you could cook."

"Did he?" Blair's voice croaked over the words, and her cheeks pinked. She remembered the time she had brought a casserole to a potluck she'd attended with Gary. She told him she'd made it herself, when in fact she had bribed her mother's cook to fix it. One of her many lies. If she'd had any doubts, now it was certain that Gary had spoken of her to the Doyles, at least to Mrs. Doyle.

"He came to dinner once when I was serving scalloped potatoes," Mrs. Doyle said. "He mentioned that you had once prepared them for him and they had been quite tasty."

"I . . . I guess I wasn't honest about that," Blair admitted. "I had my parents' cook make them."

"I suppose it is normal for a young woman to want her beau to perceive her as the domestic sort."

"Is that all he said about me?" Blair didn't really want to know, but she couldn't keep from asking. Maybe it would be best to get it out into the open. Maybe she should admit she had deceived him in larger matters than scalloped potatoes.

But the moment was lost as Hope and Claudette burst into the kitchen with a basketful of ripe fruit they had just picked. They were chattering and laughing.

"Hope, is that how you enter a room?" remonstrated Mrs. Doyle, her stern self once more. "Blair and I were having a peaceful conversation."

Both girls apologized humbly.

"Just remember it next time. Now, what have you there?"

Blair felt reprieved and did not try to return to the earlier conversation.

35

DESPITE EVERYTHING, Blair found life at the mission to be surprisingly pleasant for her. It had been weeks since she had known such peace. If she was honest, she'd have to admit it might even have been years.

She did find herself using Mrs. Doyle's "quiet time" to reflect, as she did this particular evening while seated on the bed she shared with Claudette, who, so they could have privacy during this time, was spending her quiet time in the kitchen. Mrs. Doyle had decided on this arrangement, suggesting they switch off places each evening. The woman *was* serious about making the best use of the time!

Since Claudette seemed more than willing to accept the arrangement, Blair wasn't about to fight it herself. All her life she had worked hard not to be the reflective sort, not to ponder life's mysteries, or her own actions for that matter. Now she wondered if that had contributed to her many troubles. At any rate, she didn't see the harm in using the time thus now. If she got bored, she would just crawl under the covers and go to sleep. Who was to say she wasn't just praying or something? Yet something told Blair that "Mrs. Nazi" would know.

So each night she sat there and forced herself to think about "things." For the most part this involved pondering her past. Her wild life, her rebellion toward her parents, her father. For all Meg Doyle's stern, critical nature, she could never begin to compare with Keagan Hayes. At least Meg had moments of kindness and generosity. It was almost as if there were two warring factions inside the woman that even she wasn't quite certain which ought to win.

Keagan, on the other hand, had never indicated a glimmer of inner conflict. Well, he had walked her down the aisle on her wedding day. Blair marveled at the thought. Could it be there was more to her father than she had ever imagined? She hated to consider such a question. So much of who she was seemed to be built on her antipathy toward that man. What would she be, who would she be, without it? She did not want to become some spineless, namby-pamby sort, gushing and sweet—no matter what she imagined Gary might want in a woman. In a twisted way, despite her frequent ire toward Mrs. Doyle, Blair admired the woman. Here was a Christian who was definitely not gushy. Her edges could use some softening, but it was heartening that there was room in the Christian faith for the sort of person Meg was. Maybe there was room for Blair, as well—without changing the essential person that she was.

The only problem was that Blair was still not entirely sure who that inner person was. She wasn't comfortable with being kind and sweet, but neither did she wish to be the critical sort, for who was she to criticize anyone?

She recalled one of Mrs. Doyle's after-dinner devotionals about being refined by God. She couldn't remember the exact words. . . . Suddenly Blair jumped up and began rooting though her things and Claudette's. She had become a bit restless just sitting, so this was mostly a diversion, but perhaps she could find the passage that Mrs. Doyle had quoted from the Bible. Blair didn't enjoy reading any more than she did reflecting, but she did like the challenge of wading through the biblical maze.

She found the Bible Meg had loaned her and Claudette. Scratching her head and screwing up her face in thought, she tried to remember where those verses were. Someone had mentioned they were in the last book of the Old Testament. She flipped to a book called Malachi, relieved to find that it was a short book. Scanning the four relatively brief chapters, she found it. Chapter three, verses two and three.

> *But who may abide the day of his coming? and who shall stand when he appeareth? for he is like a refiner's fire, and like fullers' soap. And he shall sit as a refiner and purifier of silver: and he shall purify the sons of Levi, and purge them as gold and silver, that they may offer unto the Lord an offering in righteousness.*

Blair shivered despite the tropical heat. Maybe these verses weren't so great after all. It didn't sound like it would be fun to be the object of this "refiner's fire." Not fun at all. But then, that was Mrs. Doyle's idea of faith. Fun had nothing to do with it in her mind. All fun was bad. Blair was not about to accept that! She often wondered what Reverend Doyle's view of this was and sensed he might think differently, since he seemed a fun-loving person at heart. She thought she might ask him someday but for now didn't feel as if she knew him well enough for such a personal discussion. Besides, he was away from the house a lot during the day. If the women had many chores, he seemed to have just as many that kept him busy outside. And Mrs. Doyle had mentioned he had a small office in the church where she said he was writing a book.

Yet there must be more to it and to this verse. Mrs. Doyle had said that the fire would remove all that was bad, and Blair did want that. She wanted to get rid of the garbage in her life. And just maybe, when that was done, she might discover who the real Blair was.

Suddenly Blair realized that in all of her reflecting just now, she hadn't once thought of Gary. She started to chide herself for being selfish again, but then a new idea occurred to her. Perhaps she was finally approaching faith in God on her own, apart from Gary. That was good. Still, she couldn't deny that a small part of her was afraid to think too much on her relationship with Gary. It conjured up too many of the lurking fears inside her—fears for him, fears for their future, and fear that she might never be able to change enough for him. On impulse she laid aside the Bible and bowed her head. She knew about "giving your fears to God." Jackie talked about it, as did Gary, and so did the Doyles. A bit of prayer had worked for her in the past. It certainly couldn't hurt now.

Blair soon discovered another source of pleasure at the mission. One day she found herself alone in the house—a rare occurrence to be sure with so many people there. Alone and—wonder of wonders!—done with her daily chores. It was three o'clock in the afternoon. She wandered up to the piano. She'd been at the mission for some time by then, but she still hadn't dared ask to play. Though she had performed professionally to large audiences, she somehow felt reticent about playing here at the mission. But feeling safe this day because no one was around, she slid onto the bench and lifted the cover over the keys. On the music rack there were some sheets of music. Blair knew many songs by heart—a good memory was one of her few useful talents, one that served her both as an actress and as a musician. She could also read music quite well and could play nearly any piece of music presented to her. Classical music was a bit more difficult than popular tunes, but with practice she could even adequately manage Bach or Beethoven.

Shuffling through the sheets of music, she saw all were hymns—no surprise there! There was a hymnbook, as well. She had nothing against hymns and in fact thought many were quite beautiful. That had been the only part of attending church she had really enjoyed.

She paused in the book at "For the Beauty of the Earth." She'd always liked that one. She played two verses and, as always, became completely absorbed in the music. She had heard of the saying "Music has charms to soothe a savage breast" and thought this must surely apply to her for all the calming effect the act of playing and singing had upon her. The thought came to her that if she ever did find herself, it would be in a song, not in a refiner's fire—yet she knew she needed a fire to clean out all her many impurities. Perhaps the enlightenment through song would come later. She hoped so. She hoped God would not take that away from her.

Next she chose a newer tune, "Morning Has Broken." She had never heard it before but thought it could easily become a favorite. She was starting on the second verse when a voice made her jerk her hands from the keys as quickly as if she had been caught stealing. And why not, since that voice was filled with scolding?

"Hope, I thought you were supposed to be helping your father—"

Meg Doyle's voice had begun from a distance, somewhere in the back of the house from the direction of the kitchen, and had drawn closer, then stopped abruptly just as Blair turned on the bench and saw her come into the living room.

"Oh, was that you?" Mrs. Doyle said, a perplexed look on her face, as if she could not believe what she was seeing.

"Yes . . . I'm sorry if I shouldn't have." Blair could not imagine why what she was doing could be wrong, but she always had the impulse to apologize to Mrs. Doyle.

"No need to apologize. I did tell the girls I wanted some quiet time, but I failed to mention it to you, so it is nothing for you to worry about."

"I'll stop if you were praying or something—well, I'll stop no matter what."

"Don't, please. To tell the truth, I found it rather nice and only came out because I thought it was Hope shirking her duties." Mrs. Doyle came up beside Blair. "You did very well with 'Morning Has Broken.' It is such a beautiful song. Hope has been trying it but not doing very well. That's another reason I should have known it wasn't her playing. Since she had to leave school because of the Emergency, she hasn't had her lessons. Unfortunately, I am not musical, so I can't help her. And Patience has only a rudimentary knowledge, as well. My older daughter has inherited my ineptitude in that area I'm afraid. Hope is . . . well, our only hope of having a musician in the family."

"I'd be happy to help her if you wish." But Blair hurriedly added, "But I must warn you, I have never taught anyone anything, so I'm not sure if I can."

"I'm sure she will appreciate any help you wish to offer." There was a formality in the woman's tone, almost as if she didn't like having to accept help from Blair. "Now I must get back to what I was doing before the paint dries."

For the first time Blair noticed Meg was wearing a muslin smock that had drips and smudges of paint all over it.

"You were painting?"

"A little hobby of mine." Her tone was almost self-effacing, as out of place with Mrs. Doyle as a toothy grin would have been.

"Did you paint the pictures I've seen on the walls about the house?"

"Most of them. I know it is vanity to display my work, but I have thought it would be wasteful to spend money on paint, paper, and canvas and then leave the results in a closet. I have yet to find Scriptural clarification on this dilemma."

Blair, with much difficulty, restrained a smile. It seemed rather silly for the woman to wrestle over such a thing, but knowing Meg Doyle as little as she did, she knew she had probably struggled over this "spiritual" issue long and hard. To Blair it was simple—you paint a picture, act in a play, sing a song, and the effort should be appreciated by others. She remembered something she'd once heard about hiding your light under a bushel. That just didn't seem right. But she didn't dare comment on her musings to Mrs. Doyle. Surely this spiritual paragon would be able to poke a hundred holes in Blair's reasoning.

Instead, she said, "Your work is very nice. I thought someone at the mission must have done the pictures, because I noted the scenes were of the mission. I especially like the one of the front porch with all the plants."

"My plants and painting are among the great joys in my life—of course besides my faith in God."

"Of course." The minute the words were out, she hoped Mrs. Doyle didn't detect the hint of sarcasm in them. But wasn't it okay for Christians to have other joys in life? Mrs. Doyle had sounded almost defensive about it.

Mrs. Doyle seemed about to comment, and in fact opened her mouth with a rather censorious look in her eyes, when yelling from outside cut her off. They exchanged questioning glances. Everyone had gone down to the spring to help Reverend Doyle with the problems they had been having there. Overgrown brush was clogging the drain and had to be cleared out. Could someone have injured himself during the clearing work? The sound they heard was surely one of alarm.

The screen door burst open. "Mrs. Doyle!" It was Dominador, the young man who helped around the mission. "It was my turn to patrol today, and I saw some Japs."

"Are you sure?" asked Mrs. Doyle.

"It was from a distance, but I am as sure as can be."

"Then why are you out there yelling so they can hear?" chided the minister's wife. Blair wondered the same thing.

"I'm sorry. I . . . I . . ."

"Never mind, Dominador. How far away are they?"

"I was down by the big curve of the river and saw a half dozen or so of them across the river. I ran all the way back. But it's maybe two miles or so from there."

"Dominador, run down to the spring and get everyone up here. Tell them to hurry." She swung to face Blair as the young man ran from the living room. "Come, let's gather what supplies we can." She hurried first to the kitchen, and as she moved she murmured, "Dear God, please keep them from spotting us!"

Blair followed her and found herself silently repeating the same prayer. Japs five miles away! How could that be? The mission was supposed to be a safe place. Gary had promised Blair she'd be protected here. Now was her peace and comfort about to ripped away from her again? What would they do? Where could they go? Her stomach lurched as she thought about fleeing once more into the jungle. Please, God, not that! But what else was there besides capture? But Meg Doyle at the moment didn't seem to be a woman preparing for that possibility.

"THERE'S ONLY A FEW HOURS of light left," said Reverend Doyle when everyone was gathered in the living room. "But we must take time to pack supplies."

"Where will we go?" asked Juan.

"Gethsemane." The reverend smiled at the puzzled looks of the newcomers. "That's a little retreat we have in the jungle. If we're careful, the enemy won't track us there."

"I think I should confirm this report," Juan said. "Dominador, take me to where you saw the enemy."

"That will just waste time," argued Dominador. "Don't you believe me?"

"Juan is right," put in Reverend Doyle. "We need to make sure. We will continue to pack while you are gone, but don't be too long."

"If we are not back in an hour, go to the retreat," Juan said. "We will join you there later. You know the way, Dominador?"

"Yes, I know the way." Dominador's tone was sulky. "I also know there are Japs out there."

Reluctantly he went with Juan. Everyone else turned to the task of packing. Mrs. Doyle's skills at ordering people about came in quite handy now. Everyone was given specific instructions and a suitcase or knapsack to fill. Food, medical supplies, a change of clothes for everyone, soap, and blankets. The retreat had some basic supplies already, but Mrs. Doyle hadn't checked the place recently and didn't want to trust the condition of things. She also was not going to let the soup she had been preparing for dinner go to waste, so she had Hope fill canning jars, and these were also distributed among the packs.

In an hour they were ready to leave. Blair could tell the reverend was struggling about what to do since Juan and Dominador hadn't returned. Blair hoped he would give it a few more minutes, especially for Juan, whom she didn't want to desert after he had done so much for her.

They waited fifteen minutes past the agreed time before the two men returned. Dominador's head was down, and he was dragging his feet.

"We saw no sign of Japanese," said Juan.

"I tell you I saw them!" burst Dominador, lifting his head momentarily to make his defense.

"It is possible they were farther away than you thought," appeased Juan. "From where the boy said he was standing on a small hill, I could see several miles down into the valley, maybe five or six miles."

"Well, whether or not there were Japs," said Reverend Doyle, "maybe this false—" he stopped when Dominador opened his mouth to make a protest of the word *false*. Doyle quickly corrected himself. "This preemptory alarm might be for the best after all. We've heard reports before of the nearness of the enemy, but I hoped they were exaggerated. Now I think we should continue with our plan to leave."

"Shall we still leave today?" asked Mrs. Doyle.

"Even if the Japs are five miles away, or ten, we best not push it by spending the night here. We can take a couple of minutes, though, to take a breath and make sure we haven't forgotten anything."

Those minutes were hardly necessary because Meg Doyle had done her job of organizing well. She obviously had thought out such a "moment's notice" evacuation plan earlier. The girls did manage to stuff a few more luxury items into their packs, but less than two hours after the original alarm, the group was ready and gathered at the door.

Before leaving, Reverend Doyle paused at the front door of the house. "We had a pretty nice home here. I hope if those Japanese come, they don't destroy it all."

"Conway," said Mrs. Doyle, "don't forget, 'Where your treasure is, there will your heart be also.' "

Blair thought it was rather a harsh thing to say just then. She knew it was from the Bible. She'd heard it before. But she thought a person had a right to feel regretful on leaving, perhaps forever, the home they loved. The reverend didn't need Scripture thrown into his face just then.

But he surprised Blair by placing an arm around his wife and smiling. "Thank you, dear, for reminding me. My treasure is with me—you, my daughters, and our friends. Let's go, then."

Reverend Doyle led them to a narrow path behind the house. He said they could not take the mission vehicle because the only road to the retreat might be patrolled by the Japanese. Blair cringed at what that meant. Nevertheless, they were a dogged, determined group that departed the mission. Juan and Ruberto brought up the rear and carefully covered the party's tracks. Blair hoped that would help. She was still trembling at the thought of the Japanese even ten miles away! Still, no one was certain if the mission had been seen by the enemy. The reverend berated himself for not leaving sooner, rather than waiting until it was under such duress. But Blair had sensed all along from both the elder Doyles a certain denial about the war—from calling it only the Emergency to expecting every day that their congregation would return. Their ministry was to the people who lived deep in the hills surrounding the mission. These were mostly pagans who had not even been touched by the Catholic Church. Patience had proudly told Blair that they had about two hundred converts. Yet when word of the Japanese invasion reached the hill people, they had retreated to their homes deep in the mountains, fearing to venture out even for an occasional Sunday service.

Blair hated being forced once again to trek through the jungle. The mission had been far from opulent, but she had come to enjoy even its spare comforts. Now she was thrust back among snakes and bugs and mud and annoying flying insects. She whimpered every time something brushed her skin, fearful of what horrid critter it might be. She cringed when darkness fell and they were forced to make camp out in the open. But she had to grudgingly admit, even if just to herself, a gratitude toward Mrs. Doyle for remembering to pack mosquito netting. It wouldn't keep a poisonous snake out of her bedding, but it did offer some protection against other creepy, crawly things. She also was grateful for the half-cooked soup. Even cold with crunchy vegetables, it was tasty.

Early in the morning before the sky lightened, Mrs. Doyle roused everyone, and with only a slice of bread and a drink of water for breakfast, they headed off. There was still no sign of the Japanese, but Juan and Ruberto continued to take precautions against being followed.

On the final stretch of their journey they came to a steep hill, nearly a cliff, which Reverend Doyle announced they had to scale. Juan, ever resourceful, climbed up first and rigged up a pulley with rope with which they hauled up packs and suitcases. This wasn't strong enough to bring up people, so for them, it was simply scaling the height with hands and feet, with someone at the bottom pushing and someone at the top reaching down a hand. There were enough footholds and handholds to aid the climb, but Blair was nevertheless relieved to clasp Juan's hand on the last stretch.

"Well, at least the Japs aren't going to guess this leads to a trail," she said.

They reached their destination by noon. The sun was high and hot. Blair was sweating and drained more from the heat than the walk, though Reverend Doyle had set a hard pace. The place they called Gethsemane was a compound of about five nipa huts. Several people were already there. Blair hadn't realized this place would be occupied, but Reverend Doyle explained that some of their congregation who lived in the valley had been forced from their homes by the enemy and had come here for safety. There were about twenty in all, and the reverend tried to make introductions. Blair promptly forgot most of the names but did grasp that all these people were related in some way. Ruberto's brother was among the group.

The Doyles' party took a vacant hut, one of the larger ones that had apparently been specifically earmarked for them in the event they must evacuate. It consisted of one huge room and another smaller one partitioned off with a curtain. It had a rustic kitchen area but no indoor plumbing. Crude latrines were built several paces from the compound, and water for cooking and washing had to be brought in from a nearby creek. Since the water had to be boiled before use, Reverend Doyle said they would risk building a fire in the old-fashioned wood stove. Blair was relieved to hear that, since it also meant cooked meals. But she was not pleased that there was only an outhouse. How she had come to practically adore the Doyles' lovely bathroom back at their house with its flushing toilet and wonderful bathtub!

But since no one else was complaining, Blair kept silent.

Mrs. Doyle almost immediately resumed her schedule of chores—barking orders and giving tasks to everyone as if she were a drill sergeant. Only then did Blair grumble. Her feet were killing her from the hike, and she fairly ached all over, with a headache to boot. She thought a few moments of rest wouldn't have been expecting too much.

"Blair, we all have to work together. Only then can we make this place comfortable." At least the woman sounded more patient than usual.

"Yes, of course," sighed Blair and took the bucket to go fetch water.

Patience, who knew the way to the creek, took another bucket and accompanied Blair.

"I'm sorry we don't have better to offer you," Patience said as they plodded through the jungle a short distance from the hut. Her tone was completely sincere. She was just the kind of sweet Christian Blair associated with religion, yet she was so nice you didn't mind.

"What?" Blair might have complained, but she never expected an apology. She didn't know what she expected. But she didn't blame her hosts. They were suffering as much as she.

"You are not as used to this kind of thing as we are. If you'd like, I'll speak with Mother and have her ease up a bit on you. We'll understand—"

"Do you think I am weak and inept?" Blair asked, affronted. Then she hurried ahead. She didn't know the way but could see a clear path and followed that. She didn't know why she was so furious. Patience had not in the least spoken condescendingly. She really did understand, or she wanted to. Sometimes, however, it was just the "niceness" of these people that pricked at Blair. Except for "Mrs. Nazi," everyone was kind, thoughtful, and pleasant. Mrs. Doyle, as well, had her mild moments, though even when she was being her usual harsh self, Blair had to admit the woman was almost always fair. Blair might have sensed she was getting picked on, yet she never worked more than the others.

She reached the creek and paused for breath when she heard Patience come up behind her.

"Put down your bucket, Blair. The water can wait a few minutes. Can we sit down and talk a minute?"

With a shrug Blair dropped the bucket and plopped down in the grass. It was wet, but Blair hardly flinched. She supposed she was getting accustomed to such discomforts. She knew the sun would dry her out quickly.

Patience joined her. "I have been so happy to have someone near my own age around. Since I finished school, it's been lonely. Some of the women in our congregation are my age, but they are mostly married with children, and I don't have anything in common with them."

"And then you had to get stuck with me," Blair replied, trying to make a joke but falling short because she believed it was true.

"That's not what I am getting at, Blair." Patience said just a little impatiently. She plucked up a blade of coarse jungle grass and twirled it in her fingers. "I am not saying this well at all! I'm just trying to assure you that no one here is merely putting up with you. I feel you are a gift from God to me, and I think Hope feels the same way, especially since you brought Claudette. Hope has never had a close friend, either." Patience studied the blade of grass a moment then tossed it away. "Mother can be a little hard, I know."

Blair tried hard to restrain eager agreement to that, but Patience glanced at her and saw her barely restrained grin. Patience smiled, and that broke Blair's self-control, and her lips twitched. Patience giggled. In a moment, they were both giggling.

"Okay," Patience said through her mirth, "Mother is more than hard at times, but she means well. Honestly. Though I can understand if you find that hard to believe. Maybe she'll grow on you."

"Like a jungle fungus!" Blair blurted, then gasped and slapped her hand over her mouth. Through her fingers she said, "I am so sorry. It just slipped out."

But Patience was giggling all over again. "If Mother had heard that, she'd wash your mouth out with soap."

"You won't tell her!" Blair didn't know whether to be laughing still or to be horrified. She could not read the source of Patience's amusement.

Apparently sensing Blair's discomfiture, Patience shook her head as she tried to still her laughter. In a moment she was able to speak. "Oh, Blair! Thank you for a good laugh. But trust me, I will never tell my mother. I don't know why she treats you the way she does. She doesn't act that way around Claudette."

"I didn't want to think she was picking on me in particular."

"I'm sure she isn't. But . . ." Patience gave her shoulder a shake to complete her thought.

"I'm sure she doesn't approve of me."

"Whyever not? Because you are from a rich family and aren't used to hardships? No, she would never hold that against anyone."

Blair knew it was more than that, and she now was certain Patience, and probably Hope, knew nothing of her situation with Gary. Apparently he had been somewhat circumspect in spilling his troubles to strangers. It angered her a little that he had done so in the first place, yet she could understand his need to talk to someone. Perhaps he was closer to the Doyles than she had thought. Why shouldn't he have friends she knew nothing of? Nevertheless, she began to wonder if it would help her to talk to someone. There had been Jackie, and she had helped despite her age and inexperience. Patience was the same age as Jackie and surely no more experienced. Maybe that didn't matter as much as just having someone to listen.

"I think I know why your mother doesn't like me," Blair said, forcing the words out. She didn't want Patience to think ill of her, yet she had a strong sense that this young woman, so much like her name, would accept Blair anyway. "I think Gary talked to your parents about some things I did that . . . well, I am not proud of. It's . . ." She was losing her nerve. "It's really hard to talk about."

"You don't have to tell me if you can't." Patience's tone was full of encouragement. Then she said, "Have you talked to my mother about it?"

"No!" That was the last thing Blair would have done, though she didn't admit that much.

"You don't know for sure, then?" Blair nodded and Patience went on. "I don't think my mother would hold something against someone without talking to them." Her brow was furrowed. She obviously didn't want to think her mother would do that, but she wasn't entirely certain.

"It's okay." Blair wanted to set the girl at ease. "I understand why she would feel the way she does about me. I know there are some things that are just so awful even God can't forgive them—"

"That's not true, Blair!" All uncertainty fell away from Patience now. "God forgives everything."

"I know that's what people say, but I think you can push Him too far—"

Patience gave a firm shake of her head, her long auburn braid flapping back and forth against her back. "Impossible!"

"But—"

Just then they heard the clamor of someone striding through the brush. "Hey, you two, where's the water?" It was Mateo. "Mrs. Doyle wants to make lunch."

Both women jumped up just as Mateo came into the open. They grabbed their buckets and hurriedly dipped them into the water. They knew they couldn't talk further about this subject in front of Mateo.

But Patience did say quietly, "Let's talk again later, Blair. Or better yet, talk to my mother. She is really a wise person."

Blair considered following Patience's advice about talking to Mrs. Doyle. The woman's overture back at the house in attempting to teach Blair how to cook and later her acceptance of Blair's piano playing was still fresh in Blair's mind. Maybe she could be approached. But the next day Blair was given the job of tending a pot of beans cooking on the stove, and she let the fire get too hot. Actually she had become distracted in talking to Claudette. The result was burned beans. Mrs. Doyle was upbraiding her over that when Juan came in, quite upset that the fire was smoking too much. They had to be careful in case there were any Japanese in the vicinity.

Blair felt awful, especially at dinner. Mrs. Doyle refused to waste precious food, so everyone had to eat the charred beans. As usual the others were too kind to say anything, but Blair could see they were not happy with her by the way they avoided her eyes.

To make matters worse Mrs. Doyle chose stewardship as the topic of that evening's devotion. She asked everyone to open their Bibles and follow along. Of course everyone had brought Bibles, for this was one item in the hurried packing that Mrs. Doyle made sure was included. She read verse after verse, flipping expertly through the pages. She seemed to know this topic especially well. One verse she uttered with special relish, her eyes flickering in Blair's direction.

" 'Moreover it is required in stewards, that a man be found faithful.' " Then she flipped back a few pages in her Bible and said, "I will close with this parable, spoken by our Lord Jesus. 'For the kingdom of heaven is as a man travelling into a far country, who called his own servants, and delivered unto them his goods. And unto one he gave five talents, to another two, and to another one. . . .' "

Blair vaguely recalled hearing in Sunday school something about the parable of the talents. She certainly did not recall what it was about, but she'd known then her musical ability was a talent. Grudgingly, with just a touch of curiosity, she listened to Mrs. Doyle. The man with five talents turned it into five more, while the man with two, into two more. But the fellow with only one talent buried his and thus had no increase.

Mrs. Doyle went on. "The master said to the first two men, 'Well done, thou good and faithful servant: thou hast been faithful over a few things, I will make thee ruler over many things: enter thou into the joy of thy lord.' But to the last man, who had hid his talent, the man said, 'Thou wicked and slothful servant . . .' "

Blair knew these words were directed at her alone, though she refused to look at Mrs. Doyle to see if the woman was looking at her. She let her mind wander at that point because she didn't want to hear more. As far as she was concerned, it had nothing to do with burning the beans. The woman just liked to hear herself say words like *wicked* and *slothful*.

Unfortunately Blair's attention returned just as Mrs. Doyle was reading, " 'And cast ye the unprofitable servant into outer darkness: there shall be weeping and gnashing of teeth.' "

Blair wanted to get up and leave, but that would only be admitting her guilt. She wasn't guilty! She'd only burned dinner, for heaven's sake. Suddenly, though, she realized another meaning to Mrs. Doyle's words. Blair *was* guilty, of something far worse than wasting food. This was no doubt the woman's not-so-subtle way of pressing that fact upon Blair. Blair had lied to and deceived her own husband, and that had to be, especially to a woman like Meg Doyle, a sin worse than any other. One surely worthy of being tossed into a place where there would be eternal weeping and gnashing of teeth.

Blair made no attempt to talk to anyone that night. She did see Patience and her mother step outside together for a time. Maybe Mrs. Doyle would set Patience straight on a few things. The younger woman was obviously misinformed on several points of Christianity that even Blair knew about. Forgiveness must have limits. The master certainly hadn't shown the man with one talent much mercy.

The two women returned to the hut well after dark. Everyone was by then rolled into her blanket—the females in the front part of the hut because it was larger and because they were usually the first ones awake in the morning, and the males in the partitioned section. There were no beds, only mats on the floor. They used no lights at night, electric or candle, in case Japanese planes flew overhead.

Blair heard the door creak open and peeked out covertly from her blankets. She saw the shadowed forms of both women. She thought there was an odd look of humility on Mrs. Doyle's face but was certain she must have seen wrong.

When the two tiptoed to their own blankets, which were next to Blair, she clamped shut her eyes, unable to face either of them. She fell into an uneasy sleep, dreaming about gnashing teeth and herself weeping, an eternity of tears washing over her. And, lost soul that she was, she thrashed around in agony, bound and nearly gagged with a heavenly cloth that looked suspiciously like mosquito netting.

Somewhere in her dreams—it must have been a dream—an angel ministered to her, but the angel had a long, angular face, not pretty but handsome. This heavenly being was a glow of light as she tried to wipe away Blair's tears with a cool cloth. Ah, the cloth did feel so good, but how could anything cool the fires of hades?

Voices wove around Blair, not angel voices, not songs of heaven.

"Jap patrol . . ."

"We have to leave."

"Not with her like this . . ."

"We must."

"You go. I'll catch up—"

"Don't be foolish."

"Mother, I'll stay."

"I will not leave her, either!"

"Trust in God. . . ."

A great battle of angels. But what were angels doing in hades?

Blair tried to speak. Words formed and sounds were uttered, but even to her they did not sound right. "Better off this way . . . Gary left, too. . . . I don't deserve . . . cold . . . so c-cold . . . p-please . . . g-go . . ."

She felt the weight of blankets being laid over her, but that didn't seem to halt her shivering. And it wasn't long before she was throwing off those blankets, suddenly consumed by heat. She was burning up, as if the flames of hell were licking up all around her. She emptied her stomach a couple of times, too, and the angel who wasn't pretty gently cleaned up the mess and changed Blair out of her soiled and soaking clothes.

"There, there . . ." the angel soothed.

"How long will this last?" came another voice. It was trembling and tearful. Claudette? Or another angel with a nut-brown face?

"Claudette . . . are you sick. . . ?" Blair murmured.

"No, Blair. You are sick," said Claudette's welcome voice.

"No . . . I'm . . . burning . . . gnashing and weeping . . ."

"No, you're not!" said the ministering angel. The voice was harsh but not angry. "Oh, God, please forgive me for my judgmental attitude! If anything happens to her . . . If I don't have a chance to right this wrong . . ."

"Now, now, Meg."

A male voice. Blair had heard it before saying they had to leave. Why hadn't they left?

"God has His hand on you and the girl. I know it."

"I know, too. But why was I—?"

Just then Blair got sick again—all over the fresh clothes and bedding. The angel—Meg?—cleaned it up again, still as gently, as if Blair deserved to be treated so. She lifted a cup of water to Blair's lips.

"You must drink," Meg said. "I know your stomach is tender, but you must have liquids."

How long this went on, Blair could not tell. Eventually the voices faded, and her shaking, sweating body seemed to calm. The dreams seemed less real, more like those of true sleep.

37

THE FIRST THING Blair saw when she woke was Meg Doyle seated on the floor next to Blair's bedroll, which was also on the floor. She saw that she was in the partitioned part of the hut now, and two other mats were near hers. But no one else was present except Mrs. Doyle, whose back was resting against the wall of the hut, her head lolling back, her eyes closed.

Blair felt weak all over. She tried to lift her hand from where it rested on a blanket, just to see if she could, and managed only to wiggle it a little before it flopped back to the covers. Sudden fear overcame her. Was she paralyzed?

"Mrs. Doyle!" she cried, though her voice was no more than a hoarse whisper.

The woman's eyes popped open. "Yes, Blair."

"What's wrong with me? What happened?"

"You are finally awake, and coherent, I think."

The woman smiled, not a smile like sunshine, which surely would have looked ridiculous on that face, but it held a clarity and warmth that Blair had never seen before in that woman.

"You've had a bout of malaria. You have been nearly two days with it, but the quinine has finally taken effect."

"Malaria!" To Blair this was some horrible exotic disease. It was why everyone on the islands used mosquito netting. But she'd never believed she could get it. "Will I die?" she asked miserably.

"No," Mrs. Doyle said soothingly. "If properly tended, it is rarely fatal. But you could have future bouts, especially since we are low on quinine. I am afraid those days you spent in the jungle unprotected have caught up with you."

"Blair! You are awake! You are okay?" Claudette appeared in the doorway. Her voice was still trembly, as it had been in Blair's dreams. She knelt down beside Blair's bed. "I was so afraid."

Blair wanted to take her friend's hand to comfort her but could not manage the effort. Instead she smiled. "I'm okay, just a little weak."

"Claudette never left your side," said the minister's wife. "I heard her praying for you."

"Yes, I did pray." Claudette glanced shyly toward Mrs. Doyle. "And, Mrs. Doyle, you only heard because you never left her side, either. Blair, she was better than a doctor! I didn't know anything to do except pray."

Almost at a loss for words, Blair thought she might cry . . . again. She remembered doing a lot of crying in her tangled dreams. They had been tears of agony, she was certain, but what the cause was, she wasn't sure. Awe, she supposed, that two people would take care of her so. And one of those was Meg Doyle! She didn't understand it. She knew she didn't deserve it.

"Thank you," she finally murmured.

"You must rest," Mrs. Doyle said. "I'll fix you some tea and some rice if you think you can tolerate it."

"I am kind of hungry."

Mrs. Doyle rose. "Come, Claudette, let's give Blair a chance to rest while we fix her something to eat."

"Mrs. Doyle," Blair said, "I remember hearing something about a Japanese patrol. Are . . . we safe?"

"God is protecting us. About half the people that were here when we arrived left when one of the men spotted a patrol several miles away."

An edge to her tone and a twist of her lips when she said this seemed more like the woman Blair knew. She was obviously perturbed at the lack of faith of those who had departed.

"But there have been no further sightings. You have nothing to worry about. Trust God, Blair."

"I'll try" was all the response she could think of.

Mrs. Doyle opened her mouth to speak, then apparently thinking better of it, clamped it shut and turned to leave. Blair expected the woman had been about to berate her lack of faith. It was surely something that she opted to restrain her comments. Maybe she realized for a person like Blair, clearly a godless woman, *trying* was indeed an improvement. Regardless, Blair refused to think ill of the woman. Very likely Blair was alive because of Meg Doyle's ministrations. A ministering angel.

Blair dozed for a while, ate a little rice and tea, dozed some more, and received visits from each of the other Doyles, Mateo, and even Juan. She dozed again. No one wanted to burden her with information about their status, but she did glean the impression that they were just going from day to day, ready to evacuate on a moment's notice. A few days after her recovery Mateo mentioned that Juan had made a reconnaissance mission—the boy seemed to enjoy using such military jargon—to the mission and had discovered the Japanese had taken it over, apparently using the place as some sort of headquarters. But from what he could tell, the enemy hadn't arrived until days after the evacuation. Mrs. Doyle was upset at Mateo for telling Blair and risking upsetting her. He came in later with a hangdog expression to apologize. That made Blair feel worse than the information ever had.

She did take Mrs. Doyle's advice and prayed a little but only silently. She also tried to trust God, which was really rather easy just then because she was too weak to do anything else.

Their food supply, even with Mrs. Doyle's strict rationing, ran out in two weeks. Some of the men took turns, under cover of darkness, trekking down the mountain to farms where they could buy or, Blair suspected, steal food. They could not hunt with rifles because of a shortage of ammunition and also because of the risk of alerting patrolling Japanese. So meat was in short supply. Once the foragers came back with carabao meat they had bought, but it was only enough to make a very thin soup. Juan set snares for smaller animals but with little success.

The men brought back bits of news, as well—none of it good. The Japanese had overrun most of the northern reaches of Bataan. Even Gethsemane wasn't entirely safe. They continued to hear the message from America, "Hang on, Bataan. Help is on the way." This broadcast came from outside the islands on the "Voice of Freedom" to the few radios still operating on the island. But the message was starting to sound as thin as the soup. The Army was keeping up the defense of Bataan, but their supply situation was even worse than that in Gethsemane. How could an army continue to fight if they had no food?

Blair worried more than ever about Gary. Was he alive? If so, was he suffering? Would she ever see him again?

Of only one thing was she certain: When she did see her husband, she might finally be the kind of wife he had always wanted. Daily she was changing inside. And what was most astonishing, she was not doing it to win him. The desperation of their situations had made the idea of winning a man seem rather trivial. In one sense, she no longer cared if she *won* Gary. Her only desire was that he was alive and safe, and beyond this, that she might see him just to have a chance to ask his forgiveness.

That was the most amazing change of all in Blair. She was discovering the truth of forgiveness. This thanks to, of all people, Meg Doyle.

One day Meg came to Blair's bed, which had been moved back into the main area of the hut as Blair's health improved. They were alone. Everyone else was out and about doing the many chores assigned to them.

"I've got your medication." Mrs. Doyle knelt down and put a quinine tablet into Blair's hand, then gave her water.

Blair was taking the medication three times a day. She knew she needed it but worried about using up the limited supply. Mrs. Doyle told her she would reduce the dose to once a day in a few more days.

"I think I am strong enough to get up and about," Blair said after she swallowed the pill. She'd already tried to get up a couple of times but would have toppled over without the aid of others.

"Don't push yourself." Mrs. Doyle crossed her legs under her, tucking her skirt around her knees as if planning to stay awhile. Since Blair had nearly recovered, the minister's wife had no longer been at her side constantly; in fact, it almost seemed to Blair that she was avoiding her—as much as one could avoid anyone in a two-room hut.

Did she find Blair's company that odious? Blair had started to think Mrs. Doyle had changed her judgmental attitude toward her, but now she began to question it again.

"Conway and I have been discussing whether to head south," Mrs. Doyle said. "We thought we could wait out the Emergency here, but . . ."

Blair thought the woman actually looked humble!

With a heavy sigh, she went on. "Oh, I must face it. We must accept the fact that this . . . *war* . . . is worse than we thought. We didn't want to desert our congregation, but now the safety of our girls takes precedence over that."

"Do you think it would be safe with the Army?" Blair asked. "Gary wanted me to come here because he wanted me away from the fighting."

"Yes, that was true initially, I am sure, but things have changed. If the Army can't hold Bataan, Conway says they will likely evacuate as many people as they can to Corregidor Island. We think if we can get to Mariveles, they will take the females at least. That means you and Claudette, as well." She smoothed the folds of her skirt. Blair had never noticed before that the woman's hands were brown and rough. They had seen much work. "It means taking some risks, though, so we are not sure. We won't do anything until you are strong enough."

"I don't want to hold you back—"

"Hush," she chided, "no one is going to listen to that kind of talk. We are all a team now, like the Musketeers—all for one, one for all."

"You don't know how that makes me feel, Mrs. Doyle. I know I don't deserve—"

"And none of *that* talk, either!" Her tone was almost at its old hard edge, but there was a gleam in her eyes. "I feel bad enough, you know. And I want to talk to you about that if you feel up to it."

"You feel bad? I don't see why."

"I judged you from the minute I saw you, Blair." She arched a brow and added wryly, "I see you don't deny that!" She smiled. "I prayed for you, but my prayers were along the line of, 'Oh, God, make her see the error of her terrible ways!' I tried to be hard on you because I felt that would drive you to God. I well know the love of God, but I also know the wrath of God, and I believed at the time you needed a larger dose of wrath than love." Self-consciously clearing her throat, she added, "I suppose wrath is easier for me to dish out than love."

"I do deserve wrath," Blair said. "I've done terrible things. I was horrible to Gary. If he never forgives me—"

"What? Goodness, Gary forgave you long ago. If he didn't tell you—"

"He might have tried to, but I wasn't listening, probably thinking that forgiveness wasn't enough. Back then I wanted him more than mere words. I wanted everything to be normal between us—like when I was lying to him. But even after he said he forgave me, he was still distant."

"He was a very confused young man."

"Because of me."

"I didn't help."

"What?" Blair was certain she had heard wrong. What could Meg Doyle have had to do with it?

Mrs. Doyle grew even more tense than before. "Do you want some tea? The water is still hot from breakfast."

"No, thanks." Blair laid her hand on Mrs. Doyle's arm as she started to rise. "Please tell me what this is all about. I know Gary talked to you, but how could you have had anything to do with his confusion?"

Reluctantly Mrs. Doyle settled back. She inhaled a breath. "Yes, Gary did talk to us. And I want you to know that he spoke to no one else. He considered us friends, though we had known one another for only a few months. He'd heard about the mission, and as we are the same denomination as his church back in the States, he came for a visit. He brought a truckful of donations, too, that he had scrounged around the base." A fondness momentarily softened her sharp features. "He is a remarkable man, not given to confusion normally, I would say. I suspect he usually knows what he is about."

Blair grimaced at that, knowing its truth, knowing she had been the one to shake his steady foundation.

"It's all right, Blair." Meg patted Blair's shoulder. "I didn't help. I made it clear I didn't approve of you—without even meeting you! He wanted to try to make the marriage work, but he also respected my opinion. How could he be with such a horrible person as you? How could he *love* such a person? Imagine the poor young man's confusion! I greatly added to Gary's heavy burden, and for that I am so sorry. And I will tell him so the first time I see him."

Blair's heart clenched as she saw the situation now from Gary's point of view. She forced out her next question. "Do you think he would have annulled the marriage had I not arrived here to further muddy things?"

"He did not know what to do, but I am certain his primary concern was doing the best thing for you."

"Oh, Gary!" Blinking back tears, Blair fumbled around for a handkerchief, finding only the blanket. She dabbed a corner against her eyes.

"He loves you, Blair. And he held firm to the belief that your actions were never malicious."

Blair sniffed loudly. Mrs. Doyle rose, rooted in her pack, and came up with a clean handkerchief, which she gave to Blair.

"Th—thank you," Blair stammered through her emotion. She blew her nose. Calmed, she added, "I still don't see what you did wrong."

"Nothing Gary said would make me think you more than a lying little brat," Mrs. Doyle confessed, clearly hating to make the admission now. "When I saw you, I held to that impression. Nothing you could do would make me think otherwise. But I couldn't forget that I had added to his confusion. Your presence in the Philippines and other things you said told me Gary was probably not going to leave you. So if a fine man like Gary was going to ruin his life, I decided it was my job to make a good Christian woman of you. I did not think you deserved to have it done gently. It was my godly duty to pound the fear of God into you—with a two-by-four if necessary!" She sniffed, too, and it seemed as if moisture was rising in her eyes, as well. "Blair, will you forgive me?"

"There is nothing to forgive—"

"I knew from the first day you came to our house that you were a basically decent girl. You are not the evil wench I conjured up. I should have known that just from the fact that a man like Gary loved you so. But I wouldn't let go of my preconceptions. Down deep I knew I was wrong, but instead of letting go, I made you pay. For that I hope you can forgive me."

"I have one question, Mrs. Doyle. What changed your mind? Is it because you feel sorry for me for being sick?"

"I guess it looks that way. But it was actually the night before you got sick that I had some sense knocked into me. It was Patience—"

"Patience?" Blair could hardly picture that sweet girl "knocking" sense into anyone, much less her mother.

"She told me about her talk with you by the creek. She asked me if I held your pampered upbringing against you." Meg Doyle chuckled softly, as if remembering the encounter with her daughter. "When I rather grudgingly admitted I was holding some things against you, she actually confronted me with one of my own Scripture verses that I'd used in my devotional on stewardship. Patience, by the way, thought it was awful the way I singled you out so obviously that night. I guess I need your forgiveness about that, too. The Scripture was the one in

Corinthians." She got up again, this time to fetch her Bible from the kitchen table. " 'Moreover it is required in stewards, that a man be found faithful,' " she read as she resumed her seat by Blair's mat. "Remember that? Patience wondered why I hadn't finished reading the passage, especially verse five, which says, 'Therefore judge nothing before the time, until the Lord come, who both will bring to light the hidden things of darkness, and will make manifest the counsels of the hearts: and then shall every man have praise of God.' " Placing a finger in the page, Mrs. Doyle lifted her gaze. She seemed to be looking more inside herself now as she spoke. "My dear Patience gave *me* quite a devotional that night! She said in that passage the apostle Paul did tell his readers that they should be faithful stewards, but even he was not worthy to judge them—nor even to judge himself. Only God was worthy, and when God judges, *He* looks at hearts. Patience does not know the particulars in your situation, but she knew me well enough to perceive what I was doing and know that it was wrong. I am so thankful my daughters turned out better than I."

"Well, it says something about you that they did," Blair replied. "And I do forgive you, though it feels really strange and unnecessary to do so. I can see where it is important to speak the words sometimes. I hope I can say them to Gary someday."

"I am sure you will. I cannot believe that God has brought you this far and will not give you that opportunity."

"Mrs. Doyle, would you show me some good places to read in the Bible for . . . well, to learn more about faith?"

"I would be happy to. But first, I think you should rest." There was a small hint of triumph in the woman's eyes, as if she had won a personal victory. Maybe it was the first time in her life she had declined pushing her faith on another, especially when that person was so willing.

Blair took it as a good sign. She wondered if it also might mean that Mrs. Doyle was not worried about Blair's spiritual path anymore. Blair wasn't much worried, either. She knew where she was headed, in this one area at least. Her path was going to lead to God.

38

THE SOUND HAD COME to be eerily familiar to Gary. A whine, like the scream of the wind through a narrow canyon. He'd learned to react instantly to that sound, and he did so now, diving headfirst into his foxhole.

Artillery shells burst all around, eating up the earth and shaking the ground, though the blast had been at least a hundred yards from his position. He felt a little foolish for jumping the gun until he heard a grunt a split second after his body hit the side of the hole. Sergeant Senger had taken cover in the same trench. Gary figured there was no shame in ducking for cover when the sarge had, as well. Sarge had a reputation in the unit for pushing caution to the edge, waiting until the whine—a longer, lower pitched sound—indicated the explosions would be much closer. Even he was getting jumpy with the almost constant bombardment the last couple of days. Gary had learned from Senger the trick of judging the distance of incoming shells, but sometimes a quirk of the terrain or a trick of the wind threw judgment off. Best to suffer a bit of embarrassment than to have your head blown off.

"You know," said Senger, his voice barely audible over the explosions, "it's a shame General Homma is wasting all those shells. If he is patient, he can starve us into surrendering."

"I have a feeling he wants a more decisive victory than that." It was difficult to talk, but Gary needed the distraction. He shifted around into a more comfortable position. Shells were still exploding, and they might be in the foxhole awhile. "I hear the Japanese put much stock in saving face, and it can't make him look very good that, with superiority on all sides, he can't get us to give up."

"You think the rumors of another big Jap offensive are true, then?"

Grimly Gary nodded. "We have to brace ourselves. Homma will want a decisive victory if he can get it."

"We can't put up much of a defense, not on less than a pound of rice a day and whatever else we can scrounge to eat. How much weight have you lost, LT?"

Gary didn't want to think of that, nor that he was so weak it would be an effort just to climb out of the foxhole. "I was around one-ninety when I came to the Philippines."

The sergeant eyed him up and down. "You look about one-fifty now. I'm about the same, but I'm a couple inches shorter than you. Most of the men don't have the strength to forage for food anymore. And half our regiment is down with malaria and dysentery. I'm worried, LT."

"Listen, Sarge, the men are counting on you. I hate to put that on you, but it's true. They look to you more than to me, and you can't break down, not now."

"I just said I'm worried." The grizzled noncom rolled his eyes and grunted. "I ain't about to go psycho. But don't you underestimate yourself. You're their leader, and they respect you."

Gary knew that, but it was nice to be reminded, which was why he had said the same to Senger. He knew the man would never go over the edge. Not that the present situation wasn't pushing them all to the brink of that edge.

The little Bataan Peninsula, twenty-five miles long and twenty miles across, was well suited for defense. Its dense jungles provided good cover for ground operations, especially from an enemy with air superiority. The central mountains were rugged and inhospitable, but that was as much a difficulty for the enemy as for the defenders. But the American and Filipino troops could not defend with only grit and determination, though at the moment they were trying mightily.

Though retreat into Bataan had always been the Army's battle plan, Gary had been shocked to discover what little supplies had been stockpiled. A few days ago he had asked the quartermaster how many day's rations there were left. He'd been told two or three weeks' worth and been sworn to secrecy about this information. What the big secret was, Gary didn't know. It had to be obvious even to the lowest private that their days were numbered. They had already begun to draw on Corregidor's supplies. About a month ago they had established trade with some fishermen and had fresh fish for a short time, but when the Japs learned of this, they cut off contact with the fishing boats. Rumors had surfaced that the Navy was outfitting some submarines for supply runs, but the Japanese blockade had tightened, and the subs had thus far not materialized.

Scarcity of food was only part of their worsening situation. The blockade and the difficulty in keeping supply lines open due to enemy bombardment also was causing a serious shortage of ammunition and gasoline, making the possibility of any kind of major offensive by the Army quite slim. Medical problems were also mounting. Starving men were simply unable to fight malaria, dysentery, dengue fever, and other such major tropical illnesses. Smaller complaints were also growing dangerous. Jungle rot was incapacitating more men than he wanted to think of. He'd told his men countless times to sun their feet and air their shoes, but often there simply wasn't time for that. No one wanted to get caught in an attack barefooted. Gary himself was having a terrible problem with the itch, and if his bouts of dysentery hadn't taken his mind off it, it might have driven him crazy.

When the shelling stopped, Gary climbed from the foxhole. Before the attack he'd been on his way to confer with his medic about supplies. He planned to send someone to the rear soon to see what could be scrounged for the unit. It probably wouldn't do much good, but at least it gave the men the sense they were doing something. Gary had always hated what his mother called busywork, but he resorted to it now as a means to keep his men from focusing on their larger problems.

"Lieutenant Hobart, that you?"

Gary turned, recognizing the man calling him as a clerk in Colonel Reese's office.

"Yeah. Watkins, right?"

"Yes, sir. The colonel wants to see you."

"Right now?"

"As soon as you can get away. By thirteen hundred hours at least."

"I was planning to send someone to the rear anyway. First I want to see if my medic needs anything."

"That'll be fine, sir. I have to see someone down the line, so don't wait for me," said Watkins, who, after a nominal salute, hurried away.

Discipline was getting pretty lax. It drove some officers to distraction. Gary supposed, with his West Point background, it should especially goad him, but with everything else hanging over him, he could not get too worked up over a sluggish salute.

After a few moments with his medic and a couple of words with his sergeant, Gary made his way to headquarters. As he strode into the compound, a jeep sped in, raising a choking dust cloud in its wake. It braked to a screeching stop right in front of the nipa hut that served as HQ. Reese, a stocky man several inches shorter than Gary but sinewy like well-worn leather, jumped out of the vehicle. Reese was notorious for doing his own driving and was a legend in the unit for driving like a maniac. He always seemed to be in a hurry. Now the man quite literally sprang from the jeep. He was suffering from low rations as much as anyone, but he still seemed to vibrate with energy.

"Good timing, Hobart," the colonel said briskly. "Come with me." Gary had to jog to catch up with the colonel's pace. Reese fairly burst through the door as he slapped dust from his fatigue jacket. He only paused in his vigorous stride for a moment at a clerk's desk. "Lieutenant Acosta, you got word out to my company commanders about the briefing at thirteen hundred hours?"

"Yes, sir. Some have already arrived."

Reese glanced at his wristwatch. "Good. Notify me when they are all here." With a brisk look at Gary, he added, "Follow me, Lieutenant."

Gary had been wondering what was up ever since he'd been told to come to HQ. He seldom had direct communication with the colonel himself, though Gary and the colonel's son had been in the same class at West Point. Peeling off his gloves, Reese tossed them on the desk, then began to rifle through some papers. He did not sit, and neither did Gary, who was told to stand at ease.

"I don't know if you have heard, Hobart, but Captain Smithers was killed this morning," Reese said as he continued to search for something on his desk. His tone was matter-of-fact, perhaps from being distracted with his search or because he'd grown accustomed to making such announcements.

Shocked, Gary replied, "No, sir, I hadn't heard."

"Took some shrapnel in his head. Bled to death before he got to the aid station."

"He was a good commander, sir. It's a loss for the company."

"Naturally that means a change of command in the company." Reese seemed to finally find what he was looking for and picked up a white envelope. Gary nodded, his throat tightening at what he thought was coming. "Here you go, Hobart, your captain's bars. I'm making you company commander." Opening the envelope, he dumped out the gold bars and handed them to Gary.

"Yes, sir," Gary rasped, taking the bars. He'd expected a promotion to come along soon but not at this moment and not in this way. He and Smithers had not been close, but he liked the man well enough as a person and as a leader.

"Smithers put in for a promotion for you a month ago, so this is more than a battlefield promotion. You've earned it."

"I wish it didn't have to be like this, though, sir." Surprised that his fingers were shaking a little, Gary pinned on the captain's insignia.

"So do I. As you know, there is a real shortage of officers now." Reese took another envelope from the pile of papers on the desktop. "This is for Sergeant Senger. I'm promoting him to lieutenant. I know the man takes pride in being an old noncom, but we need him for command. If he balks, you tell him I promise to demote him when the war is over."

Gary allowed himself a small smile. Senger had a sergeant's natural disdain for lieutenants, especially green ones, though for some reason he'd always been more than generous toward Gary. But even as a newly promoted lieutenant, Senger would never be green at anything he did.

"Now head on over to the mess tent for the briefing," said Reese. He gave Gary a smart salute. "Congratulations, Captain Hobart."

Gary returned the salute. "Thank you, sir."

At the briefing Reese announced that two days previously General MacArthur had departed Corregidor for Australia. Rumors about this departure had already made the rounds, but hearing it officially was no less dismaying. Gary knew this was going to be especially hard on the Filipino troops who looked upon MacArthur as nothing short of a living legend. MacArthur had been part of the Philippines for many years, and his father before him had had a huge role in establishing America's presence in the Philippines.

Reese emphasized that the general had vowed to return to the islands, but the announcement was still demoralizing. Tactically, the reassignment of the general made sense. With the successive falls of

Hong Kong, Malaysia, Singapore, and the Dutch East Indies, Australia was left vulnerable. Thus, it was determined that all military effort must be focused on defending this strategic area. The Philippines was going to have to hang on the best it could. Though no one said anything, they all realized this meant that the promised reinforcements from the States were probably not going to materialize.

In the following days, Gary never heard anyone speak the word *surrender*. Everyone he knew had no other thought in mind but to fight as long as they had to. Yet after the departure of MacArthur, there was a strong sense that the heart, if not the physical motions, had gone out of that fight.

Malaria hit Gethsemane hard in the next weeks. Mateo had a mild bout, as did three of the other residents at the compound. Blair also had a couple more attacks. The quinine ran out.

As Blair lay on her mat one morning fighting intermittent attacks of fever and chills, she heard Conway and Meg discuss what they must do. They seemed to agree on one point—that Blair needed the attention of a doctor.

Blair tried to argue with them from across the room. But her weakened voice was little more than a rasp. "No . . . I'll be okay. . . ."

Meg glanced in her direction but gave her only the merest shrug in response, then returned her attention to her husband.

"You can't do this, Conway. I won't have it!"

"I won't leave you and the girls stranded," he replied. "I'll see you girls to safety first."

Meg just snorted derisively at this, making clear just what she thought of needing such protection. "You don't know the first thing about the Army. You'll get yourself shot the minute you put on a uniform."

"Meg, you know very well that if we were in the States, I'd be enlisting in the chaplains' service. It's my duty. I would have done so sooner than this, but . . . events got away from me. And I felt your situation was too uncertain for me to leave you. But if we go south and can get you evacuated—well, you can't expect me to run away when all able-bodied men are fighting!"

Meg leaned back in her chair and gave her husband an incisive appraisal. "You are determined to do this?"

"I am."

"Then I must trust you are following God's will."

He nodded, with just a hint of triumph in his eyes. "I believe this is the Lord's will for me . . . for us."

"I will not stand in your way." Blair thought the woman had conceded too easily. She had a look about her that Blair knew well, that of a woman giving in but knowing full well she would do what she pleased, what she thought was best, anyway. Blair wondered what exactly Meg Doyle had in mind to do.

The door burst open a moment later, and Mateo, with Claudette sharp on his heels, strode into the hut. "I am sorry, forgive me," he said in an agitated tone that hardly sounded contrite, "but I was listening outside by the window. I heard what you said—"

"Don't worry, Mateo," Reverend Doyle broke in, "we won't leave you stranded. I will see that you are evacuated, too."

"That's not what he wants," Claudette said, clearly distressed. "Reverend, you have to stop him!"

"Be quiet, Claudette," admonished Mateo. "This is none of your business." He focused eyes full of fire and determination on the reverend. "When we go south, Reverend, you must speak for me so that I can join the Army. I am seventeen now; it is my duty to fight for my country."

Blair realized that since leaving Manila, both Mateo and Claudette had had birthdays. Celebrations had been small with everything else going on, but Mateo indeed was now seventeen, and Claudette, though she still looked much younger, was fifteen.

"I will, son," Reverend Doyle said.

"What!" exclaimed three female voices all at once.

"Please, Reverend Doyle, you can't let him do this!" Claudette's protests rose above the rest. Tears were spilling from her eyes. Blair had sensed a romance blooming between the two young people but had never taken it very seriously. The passion now displayed in Claudette's voice indicated something far deeper than puppy love.

"Stay out of this, Claudette."

Mateo's voice had a passion of its own and something else Blair had not noticed before. It was the voice of a man. Had he grown up overnight?

Claudette's lip trembled as tears rolled down her cheeks. She couldn't seem to get further speech past her emotion, so she said no more. Blair tried to stand to go to offer her comfort but got only as far as her knees when Mateo strode to the girl and placed an arm around her shoulders. He'd never really shown before that he returned Claudette's affection, but there was at that moment something in his eyes that surely was more than concern.

"Claudette . . . Aquilina . . . I don't want to leave you," he said. "But you can't force me to be a coward. It is my duty to fight. I gave my word that I would see you to safety, and I will, but then I must go serve my country. I must!" He glanced toward Blair, as if for confirmation.

Blair felt as if she were reliving her final parting from Gary. Duty! Men spoke of it so easily. She wondered if all women hated that word as much as she. Surely Claudette did, and even Meg was none too pleased with her husband's sense of duty. It was wrong that men should go into danger and leave the women who loved them to worry, to be helpless, to be alone. But Blair had been learning of forgiveness lately, and she realized she must forgive Gary for leaving her, as must Claudette forgive Mateo. She was learning to see matters from perspectives other than her own and could now see how these men felt justified in what they did. It was the only way they knew how to protect the women they loved. Even if it meant the ultimate sacrifice. It was noble. But no less maddening for their women.

"Claudette, come here," Blair said gently, holding out an arm.

When Claudette came and hunkered down by Blair, Blair wrapped her arm tightly around the girl's shoulder. Claudette laid her head against Blair, still weeping and sniffing and trembling a little.

"Honey," Blair said softly, tenderly, "we must let our men go. I think it is the way *we* do our duty. Okay?"

Claudette could only nod.

As soon as Blair was strong enough, the residents of Gethsemane made ready to head south. But the group of travelers had dwindled down to a small core. All of the hill people opted to remain at the retreat or to return to their villages deeper in the hills. Ruberto joined this group because many were his relatives. Thus only the Doyles, Blair, Claudette, Mateo, Juan, and Dominador gathered in the yard early on the morning of March 28 with packs and gear ready for the trip. The packs were lighter than they would have hoped for, since food supplies had diminished greatly.

Blair did not look forward to another trek through the jungle. But with everyone being solicitous toward her, she tried not to complain. Still, she could barely tolerate the thought of the little creepy critters the jungle teemed with—she didn't even want to think of the larger critters on the loose. Once, after the journey began, a gecko slithered into a hole in her sneaker, and she screamed so loud that everyone feared she'd bring the Japanese down upon them.

The Japanese were another problem to be dealt with. For a good two days of their journey they were in enemy-occupied territory, and after that, it was anyone's guess as to who was in control of the land. The artillery fire they often had to dodge as they pushed farther south could have easily been either Japanese or friendly.

At night Blair was too exhausted to do more than collapse on the spot the men chose for their camp. Mrs. Doyle still kept assigning chores for everyone, Blair being spared only because her illness left her little strength for more than the day's hike. Yet as much as Blair had grumbled about the chores before, she hated even more not being able to do her share now. Often she would pitch in, only to be sharply admonished by Mrs. Doyle.

"Your body is the temple of God, Blair. Do not abuse it!" Her tone was just as severe as when she had yelled at Blair for being wasteful. Blair simply could not understand the woman.

Dejectedly Blair went to a corner of the camp, out of the way of the activity, and plopped down in the grass. She felt so drained, her limbs like rubber, that she didn't even try to argue. But that same day Mrs. Doyle—to be sure, after the camp was organized and settled—strolled over to Blair and sat beside her.

"I wish I knew how to be a gentle sort," Mrs. Doyle said.

"Oh, I deserved it. After all you have done to get me well, it is ungrateful of me to push myself."

"Here, take these."

Blair noted then that Mrs. Doyle had a cloth bundle in her hands. Opening it, Blair found several mangos and bananas.

"Juan found a banana grove not far from here. And the mangos are finally ripe."

"I'm not really very hungry."

"You must eat, Blair!" Mrs. Doyle's tone held its usual edge, then she wryly arched a brow and let a smile slant her lips. Her voice softened. "You need to eat. You truly do."

Blair lifted a mango from the cloth, and with the small paring knife Mrs. Doyle offered, she carefully cut into the skin. Juice trickled down her fingers and hands. "It is ripe!" She popped a slice of the fruit into her mouth.

"Blair, you do understand that it takes all kinds to make up . . . well, any group, don't you?" Mrs. Doyle asked.

"Yes . . ." Blair wasn't quite certain what was the meaning of the sudden inquiry.

"There are all kinds of Christian people, and I'll venture to say that none of us is perfect."

"Yes, I know that." Blair put a finger in her mouth to lick off the sweet mango juice, then added, "What are you getting at, Mrs. Doyle?"

"I just want to be sure you realize that people can be squeamish about bugs or speak sharply and still be Christians."

"I understand that, I think." Blair ate another wedge of fruit. "But I'm not sure if I am a Christian—yet I am learning that I could be even if I can't stand having—" she paused and gave a shudder, still remembering the feel of that gecko wiggling around in her shoe—"bugs touch me."

"I wasn't referring only to you," confessed Mrs. Doyle, and her tone suddenly became truly like a confession. "I meant myself. I try to be patient and kind, but it doesn't come easily for me. Still, I don't want to be a stumbling block to you."

"You're not, honestly . . . well, not anymore. Maybe you were a little before I got sick and we talked. But that's not holding me back anymore."

"What is, then, Blair?"

"I don't know." This admission came as a surprise to Blair, because she only then realized she *was* holding back. She knew she wanted to commit her life to God, yet she had held off saying the words. She had not prayed the prayer of confession that Jackie had often told her about. Perhaps it was only her illness preventing her. When she was stronger . . . No, she knew that was an excuse.

Then it hit her. Her reticence still involved Gary. She wanted faith for herself, not because of Gary. She was finally certain she was at last in that place, yet there was still a small part of her that couldn't take the leap without knowing that she would get Gary in the bargain. It was almost as if she wanted to make a trade with God. She'd make the commitment when she was certain Gary would have her back. What a sick, horrible attitude!

She lifted her eyes to meet Mrs. Doyle's. She knew they were filled with surprise and just a hint of revulsion at her nerve.

"What is it, Blair?" Concern marked Mrs. Doyle's tone.

"I know why I have been holding back. But it's hard to admit I could be so awful after all God has done for me—"

"Everyone! Hurry! Into the jungle!" Dominador ran into the camp, his voice urgent but soft. "A patrol is near."

There was no time to gather their belongings, despite the fact that leaving them would give them away to the enemy. They could only hope to outrun the Japanese or, if they were lucky, to elude them in the dense jungle growth. Neither option seemed likely to end in success, and Blair, struggling to her feet and forcing her tired legs into motion, wondered if they had finally reached the end of their luck.

Blair stumbled and fell, then was scooped up by Reverend Doyle and slung over his shoulder like a sack of wheat. He murmured an apology for his rough treatment as he sprinted after Juan, who had been bringing up the rear of the party. A few minutes later, when everyone else was nearly out of sight, Juan paused and turned.

"I hate to leave our packs," he said to Reverend Doyle. "I'm going back to make sure of the danger and to get our possessions if possible. I'll catch up with you soon."

Blair wanted to make him stop. He could be walking into a nest of Japanese. But he had already turned and Reverend Doyle was again jogging in the other direction. When he reached the others, he told them to stop.

"We'll wait here for Juan." He slid Blair from his shoulder. As she tottered on her own feet, she was nonetheless thankful, because all the blood had rushed to her head.

"But the Japs!" argued Dominador.

"Are you sure they were Japs? Maybe they were farmers—"

"I saw uniforms."

Now that they had slowed down enough to think, Blair wondered about the wisdom of them running without first confirming Dominador's report. Blair admitted to herself that she, too, had panicked, but could they really trust Dominador? There was still a great deal of uncertainty about when they left the mission. Despite that, Blair had never felt much confidence in the young man. He seemed flighty and immature for his age. She hated to compare people, but Mateo, even at a few years younger, was far more responsible.

"Nevertheless," said Doyle, "we shouldn't have gone off half-cocked and left our things." He gave his head a shake, obviously disgusted with his own actions. "I'm going back after Juan. You all just wait here."

Before anyone, especially his wife, could argue, Reverend Doyle was jogging back toward camp. Their wait after that could not have been more than five minutes, but it was agonizing. Blair found herself straining to hear, though she wasn't sure what she was listening for. Yells? Gunshots? What then? If Juan and Reverend Doyle were captured, what should they do? Surrender as well or keep trying to run?

Blair started to pray, then she heard yells. But not the ones she had feared.

"Come on, it's all right!" That was Reverend Doyle.

No one debated the possibility that it might be a trap. As one, they bounded back toward the camp. Blair did not exactly *bound*. It was more a stagger. She came into the clearing well behind the others and was greeted by the most beautiful sight that the jungle could possibly hold—good old American khaki.

39

THE AMERICAN SOLDIERS were surprised to find so many Americans among the group that crowded into the clearing. Everyone clamored with greetings and questions. All Blair could see at first was that none of these soldiers was Gary.

When Reverend Doyle told the men where they had come from and that they had been traveling through the jungle on foot for three days, the men expressed surprise that they had come so far unmolested by the Japanese.

Meg Doyle murmured, "God's hand was upon us."

"Some of my people need medical attention," Doyle said.

Blair was grateful he hadn't singled her out.

"We can get you to some transportation and have you to one of the hospitals in a couple hours," said a tall, thin corporal.

Blair saw that all the men were extremely thin, gaunt, and appeared generally battle weary. She thought once more of Gary, and her heart quaked. As if sensing her dismay, or perhaps just seeing that Blair was swaying on her feet, Claudette sidled up to her and put an arm around her shoulders. Blair smiled her thanks at her friend. She had been so angry that Gary had deserted her, but now she saw how God had taken care of her, providing friends to lend support and love. Gary must have known that would happen; at least he must have trusted God to care for her.

They were thankful to find a road not far distant and an Army truck to take them south to a hospital. There were two main hospitals on Bataan, both intended to be thousand-bed facilities but now bursting to nearly double that size. Hospital #1, as it was called, served surgical patients and was located on the slopes of Mariveles Mountain, about two-thirds of the way down the peninsula in an area the nurses called Little Baguio because of its resemblance to the mountain resort in the north of Luzon. Hospital #2 was some fifteen miles south of that, closer to the coast near Cabcaben. It was to this second hospital, specializing mostly in medical patients, though many surgical patients came here as well, that the soldiers took Blair and her companions.

Blair, who had begun to experience chills once more, was immediately given a dose of quinine, but the nurse regretfully informed the others that the Army had suspended the administration of prophylactic quinine a month ago because of dwindling supplies. She then found a bed for Blair.

The next day or so passed in a blur for Blair. Though the quinine suppressed the attack quickly, she was so exhausted she slept much of that time. Vaguely she recalled brief visits from her friends. Claudette told her that she and the Doyle women had been put to work in the hospital and were so busy they could not spend as much time with

Blair as they wished. Blair mumbled for her not to worry, then promptly fell asleep. She didn't find out for two days that Reverend Doyle, Mateo, Juan, and Dominador had been inducted into military service. They had been to see her before going on their various assignments, but she could not recall their visits.

Blair woke on the second of April feeling oddly refreshed—odd, because she could not remember feeling so rested even before her bout with malaria. She crept from her bed, nothing more than a mattress on the jungle grass with a flimsy bamboo partition around it, and slowly stretched to her feet. She was still wearing the same clothes she'd had on since leaving Gethsemane. The tropical climate seemed hard on clothes, wearing them out faster than normal. Her beige trousers and white blouse were quite tattered and soiled, as were her sneakers. Her last bath had been a dip in a river days ago before encountering the soldiers who had brought her to the hospital. She suspected she smelled frightful, even as the heat of the day caused more sweat to drip from her body. She wondered if there would be a chance for a bath here.

Moving around to the other side of the partition and glancing around, she thought it all looked—rustic was a kind word for the scene. She saw now that her bed was the only one with a partition because she was the only female in a sea of male patients. Hospital #2 was an open-air facility. The jungle canopy provided excellent cover from detection by Japanese air patrols, but Blair saw that this was also the only cover for patient beds that stretched as far as the eye could see. Some of the beds were cots like regular hospital beds with adjustable backs, but many were simply mattresses lying directly on the ground, as was hers.

"Quite an operation we have here, isn't it?" came a voice from behind Blair.

She spun around to see a familiar face. "Alice Wharton!"

"It is a small island, isn't it?" The nurse smiled. "You are looking so much better than when they first brought you in."

"I better be after sleeping—how long has it been? It feels like days."

"Almost two days."

Blair remembered the perky nurse who had comforted her so long ago. A little over three months ago! Christmas Day. She didn't want to think how long it *felt*. Those three months had been no less kind to Alice than they had been to Blair. The young nurse looked to have aged five years, at least. Her once shining dark hair was now drab, in need of a good washing and combing. Her pretty face was smudged with grit and gaunt with hunger, her eyes framed with dark circles, and her skin pale. Blair wouldn't be surprised if Alice had been hit with malaria or some other jungle disease. Her dark-rimmed glasses were taped together at the bridge and at one temple. Her Army-issue trousers and pullover shirt hung on a thin body.

"Would you like something to eat?" the nurse asked after a brief silence.

"I'd rather have a bath."

Alice smiled, and there was at least some light left in the smile that touched her eyes behind the smudged lenses of her glasses. "If you are really up to it, I can take you to the nurses' private bathhouse."

The woman's wry tone made Blair wonder if there was some joke in this, but she shrugged and let Alice lead the way.

As they walked, Alice filled Blair in on the war news. Nothing had improved since the last time she'd heard reports. The Japanese had begun what some feared would be their final offensive against the beleaguered defenders of Bataan. No help had ever arrived from the States. MacArthur had gone to Australia, and only the most optimistic saw that as a good sign.

"Some say maybe now he can get those supply convoys through to us," Alice explained. "But . . ." she just shrugged and gave her head a shake. "Fill that in any way you want," she added. "Most of us have given up speculation. We just do our jobs the best we can."

"That must be hard to do under these conditions." Blair lifted a hand to indicate the open-air ward they were passing through.

"We don't think about it. We can't. We'd go insane if we did. We just continue on day by day. But I do think I'd sell my soul for a shipment of quinine. Malaria is bringing us down faster than the Japs. It's not uncommon for a doctor to get the shakes right in the middle of surgery. I nearly passed out the other day changing a dressing."

"Than you have it, too?"

"Few of us don't."

"What's going to happen to everyone, Alice?" despaired Blair.

"Remember, no speculation. One day at a time."

Blair nodded. But the thoughts continued to bombard her mind. Mrs. Doyle would tell her she must trust God by placing her fears into His hands. But Blair suspected that even after doing this, one might still worry. The important thing, she thought, was to not let those worries paralyze you—and that's no doubt where God would help.

They had left the hospital wards and were coming into an area set well apart. Here, blankets were hung among the trees as partitions, while some served as rather lopsided roofs. Other branches were hung with various articles of clothing. A few women were walking about, while some were lounging on mats or leaning against tree trunks.

"This is our nurses' quarters," Alice announced, her voice tinged with an odd mix of pride and amusement. "Your friends have a place here, and we'll move your bed in with them now that you are better." Alice paused to greet some of the women and to introduce Blair. All were friendly and welcoming. None seemed in the least concerned that Blair represented another mouth to feed and another person to care for.

"This place is amazing!" Blair said in awe. True, she'd spent her share of time roughing it in the jungle, but she could not keep from imagining nurses in only pristine white rooms and treading down whitewashed corridors filled with the scent of antiseptic. This was a far cry from that.

"Home sweet home," Alice replied drolly.

The "bathhouse," as Alice had so euphemistically labeled it, was merely a place in the nearby river that formed a shallow pool. She assured Blair there would be no prying eyes, but in any case Blair took her dip in the pool fully clothed, reasoning that her clothing needed rinsing as much as she. Once out of the water the hot sun dried her quickly. But the heat and the exertion also wore her out. Alice took her to the "tent" occupied by her friends and promised that she'd have a mat moved in soon. In the meantime, Blair stretched out on one of the other mats and fell asleep.

When she woke some time later, the sun had set, and monkeys were chattering merrily in the trees overhead. She had grown accustomed to the jungle sounds but just then realized how soothing they were. She remembered times in the jungle when all was silent and Juan had worried. So she took comfort now in the cacophony of sounds, especially since it seemed to be accompanied by a lull in enemy bombardments.

As she sat up in bed, her stomach growled. She was about to go in search of dinner when Claudette came into the "room." For the first time Blair noted how worn and pale the girl was looking. Blair berated herself for thinking so little of her friends over the last few days. She didn't think being ill herself was excuse enough.

"I brought you something to eat," Claudette said, and Blair saw she was carrying a basket. "It isn't much, some rice and tinned tomatoes. No meat. Someone was stewing a monkey, but I don't recommend that."

Blair shuddered. It would have been awful to eat something that had provided such comforting music a moment before. "The rice and tomatoes sound great. Thank you. Do you have time to sit with me awhile?"

In response Claudette sat down on the mat beside Blair. "I tried monkey meat the other day," she said. "It tastes awful. It's tough, and it seems to grow in your mouth as you chew it. Ugh!"

"Do you want some of this?" Blair lifted the bowl of rice and a spoon from the basket.

"No, I've already had dinner. But Mrs. Doyle said to see that you eat every bit."

Blair dug the spoon into the rice, waving away a swarm of flies as she did so. She'd already discovered that eating on Bataan could be harrowing with the abundance of flying insects, but here at the hospital it seemed especially bad, most likely because of the presence of open wounds, disease, and latrines. If Blair hadn't felt so hungry, she might have lost her appetite.

"How is everyone, Claudette?" Blair dumped the tin of tomatoes over the rice to give it flavor. "I feel bad that I haven't been paying attention to anyone."

"You could hardly help it, Blair. We've been feeling bad that we have ignored you so much. But they are so desperate for help here."

"I'm going to start to work tomorrow—"

"You don't have to, Blair."

"I want to!" Blair said around a mouthful of rice. "One of those men could be Gary—" She grasped Claudette's arm. "You haven't seen him, have you?"

"I would have told you if I had!" Claudette looked away, but Blair thought she saw a hint of moisture in the girl's eyes.

"What is it?"

"It's only that—" Claudette sniffed as the moisture became real tears—"I understand a little better what you have been going through now that Mateo has gone."

"So he finally enlisted."

Claudette nodded, sniffing again. "He tried to say good-bye to you, but you were asleep." Biting her lip, she added, "They gave him a gun, Blair. He's really going to be fighting! I don't know if I can stand the worry."

"You really care for him, don't you?" She studied her friend as she added, "I mean, I care for him, too, but you feel something more."

Claudette's pale cheeks flushed pink. "Do you think I am too young to know of love?" Her question was part sincere, part defensive.

"I don't even know much about love!" Blair snorted with self-derision. "I am certainly not going to tell you how to run your love life. But fifteen is young, don't you think?"

"I don't want to get married now, even if we could. But I can't help how I feel. Though I am angry at him, too. He didn't have to go to fight. He's too young."

"Well, if it's any comfort, I can't believe they will send him into battle without training. They will probably just have him delivering messages and such things."

"Still . . ."

"I know," Blair said sympathetically. "No one is truly out of danger here. Claudette, I think it is time that you and I do something we have been putting off."

"Do you mean pray?"

"That, of course, but I mean more." This was almost as difficult for Blair to suggest to another as it was to do for herself. She had no right to tell others how to run their lives. Yet she and Claudette had enough of a relationship that maybe she did, just a little. Studying her friend a moment, she realized her words would be received openly, perhaps even be welcome. "Claudette, I'm going to commit my life to God. I've thought about doing it for a long time but have put it off for various reasons. It's finally time to lay aside my fears. What do you think?"

"If you do it, I will!" Claudette said eagerly.

"But you have to do it for yourself, because it is what you want."

"I know." Claudette smiled through her moist eyes. "And it is, Blair. I guess I just needed a little boost."

Blair scraped the last of the rice from her bowl, surprised she'd eaten it all so quickly. She popped it into her mouth, and when she finished chewing, she asked, "Do you want to do it now?"

"Just you and me? Don't we need a church or at least Mrs. Doyle?"

"I . . . I don't think so. . . ." Fear crept over Blair. She'd been through so many frightening situations in the last months, but this was no less scary than meeting the enemy or seeing a snake. "We could wait for her. Maybe we should."

"She was pretty busy when I left her. She may not be back for hours. But there is always tomorrow."

That made the decision for Blair. "No!" Blair still had to struggle to find her confidence. "It is too easy to put it off. We must do it now. A bomb could fall on this hospital five minutes from now, and then where would we be?" She made herself remember what she'd learned about God's love, His peace, and His caring. "Why should we go another minute without Him?" Smiling with assurance, though her heart was thudding, she set aside her empty bowl and grasped Claudette's hands in hers.

"Do you know the words?" Claudette asked, a slight tremor in her voice.

"Any words will do, I suppose. God isn't picky about that. I think even Mrs. Doyle would say that He is looking into our hearts." Nevertheless, Blair tried to say the words she had heard from others. And Claudette repeated them after her as if Blair knew what she was doing.

"Dear God, I come to you with a seeking heart. I ask you to forgive my sins, and I now give my heart to you. Please help me to follow you always. Thank you, Jesus!"

PART VI

"A Jap's a Jap . . .
It makes no difference whether he is an
American citizen or not . . .
I don't want any of them . . .
There is no way to determine their loyalty."

General John DeWitt
Head of the Western Defense Command, 1942
(*V Was for Victory* by John Morton Blum)

40

April 1942

TRUDGING UP THE ROCKY SLOPE of Trail #4, Gary gripped his rifle and tried to peer through the darkened jungle. Night blindness, from vitamin A deficiency, the medic said, hampered him greatly. A corporal with better vision was point man, and Gary kept his eyes on him. Each man in the line had a white handkerchief hanging out of his back pocket to help the man behind him see. It was all any of them could do. The jungle was crawling with Jap patrols, and Gary just hoped they didn't stumble headlong into one.

Before that thought fully formed in his mind, gunfire ripped through the night not more than two hundred yards away. Everyone dove into the jungle for cover.

Counterfire from his men sprayed the foliage in the direction of the initial fire. Gary barely heard the sharp snap that stood out oddly from the shots. He twisted toward his flank, saw the enemy uniform flicker among the foliage, and fired, killing the Jap attempting to circle around them. Silence, almost as sudden as the initial tattoo of rifle fire had been, then engulfed the area. A moment later that all too familiar and dreaded cry pierced the silence.

"Medic!"

Quickly the cry was followed by the sounds of feet scrambling through the trees. The sound was close, and Gary followed it. On the way he ascertained from his men that the area was secure—for the moment. He found his medic crouched over another man. Ruiz was standing over both of them.

"They got the sarge," Ruiz said in a shaky voice. Gary understood the young man's distress. Senger had seemed invincible to all the men.

Gary's stomach clenched. Senger was also his best friend in the unit. He might outrank the man, but he still looked to him not only for friendship but for support and advice, as well. To lose him now . . .

"I'm okay," came Senger's raspy voice. "And I'm lieutenant now, Ruiz, not sarge. Now get back to the unit! They need you more than I do."

Gary fought back a smile. Ruiz glanced at him, and Gary gave him a quick nod, slapping the young corporal's shoulder as the man jogged past. Then he knelt down by the medic and his patient. Senger was grumbling and twisting so much the medic was having difficulty treating the man's wounds.

"Captain, can you order him to be still so I can get a bandage on him?" the medic said.

"Give the doc a break, Ralph, okay?"

"It's just a flesh wound. I saw the major get it just before me, and he looked hurt much worse—"

"And he's being tended," cut in the frustrated medic, "as I'm trying to tend you. The faster I can get a bandage on this, the faster you can get back to the line."

"You sure of that, Doc?" Gary asked. As much as he needed Senger, he didn't want him to jeopardize his life.

"You don't think I'm going to the hospital, do you?" snarled Senger.

Gary arched a brow so Senger could clearly see. Hardly a stickler for military protocol, he deemed this an appropriate time to remind the lieutenant who was in charge.

"Sir!" Senger added belatedly.

"I'll let you know if you are fit for duty," Gary said. "Doc?"

"Yeah—I mean, yes, sir, he's fit. His shoulder is gonna hurt, but he's as fit as anyone else."

"You bet I am . . . sir!" agreed Senger.

"Well, it looks like we've cleared the area, so as soon as you get back to your unit, try to get them to bed down for the night." Gary judged it to be nearly midnight. "I'm going to go see about the major."

Major Perkins was dead, but the toll of dead Japs would have to make that loss worthwhile. Gary tried to convince himself of that now, as he did every time they lost a man. A half dozen enemy had been killed. Gary tried to regroup Perkins's outfit, though they had taken heavy casualties in the ambush. The best he could do was combine them with another outfit. Then things settled down for the night, as much as sporadic gunfire in the distance would allow.

Gary would not have slept much that night even without interruptions by several of his unit commanders who were also having a hard time sleeping. But he did doze about an hour before dawn. He woke on April 3 cold and stiff just as small tendrils of light were penetrating the jungle canopy. His fatigues were still damp from the previous day's sweat and the night's dew, sending a chill deep into his bones. He would welcome the day's searing heat for a change. His stomach rumbled, but food would have to wait, for he had nothing with him, and he couldn't spare the time to scrounge up something.

As he stretched out the kinks in his body, he realized it was Friday—Good Friday, actually. He knew this was also a holiday for the Japanese, something to do with one of their ancient emperors. He had a feeling the enemy would celebrate their holiday in warrior fashion—with death and destruction. Gary would probably have to do the same. There might be a church service at HQ, but he would have to miss it. All he could do to acknowledge the holiday was allow himself a moment to think of his family. Would they go about their usual traditions? A noon church service followed by a simple family dinner of bread and beans. His father would say that the plain fare was to remind them of the suffering of Christ. For a long time growing up Gary could never understand his father's words because he actually enjoyed his mother's beans.

Then would come Easter, another special time for his family. Before going away to West Point and even after when he was home, he'd always enjoyed the task of hiding Easter eggs at church for the kids. His dad never failed to hide a raw egg somewhere, and he made sure one of the older and more ornery of the kids found it. Everyone always had a good laugh when the egg cracked open in the eager kid's hand. Would his grandparents and aunts and uncles and cousins come for Easter dinner, as they often did? Would his mother cook ham or turkey for dinner? With sweet potatoes dripping with butter and brown sugar? He forced away thoughts of food. That did him no good at all. But it was nice to pause just a moment in the hellish world in which he now existed and think of something normal, something not tinged with death or marred by the horrors he'd witnessed in the last months.

Things like his mother's smile and gentle words, his father's laugh and funny stories.

Thoughts of his family quickly turned to thoughts of Blair. He'd barely had time to think of her as family, but how he wanted her to become part of those traditions! He still wasn't certain if that would happen, but he wanted it desperately. He had never yet felt ready to give up on her and still wasn't. He might have been foolish enough to fall for her little deceptions, but there was one thing he felt sure she hadn't lied about, and that was her love for him. When she had told him that last day in California that she didn't love him, he'd known for certain that was her biggest lie. Another surety he could not deny was the sense he'd had when they had married, the assurance that God wanted them together. It might still be. It might—

His thoughts were shattered by artillery explosions. So much for holiday peace.

The day passed filled with hours of heavy shelling. Gary knew this must be the expected Japanese offensive. The final offensive? The company was hit on every side, and finally the enemy punched a hole into the left flank. He regrouped his unit a few miles east of their last position, then miraculously they held their ground this time, but barely. Gary heard that a couple of Filipino regiments had been pressed so hard by unceasing artillery fire and the onslaught of enemy infantry that they broke and ran in a complete rout. Gary's company held on but with high casualties. That's what he made himself call his wounded and dead—casualties—some of whom were his friends but all of whom were his comrades. They became merely percentages when he reported to HQ. But with each death it became harder and harder to detach himself. It wore him down, as did the hunger and dysentery and bouts of chills. The temperature in the jungle was at least ninety-five degrees—some said this was the hottest year in memory. Yet a couple of times he found himself shaking so badly it might have been the dead of winter, like those he'd experienced at the Point. He knew he had finally contracted malaria, yet it almost felt as if his inner fears were materializing and causing the trembling, rather than some physical ailment.

He forced himself to go on, to forget that he was half dead physically, until he stumbled upon young Ruiz's body. His face was so bloody and shattered that the only way Gary knew it was the corporal was by his dog tags. Gary suddenly wept. He was too dehydrated for any tears to leak from his eyes, yet his shoulders jerked spasmodically with emotion. He stalked away from the scene so his men wouldn't see. A casualty, part of the forty percent rate they were quickly reaching. That's all.

But when he was alone, he sank down against a big bahite tree. The huge roots could hide two or three men. How he wished he could hide forever. Instead, he took out a map tucked inside his jacket, opened it, and pretended he was studying it in case any of the men happened to see him. He couldn't let them see that he was hanging by only a thin thread.

Senger strode up to him, plucked the map from his hand, and flipped it around. "Sometimes they're easier to read if they're right side up," he said dryly.

Gary could only manage a grunt in response.

Senger hunkered down beside him. "Some Filipinos say these trees are inhabited by evil spirits."

"Thanks, Ralph. I needed to hear that." Even Gary's sarcasm was halfhearted.

"Good reason to get off your behind and get back to commanding this outfit." His words were peppered with a string of oaths.

Gary blinked at the salty language, but his reply was nearly as edgy. "So I'm not allowed to sit for a moment and survey a map—" he barked a dry, humorless laugh at his thin ruse—"or try to find a reason to go on."

"No," Senger said flatly. "You ain't allowed any of that."

The truth of those words finally penetrated Gary's grief and despair. He had no other choices, really. There was, of course, that time-honored option of shooting himself in the foot. A couple of days ago he'd stopped by Hospital #1 to visit some of his wounded, and a medic had told him that the incidence of foot wounds was increasing dramatically. He'd been proud of the fact that he had no such malingerers in his outfit. He wasn't going to be the first. He owed that to his men.

Using his rifle as a support, he pushed himself to his feet. "Okay, LT, let's go."

In the afternoon he, too, became one of those casualties. Shrapnel grazed his head, but he held a rag to it to stop the bleeding so he could keep moving. Funny, when it happened, he didn't even think of using it as an excuse to escape to one of the hospitals. His only thought was that medics were swamped with real injuries. A little dizziness was nothing compared to his stomach cramps and intermittent bouts of chills.

Finally late that night orders came through to withdraw. After that it seemed impossible to hold any position. The enemy pushed them from every side. And the company was all but on the run—he managed to prevent a rout, at least, and they fought and made the enemy regret every step back they took. In addition, all radio communication was lost, and wildfires sprang up in two or three positions, belching smoke everywhere. Visibility plummeted as the smoke permeated the jungle. With no radio and limited visibility Gary was desperate to know what was happening with the other units. How were they faring? What were current positions? Everyone dreaded shooting his own comrades, or taking "friendly fire" himself, though it wouldn't be the first time it had occurred.

He'd sent word down the line to see if anyone could be spared to run a message back to the command post, though he thought he knew the answer. There were already too many holes in their line to spare a single man. It wasn't until late afternoon that a messenger finally jogged up to his foxhole.

"Captain Hobart, I've got some orders."

At first all Gary heard was a voice that sounded way too young. And he was too concerned about the boy standing over the foxhole like a target to notice anything else. There was a lull in the shooting at the moment, but one never knew when a sniper or stray shell might materialize.

He yanked at the boy's pant leg. "Get down!" he snapped.

Realizing his carelessness, the messenger scrambled into the foxhole. "Sorry, sir. I—"

"Where are they finding replacements now? Nursery school?" Gary grumbled. It was bad enough to lose half his unit; he didn't want the death of a child on his hands. "Never mind me," he said gruffly by way of apology. "What do you have?"

"Orders from Colonel Reese, sir," the boy said, holding out a pouch.

"It's about time." Gary took it, for the first time taking a real look at the messenger. The face was smudged and a too-big helmet shadowed the eyes, but he knew that face. "Mateo?"

"Yes, Captain Hobart, it is me."

"I'll be . . ." Gary just gaped at the boy. It was almost unreal, as if he were dreaming—it wouldn't be the first time he'd fallen asleep on his feet. "It's really you?" he added, still bemused. Then panic gripped him. "Why aren't you with Blair? What's happened?"

"Sir, she is all right. We had to leave the mission. I saw her to the safety of the hospital, then Reverend Doyle helped me get into a fighting unit. They only have me running errands—"

"In the hospital?" He wasn't sure what to think of that. Both hospitals were only miles from the fiercest war zones.

"She got malaria and we needed quinine."

Gary pushed his helmet away and raked a hand through his sweaty hair, nearly knocking off the makeshift bandage he'd wrapped around his head wound. Just thinking of her sick and suffering made him knot up inside. Malaria! Was she really okay? He suddenly had a wild thought. Maybe his wounded head did need medical attention. He could go to the hospital. No one would question him. Maybe he could stop by HQ as well if he needed more excuse.

"Which hospital?" The idea was so tempting, even if in the back of his mind he knew it would be impossible.

"Hospital #2."

He was almost relieved to hear that because that facility was farther away than #1. Not that he could have gone anyway. Forcing his mind away from such futile fantasies, he said, "Mateo, I need you to get to HQ and inform them of my position. Tell them my radio is out, and I have no idea of the positions of the other units. Tell them I am holding on, but I've lost more than thirty percent of my men. You got that?"

"Yes, sir."

Gary showed Mateo the map so he'd know exactly the position to report, then he read the material in the pouch to make sure it needed no response. The colonel wanted them to continue to hold. That wasn't good news. Gary had been hoping for an order to retreat.

"That's all, Mateo," Gary said. "It was good to see you."

Mateo climbed out of the foxhole, started to turn, hesitated, then turned back. "I am glad I saw you, too, sir, and that you are okay. We've all been praying for you."

All? Had Blair been praying for him, also? Was it too much to hope for?

"Thank you, lad. Now keep your head down and your eyes open."

He watched Mateo jog away, then forced his mind to matters at hand. He gave no more conscious thought to Blair. He couldn't. Someday . . . maybe . . . if God willed . . . he could spend a lifetime thinking of her, being with her.

But not now.

Throughout the day, Gary drove his troops to hold their position. Each time the enemy broke through he set up a new line of defense. Inch by inch he was being pushed farther east. How much longer could they keep this up? The men were exhausted, weak with hunger and sickness. Gary hated himself for pushing them so. Every casualty he took personally. The responsibility of command weighed on him worse than the fear of his own death, tarnishing his lifelong dream of being an officer in the United States Army. When Mateo returned—thankfully he found them in their new position!—word from HQ was to fall back to Limay. But the enemy still pushed at them, so even the retreat was hard won. He felt as if he were hanging on to a cliff with his hands and the Japs were trouncing on his fingers.

On April 8 they were ordered to establish a final defensive line at Cabcaben, fifteen or twenty miles south of Limay and nearly as far south on the peninsula as you could go. Only vaguely was Gary aware that this was much nearer to where Blair was supposed to be. He could not think about her yet, but he had a sick feeling that if he survived this day, he'd have all the time in the world to think of her while rotting in a Jap prison camp.

By now hope was as ethereal as the promised help from the States. Some of the men sang a ditty concocted by the correspondent Frank Hewlett.

"We're the battling bastards of Bataan,
No mama, no papa, no Uncle Sam,
No aunts, no uncles, no nephews, no nieces,
No pills, no planes, no artillery pieces,
And nobody gives a damn!"

Gary didn't hold with all the colorful language in it, but even he could not deny the truth of it. They had been abandoned by their country. A few of the most naïve still spoke of "When help comes from the States," but Gary knew that was a dream. So he let his men sing the ditty—amazed and not a little proud that they could sing anything at this time.

Military organization was by now in chaos. Communications were often down, and rumors were more frequent than real orders. But his men were still fighting. He wished he could tell them how proud he was of them, but there was no chance. They knew. They must know!

What amazed him even more than his own men's stamina was the fact that the enemy just kept coming. There seemed no end to the Japanese infantry nor of their bombers or artillery. That day the shelling was like the biggest Fourth of July fireworks display he'd ever seen. And, as with a fireworks show grand finale, everyone knew this was the end. They knew even before the order came that all guns, ammunition, and matériel were to be destroyed before seven o'clock the next morning.

"At that time cease all hostilities," the order read. "Units are to lay down weapons and re-form at the nearest road. The allied Army will surrender at 7 A.M. April 9."

This communiqué came as no huge surprise, despite the fact that he knew the orders straight from Washington just a few weeks ago had been "No surrender." Still, knowing the certainty of it made it feel no less like a kick in the gut. Tears stung Gary's eyes when he heard it. Four months and a day from the catastrophe at Pearl Harbor. Fighting nearly every moment of that time, watching his friends and comrades fall and die—what had it been for? He tried not to fall into despair, though avoiding it might have been easier if every ounce of grit had not been drained from him. He tried to grasp at his faith for comfort, but even that was hard.

"Captain," Senger sidled up to Gary. "I'm heading for the jungle. You ought to come, too." The men were allowed—at least it was tacitly understood—to decide for themselves if they wanted to keep up a resistance against the enemy rather than face prison. There weren't many interested, for they simply had no more fight left in them.

"I can't leave the men," Gary replied.

"I thought about that, too, Gary," Senger replied, dropping all pretense at military formality. "But now I'm thinking more about living to fight another day. The majority of the men are too sick and exhausted to keep it up, and I don't hold it against them. Still, I think I got a little left in me. And I don't believe any of them are going to hold it against me, or you, for that matter, if we take off."

Gary knew a few others were thinking of taking this route, as well. But he didn't see himself as a guerilla warrior. He'd been trained to command his men, and he could not leave them now. Maybe the real reason was that despair had indeed won him over. He was so tired of fighting.

He thought that maybe as a reward for his cursed sense of duty he would trot over to Hospital #2 and find Blair. It wasn't far away, and in the current chaos no one would miss him for an hour. But he'd heard the nurses had been evacuated to Corregidor. He hoped that meant Blair had, as well. Dear God, let it mean her. Let her be safe.

But how safe was Corregidor? The Japanese were not going to stop with Bataan. They must have the Rock, as Corregidor was called, for only then could they control the true prize they sought—Manila Bay. But if Blair could make it to the Rock, there was yet a chance for her. Maybe a submarine might still come from Australia and rescue the women.

He snorted a dry laugh that lacked even elemental mirth. Maybe hope wasn't entirely dead after all.

41

IF THE JAPANESE were not stopped, Hospital #2 stood directly in their path. But with the jungle floor swelled with thousands of wounded—at one point there were seven thousand patients—there was no time to think of such minor details as the nearness of the Japanese. Blair didn't think she'd notice if they marched right into the hospital that minute! But she did notice gunfire coming closer each hour, yet even that she shoved from her mind, instead keeping doggedly at her work. She didn't get sick anymore at the sight of blood or of gaping wounds and—goodness!—she'd assisted at an amputation that morning and turned right around when it was done and cleaned an infected head wound.

She'd performed a gastric lavage on a patient when her hands were shaking so hard from chills that she dropped the tubing three times before making the proper insertion. She worked through a burning fever and a rumbling stomach. She wanted to complain, she wanted to retch, but . . . there just wasn't time. Besides, no one had time to listen to her complaints, anyway. Even Mrs. Doyle had called Blair a real trooper. If only the woman knew of the horrified thoughts assailing her mind. Blair had confessed her guilt over this to Patience, and the younger woman had just laughed and said she was screaming silent "Ughs!" constantly herself. The sense of horror didn't stop Patience, and neither did it stop Blair.

Word came that Hospital #1 had been bombed and some seventy had been killed, including three nurses. The fear of the same happening to them hung over everyone, Blair was certain, but no one stopped working.

Finally one thing did stop the work of the nurses. Around sunset on April 8 all American nurses were ordered to evacuate to Corregidor. They had an hour to gather whatever they could carry and meet at headquarters. It was only then that Blair even remembered that it was her birthday. She said nothing to anyone. There wasn't time for birthdays.

"Nearly all the nurses wanted to refuse to evacuate," Alice told Blair as she threw her last few personal possessions into her pack. They were in the "quarters" Blair shared with Claudette and the Doyle women. Alice was helping them pack. "They expect us to leave our patients, just like that."

"I don't know how you can bear the military, Alice, and all their orders." Blair was learning about forgiveness, but she still needed to lay blame *somewhere* for Gary having to leave her. The Army seemed a safe target for that.

"The Navy has been good to me." Alice then grinned. "But you should hear what Josie did—"

"Girls, quit dallying," barked Mrs. Doyle. "There isn't time for gossip, and even if there were, I won't have it!"

"Wait, Mrs. Doyle, you'll want to hear this, too," persisted Alice. The others also paused to listen. Everyone liked the feisty head nurse, Lieutenant Nesbit, whom the entire staff called Josie. "When the colonel told her that only American nurses were to be evacuated, she told him that if her Filipino nurses weren't going, neither was she.

Well, the colonel got on the phone and got the order extended to include the Filipinos."

"Good for her!" said Mrs. Doyle. "It would have been heartless to do otherwise. The Japanese despise the Filipinos, and I am sure they would be especially harsh toward the women."

"You are sure the commander won't stand in our way, Alice?" Blair had mixed feelings about leaving Bataan; after all, Gary was still there somewhere. But she also knew when to be reasonable, and it was just sensible to evacuate.

"You are all American women. No one is going to hold you back even if you aren't technically nurses. And Claudette will just blend in with the other Filipinos."

Blair ventured a glance at Mrs. Doyle. She was pulling the buckle closed on Hope's pack. She had a taut, determined set to her expression. So did Hope and Patience. They did not want to evacuate and leave their husband and father behind. Mrs. Doyle had agonized over the decision and in the end decided to go only because of her daughters' safety.

They just made it to the trucks, which were waiting with motors running and drivers anxious to leave. Many nurses were running up at the last minute, some with their clothes in disarray from their haste. One nurse had curlers still in her hair. Many possessions were left behind. Blair thought the medic racing up to the truck intended merely to say good-bye to the nurses, but instead he stopped in front of Meg Doyle.

"You're Mrs. Doyle, aren't you?" he said breathlessly. "The chaplain's wife?"

"Yes . . ."

"I just brought the reverend in, Mrs. Doyle, and thought you'd want to know before you left—"

"He's dead!" Mrs. Doyle gasped, swaying back against Blair, who slung an arm around her to hold her steady.

"He's been wounded, ma'am. It's serious, but I think we got him here in time."

"Take me to him," she said without hesitation, then started toward the hospital only to stop abruptly and turn toward Blair. "Blair, you'll take care of my girls, won't you?"

"Mother, we're going with you!" cried Patience.

"No, you're not. You are both getting on that truck. Blair, I am counting on you to see to them."

"Mama, don't go!" Hope pleaded tearfully.

"You both know I must, but your father will rest better if he knows you are safe."

The girls looked at Blair, perhaps for support. For herself, Blair wondered why suddenly she had been thrust into such a position by both mother and daughters but especially by Mrs. Doyle, who despite recent confessions had never indicated she thought Blair a pillar of responsibility. Yes, she had been thrilled when she had learned of Claudette's and Blair's confessions of faith, that is, after her initial surprise over the unconventional manner in which they had done it, without even another mature Christian present. And she had acknowledged Blair's labors in the hospital. But her comments had never been flowing with flowery praise. They had merely recognized her effort, even a bit grudgingly at times. Certainly they had never indicated she'd entrust her daughters' lives into Blair's hands.

One of the trucks had already taken off. The driver of the second truck was blasting his horn.

"Blair?" Mrs. Doyle's tone was as incisive as her gaze.

"Come on, girls," Blair finally said, her voice none too steady. After the girls hugged their mother, Blair gathered them together and prodded them into the back of the truck. Claudette climbed in last.

The truck bounced away a moment later, leaving Mrs. Doyle in a cloud of dust, waving a forlorn hand. Everyone waved back, and the Doyle girls were not the only ones weeping. Blair, Claudette, and many of the nurses were emotional, as well. They were all leaving behind people they cared about.

Blair wondered about the hurried departure shortly after when they were caught up in the choking mass of traffic on the road to Mariveles. Clogged by retreating soldiers, their equipment, and civilian refugees, the hospital trucks moved at a snail's pace. Most of the time they sat motionless on the road. The launch was scheduled to leave Mariveles for Corregidor at midnight, and the clock was inching closer to that time.

A convoy of tanks broke down, blocking the road for an hour. After that the truck Blair was in started creeping forward, only to lurch to a stop. Poking her head out from the back, Blair saw a billow of steam rising from the hood. When Reverend Sanchez's DeSoto had experienced that malady, it had held her up for days, but the soldiers seemed to know how to deal with such matters. They were under the hood and tinkering for only an hour before they slammed the hood shut and started up the engine.

It was after midnight.

Suddenly horrific explosions lit up the night sky and shook the earth. The trucks stopped, and everyone ran to take cover on the side of the road. Soon one of the drivers assured them it was just their own troops blowing up ammunition dumps on the docks so the enemy couldn't take them after the surrender in the morning. Unfortunately, that would delay the trucks further because it made the docks too dangerous to approach.

Stomach cramps forced Blair to race into the jungle a couple of times. Other nurses joined her. One said she would be happy if they just left her to die by the side of the road. Blair felt the same. Exhaustion, hunger, and various physical distresses had turned her into a zombie. The pounding explosions simply punctuated her miseries. She tried to keep her suffering to herself, burying her face in the dirt so that none of those she was responsible for would see. Claudette, clinging close to Blair, had fallen asleep, apparently too exhausted to be deterred by the fireworks.

Eventually the explosions quieted, and the driver told them to get back into the truck for another attempt to get to the docks. The midnight launch might have departed, but there might still be other vessels to get them across. Blair nudged Claudette awake, then turned to urge Patience and Hope into motion.

They were nowhere in sight. She ran into the jungle to see if they had gone there to relieve themselves, though she doubted they would go together. But she called their names. Claudette followed, still groggy from a difficult sleep, and tried to help. Back at the truck Blair questioned everyone without success. She also ran after the second truck, moving sluggishly along only a few yards ahead, in case the girls had boarded it by mistake.

"Some of the nurses left a little while ago," one of the nurses said. "They thought they could walk to the docks faster. But I don't know if the girls were with them."

All the nurses knew the Doyle girls and would have recognized them if they had seen them leave. But what reason did they have to attempt getting to the docks alone, leaving behind Blair and Claudette?

Blair was left with only one possibility. They must have gone back to the hospital to be with their parents. Her heart sank. She had been given one important responsibility, and by a woman she wanted to please, and she had thoroughly flubbed it. But how could she have known the girls would do something so harebrained? Patience and Hope were the most obedient, well-behaved girls Blair had ever known.

"I've got to go after them," Blair said.

"If they have gone to the hospital, how will you get them to come back?" Claudette asked reasonably. She was such a sensible, level-headed fifteen-year-old. Blair wished she could be more like her.

But she was only Blair, unreasonable, impulsive, crazy. And she simply could not make herself do anything but what her heart and gut told her to do.

"I'll drag them back by their hair if I have to! Mrs. Doyle trusted me!"

"Then we will go," said Claudette, turning from the truck.

Alice interceded. "You can't do this. You cannot drag them back, Blair, no matter what you say. Maybe they have a right to be with their parents, now of all times."

The driver yelled back at them, "Come on, the traffic is starting to move. We have to go."

"Blair," Alice continued, "you especially can't risk Claudette's going back. It's possible the Japanese have advanced as far as the hospital. You can't let Claudette fall into their hands. They treat Filipinos like dirt. And Filipino women—! Blair, she cannot be captured."

Blair rubbed her hands over her face, feeling grit and dampness from tears she hadn't even known she was shedding. The driver was yelling, the nurses urging them to hurry.

Finally she said, "Claudette, you stay with the nurses. I'll catch up. I'm sure the girls haven't gone far. I'll find them and hitch a ride to the docks on another truck. I'll be there, I promise."

Claudette nodded dismally, then was pulled onto the truck by the hands of the nurses. A break in the traffic jam allowed the truck to lurch forward at more than its usual crawl.

After having retrieved her pack from the back of the truck, Blair started to jog off in the other direction, but after a few steps, fatigue forced her to a plodding walk. She searched through the mob on the road but didn't see the girls. After an hour she knew she should give up and make her way to the docks. The Doyle girls would make it to the hospital, and then their mother would look after them. In a way, they would be much better off. But Blair knew that would be shirking her responsibility. She must at least see that they were all right, then if she could not convince them to come to the docks, she would know she had done all she could.

She continued her futile trek, and within a few minutes, chills wracked her body. She'd worked through malaria attacks before, but this one struck so hard it literally knocked her off her feet. She had nothing left to fight it, and slipped down into the ditch at the side of the road. Maybe if it hadn't been so deep, someone would have seen her and helped, but with all the chaos and confusion on the road, it was unlikely that anyone had even been looking.

The attack must have lasted an hour. She took a couple of aspirin—it was all she had—with a swallow of water from her canteen. When the worst had passed, she tried to crawl back up to the road but had no strength for the climb. Helplessly she fell back into her hole, noting that dawn was close at hand and the traffic on the road had thinned considerably. In another moment sleep consumed her, the first time since the previous night that she had closed her eyes.

The heat of the sun beating down on her finally woke her and gave her strength to climb out of the ditch. The traffic on the road had thinned, but there was nothing heading east. She was offered a couple of rides to Mariveles and knew she would regret refusing them, but something made her doggedly continue to the hospital. Likely it was knowing there would be no escape from the dock now, but mostly she was just too dazed to think straight.

Japanese aircraft winged overhead. Several times the refugees on the road dove for cover as the planes circled low. In the distance Blair saw planes drop bombs on what must be the docks; at least they fell in that direction. Wasn't there a cease-fire in force with the surrender? Perhaps the enemy considered the bombing justified as part of the continued campaign against Corregidor. One thing was certain, Mariveles was no longer a safe haven.

Sensing she needed to take more care now than ever, she left the road a few miles from the hospital. If it was true that the Japanese had advanced this far, she didn't want to risk encountering them. She prayed she wouldn't get hopelessly lost in the jungle. At last she stopped to rest in the cover of a large patch of vines and roots. The heat was sapping what little strength she had left.

At the faint sound of rustling leaves, she caught her breath. There was not even a hint of a breeze in the air. Her heart thudding like a drum in her chest, she froze and listened. The distant tread of footsteps neared. They were cautious but hardly stealthy. Peeking out from her hiding place, she saw the form of a man in civilian clothes. Certainly no Jap. She watched him for a few moments, then he turned toward her.

"Dominador!" she breathed.

The man jerked at the sound, pistol suddenly in hand.

"Dominador," she cried, as quietly as her urgency would allow. "It's me, Blair Hobart."

"Show yourself," he said.

Cautiously she moved into the open.

"What are you doing here?" he said, lowering his pistol and jamming it into his belt. "Mrs. Doyle said you had all gone to Mariveles."

"You've seen Mrs. Doyle? Were the girls with her?" She had so many questions, but this was foremost.

"No, the girls went to the docks, didn't they?"

"They slipped away from me." The admission was agonizing for her to make. "I am almost certain they wanted to come back to the hospital to be with their parents. You are certain you didn't see them? How long since you were there?"

"I escaped about a half hour ago. They were not there then."

"They should have gotten there already," Blair despaired. What could have happened to them? "I need to go. I need to find them!" She started forward, but Dominador grabbed her arm.

"You cannot go there!"

"Why?" Then something registered with her. "You escaped? What do you mean?"

"The Japs are swarming the hospital. I managed to get away after— It is just as well the girls did not make it back."

"Are Reverend and Mrs. Doyle okay?"

"We cannot stand here and talk."

"Please, tell me." He was hesitant, and her hopes crashed. "Please . . ." she urged, though she feared the worst.

"Reverend Doyle had a leg amputated. He was conscious when I saw him. And Mrs. Doyle was also . . . alive. We must get as far away from here as we can. You must not get taken."

All Blair could hear was that slight pause in his voice when he said Mrs. Doyle was alive. What could have happened? "Tell me, Dominador, what is wrong with Mrs. Doyle?"

"For a time the Japs rampaged through the hospital, mistreating the injured. Mrs. Doyle tried to stop them. They beat her up badly."

"Dear God, no!" she breathed. How many times had Blair thought she would pity anyone who got in Meg Doyle's way when she was determined about something? She could vividly picture the formidable missionary, hands on hips, railing at the enemy. Yet even she was no match for a horde of Japanese soldiers.

"No one could help her," he forced out.

Blair wondered if anyone had tried. What had Dominador done? She didn't ask, for it seemed useless now to judge anyone.

"We must go," he added dismally.

"The docks—" But Blair remembered the bombing she had seen earlier. There would be no escape from there now. "Where can we go? The Japanese must be all over."

"We have to try. There are ways to hide in the jungle."

She didn't have a lot of faith in Dominador's words. He was not exuding confidence. Unlike Juan, he seemed almost as ignorant of the wilds as she. Yet as inept as he might be, he was all she had. She could not survive in the jungle alone. All at once she remembered what she and Claudette had done a few days before. She had really had little time to give her new commitment of faith much thought except for hurriedly murmured prayers. She was almost certain God would not hold that against her. But she was even more certain of something else—she had never been truly alone in all that time, and she still wasn't. God was with her and would be even now as she plunged once again into the hated jungle.

42

TWO DAYS AFTER the surrender Gary was in Mariveles sitting in a holding area for officers. The sun had risen a couple of hours earlier, beating down its relentless heat on the defeated men. Like all the others, Gary had not eaten a thing since the surrender. Water was supplied in a communal bucket, which by now was swarming with filth.

The burden of defeat was still heavy upon him, perhaps more so now than when he had first learned of it because now he had begun to experience the degradation of the defeated. First had been the rough search of his ragged clothes by his captors. The Japs had taken anything of value, not that he had much. But the most precious thing had been Blair's wedding band. When they took that, it seemed as if they were robbing him of his last vestige of hope. Reuniting with Blair one day, giving her back that ring, coming together truly as husband and wife in their hearts and in the spirit of God—this was a fantasy he had clung to in his darkest moments. The loss of the ring nearly shattered that.

It was worse than the beating he'd received for helping one of his comrades who had stumbled on the way to the holding area. But certainly equal in its demoralizing effect was when a couple of men had been shoved into the compound through the gate last night. They were both badly beaten and both crumbled into a heap in the dirt. Only after the guards had locked the gate and turned their backs did several of the prisoners dare go aid the newcomers.

One, half conscious, was rolled over. Gary did not recognize him. He had the insignia of a captain with the 41st Field Artillery. The second man rolled over on his own, shaking his head, grumbling and cursing under his breath.

The sight made Gary smile for the first time in days. "Sarge!"

"Lieutenant, you knucklehead—" Senger blinked and saw who had addressed him. "I mean, you knucklehead, sir!"

Gary chuckled, then realized there was nothing to laugh about. Senger had attempted to escape capture but obviously had failed. His face had been bashed and bruised. His eyes were swollen slits. Yet still he could make a joke! Gary jumped up, and while some of the others were tending the captain, he went to the water bucket, dipped in his cupped hands, all he had to use as a ladle, and carefully brought the water back. When he reached Senger there was only enough left in his hands to drip a few drops onto the man's parched and bloody lips. But he lapped gratefully at it as if it were an artesian spring.

"Thanks, Gary." After a few minutes Senger found the strength to sit up and tell his story. "Me and a couple others were doing pretty good dodging the Japs. They just don't have enough men to keep everything under their thumbs. I was crossing a rice paddy—I know it was a stupid thing to do, putting myself out in the open like that—but there was a mango grove on the other side. I was starved, and those ripe mangos were too tempting to resist. I boasted to my buddies that I'd bring back a fine dinner. I got across okay, ran into the grove, right into a Jap patrol. They were picking mangos, too. Their weapons were leaning against the trees, so I was able to draw my sidearm. Then I got hit with an attack of the shakes." He added a few choice curse words to further describe that crushing moment. "My gun fell from my stupid shaking hand, and they had me. At least I was able to convince them I didn't know anything about the surrender. It might have gone worse with me if they'd thought I was a fugitive."

"That's a rotten deal, Ralph," Gary commiserated.

"Nothing ventured, nothing gained," he said with an airy derring-do that would have looked ridiculous on anyone else. "I'll give it another try first chance I get."

"I don't know where you get the nerve," sighed Gary, feeling like a shriveled old man.

"You got nerve, too, Gary. I know it. You're worn down now, that's all. But I'm certain we have just as good a chance of surviving in the jungle as we do in a Jap prison camp. After I was captured, there was an officer who questioned me. He let slip that they never expected this many POWs. They thought maybe there'd be twenty-some thousand. There's gotta be close to seventy thousand. What're they gonna do with us? Do you think they can feed and shelter all of us? I think they'd be perfectly content if a good number of us died one way or another. Maybe a mass escape attempt in which they had to gun us down."

"You may be right." But Gary could still find little enthusiasm for it.

That had been last night. Nothing had changed since then. Except rumor had spread through the compound that the prisoners would soon be moved. Where, he did not know. Some thought north. Gary tried to think about escaping. After all, a prisoner of war's duty was to escape. A move would be the perfect time to do so, during the initial disorder. He believed what Senger had said about the enemy's miscalculation of the POW numbers. If they planned some kind of forced march north, they couldn't possibly have enough men to adequately guard their prisoners and to maintain an occupation force on Bataan, as well. And they still had to keep up the attack on Corregidor, which was mostly an air and artillery bombardment for now, but they would have to hold a reserve for invasion if it came to that.

Gary tried to find within himself that nerve his friend had. He prayed but still felt empty. Then he remembered the one item the Japanese had not taken from him—his small New Testament. Apparently they had not considered it of value. He hadn't read it in a long time, and lately he was finding it harder and harder to cling to his faith. On an intellectual level, he knew God didn't cause suffering, yet it was hard not to question God after all the misery he'd seen. He couldn't help but wonder if God had abandoned them the same way their country had.

But he knew in his heart God wouldn't do that. He'd made promises, though now those promises were blurry in Gary's mind. He tried to call to mind verses he'd memorized as a kid. He couldn't get beyond *Jesus wept.*

When he was eleven or twelve, he'd tried to make a joke in Sunday school by telling his teacher he'd memorized a verse. Everyone had laughed when he quoted the shortest verse in the Bible—everyone but the teacher, that is!

What an irony that now that was the only verse he could bring to his numb mind. His Sunday school teacher had delivered an impromptu lesson on that particular verse. *"Do you know why Jesus wept, Gary?"* Of course he hadn't read the entire passage so he hadn't a clue. She explained, "It wasn't because Jesus' dear friend Lazarus had died—after all, He surely knew He planned to raise the man from the dead. No, instead, Jesus wept because of Mary's and Martha's lack of faith in Him. They had seen Him work so many miracles, but they had called Jesus to the grave to share their grief, not to work a miracle for them. The Bible said He was troubled, and I believe that was why He wept."

Gary blinked. He hadn't realized he even recalled that memory. How he wanted to have more faith than Mary and Martha! To know in his heart that his Lord had not abandoned him to his grief but was there, fully prepared to work some miracle. Yet he was a mature enough Christian to know that God's miracles were not always what one might expect. Not, perhaps, deliverance from a POW camp. But . . . what? What did God have in mind?

Gary took the New Testament from his pocket. There had always been answers in God's Word before. He opened to a verse he could find easily because it was the last thing Christ had said to his disciples. Before reading, though, he heard movement. A few men shuffled toward him.

"Looks like the Japs left you with something," one said.

Ralph Senger was among the men. "Captain, why don't you read something out of there to us?"

That idea had not occurred to Gary, and he couldn't hide his surprise it had come from his salty ex-sergeant.

"I was going to read a verse I thought I needed to hear right now," Gary said. Glancing at the page open before him, he read, " 'Lo, I am with you alway, even unto the end of the world.' "

"That's a good one," said Bob, a young lieutenant. "It's kinda like the end of the world for us, isn't it?"

"I always liked the Twenty-third Psalm," another young man said. "Read that."

"Sorry, I only have a New Testament," Gary replied. "But I did memorize it as a kid. Let me see . . ." He silently prayed the cobwebs would fall from his brain, if not for him, then for the men. And that was the first miracle he was to witness as the words of old came back to him. " *'The Lord is my shepherd; I shall not want. He maketh me to lie down in green pastures: he leadeth me beside the still waters. . . .'* " Gary paused, unable to recall what came next.

Bob chimed in. "I memorized it, too, once . . . long ago. *'He restoreth my soul: he leadeth me in the paths of righteousness for his name's sake. Yea, though I walk through the valley of the shadow of death, I will fear no evil: for thou art with me; thy rod and thy staff they comfort me. Thou preparest a table before me in the presence of mine enemies: thou anointest my head with oil; my cup runneth over. Surely goodness and mercy shall follow me all the days of my life: and I will dwell in the house of the Lord for ever.'* "

"Wow!" breathed hard-bitten Ralph Senger. "I would've never thought the Bible had anything in it about *us*! Read some more, Gary."

Gary did so until, not long after, the guards flung open the compound gates and began shouting orders. They couldn't be understood, of course, until they used the "universal tongue," in this case the prods of their bayonets. In that way, the men got the message they were to depart the compound and form up again on the road. The weak prisoners stumbled and fell and were forced to their feet by the painful pricks of bayonets.

Gary wondered if the men he had just been reading to remembered a table being prepared for them in the presence of their enemies. Or if in the depths of their souls, they felt the comfort of the Lord's rod and staff. He hoped so. He knew he was finding comfort in those words. And he realized *that* was a true miracle!

Column upon column of prisoners formed on the road. The line of bedraggled men strung out as far as Gary could see, and as they plodded up the road, they were joined by more. Thousands of men, perhaps all of the seventy thousand who had become POWs, would eventually join up with them. Considering the proportions of the defenders of Bataan, Gary figured sixty thousand were Filipinos and about twelve thousand were Americans. Such a breakdown didn't really matter. They were all comrades and always had been.

Gary learned from one of the guards, who spoke halting English and seemed friendlier than most, that all the prisoners were to be marched north to an assembly point in Balanga, which Gary knew to be about twenty-five miles from Mariveles. Here, the captives would be fed and then marched to San Fernando, which was an additional thirty miles, where there was a rail junction. From there they would be transported by train to Camp O'Donnell.

Gary had gleaned a bit of knowledge about the Japanese military at West Point, and he had once heard a lecture by a man who had spent time with a Japanese infantry outfit before the war. For the Japanese infantry soldier, twenty-five miles was considered a day's march, whereas a day's march for an American infantryman was only twenty miles. And it was not uncommon for the Japanese to "round out" their march with several laps around a track field. Thus, the Japanese were expecting no more from their captives than they did from themselves. To them, making the captives march to Balanga in one day was quite reasonable.

But apparently no one had taken into account the totally debilitated state of the prisoners. Not even the hardiest among the captives could make twenty-five miles in a day, probably not even in a week! However, in expecting the trip to take only one day, the Japanese had made no provision for food along the way, and for water the men were forced to find it where they could, often drinking from streams or dirty puddles in ditches. Not a few men died from that alone. Moreover, the searing heat and oppressive humidity beat upon the men almost more mercilessly than their captors' clubs.

Gary witnessed the stuff of nightmares on that tortuous march. Once, a woman on the side of the road, her stomach swelled with pregnancy, offered a cup of water to one of the captives. A guard stepped between them, bayoneting both the woman and the hapless captive who had reached for the water. It was a sure lesson for other spectators not to interfere.

The guards were especially brutal toward the Filipino prisoners. Gary witnessed executions and beatings that made him thankful he had no food left in his twisting stomach. If the Americans were not singled out as often, it was likely only because there were fewer of them to attract attention. But even without the abuse of beatings and such, the trek would have been no less harrowing. Men fell to the road, weak and exhausted, and if their companions tried to help them, they were beaten senseless. Gary watched Bob, the young lieutenant who had quoted the Twenty-third Psalm, stumble to the ground. Defiantly, Gary slung an arm around the man and prodded him to his feet, dragging him a short distance before he himself staggered to his knees under the man's near–dead weight. A guard watched the scene with an amused smirk on his face, and when Gary finally crumbled, the man pounced on both Gary and Bob, clubbing them with the butt of his rifle. Bob was dead by the time the guard finished. Somehow Gary found the will to struggle back to his feet and continue.

Besides the captives, Japanese troops and equipment heading south to continue the battle against Corregidor filled the road, causing congestion and havoc. The Japanese riding in trucks took up the game of trying to knock off prisoners' hats with sticks. It was a lethal sport, knocking senseless many of the already defeated men, some stumbling in front of the oncoming vehicles and getting crushed under their wheels. But those moments of sheer chaos springing from the confluence of the POWs and the advancing troops did have a positive side, one of which Lieutenant Senger was quick to take note.

He sidled up to Gary and in a low voice said, "We could make a break now, and no one would notice."

Gary gaped with shock at the sarge—he'd always be that, even to Gary. How could the man think in those terms? He was still limping from the beating he'd received after his capture, now three—or was it four?—days ago. Yet despite his own horror at what was happening around him, Gary had not slipped back into his previous benumbed state. In fact, the sheer hopelessness of the situation had oddly injected him with a kind of drive, if not exactly hope. He did not expect to make it to Limay alive, much less to Balanga at the top of the Bataan Peninsula. He had absolutely nothing to lose by risking an escape attempt.

"Yeah," Gary grunted. "When?"

"Before we die," the sarge said wryly. "You make the first move. I'll follow."

Gary nearly laughed at such a flimsy plan. But they didn't really need one more elaborate. All they had to do was wait for one of the many moments of confusion and disorder. The guards were cruel, monsters at times, but they didn't have eyes in the backs of their heads. Nevertheless, Gary waited until the sun was sinking behind Mariveles Mountain and the dim light could offer some aid.

When the nearest guards were looking in the opposite direction at a line of tanks coming toward them, Gary simply dropped from the line, smoothly and quietly. Anyone watching might have thought he had just dropped from exhaustion, as so many had. One man near him reached out to catch him, but Gary gave a quick shake of his head and a wink before slithering into the ditch. He'd caught Ralph's eyes a moment before and hoped he, too, was making his move, though his vision now was cut off by the side of the ditch. Gary worried when a moment or two later, the sarge still hadn't dropped out. Gary waited, unable to make out details among the men on the road. He rubbed his eyes and bemoaned his night blindness in the encroaching darkness.

He waited, hearing only the sound of boots tramping on the road a few feet above him. Where was Senger?

Suddenly a hand grasped Gary's shoulder, and he jumped.

"It's me" came the raspy bass of the sarge.

"You are lucky I didn't scream."

"I knew you weren't the screaming type." Senger grinned, the gesture especially bizarre, framed as it was by his cuts and bruises. Here they were, two escaped POWs, half dead, mere feet from their captors, and the man grinned!

Against all reason, Gary grinned back.

Blair crawled to the edge of the cliff. Dominador had beckoned her to come and look at something. She was glad to see when she reached the edge that they had climbed a bit and must have covered several miles since they left the vicinity of the hospital a few days ago. Even a few miles was quite a feat considering much of the time had been spent hiding from the Japanese.

Now Blair wondered what had caught the Filipino man's interest. The sun was setting behind them, so she had a fairly decent view toward the east, where her companion was pointing. Down below wound what she thought must be the road from Mariveles to Cabcaben. A long line of men were marching on the road—hundreds, maybe thousands of them. From her vantage, she could make out few details, but she could identify American and Filipino uniforms, though most of these were in tatters.

"They must be marching the prisoners north," Dominador said.

She grasped Dominador's arm. "Oh, those poor men." She'd seen enough of the soldiers in that last week before the surrender to know they were in miserable physical condition. Was Gary among them? Or Mateo? Or Juan? She supposed it was a good thing if they were. It meant they were still alive.

Gary, you must be alive! I will not accept anything else!

Dominador was about to turn away from the scene when Blair clutched his arm again. "Let's pray for them."

Later, she hoped someone was praying for her, as well. Her

strength gone, she crumbled into the damp grass and wouldn't have been able to move another step, even if a malaria attack hadn't suddenly gripped her.

"I'll go find help," Dominador said.

"N-no! P-please don't leave me!" Her teeth chattered so with chills that she could hardly get out a single word.

Dominador's gaze swung wildly around, as if he expected to see an enemy patrol rise up from the grass itself. She knew he was afraid and had been the entire time. She knew she was holding him back. She knew she would get them both captured, and she wanted to be noble and tell him to go on without her. That's what heroines always did in the movies. But she was too afraid. The idea of being all alone, stranded and helpless in the jungle, threw her into a panic. Part of her realized she wouldn't be really alone—God was with her. But . . .

"I go for help." Dominador sounded all too eager to do so, and he scrambled away as if he had an army on his tail.

Blair found only enough will left in her to crawl on hands and knees to the cover of some vines and roots. She hated the jungle, but she did think this little nook was green and pretty—a good place to die in.

She waited. Wracked by fever and chills, she lost track of the number of times the sun rose and set. Once, maybe twice. She knew Dominador was never coming back. She couldn't blame him. Yes, in the movies the heroines always told the heroes to go on, but of course the heroes never did. They never gave up on the heroines. But then, Dominador wasn't really Blair's hero.

Gary . . .

He rode to her on a shining white stallion. Leaping from his sinewy mount, he lifted her frail form into his strong arms. A rainbow arched over his head. A song floated through her mind. Yes, she had found it at last. The land in the lullaby where dreams come true, where troubles melt, where love is finally hers. *Somewhere . . .*

Oh, Gary, you have rescued me! I knew you would.

Hands jostled and lifted her from the grass. Gentle hands, she thought.

Japs!

No . . . gentle hands. Gary . . . but the faces she saw through the blur of fever were brown and round. Not angelic. She remembered the angelic features she had attributed to Mrs. Doyle once . . . oh, poor Mrs. Doyle . . .

Not Mrs. Doyle. Not Gary. Not the Japanese!

"Who. . . ?" she rasped but could get no more from her parched throat.

"Shush . . ." came a whispered response, like the wind parting the jungle vines.

Blair did not try to speak again. Did it matter if she was being rescued or captured or carried away to her heavenly home? At least she was ready for that now. Perhaps she was ready for anything.

Los Angeles, California
April 1942

THE STUDIO APARTMENT was small but perfect for a newlywed couple. Jackie had fixed it with homey touches—a plant on a hand-crocheted doily, two framed prints on the walls, one of an English garden with flowers in full bloom, another of laughing children dipping their bare feet in a country stream. Idyllic scenes like the life Jackie dreamed of for herself and her new husband.

Jackie and Sam were happy when ensconced in that little studio—very happy. Knowing Sam before as a friend, even as a boyfriend, had been wonderful, but now sharing a life with him as his wife . . . the joy of it was beyond words. Each passing day made her more and more certain they were perfect together.

If only the outside world did not intrude.

But from the moment they had returned to California, it tried to batter them. First no one would rent them a place to live. Landlords would have sooner defiled their precious apartments with bands of criminals than with a Japanese man and a white woman living in so-called sin. Seeing their marriage license did not change anyone's perception of the matter. They spent the first two days with Sam's family, but the little house was already overcrowded. And Sam's father refused to speak to Jackie. When Sam questioned the man, he admitted that he had given his blessing to the marriage at first, but suddenly he found he could not bring himself to acknowledge his son's white wife.

Finally Jackie was forced to resort to asking her father for help. That was difficult beyond words. He, too, had given his blessing, but that made it no easier for him to accept a Japanese son-in-law. Keagan did own some real estate, among which was an apartment house in a run-down section of East Los Angeles. So a place to live was secured for the couple. There was no landlord now to abuse them, but that didn't prevent the mean stares and unkind words from the other tenants.

Still, Jackie tried to be the wife she'd always dreamed of being. In a yellow apron, printed all over with bright red cherries and tied around her waist, she stirred eggs in the skillet. They couldn't afford bacon, but she'd chopped some onion into the eggs, and the fragrance mingled nicely with that of the brewing pot of coffee. At least she thought it might be a nicely domestic odor. But lately the smell of cooking eggs had not been settling well with her, though she still cooked them every morning because it was the wifely thing to do.

Sam was making up the bed. She had a perfect view of him because the bed was in the same room, separated from the kitchen only by a short counter. He was dressed in a plaid work shirt and denim trousers. He was still going to UCLA and working on his parents' farm—what work there was now. They were finding it difficult to sell their produce these days—some people actually feared the Japanese farmers might poison their harvest! Mostly Sam was helping his parents pack and dispose of their possessions. By now everyone knew the evacuation of the Japanese was inevitable. On March 18, the War Relocation Authority had been established, so the order to depart their homes could not be far behind. At the end of February, all the residents of Terminal Island had been evacuated. They had been given only forty-eight hours' notice.

"Sam, breakfast is ready." Jackie took dishes from the cupboard—they were extras her mother had packed for her, along with a box of other kitchen items. Jackie didn't have the array of wedding gifts a girl expected to have after her wedding day. She didn't mind and was just thankful for her mother's generosity. Everything in the apartment was hand-me-down, most from her mother, a lot from secondhand stores. But she didn't have a great deal, even at that. They had known the evacuation was coming, so even if they'd had the money to spend, the expenditure didn't seem practical when all was so uncertain.

Sam put the last touches on the bed, straightening the crocheted bedspread. It was the most extravagant thing in the place, a true wedding gift from her mother, and it had belonged to Jackie's grandmother, handmade by her fifty years ago.

Striding the few paces to the kitchen, Sam got there in time to help carry the plates of eggs to the table. Jackie brought the coffee. Standing back for a brief moment to survey the scene, she sighed. It was so perfect. Much like playing house as a little girl but real, too, and in so many ways better than the child's game.

She sat down and lifted her fork. Sam did the same, popping a forkful of eggs into his mouth.

"Hmm . . . wonderful!" He swallowed and smiled. "There's something . . . uh, different in the eggs, isn't there?"

"Oh my goodness!" she gasped. "You don't like onions?"

"Well . . ."

"I am so sorry. I didn't think of them as vegetables."

"It's okay. Actually, not bad . . . not bad at all." To prove his words he scooped another huge forkful into his mouth. "Yes . . . I love them!"

"And I love you, dear!" She smiled, actually grinned, as the truth of those words struck her once again. "You'll have to tell me what nongreen vegetables you don't like."

"I sound like a kid, don't I? Guess I'll have to learn not to be so picky, eh?" A lightness in his tone belied the shadowed implications of his meaning.

"Have you heard anything definite?"

He looked away a moment.

"Yoshito Okuda! I thought we had a marriage of complete honesty," she chided him.

"It's not that I want to be dishonest with you, Jackie." He looked abashed. "It's just that . . . I'm a dope, that's all. I don't want to think about it. I want our life to continue forever as we have had it these last five weeks. Please try to understand."

She laid down her fork and eyed him tenderly. "I do understand.

But tell me now what you know. We can't hide from it."

"My parents received the order to evacuate two days ago. They are to dispose of their goods and go to the holding area at the Santa Anita Racetrack on April 19."

"That's only ten days away!"

He nodded grimly. "My mother is frantic. And she has been chipping away at things for a time now, whereas many haven't. They are selling their belongings at fire sale prices. The Fentons are storing as much as they can, but we will have to sell much. My dad will have to get what he can for his truck. Do you remember that neighbor of ours, Mr. Compton? He offered Dad a hundred dollars for the truck! It's worth three times that. Then there are the tools and the tractor to sell."

"Is there anything I can do to help?"

"I'll tell my mother you offered, but . . ." he let the thought trail away, obviously not wanting to bring up a tender issue. Jackie well knew that her presence would only further stir the existing tensions. Mrs. Okuda tried to be nice, but she was torn between her husband and her son's wife. Best not to be a thorn in the family until it was absolutely necessary.

"Sam, maybe it's best if I don't go to your house now, but there is a huge garage at my parents' place and plenty of extra space. I'll bet half your furniture will fit."

"Well, there is a big oak hutch that the Fentons have no room for, and my mother is sick about selling it because she got it when she and Dad married. There are also a few other things they don't want to have to sell. I'll tell my parents about your offer. I'm sure they'll be happy to hear of it."

They returned their attention to the eggs, which had grown lukewarm, but Sam ate every last morsel. Jackie merely pushed the food around on her plate. She thought about a marriage based on honesty. Sam had his reasons for withholding the news of the evacuation order. She wondered if her reasons for keeping her little secret were good enough, as well.

"Sam, I have been thinking a lot about the evacuation," she said slowly, thoughtfully. "And I know we have discussed what we'll do."

"Yes, we have, Jackie." He eyed her over the rim of his coffee cup. "You will stay here and finish student teaching. Then in June, we will reevaluate."

"I never much liked that plan." Yes, they had talked about it but only in the vaguest terms, since neither wanted to accept what might happen. But she had a strong feeling that *reevaluate* meant she would not join him in June.

At first she'd thought agreeing to finish school would be fine because she kept hoping there would be no evacuation, at least not until after June. Now the situation had changed. In less than two weeks she and her husband would be forced apart. True, the small percentage of white wives among the Japanese would be permitted to join their spouses in the internment camps. If, however, the husband was white, especially if he was in the military, his Japanese wife would not have to go to a camp at all. The reasoning here was that the man, being the head of the house, had a strong influence over the woman. So if the husband was white, his Japanese wife was no doubt more loyal to America than the reverse. Which meant in Jackie's case that she had less influence over her Japanese husband, so he was required to go to a camp. She could choose to do what she wanted. It was all hogwash as far as Jackie could see—a bunch of government bureaucrats trying to justify a completely faulty law.

The idea of her being able to choose wasn't entirely true, anyway. She must do what Sam wanted, and he wanted her to finish the semester. She wanted to finish also, but there were other considerations. She debated about the fairness of using these other considerations to attempt to sway him to her way of thinking.

"I don't want to be separated from you, either," Sam said. "We might be able to move to the Midwest—"

"I'm not going to make you do that!" she cut in firmly. "I won't make you leave your family. They need you. Your father doesn't understand the law and the workings of the government as you do, and his poor English makes it hard for him to communicate. If only for that reason they need you to see that they are treated fairly."

But they both knew there was more to it. Though the Japanese might have a quasi freedom to evacuate on their own to areas beyond the Western Defense Zones, many of those states did not want the Japanese either and would not make it easy for any to relocate; otherwise there surely would have been a mass exodus.

"You are making it hard on me," Sam added, "making me have to choose between you and my family." She knew the edge of his tone came more from frustration than anger. She knew another part of his frustration was that his own education would be interrupted. The college was going to give the Japanese students full credit for classes not finished in the spring semester, but they were still being deprived of a completed education.

"You don't have to choose," she gently suggested. "I will just go—"

"No!" Now there was no doubt about the edge. "I will not see you locked up because of me." It was the first time he had stated his feelings directly, without speaking of the reevaluation business.

"It's not because of you."

"Semantics, Jackie, and you know it."

She bit her lip and suddenly caught a whiff of cold eggs. Her stomach churned. With a jerk she shoved back her chair, jumped up, and raced to the bathroom. When, a few minutes later, she came out, dabbing a tissue at the corners of her lips, Sam was standing by the door, a concerned look on his face.

"I was eleven years old when my little sisses were born," he said. "I can still remember my mother racing to the bathroom every morning—"

"Oh, Sam!" She threw her arms around him, tears erupting.

"Are you upset about it?"

She jumped back from the embrace. "Upset? Why? Are you?"

"No, never," he murmured, then grasped her hands. "It's true, then?"

"We're going to have a baby, Sam."

"Oh, wow!" He actually swayed a bit, but she was pleased at the tone of wonder and pleasure in his tone. "I've got to sit down." But as he led her to the bed—the only place to sit in the apartment besides the kitchen chairs—a wide grin spread across his face.

She was thankful he had chosen the bed. She could not bear to look at those eggs again. But despite her queasy stomach, she was smiling, too.

"I couldn't be happier about this," she said. "You believe that, don't you?"

"Me too. But it doesn't change anything. You still have to finish school. Then . . ." He rubbed his chin. His hand was shaking. "We're going to be a family! I'm going to be a father. I want to be a wise one. I want to do the right thing. The best thing for you and . . . our child." As he said *our child* his eyes glowed, and he couldn't completely lose the grin even if he was trying to be serious.

"Sam, the best thing for us, for me, for this baby, is for all of us to be together."

"He could be born behind barbed wire."

"He . . . or she . . . will never notice. But he . . . or she . . . will notice if her father isn't there. Please, Sam!"

"My father was the master of compromise," Sam replied. "Perhaps all good fathers are. Here, then, is a compromise. You finish school. Then in June you will join me wherever I may be."

"I can accept that!" Her grin broadened. "I don't care what is happening out there in the cruel world. I am so happy right now to share this with you."

"As am I, my little mama-san!" His smiling eyes roved lovingly over her, as if seeing her in yet another new light. "When can we expect this bundle of joy?"

"I haven't been to a doctor yet, but I found a book in the library that explained how to calculate, and I figured it should be in December."

"Imagine that!"

"I am so glad you are happy about it."

"You thought I'd be otherwise?"

"Not really, but the timing isn't perfect. I was so afraid of complicating everything."

"My mother says children always complicate everything, but that it is the kind of complication you wouldn't want to live without. And we have faced far worse things. Why, after facing your father, being a father myself will be a breeze." He laughed. "I can't help it, I feel absolutely giddy. The world is spinning out of control, but we are going to have a baby! And I feel like laughing!"

He took her into his arms again, murmuring that his mother's packing could wait. Jackie thought she might have to be a few minutes late to school, as well. She wanted this joyful interlude to last as long as possible.

Sam was glad Jackie had listened to him and not come with him and his family to the racetrack. They'd said their good-byes where they had been happiest—in that goofy little apartment. And that's how he wanted to think of her during the weeks of separation they must endure.

But he'd had another reason, as well. He didn't want her to see his family's shame, rounded up like a herd of animals in a pen, stripped of self-respect.

True, the scene outside the Santa Anita Racetrack didn't exactly resemble a wake. The kids, especially, made it seem more like a fair. Miya and Mika, Sam's ten- and eleven-year-old little sisses, raced all around, greeting their friends, playing games. They seemed to look upon what was happening as the stage of a huge slumber party. Even Toshio, Sam's sixteen-year-old brother, seemed to be enjoying seeing his friends. He'd been pretty quiet and sullen since the war began, refusing to talk about it to Sam or to anyone. So it was nice to see him joke around with his school friends. Only Kimi, at eighteen, was rather subdued. Her fiancé, Susumu, and his family had been evacuated a week earlier, and she didn't know if or when she'd see him again.

Sam's mother was also making the most of the situation, flitting about greeting her friends, gossiping and speculating on what lay ahead. The women talked about what they had managed to stuff into the suitcases they were allowed to carry—the rule being to bring only what you could carry. Some were "carrying" a huge load, dragging big trunks and duffels besides.

Of the family, only Sam's father appeared truly daunted. He stood saying nothing, barely acknowledging the greetings of friends. His eyes roved over the crowds as if he could not believe what was happening. Sam had noted similar reactions in other men, especially the older Issei men. Of everyone, they were losing the most in this vast upheaval. In Japanese culture, even more so than in Western culture, the men ruled their homes. Now they were being stripped of all vestiges of authority. From now on the U.S. government, not the Japanese man, would be the true authority. The government would say "come" and "go" and "do this" and "do that." The government would provide the food, the shelter, everything to sustain life. The Japanese man would be no more than a figurehead, if even that.

Sam stood near his father. It seemed all he could do to support the man, to show him the respect he deserved.

When Sam saw his friends Charlie and YoYo standing with a group of others from their high school class, he waved. YoYo had been looking in his direction, but when Sam acknowledged him, he jerked his head away as if he had not seen him. He whispered something to the others, and they all deliberately diverted their gazes away from Sam.

Sam had felt their alienation in the last weeks in the form of unreturned calls and outright avoidance at school. He knew some thought him a traitor for marrying a white girl. But he hadn't wanted to believe his best friends thought the same.

He clung closer to his father, if not physically, then emotionally. They were both like boats cast adrift in what should have been a friendly sea. What would it be like when he was locked up with his own people in close contact but forced to be apart from them?

"You don't have to stand with me," Sam's father said suddenly. "Go be with your friends."

"I don't mind, Papa. Besides, they aren't interested in me."

"They have abandoned you?"

"I suppose so."

Hiroshi Okuda placed a hand on Sam's shoulder. "It isn't right." It seemed an odd sentiment from a man who himself seemed to have problems with Sam's choice of a wife. Yet the words had been spoken sincerely, and Sam sensed they referred to so much more than the issue of Jackie.

None of this was right. Why didn't they all just refuse to go? If all of them right now got together and staged a rebellion . . . but it would never happen, because these people were simply too loyal to this country to consider rebelling against it. An odd turn, really, that in order to prove their loyalty they must give up their rights as Americans.

Everyone, even the children, did seem to sober a bit when they were finally instructed to move forward and they saw the armed guards at the racetrack gates. The idea of being *imprisoned* seemed to finally register. Suddenly Sam felt the need of his father every bit as much as he thought his father needed him. Anger rose up in him as they were herded through the gates, registered, then led to what would be their quarters—horse stalls! The authorities said these were temporary until transfer to a permanent camp was arranged. Did they think the word *permanent* helped? But some of the women took hope at the news that camps were being built for them. They would be new, maybe nice, too. Perhaps it would not be so hard to stay in a horse stall when better accommodations awaited them.

Sam bought none of it. Even if palatial hotels were offered them, it was still imprisonment. It was still forced. He wanted to scream, "I am an American!"

But he swallowed the gall of his anger. Little Mika wanted to hold his hand. Fear had finally settled into her big, round black eyes.

When two nights had passed in their strange new quarters and Mika said, "I'm ready to go home now," it was up to Sam to try to explain why she couldn't. He knew, for her sake, his explanation could not be tainted with invective. As angry as he was, he still did not hate his country, and he certainly didn't want to pass even a hint of hatred on to his sister.

Someday the war would end, and he would still be an American. He would proudly raise his child as an American. He had no doubt about that. Even if Japan, by some miracle, won the war and ruled the world, Sam would still consider himself American. Because that's who he was. He didn't know how to be anything else.

44

Kuibyshev, Soviet Union

CAMERON ATTENDED the soirée at the British legation in Kuibyshev mostly for the distraction it provided. The talk that evening was largely of the recent visit to London by Molotov. Of course, the journalists had only learned of it after the fact because it was touted a "secret" mission.

When asked what he knew of the visit, Bill Tramble, a British embassy attaché, spoke wryly of the event. "It is said Molotov knows only four words of English: *Yes*, *No*, and *Second Front*."

"From what I hear, Churchill was not accommodating where the Second Front is concerned," Cameron rejoined.

"Churchill is of the mind that Russia is an expendable ally. And for that reason he is in no hurry to attempt a cross-channel invasion. He is still smarting over the disaster of prematurely landing troops in

France during the Great War. He wants no repeat, I daresay, and is quite willing to wait years, if necessary, to wear away the Krauts—at the unfortunate expense of the Russians."

Cameron winced inwardly at this cavalier attitude. She was immediately aware of just how attached she had become to this country when a slight against it affected her so personally. It wasn't healthy.

Slipping away from the group surrounding Tramble, she sought out Johnny. He was standing alone, rather sullenly nursing a martini. She'd noticed all evening he hadn't been his usually obnoxious self.

"Goodness, Johnny, can't you do something to liven up this party?" she said half sarcastically.

He shrugged with little enthusiasm. "Not much to be done, I'm afraid."

"Whatever is the matter with you?" She eyed him with sudden concern. Was something wrong?

"Nothing. I'm just not in the mood."

"I know you better than that, Johnny. Something is amiss, isn't it?"

He blew out a sigh between pursed, taut lips. "I tell you, everything's fine—aw, I just don't want to ruin the party."

"The party's a bust already, if you hadn't noticed. Did you get bad news from home? Did someone die? Have you learned something about the war—?"

"All right! Stop! Sheesh!" He shook his head in mock disgust. "You just can't give a man peace, can you? That's one thing I won't miss. But—"

"Miss? What do you mean?"

"I got a cable from Harry just before coming here. My transfer came through."

She stared, shocked on several levels. First, that he was actually leaving, and second, that he didn't appear ecstatic over it. Squinting with perplexity, she asked, "Okay, Shanahan, why the long face? You have been wanting this for months."

"You know what they say, 'Be careful what you ask for,' " he replied glibly.

"I don't get it."

"It's not as easy to leave as I thought. I put a lot of myself into this assignment. I've become fairly expert in Russian politics and culture—"

When she smirked at his lack of modesty, he just quirked his shoulder and smiled. "I'm also gonna miss everyone here. You're all like fraternity brothers—and sister. Okay, I'll be honest. I'm gonna miss you, Cameron. Happy? Well, it's true, and I guess I'm not ashamed to admit it."

"Well, Johnny . . ." she tried to sound glib, but a lump in her throat made that difficult.

"Hey, enough said. Okay? We know how we feel. That's good enough."

That's what she liked about Johnny. He made things simple. And she tried to accept that. No sense in beating their feelings to death. No sense in acknowledging the wrenching of her stomach. "When will you be leaving?"

"In the morning."

"What! You won't be returning to Moscow first?" The journalists had just received word that they would be flown back to Moscow in three days.

"There's no point in waiting around, is there? I was lucky to get a flight tomorrow heading east. Who can say when another will be dispatched?"

She could not believe his glum aspect. "Johnny, you know you should be wildly excited about this! You'll finally get some combat reporting. It's an assignment that's the stuff of journalistic dreams. You should be dancing in the streets. I'm the one who has a right to be glum. You're my main source of entertainment around here."

"Aw, you are too kind, sweetheart! I am thrilled about the assignment. I suppose what brought me down was I didn't know how to tell you." He was obviously abashed at this admission.

"You are the sweetheart. You know that. You were sensitive of my feelings, and I appreciate that."

"You do?" He whistled between his teeth. "Time was, you would have chewed my head off for worrying about you that way."

"That's true, isn't it?" They both knew she wasn't the same person she had been a year ago. They both had changed considerably and had come to appreciate and understand the value of true friendship.

Johnny was gone before Cameron woke in the morning. He'd left her a note explaining how he hated good-byes. But he reminded her that she could be following him if Max was really intent on keeping up the game he had started over a year ago. She wondered, as she had every time Johnny had talked about a possible transfer, if that's what she wanted. The Pacific was the hot spot of the war. Yet, she reminded herself, Russia was still a key player. And there were other things keeping her in this country.

She was more relieved than she wanted to admit when no cable arrived from Max Arnett. And even more so when she finally returned to Moscow. Still, she had to admit that she felt a deep emptiness with Johnny's absence. Her two best friends had been cut out of her life, and she felt the loss deeper each day. Time was not healing the wound.

Her blossoming friendship with Sophia helped fill some of the void, but there remained a great vacuum. What had it been about her relationships with Johnny and Alex? With Johnny she missed the comfort of an old friend, complete with inside jokes and the ability to read each other's minds. But mostly, she thought, he was her connection to home, to the life that was still very much a part of her. With him gone she feared she might lose an important aspect of who she was.

Alex, on the other hand . . .

Oh, Alex, why can't I let you go? I barely knew you, and you barely knew me, yet I feel as if you know the deepest, most secret part of me. When I surrendered my love to you, I gave something I had never given before to any living soul. I believe you did the same with me, and that is why the loss of you cuts even deeper than the loss of my dear old friend Johnny. I don't understand why, but I need you, Alex.

There was the word Cameron feared above all others. *Need*. Yet how else could she explain the yearning for him? She hadn't felt the need to run to Johnny when Alex left her, so why now did she long to seek out Alex for comfort at Johnny's departure? At every turn of her daily life she thought of Alex, wanting to talk to him, to be held by him, to simply have him near. She could not fathom this incredible sensation. Was it weakness? Was it love? Both? In that case, did she want to love if it made her weak?

Answers eluded her.

Shortly after settling back into her room at the Metropole Hotel in Moscow, she found herself spending a lot of her time reading Jackie's Bible. Something innately told her that the answers she sought regarding Alex were intricately wrapped up in the answers she wanted about faith in God. Alex had said she should approach this as she would any conundrum—by researching the "story." So she began to ask herself exactly what she was researching with this Bible reading. Her broad purpose had been to see what it was all about. Yet she was not the kind of person to be challenged by such a vague motive. There had to be more. Either her findings were going to have an impact on her life, or they weren't. She was not interested in learning about Christianity for the sake of learning.

That being the case, was she indeed ready to accept God as she found Him in the Bible? Was she ready for Him to change her life? The mere thought scared her to death, yet fear didn't deter her, either. She kept reading, pushing, searching.

If nothing else, throwing herself into this research project seemed to fill some of the emptiness inside her. Yet that troubled her as much as everything else about it. She had always looked upon Christianity as a crutch for the weak. Was she now turning to it out of weakness? That scared her even more than the notion of turning to it in order to win Alex. Jackie had told her that Blair was afraid of turning to God because she didn't want to be doing it for Gary instead of out of real faith. Cameron felt certain she herself was beyond that. She would be more likely to *run* from faith because of a man rather than the opposite.

The issue of Christianity versus weakness was far more disturbing. What was the answer? So often people like Sophia and Alex and her mother had talked of finding comfort in God. Lately Cameron couldn't shake the feeling that she wished she had such a connection. Was it any more a weakness to need the comfort of faith than it was to need a man? Wasn't she the greatest of fools to believe herself entirely self-reliant? Did need really have to equal weakness? She was confused. That, at least, she could admit.

"Sophia," Cameron asked one morning as the two of them were working in her hotel room, "why are you a Christian?"

Sophia's nose was buried in the *Red Star*, but she lowered the paper, and her expression reflected her surprise at the question coming out of the blue.

"That is both a simple and a complex question, Cameron," Sophia said. "The simple answer is that I love God and want to serve Him with my life."

"Why do you love Him?"

"Because He gave His son to die for my sins. That's the simple answer."

"And the complex one?"

"That has more to do with my own personal relationship with God. The way He speaks to my heart, the way He daily touches me. Things that would mean little to you because you are a different person. Things like the way He accepts my shyness when others often ridicule me for it. Some have told me, 'Sophia, speak up for yourself.' Or, 'You let everyone walk all over you.' But God has never made me feel less of a person because of that trait. And for that I love Him. There are so many examples like this, Cameron, that I cannot imagine not loving Him."

Cameron was silent, wondering if she should continue. She knew Sophia well enough to know she wouldn't pursue the topic unless Cameron pressed on. But she also knew she was treading on shaky ground. Sophia was not going to give theological answers or safe answers. The girl only knew how to talk about God in a personal way. And that daunted Cameron, because it was far easier for her to think about God on an intellectual level than on a personal one. Yet fear urged her forward; actually, a stubborn refusal to accept fear.

"I have asked myself that question," Cameron said. "Why should I be a Christian?" She paused, glancing at Sophia, who sat poised and serene. She had expected a more shocked reaction from her friend. After all, the question was quite earth-shattering to Cameron. "People talk about *needing* God; well, I just can't say I need Him. That's terribly arrogant, I know. Maybe I should say I don't *want* to need Him. In fact, if my turning to God is based on need, then I am not sure it will ever happen. Maybe I do need Him, but I just can't picture myself crumbling on bended knee and with wailing and weeping turn to God. I can't. It is just not me." She gave a couple slow wags of her head. "But then there is this . . ." She grabbed the Bible, which seemed lately never far from hand. She glanced at some notes she had jotted in the blank pages in the book, then flipped through till she found what she was looking for. "This is from Second Corinthians. 'And he said unto me, My grace is sufficient for thee: for my strength is made perfect in weakness. Most gladly therefore will I rather glory in my infirmities, that the power of Christ may rest upon me. Therefore I take pleasure in infirmities, in reproaches, in necessities, in persecutions, in distresses for Christ's sake: for when I am weak, then am I strong.' " Cameron snapped shut the book. "This sounds like the only way to be strong is by being weak first. I know I am not a paragon of strength. I have been through enough, especially in this last year, to know my limitations. But this is going almost too far. I . . . I just don't know."

"Cameron, what do you know of the man who wrote those words—the apostle Paul?"

"Just what I read the other day in the book of Acts. He was a pious Jew who was persecuting Christians, then he was converted on the road to Damascus, where he had planned more persecutions. After that he went into Christianity in a big way. It was rather impressive how he made such a hundred-and-eighty-degree turn. I remember thinking that if the Lord spoke to me like He did to Paul on the Damascus road, it would be much easier for me to admit I may not be so self-sufficient after all. I also noticed that before then, Christ's disciples had been uneducated, simple men. But Paul was different, highly educated and powerful in his profession."

"I have always thought of Paul as a powerful man, as well," Sophia added, "even to the point of arrogance. He stood up to rulers, even the emperor of Rome. He was, in fact, a Roman citizen, which made him a man above many men. I have a feeling he also had a problem with needing God—really needing him. Something had to happen to him to make him write those verses you just read. Some say he had a physical malady that forced him to learn humility. But I don't think it was easy for him to confess his weaknesses before God."

"Must be why God had to zap him with a bright light and an angel to get his attention," Cameron said lightly. Then her brow creased. "Do you think that's what it will take for me?" She almost shuddered at the thought. The logical part of her did not believe such things really happened.

"You once told me your mother used to say, 'The bigger they are, the harder they fall.' Maybe that's what she meant."

"Sophia, let's just say I do . . . this thing." She smiled diffidently. She couldn't even give the act of conversion its proper name. She continued quickly, hoping to gloss over her awkwardness. "Can God really accept a person like me? I am still going to be independent, determined, dogged even. I've been told I am stubborn, even arrogant. There's that word again! I cannot become a different person. God isn't going to expect me to become a meek and mild sheep, is He? That's okay if that is who a person is, but that isn't me."

"God doesn't want all His children to be alike. Imagine if they were all meek sheep like me." Sophia grinned at Cameron's attempt at an apology for her previous words, then continued. "He will accept you as you are, Cameron, not try to shove you into some mold."

"What about all the rules in the Bible?"

"My papa always says that the Bible is a blueprint, not a cudgel. Do you think Paul changed from the essential man he was? Oh, I'm sure he matured, grew, deepened, but he was still a strong, forceful man. Even after his conversion he stood up to leaders and spoke his mind. God didn't change those qualities. He used them. Cameron, I don't believe God is going to try to change you. And He doesn't expect you to change before you come to Him. All He wants is for you to believe in Him with your heart. Goodness, none of us could have become Christians if we would have had to fit some profile first, and we wouldn't remain so for very long if we all had to be alike!"

"So simple," breathed Cameron.

"And complex," Sophia replied. "He wants nothing from us . . . yet he wants everything, too."

"Funny, but that is one part of it I can truly understand," Cameron said. "I wouldn't want to make this kind of commitment unless I made it with all I had."

"What holds you back, then?"

"I don't know. A revelation. My own bright light, I guess. I want this to be in my heart—it has to be—not just in my head. Right at this moment my head tells me there is nothing standing in my way. But I lack something, Sophia. I lack the light I see in your eyes when you speak of your relationship with Christ. I lack the passion I saw in Alex when he chose God over his love for me. I understand that feelings are not the best basis for making a commitment to God. I don't want emotions, but I seek an assurance in my soul. And one other thing. If it is not asking too much, I want my decision to be personal. I want to encounter God as a friend. Like the old hymn I used to hear sung in church when I was a girl—'What a Friend We Have in Jesus.' "

"You are not asking too much. That is how it will be for you, I know." Sophia reached for Cameron's Bible and opened it, turning to Psalms. But she didn't look at the page as she quoted, " 'Delight thyself also in the Lord, and he shall give thee the desires of thine heart.' "

Cameron's only response was to blow a puff of air through her lips. This Bible was an amazing book. It confused and mystified her. It raised a hundred questions, but it did offer hope. And she realized it wasn't so horrible to need hope.

Cameron and Sophia returned to their work. Cameron's mind was full for the time being. She had received many good insights, yet she was still fuzzy about that issue of need. It seemed okay to accept for herself *universal* needs. But she continued to struggle on a more personal level. She still could not say why, but making herself vulnerable that way was fearsome. Hadn't she tried to do so with her father? Look where that had gotten her. And even with Alex. She had opened her entire self up to him, and even if his reasons were valid, he had left her, rejected her.

Wouldn't God do the same?

She felt as if she were staring into a deep abyss and needed a bridge to get her across. Something to shore up her fears of being abandoned once again. Paul's bright light? Probably not that much, but something to assure her she wouldn't go flying to her death if she took that first step.

45

THE LAST OF the winter's snows were nearly melted from Moscow's streets when Cameron threw caution to the crisp June wind and trekked across town to the Fedorcenko flat. She had been invited to celebrate Sophia's twentieth birthday, and she didn't care about the NKVD. She was going to attend. However, to protect the Fedorcenkos, she did take precautions to lose her police shadow if indeed she had one. She was getting quite adept at such clandestine activities.

But she was shocked when she was ushered into the apartment and found Alex standing there having a jovial conversation with Sophia's mother, Katya.

The last she had heard from Sophia, Alex had been in Kharkov during the May battle there. She had worried about him because reports regarding this battle had been, even for the tight-lipped Narkomindel, very vague. Cameron had guessed it had gone worse for the Russians than usual, this being reinforced by one of Palgunov's communiqués that listed Soviet losses as five thousand killed and seventy thousand missing. Something had gone terribly wrong. And Alex had been in the midst of whatever disaster had occurred.

But here he was, standing tall and almost regal in his crisp khaki brown uniform. His hair was shorter than usual, an Army cut, but no less golden. He was thinner than normal and his features just a bit drawn. A fresh scar sliced through the outside corner of his right eyebrow. But none of this detracted from his appeal and only added a more seasoned look to him.

Cameron's heart leaped into her mouth while at the same time it sank to her toes. The range of her emotions could barely be described. Only one emotion was absent, and that was anger toward Sophia—it had to have been her!—for arranging this encounter.

Cameron swallowed all these raging sensations as she pasted a cool, aloof smile on her face while subduing her voice into a calm, urbane tone.

"Why, Alex, is that you? How good to see you." She'd always found that taking the offensive in a sticky situation worked best for her.

His responding look was not as finely honed as hers, but then, hadn't his uncluttered honesty been one of the things that had once appealed to her? *Had once?* Her pounding heart told her nothing was in the past at all.

"Cameron . . ." His tone was as raw as an exposed nerve. He obviously had not expected her to be there, either. How foolish they both were to have been deceived so easily.

"Mrs. Fedorcenko, how good to see you again." Cameron swung her head quickly about to face her hostess because she could not bear to look at Alex a moment longer. "Ah, Dr. Fedorcenko," Cameron added as the man joined them. "It has been such a long time. But who is minding the store when two of Russia's finest physicians are here?"

She could not believe the unnatural quality of her voice, but she was helpless to do anything about it. The glib, almost oily words seemed to have a mind of their own.

With an inscrutable smile, Yuri Fedorcenko took Cameron's proffered hand and, in that old-fashioned way of his, bowed ever so slightly over it. "We are not indispensable. Russia has many fine doctors. Nevertheless, my Sophia's birthday is a special occasion, and little could have made me miss it."

Sophia came up to her father and slipped an arm around his waist. "It is appreciated, Papa." She smiled at him, then her gaze skittered toward Cameron. In that brief moment Cameron saw in her friend's eyes a little apology and perhaps a little hope as well about the success of her deception.

Cameron shrugged. It was hard to be angry at the gentle young woman. Anyway, she and Alex were sensible adults. They were certainly above displaying petty emotions.

Still, Alex had said no more beyond the shocked grunt of her name. Cameron managed to smoothly ignore him by flitting among the other guests, though she feared she resembled a slightly crazed hummingbird, talking airily about trivial matters, laughing at comments that were hardly funny, making her own jokes that most certainly were not amusing.

Everyone was present who had been in the flat the last time Cameron had been there, with the exception of Sophia's husband, Oleg. Sophia's older sister Valentina smiled prettily but said little to Cameron. Her English had not improved. Anna Yevnovona gave Cameron a warm embrace. The old woman's hold was quite sturdy, and Cameron felt an unaccountable intensity in the brief contact. Anna's eyes were probing, and her smile was knowing, though what exactly the woman *knew*, Cameron could not guess. She no doubt knew quite a bit!

Cameron was relieved to be distracted by the introduction of a new face in the group.

"Cameron," Sophia said, "I would like to present my big sister Irina. She is home on a short leave."

Irina, who appeared to be Cameron's age or a few years older, was dressed in a woman's Red Army uniform. She was much taller than the other Fedorcenko women yet had the same willowy beauty.

"I am happy to now know the entire Fedorcenko clan," Cameron said.

"Except for my brother, Sergei," corrected Sophia. "Perhaps he will come home on a leave soon, and you can meet him, too. There are also his wife and two children, who have evacuated east and were too far away to be here."

This was a congenial group and never at a loss for friendly conversation. The only silent one in the room was Alex. When Katya left him and went to the kitchen to see to some preparations, he made no move to engage anyone else in conversation. He merely stood alone, silently watching Cameron. She noted all this from the corner of her eye and made no overtures to him, either. Their behavior did, in fact, seem petty, immature. They might not be making a scene, but doing the exact opposite of that was just as disturbing. Cameron didn't know what else to do. She had made the first move. She'd greeted him in a friendly fashion. If he chose to ignore her, she certainly wasn't going to act the fool by pushing herself on him. He was the one who had left her in the first place. Obviously he had gotten over her—quite quickly at that!

Part of her knew, though, that the look of consternation he wore was not that of a man who had gotten over anything. Maybe that's what really restrained Cameron from making another gesture. She just did not know what to do with that look of his.

After a few minutes he began to make his way toward her. Only then did Cameron notice he held a cane in his right hand and was limping. What had happened to him in Kharkov? He had a new scar, a limp, that *something* deep in his eyes that turned the warm blue pale and said they had seen far more than any person should ever have to. She wanted to go to him, hold him, comfort him. But could he possibly need her comfort anymore? Had he ever needed it? Because she had lately felt her own need so acutely, she now held back, the fear of rejection shooting through her like the pain of an old wound.

At the same moment she saw him move, Cameron also spied Katya coming from the kitchen bearing a heavy tray of dishes.

"Let me give you a hand," Cameron said, moving quickly toward the woman.

"I've got it, dear. You are a guest, so just enjoy yourself."

"I really don't mind helping."

"I won't have it." Katya was firm but pleasant. She paused a single moment, then her gaze fixed on Alex. "Oh, Alex, won't you be a dear and keep Cameron entertained, or she will end up washing dishes or something."

Cameron sensed she was the object of a conspiracy, but there was no escaping now. Did she truly want to?

"We can't have that," Alex said wryly, limping toward Cameron.

Katya flitted away, as much as anyone could with a heavy tray in hand, leaving Cameron and Alex standing together like two rocks in a rushing stream. Cameron swallowed but said nothing. She had used up all her slick responses.

"I gather you are just as surprised as I about this little setup," he said. His normal voice had returned, his English accented, his tone deep and resonant, and it sent an electric charge through Cameron.

"They meant well, I suppose," she replied. Not wanting to dwell on that, she hurriedly changed the subject. "Alex, what happened to your leg?"

"The Germans failed to see the red cross on our hospital. I was cut by some flying debris and needed a couple stitches. I'll be right as rain in a few days." Except for a touch of awkwardness in his voice, his response was for a brief delicious moment almost like it had once been between them. Cameron was only reminded of the changes when he asked stiffly, "And you? Your work? It goes well for you, I hope?"

"Oh yes, very well," she answered airily, trying desperately to distance herself from the emotions clutching at her heart.

"And what of your sister?"

"We know little more than that she is alive or was when we last heard. Very little communication is coming from the Philippines now that they have fallen to the Japanese. I expect she is now in a prison camp."

"I am sorry to hear that."

"Well, nothing is certain in this world, is it?" she said coldly. She hadn't meant for it to come out that way, but she was having a terrible time masking the onslaught of emotions.

"Are you happy?" he asked, focusing a gaze upon her that was filled with such poignancy and intensity that it made her breath catch.

The question took her aback, as well. She gaped silently at first, not knowing if he really expected a reply. She certainly would not tell him the truth. That would serve neither of them very well.

"What do you think, Alex?" She seemed to have no mastery at all over her rebellious tongue as the truth nearly slipped out when a moment ago she had determined to lie. But reining it in time, she added, "I have a job to do, and I am quite content in doing it."

"Is that—?" he began but was cut off by Dr. Fedorcenko.

"Everyone!" the doctor said loudly, seemingly unaware that he had interrupted a potentially volatile exchange between two of his guests. "It is time to honor our birthday girl."

Just then Katya came from the kitchen carrying another tray with a plain white-frosted cake perched in the center. Five candles burned on top of the cake. "We have adopted Sophia's favorite American custom that we learned from Sophia's uncle Daniel."

"Oh, Mama!" Sophia exclaimed. Suddenly the grown woman that Sophia had become in the last months turned into a gleeful little girl. "What a wonderful cake! But it must have taken all our sugar rations."

"And Cameron's, as well," Katya said.

"A few other correspondents also contributed," Cameron put in, almost surreptitiously moving away from Alex and nearer to the safe center of the group. "We heard you had a sweet tooth, Sophia, and everyone wanted to give you a gift."

"You are all wonderful!" Sophia's lip quivered. "I love each one of you so much! And I will be sure to tell the journalists the same."

"Don't tell those ornery reporters you love them, Sophia. They'll die of embarrassment," Cameron quipped.

"Come," said Yuri. "Blow out your candles before the air-raid warden turns us in."

Cameron stayed long enough after the cake was served so as not to appear rude, then she made her excuses, gathered up her coat, and left. She barely reached the end of the corridor outside the apartment when she heard footfalls behind her.

"Cameron, will you truly go like this?" Alex asked, hobbling after her as fast as his wounded leg would permit.

Cameron felt sorry for him when she turned, but she forced a cool reply. "I know of no other way to go."

"Is there still no chance for us?"

"As I recall, Alex, you were the one to walk out. So I must ask a question of you. Has anything changed with you?" For once her tongue obeyed, and her words were cool, revealing nothing of the hopeful yearning she felt.

His silence seemed answer enough. His features were contorted with pain, but she could only take that to mean he was unable to give her the answer she desired. It made her glad she had bared no more of herself to him.

She spun around and hurried down the steps, both relieved and miserable when she reached the bottom and found he had not followed.

Alex watched Cameron hurry down the steps. He felt numb all over, unable to move. Part of his mind screamed, "Go after her!" but another part reminded him that truly nothing had changed.

It did not matter that he thought of her nearly every waking moment or that she often appeared in his dreams. In defiance of all reason he had clung to his memories of her during the nightmare of his first battle experience. Kharkov had been more than the usual battle nightmare, too. The secret was guarded closely by the government, and he saw no good in revealing what he knew, but that battle, if it could be called one, had turned into a complete rout for the Russian Army. Too late the Russians realized they were heading into a German trap that quickly encircled them and battered them nearly to pieces. Many good men, including some high-ranking officers, were lost before the Russians had managed to break out of the trap.

Alex had never known such terror before, and the bombardment nearly drove him insensible. The ground shook so beneath his feet at times, it hardly mattered that his hands also shook as they laid scalpel to shattered bodies. He had never before seen a wound fresh from the battlefield, and it had both appalled him and made him appreciative of the life of ease he'd known in his Moscow hospital. Even now, after two weeks' separation from it, he could still smell the stench of freshly charred flesh.

When the field hospital had been bombed nearly out of existence, he'd had to wonder if it was merely a way of escape from the carnage. Perhaps the end of the hospital meant he could join the retreating soldiers and run for his life. Only duty kept him at his post, and ignoring his own wounds, he and the other staff had managed to get most of their patients away. He tried not to think of the ones left behind. He also had tried not to think of Cameron through it all, but he was too desperate for the comfort he knew he'd find in thoughts of her for that to be possible. He wouldn't let himself ponder the reality of their separation, that her comforting arms might not be extended toward him ever again. For him the connection was still there, as if nothing had happened.

Later, while recuperating in a hospital away from the front lines, he'd had time to reflect more rationally on her. Even then hardheaded logic eluded him. She was still embedded deep in his heart, perhaps now like a poorly healed scar, painfully felt with every movement.

Yes, nothing had changed—in more ways than one. His faith in God was still strong, but so was his love for Cameron. How could that be?

Confusing matters even more were the not-so-subtle hints from Sophia that Cameron's heart was softening toward God. He'd only had a few minutes to speak with Sophia before the party, but she'd mentioned talking with Cameron about Scripture verses Cameron had read! Maybe that, after his initial shock at seeing Cameron had worn off, had caused him to expect more from the encounter. Perhaps his disappointment over the realization that she hadn't made a commitment of faith had caused him to hold back now. How could he run after her when that gulf still separated them?

Standing there in the empty darkened corridor, alone and as empty inside as his surroundings, Alex sought the Source of all comfort.

"Why bring her back into my life, God? Wouldn't it have been better to let the wounds heal first, to let the love grow cold? Maybe you know best, but I am still baffled that you brought her into my life in the first place if you knew all along she would just be torn away. What purpose have you that I can't see?"

And why couldn't he shake the feeling that in not going after her just now, he had somehow abandoned her once again? Was she reaching out to him? An odd way to reach with her cool, even cold, remarks. Yet he should know better than to be fooled by her hard shell. She had always feared being hurt, and when she had finally found the will to be vulnerable, what had he done? He had hurt her even worse than her past hurts. Not intentionally, of course.

Yet she had been hurt.

It came to him then why he so strongly felt the urge to go after her. He must try to heal that hurt. Perhaps he could never have her back, but he still needed to reach out and tend her wounds. Was it just the physician in him, or could it be the Spirit of God even more powerfully within?

46

CAMERON PUSHED OPEN the heavy door of the Metropole. Even after the long metro ride she was still bewildered by what she had done. Why had she walked out on him? Was it merely the satisfaction of being the one to walk out for a change?

No, even she could not be that petty. The answer ought to be clear to her. She ran because she would not let herself be hurt again.

Not that it had done her any good. She was still wracked with pain. If only Alex would have come after her. If nothing had changed and his faith still separated them, he could have indicated that. Given her something to ease the pain.

Now, that would have been a nice bright light, God, she thought with just a touch of bitterness. A Paul-like miracle to suit me fine. Alex showing up now to gently ease himself from my heart.

With a dismissive toss of her head, she strode toward the elevator.

"Miss Hayes!"

Cameron's heart leaped at the sound of her name, but of course Alex would never call her Miss Hayes, nor did he have the accent of a Frenchman, as did the voice that called. Quickly recognizing the voice of the night manager, she turned.

"Yes, Monsieur Billaud," she replied.

"I am glad I saw you come in. I have cables for you." He held out the papers.

With a puzzled quirk of her brow she thanked him and stepped into the elevator as it arrived. Usually the cable office at the Narkomindel notified her when cables arrived for her. The only other time she recalled one had been delivered, it hadn't contained good news. And now two in one evening! Despite her curiosity, she did not open them. She was never anxious to read cables these days.

In her room she shrugged out of her coat and kicked off her shoes before curling up on the sofa, the cables in hand. The first was from Max Arnett. It had a fatherly tone, as much as could be conveyed in the brief lines. Would she care for a little change of scenery? She was still his best foreign correspondent and doing a crack-up job in Moscow, but with the focus of the war shifting to the Pacific, he wondered if his best "man" should be wasted away from the real action.

Cameron's first reaction to this was an audible "Harrumph!"

What did the people in the States think? That the war in Russia was nothing more than a couple of skirmishes? She'd heard there had been quite a resurgence of Russian support in America of late. Surely they must know what a key player Russia was and would continue to be in this war.

At least Max was astute enough to know. Besides, the tone of the cable indicated there was more to be gleaned between the lines—or perhaps that had simply come from her experience with Soviet matters. Suddenly it came to her that Max must know of Johnny's reassignment to the Pacific. Had Johnny himself told Max? Had he discovered his feelings for her were stronger than he'd once thought? Was he off in some tropical jungle pining for her?

Outlandish!

It showed how wrought up she was over Alex that she would even consider such a foolish notion. Yet the idea of working in competition with Shanahan again was not completely repugnant to her. She doubted she could ever feel for him as she once had, but she did care for him and, at the very least, she enjoyed his company—when he didn't make her furious. They were kindred spirits. What was wrong with that? Who could tell, perhaps one day she might even shake these futile feelings she had for Alex and find with Johnny—

No! She would not fall into that abyss again. She didn't need any man.

She glanced once more at Max's cable. There was something else in it, between the lines, as well. That fatherly tone. Max Arnett had no doubt noted the erosion of Cameron's passion for her work since her visit to the States. She had begun to notice it herself. She was too distracted with self-pity and her own romantic pining. A new assignment might be just what she needed to get back her fire for her work. Get away from everything here in Russia that was bringing her down. Everything and everyone.

With a sigh, she laid aside Arnett's cable and opened the next one. She wrinkled her brow as she noted it was from Harry Landis, her old editor at the *Journal*. She read:

CAMERON STOP IT IS MY SAD DUTY TO INFORM YOU OF JOHN SHANAHAN'S DEATH STOP HE WAS ABOARD U.S. CARRIER YORKTOWN DURING BATTLE OF MIDWAY STOP SHIP SANK BY JAPANESE STOP IN SHOCK HERE STOP I KNOW HE WAS CLOSE FRIEND AND MENTOR TO YOU STOP ALL MY BEST WISHES STOP HARRY

Certain she had missed something, Cameron read the cable again. Then she went numb all over. She sat that way for ten minutes, the cable crushed within her fist. Then her mind sluggishly ground into gear, but her first thoughts were denial. This must certainly be a mistake. She was going to the Pacific to join him, to keep racing him for the big scoops of the war. He was going to pump the life back into her, the passion for her work that she seemed to have lost. They were going to be adversaries and teammates.

Johnny was dead!

The sudden realization shattered her flimsy denials. Harry always got his facts right, and if there had been even a glimmer of hope, he would have been the first to offer it.

"No. . . !" she groaned as the full impact of the truth struck her. Though she seemed to collapse inside, no responding tears rose to her eyes despite the fact they ached with the need for release. Johnny wouldn't want her or anyone to cry for him. He would laugh at such silly gestures.

Cameron jumped up and, dropping the crumpled cable on the table, strode to her closet, pulled out her large suitcase, and set it on the bed. Snapping it open, she started taking things from the closet and the dresser and throwing them into the case. She gave no thought to the irrationality of her actions. Even if she was going to leave Russia, it would be days, perhaps weeks, before her exit visa would be issued.

But such logic eluded her.

She only knew she was going to the Pacific—and even that, using the nebulous term *the Pacific* in her mind, should have indicated she was not thinking straight. She had no specific assignment. Did she think she would just plop herself down in the middle of an ocean?

None of that mattered. She would find Johnny. He would—No, she couldn't find Johnny. Johnny was dead.

But he was the only one left to help her. What was she going to do? Alex was not there for her. And God. . . ? How had He decided to help her? Not with the miracle she had wished for but rather by cruelly snatching her only remaining friend from her. Some bright light!

Well, she didn't need God or Alex or anyone. She was strong. She was steel—but the steel was finally bending. She could feel it bending . . . bending . . .

"Oh, God!" With a lurch, she dropped the sweater she was holding and stumbled back against the door of the closet.

She wasn't steel at all. She was straw.

Her head throbbed so with silent cries she almost didn't hear the tap on her door. When the sound finally penetrated, she only stared at it. She didn't want to see anyone now.

"Cameron, the key lady said you were in here," Alex called. "If you are, please answer."

His voice was desperate and pleading. Why had he come now? To taunt her with her need? Just hearing his voice made her know she would find the comfort she craved if only she opened that door.

Yet . . . oh, God, I do need him! You know that as well, don't you? Are you taunting me, too? You take and you taunt, but when do you give?

The room seemed to spin before her, and she sank to the floor. The answer wasn't a bright light, it was more like a kick in the stomach. She had asked God to bring Alex when she hadn't even known of the tragedy that lay ahead. And here was Alex!

Fear reached out like a fist and gripped her. Had Paul felt this way on the road to Damascus? Not wonder at a miracle, but stark fright? Not a desire to finally reach out to the provider of that miracle but a gripping urge to run from it? Who had said to be careful what you ask for?

Johnny had told her that. Of all people!

She'd asked for a miracle. She hadn't guessed that with it would come sheer terror.

"Cameron, can we talk?" Alex asked through the door.

She'd almost forgotten he was there. She wanted to forget, anyway, that God gave, even to one so undeserving as she. She was undeserving because she didn't think she could give anything in return.

She glanced at the door. "I . . . I can't talk." She was surprised she could even find her voice, though it sounded like an old boot scraping across grit. But she'd said it. Miracles couldn't count if you didn't accept them.

"Please don't make me beg."

And despite her fear, perhaps even because of it, she found she could muster no strength of will to keep him away. She slowly groped her way to her feet and shuffled toward the door. She flung it open, and in the next moment she collapsed into his arms, tears at last erupting from her eyes, sobs spilling from her lips.

"Cameron, what is it?" he asked, shoving the door shut with the heel of his boot, then gripping her firmly within his embrace. As if from a great distance, she heard his cane clatter to the floor, but that's all she noted beyond the fact that he was there, his arms open to her.

It took a full minute for words to navigate her sobs and hiccoughs. She was not used to crying. "W-why d-did you come?"

"I just knew I had to."

"The p-police—"

"I don't care about the police. I had to talk to you. I couldn't let it be the way it was." He smoothed back strands of her hair that had been plastered to her cheeks by her tears. "But this, Cameron, these tears can't be because of me."

"Shanahan . . ." Merely saying the name brought fresh sobs. "K-killed . . . he's . . . dead."

"Dear Lord, no!" Alex pressed his cheek closer to her. "There, there . . . let it out, my love."

"H-he'd laugh at my blubbering."

"No, he wouldn't. Didn't you know Johnny just talked tough?"

She could only nod against his shoulder.

She stood clutching Alex, crying in his arms for several minutes until she felt she could breathe normally. He gave her his handkerchief, and she blew her nose and wiped her eyes. Then he nudged her to the sofa, but he had to nudge her again for her to take the cue and sit. She curled up against him, still feeling as if she would break without him close.

"H-how come you always happen along at times like these?" She remembered how he had showed up after she had learned of her sister's being caught in the Philippines. She still could not admit the answer to her own question.

"Maybe I've got a sixth sense." When she shook her head dubiously, he added, "Do you want to hear the real reason?"

"But Alex, if I accept that God brought you here when I needed you most, then I would have to accept too many other impossible things."

"Like what?"

"Well, it is awfully kind of Him to send me comfort when it would have been just as easy for Him to prevent the painful moments in the first place."

"You know as well as I that God doesn't work that way," he replied softly, no antagonism in his tone. He realized this wasn't a debate. "What's really the problem?"

"I'm scared to death of God, Alex." The admission took as much out of her as had her previous tears. "What if I needed God as much as I need you?"

"What would be so wrong with that?"

"I can't."

"Why?" he gently persisted.

"I can't lose myself like that. I'll die inside. I'll crumble. I'll crack." She'd said the same thing once to Sophia. Was it really so horrible?

He grasped her hands in his. "But Cameron, you do need; you've said it yourself. Everyone needs. It is just human." He added, with a slightly ironic smile quirking his lips, "Anyway, you were pretty well crumbling before I came, weren't you? At least by reaching beyond yourself for help you never need be alone."

She lurched to her feet and walked across the room. Bending over, she picked up the sweater she had been holding before Alex came. Running her hand over the wool, she realized how silly it had been to pack it for the tropics. Of course she must leave all her warm clothes for her Russian friends.

"Why is your suitcase out?" There was a sudden hollowness to his voice.

"My newspaper wants to assign me to the Pacific Theater. My publisher probably wanted me to keep competing with Johnny—" Her voice caught on a sob. "But . . . he won't be there now. . . ." Another sob escaped.

Alex was at her side in an instant. She saw he was holding the cable from Max that she had dropped on the sofa earlier.

"It's only a request," he said, having obviously read the cable.

"It's just the way they do things," she lied, then turned away from him, trying to appear to straighten an item in the suitcase. Everything he'd told her about need was right. Why fight it? But fighting was her natural instinct.

Yet Alex was not going to let her get away with lies. He gripped her shoulders in his large, strong hands and spun her around to face him. "That's not the truth!" he declared. "Why don't you admit to yourself, if not to me, that you are running away?"

"Okay!" she nearly shouted into his face. "I'm running away. I'm scared . . . weak . . . needy! But I can't—" She paused, closing her eyes against the onrush of new tears. You foolish woman! she screamed inside her head. Then other words leaped into her mind, words she had recently read. *It is hard for you to kick against the pricks.* She hadn't understood that when she had read it. To her, it had seemed much easier to fight God than to accept him. But now she clearly understood. It is only easy to fight God when you don't know who He is. But now Cameron knew. He was the kind of God who would answer a foolish, undeserving woman's prayer *before* she had enough wisdom to accept Him. He was the kind of God who would give her the comfort of the man she loved, when in fact she should have been seeking *God's* comfort.

Swiping a sleeve across her damp eyes, she squared her shoulders as if the steel were back. But she knew the truth of it now. " 'My strength is made perfect in weakness,' " she murmured.

Alex stared at her, mouth hanging slightly ajar.

She went on. "Alex, I have a confession to make. When I came back to the hotel after seeing you and before I got the cable about Johnny, I asked God to bring you here to me. You came, against all odds, when I needed you more than I have ever needed anyone in my life. Yet still I fought acknowledging God. How could I deny my need when I was nearly overwhelmed with fear?"

"You know, don't you, that God understands your fear? He's watched you grow up with it."

"Do you think some of it is because of my father?"

"People are going to fail you, Cameron."

"But God won't?"

"Never."

"How can you be so certain?" There was no challenge in her question. Somehow she knew she could trust Alex's certainty, but it was still her nature to question.

"I guess it comes with experience."

"Alex . . . I am ready."

"For what?" He tried to mask his surprise but not very successfully. "Do . . . you want to—?"

"I want to do whatever I must do to give myself to God." She sucked in a breath. The words were not as difficult to utter as she had feared. They were, instead, quite a relief.

"Now?"

"Now. With you. It couldn't be more right this way."

He nodded.

"What should I do?" she asked guilelessly.

"Just let God know what is in your heart." He grasped her hands in his.

The prayer came incredibly easy. She talked to God as she would to Alex. And as with Alex, she knew God was listening. And for the first time in her life she surrendered to something willingly. But it didn't feel like surrender. It felt too wonderful for that.

Alex murmured his own prayer when she finished. "Thank you, Father, for the great gift you have given to Cameron and to me!" A placid smile slid across his face.

With her own smile of contentment, Cameron laid her head on Alex's shoulder. Oddly, the pain of the loss of her dear friend Johnny was still there. A lump of tears still rose within her when she thought of him. Yet all the emptiness was gone. She had absolutely no explanation for these sensations. She had no idea how it all worked, but it was working! She suddenly thought of something Anna Yevnovona had once told her about a seed of grain, that it had to be planted into the ground and die before it could bring forth fruit. The words had been so much drivel to Cameron then. But now she understood them! She was already seeing the process within herself.

"Goodness!" she breathed.

"Hmm. . . ?" Alex murmured.

She could tell he was too contented to say much more. She also didn't want to speak and ruin the spell over them, yet her mind was abuzz. She was stepping into a new life. This, she was positive, would be an adventure far more exciting than the one that had changed her life a year ago when she had become a foreign correspondent. Now everything was changed. Everything! She was still a little afraid, but as she felt the solid warmth of Alex beside her, she knew her fears need not crumble her. God was not only in her heart, but He had given her Alex to share it all with.

"What do you think will happen now, Alex?"

"I can't wait to see!"

"Neither can I."

They drew close to each other, as if they knew that whatever lay before them, they were now truly in it together—in their hearts and in their spirits.